The Iowa Award

The IOWA AWARD

The Best Stories, 1991–2000

SELECTED BY FRANK CONROY

University of Iowa Press Ψ Iowa City

University of Iowa Press, Iowa City 52242
Printed in the United States of America
http://www.uiowa.edu/~uipress
The publication of this book was generously supported
by the University of Iowa Foundation.
Printed on acid-free paper
Library of Congress Cataloging-in-Publication Data
The Iowa award: the best stories, 1991–2000 / selected by Frank Conroy.
p.   cm.
ISBN 0-87745-785-9 (pbk.)
1. Short stories, American.   I. Conroy, Frank, 1936– .
PS648.S5I58   2001
813'.0108054—dc21   2001033298
01 02 03 04 05 P 5 4 3 2 1

Contents

Introduction

These stories come from all over the country. North, South, East, West, both coasts, both borders, and the vast central plains, mountains, and deserts. There is as much variety in what they have to say, and how they say it, as the American geography itself. They are unpredictable and often quite surprising, and most importantly they are good.

People wonder about the state of our culture in part, I believe, because of the accelerating rate of change in almost every aspect of our society. Talking about culture has itself become political, and hence a bit loaded. Can we speak of "high culture" without being accused of elitism? Or "pop culture" without being accused of snobbism? Well, we have to speak, come what may, because nobody really knows what's happening in toto. We can only make guesses about our particular corner—in this case literature—and we can also go ahead and write the best stuff of which we are capable, as do the people contributing to this book, and let the chips fall where they may.

Much of the received wisdom about the book industry is correct. More money invested in fewer books, and fewer kinds of books. No matter the square feet of most bookstores, no matter how many shelves and how many walls covered with books, the fact is that most of the money revolves around a dozen or so "slots," as they are called in the business. Thriller. Romance. Asian American. Historical novel. Big Name Author (a number of slots). Male mystery. Female mystery, and so forth. As a book in one slot fades, it is often replaced by a similar book. At worst it is essentially the same book, by a different author and with a different cover. And of course, every once in a while someone comes in and wants the *Confessions of Saint Augustine,* and it might very well be on a shelf or a wall somewhere, which is good because after all one is supposed to be in a bookstore. But mostly it's "slots." Author, publisher, retailer, and critic conspire in this system.

Readers and intellectuals often wring their hands over this situation, assuming it is somehow destructive of quality literature. I cannot agree with them. People drawn to serious writing have always been a minority. Robert Frost never made enough from his writing to cover the groceries and the rent. Saul Bellow's first novel sold only four thousand copies. (Initially, that is. After he became a Big Name Author, and even before the Nobel Prize, every book he wrote was assured a "slot.") It is my belief that the growth of the pop market did not hurt the high culture market in books. It may even have indirectly helped, since more people read books of all kinds now than they did before. (Before the introduction of television they read less, not more, according to the statistics.)

The book you hold in your hand is not a "slot" book. But it is proof that serious writers exist, that they work to very high standards, get published, and contribute to the forward movement of American literary high culture. They give a lot of pleasure to an elite minority, who are in fact so hungry for freshness, originality, and the thrill of discovery they will crawl on their knees through a snowstorm for a taste of the real thing. You are probably one of them. I know I am.

The Iowa Award

DAVID BOROFKA

Hints of His Mortality

*David Borofka teaches composition, literature, and creative writing at
Reedley College. His stories have appeared in such journals as the* Southern
Review, Gettysburg Review, Shenandoah, *and* Massachusetts Review, *and
they have earned such awards as the* Missouri Review*'s Editors' Prize and*
Carolina Quarterly*'s Charles B. Wood Award for Distinguished Writing.
His novel,* The Island, *was published in 1997. New work has recently appeared
in* Image, Idaho Review, Mid-American Review, *and* CutBank.

*"Tersely written and marked by an exuberant and fluid prose style, both lyric
and colloquial,* Hints of His Mortality *is a serious-minded, highly refined
collection of stories by a writer of splendid talent. A sprawling, generous
anthology of stories about modern life, this book has much to admire and
much to offer to the discerning lover of good modern literature."*
OSCAR HIJUELOS, 1996

I. STEAM

Years later Ferguson would remember—as the disabled 727 in
which he was trapped as a passenger sank into the twilight of morning clouds—how his first wife had disappeared or died (he never
knew which) in the fog of the Central Valley of California. They
had been married a year. Helen had kissed him good-bye on a Friday morning following a Thursday night argument, saying that she
would return in three days after visiting her mother in Los Angeles.
From their apartment over the dry cleaner's, he watched as she
backed the Volkswagen out of the parking lot. She waved, giving
him a mock salute, forgiving him or dismissing him, he couldn't be
sure. Twelve hours later her mother called. *Wasn't Helen going to
come after all?* The police were notified, a missing person's report
was filed, but her disappearance remained a mystery. Her car was

never found alongside Highway 99, nor was her body admitted to any hospital in the state. No unidentified victims of accident or amnesia were reported during that weekend. One investigator insinuated that Helen might have wanted to disappear. Unwilling to admit the possibility, Ferguson waved the idea away as quickly as it had mingled with the smoke of the officer's cigarette. But a month later, having recognized that her return was not probable, that her disappearance would in all likelihood remain a mystery, Ferguson drove the route that Helen would have taken, drove down 99, with its tidemarks of agricultural flotsam, drove into the fog bank that threatened to swallow him in Stockton and continued unabated through Modesto, Merced, Madera, Fresno, Tulare, and Bakersfield, only lifting when he had begun the ascent through the Grapevine, drove until he had found an empty spot at a water turnout, where he could stop the car and look back like Lot's wife at the bowl of mist he had driven through. *Forgiven or dismissed?* Only then could he accept the fact that she was gone. Vanished. He assumed the worst. In front of him the tule fog—in the company of unwelcome emotions—hovered, reminding him that the first time he had seen her, she had appeared to him as something of a mirage, an image out of steam.

His father shot himself during the fall semester of Ferguson's junior year of college, and the estate provided certain bitter revelations. A romantic, Ferguson *père* had gambled every last scrap on a California cotton field, site of what the developer's brochure called New Town, a dreamer's utopian community of fresh air, clean streets, and happy children. That the cotton field was still just that, that the developer faced a shopping list of indictments for fraud and illegal use of the mails, that in order to settle the last of her husband's debts and to provide a small income for herself Ferguson's grieving mother was forced to liquidate the holdings of the trust left by her own father—it all seemed to possess the inevitability of Greek drama. A crueler joke, perhaps, was his father's farewell note, which read in part, "engendered by love, prompted by memories of a world known but never seen, it was a kind risk."

Kind or not, Ferguson was broke, deprived by his foolish father's

love, and his only recourse in the middle of that awful semester was
a financial aid advisor who directed him to a dishwashing job in the
basement cafeteria of Holman Hall. On his first evening of work,
he had descended the concrete steps with resignation. While he
couldn't claim to be political, he couldn't fail to spot the irony of
his own self-pity. Outside he had walked along the perimeter of a
rather chaotic war protest. The beneficence of a high draft number
(328) and the bad luck of having a romantic for a father had con-
spired together, and he now found himself neither in Vietnam nor
protesting it but guiltily following a conveyor belt stacked with
a trail of lasagna-encrusted plates to the bowels of a dormitory
kitchen. There in a haze of moisture, a woman, with the aid of a
pair of wooden tongs, was yanking a tray of plates out of the steaming dishwasher. Her back was to him, a sweat-soaked Grateful Dead
T-shirt, the outline of her brassiere showing whitely through. A
braid of frizzy, copper-colored hair slipped to one side of her neck,
around which a black rubber apron was tied.

"I'm here," he had yelled above the thunderstorm of the dishwasher, a stainless steel cylinder with a sliding door that seemed
more spaceship than appliance, "I'm here about the job."

She turned, frowning. Her eyes, blue agates, seemed unnaturally
bright.

"What job?" she said. Her black rubber gloves slashed through
the mist. "I don't need anyone."

"I'm a hardship," he said, speaking quickly and at a pitch higher
than the *boom, boom, whoosh* of the dishwasher.

She viewed him critically. "I'm sure you are."

"My father died."

She shrugged. "I'm sorry."

He stood, staring at her eyes, which seemed to have been clarified
by the steam, staring at her nose, a slight midwestern bump mis-
aligning it, its imperfection also its beauty. Couldn't she see that
this job wasn't of his own choice?

"Financial aid sent you?" she sighed. He nodded. "Here." She
stripped off the gloves and handed them over. Ferguson put them
on, feeling as though he were wearing another's skin. "We'll see
how it goes."

Later, when the conveyor had ground to a stop and the plates and the glasses and the institutional silverware had been returned to their respective slots and Helen had untied the rubber apron, they left the comfort of the steamy basement together, entering into the forgotten memory of the world and an evening of clear, indifferent stars. In one corner of the common a bonfire burned, marking the conclusion of the war demonstration. An effigy of the president was burning, only the nose and two fingers of one hand visible through the flames. A flag was incinerated. Cheers erupted as sparks rose.

"Fucking hypocrites, most of them," Helen said when she saw the protesters, her vehemence surprising him more than the profanity.

"I would have been a part of it if I wasn't up to my elbows in other people's food," Ferguson said, aware as he did so, that his voice had somehow ascended into his nose.

"Of course you would have. Poor baby has to wash out mama's dishes." Her hands were on her hips as she stared across the common. "Five years from now you can drive your daddy's Cadillac, excuse me, mommy's Caddy, and tell yourself that you did your part—you marched, you sang, you wrote letters, you were a part of IT, you were on the right side, the decent side, you got to rebel—and you had a terrific party besides."

"You want the war to go on?" he asked, annoyed not only by the continuing defection of his voice but by her knowingness, her certainty, her cynicism about his own best motives.

"The war stinks, but you can't hate its smell, then light some incense to cover your own."

"You'd just do nothing."

"You have no idea. Listen, hardship," the wind had shifted directions and smoke from the fire drifted between them, "I'll see you tomorrow at six. Unless, of course, you decide to become a revolutionary in the meantime."

It was not the last time she would act as his conscience, but having a conscience, whether one's own or embodied in someone else, wasn't necessarily such a bad thing, now was it? Helen was quick to judge, easy to anger, and sensitive to the faintest trace of self-interest. That she was so often right in her judgments of others' motives might have been due in part to the close scrutiny she'd given her own. At the age of sixteen, she'd rejected her father, president of an electronics firm specializing in defense applications; more importantly, she'd repudiated his money. Her mother, although already divorced from Helen's father, upbraided her daughter for throwing away the thousands of dollars she could have expected in continuing support and the possible millions in inheritance that one day might have been hers. In 1970, Helen's father's company sold $14 million of equipment to the American military, and Helen's father moved to the Hollywood hills to a facsimile of a Roman villa. Helen's mother owned her own mansion, financed by the divorce settlement. Helen lived in a studio apartment above a dry cleaner's and stamped her father's letters *Return to Sender*.

It was to this apartment that Ferguson came with Helen eight weeks after his own father's death. The room was filled with books; many of the titles he recognized as ones he was supposed to have read. Helen had read them, debating their ideas in silent conversations between herself and the images of the authors she'd created from the pages of the texts. Her interest in him confused him still. They sat on the floor, a gallon of wine between them, and talked, Helen instructing and criticizing, Ferguson listening. She seemed to need her own lectures, and if listening helped—even though his attention was directed not to the shape of her words but to the shape of her lips—what of it? She spoke of moral imperatives, personal integrity, and uncompromised interests, topics that few can tolerate, especially if one listens. He tried to listen only to the tone of her monologues rather than their substance, enjoying his intimacy with her passions more than her thoughts.

"I don't even open the envelopes," she said. "I'll live here until I die before I take his money. If I open an envelope and see a check, there's too much temptation. I'm his daughter, not his accomplice. I don't have to stink because he does. There's a better world than that inside me."

Later, because they had just come from the dishroom, they showered together before they made love. Even so, Ferguson couldn't help thinking afterward, as he wedged himself between the wall and Helen's inert form, listening to her slight, openmouthed snore, his nose buried in her wet, coarse hair, he couldn't help sensing, somewhat repelled, that no amount of scrubbing, bristle-brush or moral, would ever remove from the two of them the odor and confusion of other people's food.

And now, as the 727 pitched forward, it seemed analogous to his own life. It seemed as though he'd been living in anticipation of this moment for years, the slow rise to the top of the roller coaster's tracks, the climb, the struggle, knowing that achieving the summit would also mean the screaming descent, the wild ride, fear and pleasure indivisible, each necessary to define the other. Ferguson sat with his seat belt buckled, his wallet opened to the picture of Charlotte, his second wife, able to think only of Helen, his first. Remembering those late nights, when they had been the only ones in the dishroom, when they had worked naked in the steam, when her unreachable idealism became sentimental fantasy: "Two woodland creatures," Helen had breathed, running one finger along his glazed hip, "at play in the original world; one noble faun, one perfect nymph."

"We've been notified of a minor problem."

The pilot's voice, an intrusion, had intended comfort but in Ferguson had induced only remorse: *I'm so sorry,* he had thought, *I was wrong, I was always wrong. My poor, dear Helen.*

The ventilation system shut off, and the air became stuffy, used up. In the smoking section, a woman began to moan. If only her conscience had been strong enough to serve both of them, he wouldn't be here now. An irrational thought. Through the claustrophobic windows, he saw clouds reaching up to touch the wings. Gravity pulled at his stomach. A flight attendant made her way to the back of the plane, checking seat belts and tray tables, pulling herself along by the seat backs, the pitch of the floor as steep as stairs. Suddenly a rending. Ferguson watched, disbelieving, as the skin of the roof peeled back, the cavernous sky sucking out purses and magazines and overnight bags. The attendant fell to her knees, grabbing Ferguson's legs and the legs of his seat. His wallet flew from his hands. The stars were pouring through the tear in

the roof, swirling in chaotic order, dancing among the luggage
compartments.

The pilot announced that they were not to worry. *Just a routine emergency-type landing.* Routine?

The attendant's fingernails were digging into the meat of Ferguson's calves; her face was pressed against the floor, her skirt snapping against her legs like a flag while she intoned the same prayer over and over, "Oh God, oh God, oh God." Ferguson touched her hair. Then they were in the clouds, and there were clouds inside scudding down the aisle; the plane angled another degree toward the vertical, and recognizing that a thirty-eight-year-old man without a conscience of his own was not likely ever to own one, he gave himself up for lost.

Which was the same realization he'd had that morning standing at the turnout on Highway 99. A certain resignation to the state of his own soul. A certain disgust. For what he couldn't control, as he stood looking back at the fog, were the alternating currents of horror and joy that Helen's disappearance had caused to well up within him. If you had been standing there at that turnout, a tourist, say, driving an overheating station wagon, you might have seen him and wondered, wondered at the flickering of emotional responses that Ferguson himself could feel, like birds' wings playing around the corners of his eyes, nose, and mouth. If you had seen him there, and if you were the compassionate sort of person who was not afraid to involve yourself in another's affairs, you might have touched him on the shoulder, asked if he were all right, so extraordinarily, visibly torn was he by the depth of despair he felt over her absence as well as the gorgeous, liberating relief, the freedom he likewise felt, and then the guilt, the guilt, the guilt . . . of feeling so good when everything was so, well, wasn't it supposed to be tragic?

Without a conscience, who could tell?

Conscience, as he stared into the opaque mist below, seemed to be the tune from a forgotten song. Known once intuitively, but elusive now and forever, it recedes farther and farther the more the mind probes. Helen had known about that, of course. The night of their argument, before they had begun to yell, before Helen had begun to methodically break the juice glasses in the sink, he had found her sitting cross-legged on the floor, an open book in her lap, her mouth settling into a frown at the sound of his entrance. She closed the book, then said, "It's all just words, isn't it?"

"I guess so." Her admission frightened him.

"I used to think that the words were little cracks, and I could see through the cracks and see something really good. Really right.

"I don't think that now."

"They're the same words," he said.

"The same words," she agreed. "But things," she said, looking at him, he realized, as the violator of her perfect peace, "things are different."

So now, after he had failed—although he'd tried, he'd really tried—to find her, he lifted his hands over the valley in benediction and gave it, gave her, his blessing, that she could have loved him so much to leave without a nagging trace.

After all, Helen's father had begged him to take the money. That was the way he always told it. Her old man, bereft by his daughter's refusal of him, saw in Ferguson an ally. If he could not reach her, then through her husband he could satisfy his parental obligations. He worked out an arrangement with Ferguson, sending him a check each month, which Ferguson then deposited into a brokerage account, some of which, Ferguson was sure, wound up returning as stock in Helen's father's company. Tainted capital multiplying itself as it served its maker. He never asked specific questions while the account climbed, and it soared until 1972, the year Helen found the broker's statement on the kitchen table. A foolish thing to do, leaving the thing lying around like that, so foolish that he often wondered whether or not he secretly meant for her to see it, to infuriate her, to drive her away.

So he was going to die, his mind filled with self-recrimination, his eyes faced with the judgment of clouds.

The pilot, surely a maniac or an imbecile, announced—enthusiastically Ferguson thought—"We're not having a real good day

here, folks. A little trouble seems to have come up with the landing
gear, so we'll ask you all to get prepared as we ease her on in."

Ease? This hunk of disintegrating metal?

The plane leveled, loose objects settled back to the floor, and the
attendant rose shakily to her knees. "I'm *so* sorry," she said to Ferguson, holding in her hand a rectangular piece of his pant leg.

Murky lights shone through the clouds, through the fog, and
Ferguson allowed himself a glimmer of hope in this connection
with life lived safely on the ground. A cold wind roared through the
roof, and the plane shuddered. The engines whined in another key.
Evidently an airport was below; he could dimly see the haloes of
streetlamps, the movement of cars, the outlines of houses, the darkness of canals.

Automatically, he began mumbling, "Mary, Mother of God,"
though he had not been a communicant since college. The young
man in the window seat bit his lip until it bled; the banker across
the aisle held his head with his hands as if he were afraid it might
float away.

Then, lights and poles, cars and streets, all too quickly rushing up
from the ground. The fog would cushion them, Ferguson thought;
it would bear them up. But when they hit the runway, it was a sliding crash, with sparks flying from wingtip and engine. The control
tower skipped across the window, the terminal—they were never
going to stop. There were pieces of metal and jet engine strewn
behind them like a trail; next would come baggage and passengers
and crew until the trail unraveled and there was nothing left. Ferguson put his head between his knees. He could see the runway
through the floor. Helen would have known what to do; his only
impulse was to puke. Smoke surrounded them all. He was vaguely
aware that he as well as everyone else was screaming. Windows
broke. The seat ahead of him buckled, he heard his own legs snap
like uncooked spaghetti, then the window was filled with trees—
they must have slid into an orchard—and an attendant—*his attendant?*—was announcing the need for a prompt, orderly departure,
the taint of fright in her voice acting as contagion in everyone else.

"I can't move," he muttered. "My legs. I'm stuck." He worked his seat belt. Broken. Stuck twice. The young man near the window climbed out over him. "Could you give me—?" he began. "Help," he said. "Could someone give me a hand?" Amazingly, no one else seemed to be injured; no one else seemed to be experiencing the slightest difficulty in making the mad dash for the exits and the ramps. "Someone?"

Where was the crew? His attendant? The pilot with his false cheer?

Surely they knew he was in trouble.

"Help," he said again. "Help," this time more softly than before, under the impression that his life, his existence, hung on a fragile, precariously balanced scale.

The overhead lights blinked once, then off for good. Red lights—from an ambulance, perhaps?—flickered along the broken seat backs; shadows danced across the movie screen of this, his broken metal cave.

"Helen?" he breathed. "Help me."

Trapped, he sat still, watching her shadow braid illusory hair, listening to the sound of unknown liquids dripping in the dark.

One Sunday morning, not long after they were married, Ferguson was complaining about their lack of money, bitterly reviewing the old list of grievances against his father; Helen told him that if all he wanted to do was to get rich he should talk to *her* father, but that if he ever did, she'd be long gone. "It's a simple choice," she said. She left him sitting morosely, pondering her books, her bed, her seed of an idea now his. She was in the shower, and steam drifted along the ceiling. Framed by the shower curtain, she moved translucently, a creature alien to himself. The curtain fell away from his hand. She was standing under the nozzle, her face to the water, her closed eyes an illustration of absolutes. Light from the frosted window above the toilet irradiated her wet, copper-colored hair. As he stepped into the shower fully clothed, holding her from behind, whispering his already corrupted assurances, he knew that this moment might never be duplicated: he might never again be so transported by the elements of water and light and steam; she might never be so clothed in these clouds of glory.

David
Borofka

When she was in her dotage, Aunt Mary Brown Cartwright fell victim to a series of wasting fevers, from which she began to see visions, and her dreams bordered upon the prophetic. Her family, those nieces and nephews still alive as well as their children, became increasingly alarmed when, in her waking moments, she failed to recognize them, seeing at various times the angels Gabriel and Michael and at others the demons Beelzebub and Lilith. It was, after all, a jarring experience to visit one's favorite aunt and, upon pushing open her infirmary room door, flowers in hand, to be addressed as a creature of the netherworld and consigned to everlasting flames in the name of Jesus Christ. What may have been most disturbing, however, was that in her periods of extreme dislocation, even when blasting the most heinous of demons, her demeanor was calm and serene; it was in her lucid moments that she grew fretful and restive, as if she had been cut adrift on an uncertain sea, doubtful of ever reaching land again.

So, before Ferguson accompanied his wife from their home in Palo Alto to Aunt Mary Brown's retirement center in the Central Valley of California, Charlotte had warned him of what he would see. He was not entirely unprepared. Still, it was a shock to see this once-vibrant woman, a woman whom he'd met three times before—once at their wedding, once at his oldest son's baptism, and the last time at his wife's Uncle Farley's funeral—it was a shock to see her so wasted by fever . . . and fervor. There could not have been seventy-eight pounds left to her. The pillows supported her head; her body, however, appeared to float above the bed. Her skin was transparent. One blue-green vein, delicately tracing the hollow of her temple, seemed more decorative than anatomical. She was otherworldly. This good woman, who had served family and faith for seventy-plus years, looked as though she were nearing a point of translation—as if she were dematerializing into one of the invisible beings she so clearly saw just to the left of the wall-mounted television set, the garish images of tawdry soap operas, in her eyes, pale by comparison with the heavenly throngs peopling the airspace of her universe.

As they entered Aunt Mary Brown's room, Charlotte set her packages down—the occasion of their visit happened to coincide with Aunt Mary Brown's birthday—and then left the room again, announcing over one shoulder her intention of "finding that little shit of a head nurse." Ferguson was alone, watching the translucent skin of her cheeks and forehead, the rise and fall of Aunt Mary Brown's slight chest, the barely noticeable disturbance of blanket and sheet. Unnerved by his proximity to this woman who was so obviously a part of other worlds and glad that she was separated from him by her slumber, he sat in the one chair at the foot of the hospital bed, thinking that he would be happy to leave this flat, dusty town, happy to go home, alone, away from his wife and her dying relatives.

Together he and Charlotte had driven down the peninsula, through the coastal mountains, and three-quarters of the way across the San Joaquin Valley to this ugly, ramshackle series of expiring one-story stucco buildings inside which an old woman was noticeably disappearing. Outside the window, ancient men and women sat in wheelchairs dozing in a gray courtyard landscaped in cactus. Tomorrow morning he would leave, flying back to his own poor choice of a life. He would fly back only, he vowed, at Charlotte's express request. In the meantime, he had eighteen hours of dull regret to kill.

If he were cornered, Ferguson would have confessed himself to be an honorable man, happy in his life—his marriage, his family, his career. But he was not without misgivings or fear of exposure. If self-respect could be defined as an awareness of one's flaws and the refusal to allow either self-excuse or excessive guilt to accumulate in one's life, then, Ferguson decided, his honor was easily enough established. His own catalogue of character deficits was simple: a lethargic temperament during moments of crisis, a tendency to incite gossip among his co-workers, and, worst of all, the rather unfortunate habit of copulating with secretaries, receptionists, baby-sitters, retail clerks, nurses, etc. Any female economically and intellectually inferior was fair game. No Lothario exactly, he had discovered the

method for his own brand of seduction—the fact that women liked
to hear him confess these flaws of character; they liked to think that
they could heal him in some way, that they could convince him that
he wasn't really so lost, that they could help him find some peace
within himself. And following such confessions—*mea culpa*—he
found himself in more than one compromised position, wondering
how he could have come to such a pass: these twisted sheets, this
rank taste—not only in his mouth but even in his throat, his nose,
his eyes—of mortality.

An unfortunate habit, of course, but one that he had lived with
and accommodated. He was old enough now, however, for it to be
frightening rather than exciting. And yet as he thought of leaving
this hospital room in which a spectral wraith delayed her death, he
found himself thinking not of his crimes against Charlotte, nor of
those committed against his first wife, Helen, but of those misde-
meanors certain to be realized with Magda, the twenty-five-year-
old actress/typist/palm reader whose taste he had most recently
savored. He needed to leave this place, needed to leave Charlotte,
with her sprayed helmet of hair covering a mind bereft of imagination or soul, her clothes with creases sharp enough to cut passion;
but he also needed to end what had become a tedious affair with
Magda, who wore caftans and wooden beads in some vague, mis-
understood tribute to the 1960s, who plainly hated to wash, whose
odor during lovemaking often reminded Ferguson of the dirty
towel bin in a high school boys' locker room.

He had met her at his son's school carnival. Her hair was pulled
back in a scarf, and she was dressed in her habitual, he realized later,
gypsy style, a fashion she preferred because it required no underwear. She held his right hand, lightly tracing the lines with one
blood-red press-on nail, and he had known—at the moment when
she pronounced his love life to be one of indifference and confirmed
what he already knew—that she would invite him home with her.
He had known even before their first thrashing together that her
body—her odor, the mole on the back of her right knee, the wild
thicket of her pubic hair, which spread upward to her belly—would
fascinate him even as it repelled him, and that her exoticism, like

her dirty second-story apartment, would begin to bore him five minutes after he first thrilled to it. He had known all this for some time, but where was he to go after Magda?

So absorbed was he in the memory of her peculiarly fetid taste, now two hundred miles distant, that he failed to notice when Aunt Mary Brown's strangely clear blue eyes first opened.

"Hello," he said, struggling to surface. "You're awake."

She said nothing, staring, as if seeing everything for the first time. Her hands fussed atop the blanket.

"Charlotte went to speak with the nurse." He was aware as he spoke that, in order to be heard clearly, his voice had become loud, prissy, with elaborately precise elocution, as if he were speaking to a foreigner, but he could find no way around it. "She should be back presently."

Her eyes, blank as a movie extraterrestrial's, consumed everything—the room, her bed, himself—and saw nothing.

"Can I get you anything?" he asked.

The woman continued to look at him. Not precisely at him but near him, as if there were something other than himself occupying similar space. Spooky. For a moment he imagined that he too saw something, some disturbance in the air above the foot of her bed. The watery light from the courtyard window projected shadows at once alive yet indistinct.

"Can I get you anything?" he asked again. Just for something to say, some sound to keep that space filled.

A change seemed to fall about her features. She raised her head from the pillow, her eyes narrowed into focus, her hands reached for the steel railing on either side of the bed. Her mouth sagged. A blob of spit escaped from one corner, an unintelligible sigh from the other. Where had Charlotte gone? A cloud seemed momentarily to intrude between his eyes and hers.

Curious and, in that moment, glimpsing the depths of his own guilt, desperate for accusation and confession, believing as he did that his crimes must be evident to any who cared to look, believing even more firmly in the revelations from strangers, he asked: "What? What are you trying to tell me?"

Aunt Mary Brown's head rocked back onto her gray pillow, exposing the valley of her old woman's throat caught between the

tired cords of her neck. Jesus, he thought, don't die now.

But the old woman, with no sense of drama or irony, had only
fallen asleep, her cracked lips crossed by a look that he could only
regard as sly.

Ferguson met Charlotte a year after Helen disappeared. He had
taken to driving along Highway 99, looking for absolution. He had
fought with Helen the night before, and he could not be sure that
upon leaving—driving, she said, to her mother's house—that she
had yet forgiven him. He could also not be sure, to this day some
twenty years later, whether he was sorry that she had gone, that she
had disappeared somewhere along this highway to nowhere, that
she was for all intents and purposes dead, and that his own financial statement had benefited hugely from that fact. If there were
justice at all, he sometimes liked to reflect, he had received whatever
punishment was his due for his behavior toward Helen by meeting
Charlotte.

He had driven from Berkeley to Fresno, driving numbly without
seeing anything of the road or the country except what was necessary—the taillights of the semi in front of him, the turn signal of
the Volkswagen in the next lane. For a year he had experienced the
regret of a man unable to celebrate separation from his wife because
she hadn't simply left, she had disappeared; and on top of that, he
was afraid that she'd been right for leaving in the first place and that
his own material and emotional gains were, because they had come
at her expense, forever tainted and therefore unendurable.

In a hotel bar that night, he'd noticed a group of three women
having drinks in one of the red leather booths. Two of the women,
blond and bouncy and full of self-absorbed laughter, sat across from
the third, a straight-lipped brunette in a plum-colored suit, who
drank beer from a bottle and tapped cigarette ash into her empties.
When the blondes left in tandem to go to the Ladies, Ferguson slid
into the seat across from Charlotte. She was an accountant, she said,
when he asked. Her father was a retired air force colonel, now a
farmer of peaches and grapes. Her mother did charity work for
the children of migrant laborers. Her father, she said, was a good,

strong man, and her mother was only good. Ferguson thought that he had seen her smirk as she spoke of them.

What he couldn't know, of course—as he sat across from her in the anonymity of that red leather booth—was that what he'd presumed to be an intelligent skepticism was in reality a simple absence of imagination. The only other time he saw those straight lips change, they curled (into something like Aunt Mary Brown's sly smile) when he told her about Helen, sparing her none of the details, condemning himself as a moral bankrupt, his integrity lost, his honor forfeit. It was the first time he had used this routine with a woman—indeed he hadn't recognized it as the opening salvo to seduction until afterward, not realizing until much, much later, either, that she hadn't even understood the apparent intent of his story, much less the uncertain motive: a betrayal confessed, an act of penance and contrition. She only heard him relate the details of a pragmatic business decision and the reaction of an overemotional wife. He had thought at that moment that such a woman might be just the answer to his most pressing need, someone who looked reality in the face and did not expect anything except that which was on the surface, that which could be seen and counted and measured, someone in whom a teasing spirit could not pander.

So it was that Charlotte drove him to the airport at six-thirty the following morning. Ferguson felt as though he were strangling. A bank of lead-gray autumn clouds dropped a faint drizzle. The roadway glistened, the moisture standing on top of a season's worth of oil. They drove through fruit orchards, cotton fields, and vineyards, all recently harvested. Field workers in green slickers were pruning the fruit trees. Smoke hovered as rain floated to the earth. They drove through this dull country, and suddenly a swarm of black wings, like the black bows on a funeral wreath—the only way he could describe the objects—surrounded them, falling and fluttering in the heavy air, turning end over end and spinning the way certain seedpods do. He had heard stories of dogs and cats or slaughtered sides of beef falling from open cargo-bay doors, and he looked—didn't this sort of thing happen all the time?—craning his neck for an upward view of the sky, but there seemed to be no air-

plane, no rational explanation, visible or aural. The wings, inexplicable, swirled against the windshield, then slipped to the side, flying
upward again in the sudden wake of the automobile. If he had been
given to such sentiments he would have said that the sight made his
heart jump. Indeed, his eyes felt enlarged in their scope, as if they
now saw a deeper fact. If he could somehow know how this other
life, these heralds of other worlds, could fall and fall and spin—
if he could somehow enter into their inarticulate exaltation—he
might be able to know his own, his better self.

"My God," he breathed, "what do you think—"

"Raisin trays," Charlotte, the farmer's daughter, said.

"What?"

The wings turned and turned as they fell.

"Paper raisin trays. The grapes are set out on butcher paper between the rows. The sun dries them, then after they're taken up,
the trays are burned." Charlotte flicked the wipers into action, a
movement that physically hurt Ferguson and smeared several of the
black objects against the glass.

The mystery, little enough, was explained; the problem was
solved, and, as usual, he'd made too much out of nothing. When
he looked now, he wondered how he could have failed to see them
for what they were—burned scraps of paper. She was obviously
right. He had simply gotten carried away. Why, then, did he feel so
lost? He watched the charred wisps swirling in the updrafts, and
then, as if a direct result of Charlotte's explanation, he saw a fire
burning in the middle of an open field and a Mexican in khakis
throwing crumpled streams of butcher paper—and with them the
wings of heaven—into the center of the flames.

Not unlike the day before: a doctor, a lawyer, and a minister had
each come to visit Aunt Mary Brown Cartwright, and if Ferguson
had not been there to see it, he would have considered it the opening line of a badly told poker-night joke. The doctor had come, a
perfunctory gesture, on his every-other-day visit. He appeared tired
and not a little bit cross, and when he spoke to them he looked over
the top of his glasses. These things, he said, standing beside Aunt
Mary Brown's bed as he took her pulse, sometimes go on for

months. The family—Charlotte, her parents, a younger cousin—nodded without rebuke. The lawyer, a fat man nearly as ancient as Aunt Mary Brown herself, came with papers to deliver and a copy of Aunt Mary Brown's power of attorney for Charlotte's father. He patted Charlotte on one knee and cast a rueful look at the hospital bed, as if measuring its length and width. Dandruff fell from his ears in a cheery imitation of snow. I think we're all covered, he said to Charlotte's father. Now all we have to do is wait. Yes, Charlotte's father said, that's all that's left, isn't there? The minister came in last of all, a youngish Episcopalian wearing, for no discernible reason, a clerical collar underneath a green golf cardigan. He held Aunt Mary Brown's hand and then, seeing the straight-lipped looks on the family's faces, replaced it next to her side. She was a good woman, he said. His lips trembled from something other than grief. Yes, Charlotte's mother said, an exceptional woman, but these past two months she's not been herself at all. Last week she called me the whore of Babylon. It is so hard to see, the minister said, someone you love brought to this point. That's for sure, Charlotte's cousin said, that's for sure. She had a good life, Charlotte's father said. Without question, the minister said, an exemplary life, a pillar of the church and her community. They each stared at her, watching the sheet struggle to rise, then fall. Ferguson waited, hoping to see once again that disturbance in the air, hoping to see those invisible wings. Would you like me to pray? the minister asked. If you want, Charlotte said. Go ahead.

The air above Aunt Mary Brown's bed was absolutely still.

Ferguson wanted to scream.

At the end of the jetway, his plane loomed, a black silhouette in the rain-threatened dawn; heaven's lumbering, mechanical messenger, it bulked on the runway, dour in purpose, irrevocable by nature. It suddenly seemed that the poles of his life had become awful in their clarity: to remain earthbound in this dusty valley was to cling to Charlotte; to reach Palo Alto was to confront Magda and his own need for something new, something young and dirty. But to board—*nagging thought*—to become airborne was somehow to risk meeting Helen and her appalling idealism.

He paused for one moment, suddenly hesitant. Charlotte was
waiting, watching him from the rack of Mutual of Omaha machines. He raised his hand, drawing her eyes. "I'll come back for
you on Friday," he called to her. He had intended to say, "I love
you." Even so, while the line behind him began to bottleneck between the blue cords, his tone and expression, he imagined, were
that of a man demanding the answer to a proposal. But from her
distance, Charlotte could hear only the surface of the words, not
their intended depth. "Have a good trip," she said pleasantly. She
held her purse in both hands. Her good winter coat, her navy dress
underneath—both held their uniform press. Ferguson had to sup-
press a sudden desire to vault the blue cords, tackle his wife, and
violate the military concision of her life and imagination.

Distrusting his impulse and believing finally that such things are
best left as dreams, he did nothing. He walked into the tunnel of
the jetway, fighting an unexpected congestion of claustrophobia. A
smiling flight attendant ushered him to his place athwart the wings.
He cinched his seat belt uncomfortably tight and closed his eyes,
fearing what he might otherwise see, vowing not to open them
again until he was home.

III. SMALL FIRES

Small fires danced behind his eyes. An odd music of invitation filled
his ears. He was dimly aware of hands—hands touching his face,
hands pulling at his broken seat belt, hands fluttering like moths in
the red-stained darkness.

Helen?

They were carrying him then, holding him beneath his armpits,
telling him to walk when *goddammit* didn't they know, those sad-
ists, that his legs were brittle, broken sticks? It seemed such a long,
such an uphill climb, this blind stumble through the wreckage of
turbulence and impact. And all the while fire was licking at the corners of his eyes, the light flickering blood red, the danger of which
these sadist-angels were obviously stupid and unaware.

"Stop it," he tried to say. "You're killing me."

And then they were out, moving in the foggy fall morning, a morning unremarkable except for seventy-seven people, all with their respective burdens of conscience and guilt and fear, seventy-seven people who had fallen from a sky so murky and gray as to be nothing.

Ferguson's father had never claimed to be anything other than a failure. His own father, owner and founder of a company that built prefabricated housing, had tried to teach his son the intricacies of business and finance, two-by-fours and brackets, but proved spectacularly unsuccessful. Not for lack of trying. Ferguson remembered being eight years old and waking up into darkness, startled by his father's shadowy form above him, his father's voice whispering, "I'm sorry I have to do this." This occurring just before his father tried to leave his mother and him, going, he said, somewhere, anywhere . . . away. Ferguson never entirely understood the mechanism by which his grandfather compelled his father to stay. Only one dim memory remained: his grandfather and father sitting together in the kitchen of his grandparents' house, his grandfather silver-haired and profane, his father broken, sitting before his own father, his hands pressed between his knees, his head nodding slowly, reluctantly, as obedient as Ferguson himself. His grandfather punctuated his sentences with plumes of acrid cigar smoke while his father ducked his head yet lower and water rose in his eyes. And Ferguson had known, with the clarity of instinct, that he might never love his father more than at that moment. That rather than hating this adult child for his weakness of will, he was obligated to understand his father's deficiency of moral fiber as a prescient gaze into his own future.

And then too, he also understood, his certainty inarticulate yet profound, that the ploy his grandfather had used—condemning his father to failure, into this posture of abject servitude and responsibility—was himself.

They carried him through a wasteland of wreckage. The jagged, torn metal of the aircraft, the earth smoldering and charred. Suitcases, their contents strewn in all directions, littered the orchard of

Scotch pines in a parody of Christmas cheer. The air itself seemed

to have become smoke. Two men in stiff, buff-colored crash coats,
their arms locked beneath him, laboriously ran with their raving
burden, not looking at him, relegating his moans for the losses of
his life to that realm of nonsense common to all victims of tragedy
and anguish and horror.

Following the shot, Ferguson was the first to find his father. At
two in the frost of a fall morning, aware of the cloud of gunpowder
blown about by the night winds, he and his mother stumbled in
pajamas and bare feet into the backyard, screaming his father's
name, knowing already the outcome of their search. By the stone
bench underneath the barren apple trees, Ferguson saw the crumpled form. He waved his mother away then, feeling as though he
had become a character scripted by others, rolled his father over. By
moonlight, his father's eyes appeared startled, puzzled by the violence of this latest decision, this last disappearance. It had seemed
to Ferguson a horrible exit from one life for the sake of entry to
another, and he could only imagine the despair that had driven his
father from prefabricated housing to New Town, from wealth to
ruin, as if his choice, under the delusion of the ideal and immortal,
had been one of escape by destruction.

A door had been opened, a threshold crossed. He awoke in a
room so white as to be stripped of recognizable features. A rough
institutional sheet lay across his chest. He was clothed in a hospital
gown, his legs elevated, wired to pulleys above the bed, his wrists
shackled by IV tubes and a paper bracelet. His fingers, probing his
head, found bandages, a caricature of injury. A nurse with red hair
and white uniform entered, stacking some towels on the vacant second bed. "You're awake," she announced as though he needed the
news confirmed. She paused, reviewing his records with a skeptical
frown, and Ferguson watched, heartsick, when she turned, reveal-
ing the single, coarse braid of coppercolored hair.

"How about a little light?" She moved to open his curtains, pivot
the blinds.

"I'd prefer not." He stopped her just short of allowing this invasion of golden fire, knowing now that Charlotte would come soon with flowers and stock assurances, that Magda would call, excited to know someone so nearly dead. That everyone would announce how lucky he was to be alive, and only he would know that it was no real cause for celebration.

José del Río

Mark Brazaitis is the author of Steal My Heart, *a novel whose hero, Ramiro Caal, originally appeared in "A Detective's Story," one of the stories in his Iowa Award–winning collection. Brazaitis is a recipient of a 2000–2001 Literature Fellowship from the National Endowment for the Arts. An associate professor of English at West Virginia University, he lives in Morgantown, West Virginia, with his wife, Julie, and daughter, Annabel.*

"The stories in The River of Lost Voices *are unified not only by their vividly rendered Guatemalan settings but by the pervasive sense of folktale that is evident in both the magic of their imagery and the pleasing unpredictability of their forms."*

STUART DYBEK, 1998

I was born dead and I've never been allowed to forget it. Nor would I want to. Because I was not supposed to live, my life has been a freak occasion, free of obligation. I am a ghost and I enjoy a ghost's freedom.

I was not supposed to live. God left me in the dark room with my mother, wet and lifeless in her arms. The women who had come to help with my birth cried, and my father turned away and walked to the cantina. My mother said a hundred prayers, then fell silent, with no more prayers to say. The women went away, and my mother slept with me in her lap. I woke her with my first breath.

The women came back the next morning to celebrate a miracle, and my father, still drunk, lifted me and kissed me with cantina kisses. But that night my mother held me in her arms and whispered her amazement and fear: "I dreamed of a river and a serpent and I heard you breathe."

My father wanted to name me Lazarus and the women all suggested variations of "del Milagro," but my mother named me José del Río after her brother, who at age thirty-two drowned while swimming in the shallow river on the far side of town.

I owed nothing to God. Mine was a free life, a freak life. I was supposed to be dead.

Everyone thought I was retarded because I didn't say a word until I was fifteen years old. Concerned about the forbidding influence I might have on my three sisters, my father consigned me to a room in the front of our house. My sisters, all older than I, slept in a back room across the courtyard. They acknowledged me only when they brought new friends home and pointed me out as a zookeeper would an exotic animal: "He was born dead."

Around town, however, I was celebrated as a mentally deficient angel, one to whom everyone turned as living proof of God's existence. "Here he is, the boy who was born dead, the one our Savior rescued." Because of my sacred status, my father liked to keep me beside him whenever we had visitors.

My father was an assistant to the mayor in those days, and our house was used as a meeting place by local government and military officials. In addition to their official positions, many of these men were owners of plantations. Their coffee plants lined the mountains around town like fat, green-uniformed soldiers. My father, though, was not wealthy enough to own a plantation; instead, he planted corn on land he rented in a nearby village. But my father's voice— more radiant and powerful than a priest's—helped him overcome his low status. Because of his voice, he was, at these gatherings, a kind of master of ceremonies.

On meeting nights, my mother and sisters were sent to church or to my aunt's house. I was permitted to stay, my father always informing everyone, unnecessarily, that they needn't fear my presence because "a wall couldn't keep a secret better." My father would inaugurate each meeting by asking the men to place their guns on the table. Everyone would be silent a moment, staring at the sparkling collection of black and silver. "Well," my father would say. "Here, *caballeros*, is power." My father would lift his arms, the men would reclaim their guns, and the meeting would begin.

Between discussions of life and death, the men swigged beer and traded uncouth comments about local women. One night, a little drunk, as usual, my father described his seduction of Doña Blanca; because of his intoxication and her girth, he said, he'd needed her help in "finding the entrance." Lieutenant Rubio told of a similar experience with the same woman and declared, "I wasn't even drunk."

During one of these meetings, Mayor Gualim spoke bitterly about Miguel Cal, the owner of a sawmill. Don Miguel gave scraps of wood to plantation workers for their fires and explained to them, leaning out the window above the mountain of sawdust where they all gathered, that a plantation owner was legally obliged to pay the minimum wage of five quetzales a day, not half that, as was custom in our town. "He's a guerrilla," Mayor Gualim said. Grinning, Lieutenant Rubio asked the mayor if Don Miguel's political ambitions—he was known to be considering a race for mayor in the next election—also concerned him. Mayor Gualim said, "What concerns me is the purity of our town." He winked, and Lieutenant Rubio laughed. Then the room fell silent and the two men stared at each other, their grins gone.

"When?" Mayor Gualim asked.

On the night Don Miguel was supposed to die, I waited in his yard. Don Miguel's house had a big front window that looked in on his television, and people from town would often gather outside to watch without sound whatever Don Miguel was watching. Don Miguel's wife was dead and his two sons were grown and living in the capital, but he had recently bought a swing set and slide, which children in town had christened already with muddy feet.

I was sitting on a swing, about twenty meters from the front of the house, when Lieutenant Rubio and two soldiers pulled up in a van and knocked on the door. When Don Miguel answered, asking in an anxious voice what the men wanted, one soldier jabbed his rifle into Don Miguel's stomach. Don Miguel bent over, clutching himself, then fell on his knees. No one moved for a long time. Finally, Don Miguel looked up. The second soldier placed the end of his rifle between Don Miguel's eyes and pulled the trigger. The sound was softer than a dog's bark. The two soldiers dragged Don Miguel's body to the van as Lieutenant Rubio entered the house. In a few minutes, he returned outside and stepped into the van.

When I could no longer see the van or hear its motor, I walked into the house. In the living room, the cushions of the couch had been removed and thrown aside, and a glass cabinet next to the television had been cleared of its objects. Ceramic figures and soccer trophies lay broken on the floor. Down a hallway, in Don Miguel's bedroom, the mattress had been removed from the frame and the drawers of his dresser pulled open. A single black sock hung like a burned tongue from the top drawer.

In the last room at the end of the hall, a *bodega* full of old machetes, hoes, and scraps of wood, I smelled wax. There was no light switch, but the moonlight from the small break between the block walls and tin roof provided enough light to see. I moved past the tools and wood to the back of the room, where I saw a small desk in the corner. There was a candle on the desk; touching it, I felt the still soft wax.

Below the candle was a sheet of paper with neat numbers filling a hand-drawn column on the right edge. Don Miguel obviously had been counting his money, but the interruption had forced him to conceal it. He had not, however, done a thorough job. The end of a new bill stuck out of the bottom drawer. Opening the drawer, I reached in and pulled out a fistful of tens. Deeper in the drawer were stacks of twenties and fifties, each held together by thick rubber bands.

I was not permitted to eat with my father, mother, and sisters, so I ate on my bed, where my mother would join me after serving everyone. My mother was a tall, thin woman who wore only black or dark blue *corte*, although my father was *ladino* and wore blue jeans and cowboy hats.

My mother always smelled like wood smoke from her cooking fire. Even her breath smelled and felt like smoke, fragrant and warm. Sitting next to me, my mother would wrap her hands in her *corte* and talk to me as if I could understand. She spoke to me in Spanish, in order, she said, to prepare me to survive in the modern world, although when she got tired, she would drop, dreamlike, into Pokomchí. I loved the way the words clicked in her throat.

Often she would ask me questions. "What do you think of the

new outhouse your father built?" She would wait for a response,

smiling patiently. "He's good with his hands," she would continue. "His father was a carpenter, you know. Do you think his father would approve of what he does?"

Sometimes late at night, my mother would leave her bedroom and walk across the courtyard to visit me. Often it would be raining, and even minutes after she had sat next to me on my bed, water would trickle from her hair. She told me the stories her mother had told her, the fables of our town. She always apologized before beginning a story, explaining that her mother knew the story better. Her mother, she said, told these stories over and over and hardly altered a word from one telling to the next, her fidelity like a priest's to the Bible. My mother told the stories softly, with a whistle in her voice like a wind tickling tree branches. I liked best the story about the two priests and the serpent, and my mother must have known because she told this story more often than the others.

"A long time ago," my mother would begin, "not long after the Spanish came to our town and built the church, there were two priests who hoarded the church's money, gold and silver coins stacked as high as their eyes, in a room at the back of the church. At the end of every night, even on nights they gave mass, the priests would retreat to their room at the back of the church to count the money. One would count silver, the other gold. Then they would trade jobs to make sure the other had counted correctly.

"A great earthquake came, and everyone ran out of their houses, everyone but the priests, who had not finished counting their money. A great gap opened in the earth and the priests and all their money fell in, fell all the way to the center of the earth, where there is an underground river. The church was destroyed, but gradually the people in town raised enough money to build another. The priests and their money, however, were never found.

"But there is a serpent who knows where the money is, and he lives beside the gold and silver and the bones of the priests on the banks of the underground river. The serpent comes up to town once a year, on Holy Thursday, and only at midnight. He has one gold eye and one silver eye and few people see him, but he sees everything."

Sometimes after reciting this fable, my mother would tell me again the story of my birth and the dream she had before I breathed. "I was afraid," she said one night. "I thought it was a terrible omen, you given life with the help of a serpent." She sighed and tried to smile. "But later I thought it might be good fortune in a bad world."

One time my mother cried. This was after she said, "Your father gave me a disease and when I urinate, it hurts." She cried silently, as I would have, and her crying caused me to say, against my will, "Passion." She smiled, a quick, joyful smile, dried her eyes, and left the room. My father and sisters, staggering with sleep, returned with her. Rubbing his eyes, my father said, "You sure he spoke?" My mother nodded and repeated the word, looking at him as if she expected "passion" to set everything right. But my father merely patted my head as he would a dog's and said, "Will you speak again in another fifteen years?"

When my father and sisters had left the room, my mother said, "He doesn't believe me." She placed her hand on my head and dug her nails into my scalp until I flinched. Quickly, she removed her hand and looked at her fingers as if they had disobeyed her. "I'm sorry," she said.

She sat next to me and looked a long time into my eyes. "I'm sorry," she said again, and I knew this apology wasn't for the momentary pain she'd caused me but for giving away my secret. Forgiving her, I rubbed my knee against hers.

It was a month later that I returned home from Don Miguel's house with my shirt full of money. My room was dark, and when I went to sit on my bed, I noticed my mother. "José," she said, "I've been waiting here a long time."

I sat next to her. She must have seen the bulge in my shirt, but she didn't acknowledge it. "A mother knows things about her children that no one else knows," she said. "I know that you understand more than anyone suspects. And I know that you need your silence; it's what you have to make it all bearable. Everyone has something. Your aunt has her church and Bible group, and your father his politics and beer, and you have your silence." She smiled.

"And I have you."

She gazed at me until I smiled too. "We know each other," she said.

I sat in the room with my father, the mayor, and Lieutenant Rubio as they celebrated Don Miguel's death. In time, I heard them plot three more murders, all of which I attended, standing in shadows.

When Lieutenant Rubio and his two soldiers went to kill Don Felix, the owner of a paint store, he didn't open the door. The soldiers broke it down, their rifles punching through it like paper. I heard shots puncture the night—shots quieter and quicker than thunder—and saw the two soldiers haul Don Felix into the van as if he were a drunk companion.

I waited until Lieutenant Rubio had left the house before I entered. There was broken glass on the floor, the shards mixed with playing cards. Doña Lorena, Don Felix's wife, was spread on a couch in the middle of the room. Blood was splattered on the couch and dribbled out of her mouth like a baby's spittle. I knew she was alive, however, because I could see her pulse beating in her throat.

Before long she opened her eyes. She looked at me, then glanced quickly to her left, and I knew where to look. She tried to speak, but I slipped past her. To see the top shelf of the cupboard, I had to stand on a chair. At the back, behind empty cereal boxes, I found three old paint cans stuffed with bills.

As I walked past Doña Lorena on my way out the door, she spoke very clearly: "You devil." I waited until her eyelids fell over her eyes like heavy clouds.

I kept the money, a stack that would have overwhelmed a bank clerk, in plastic bags that I picked up on the streets: pink bags from the bakery and blue bags from the woman who sold tomatoes in front of the market and yellow bags from Doña Patricia's pharmacy. I sorted my money in the bags: the tens in the pinks, the twenties in the blues, and the fifties in the yellows. I put the bags in the corner of my room and covered them with a blanket.

I began to leave ten- and twenty-quetzal bills in my mother's purse, sneaking them in when she was bathing or sleeping or cooking. She would come to my bed nights and sit beside me, our knees touching, and speak softly as trucks rumbled past the doorway and the house shook. "Thank you," she said one night. "I bought myself some soap today, three little heart-shaped soaps that smell like roses. I don't want to use them. It's nice just to look at them in the box and smell them. Of course one day I will use them, but I'll miss them."

Another night she said: "Your father is doomed. A person can live only so long sentencing people to death like God. God doesn't like that, and besides, people don't like it either. They won't touch us, though. They think that because I'm a woman, I'm harmless. And you, they think you're a fool." She laughed, a sort of triumphant laugh, and shook her head. "They think you're a fool."

She pulled from her *corte* a twenty-quetzal bill I'd given her and rubbed it between her fingers. "We'll be all right," she said.

Three nights later, five guerrillas entered our house with rifles. When they came, I was awake, but they pulled my father, mother, and sisters out of bed and stood us in our courtyard. The leader gave a short speech, then said he would take only my father. Trembling so violently his teeth chattered, my father broke toward the back fence, and in their haste to kill him, the guerrillas shot my mother in the neck.

My father died instantly, a half dozen bullets in his back, although my sisters kneeled in the dirt beside him and cried prayers in his ears. After the guerrillas left, the neighbors arrived to watch my mother die.

Wailing, the women crowded around her bed. I couldn't get near her and saw her only through a screen of skirts. She didn't say anything. A woman tried to hold her hand, but my mother kept moving both her hands to where the blood was flowing from her neck. She didn't seem to be in pain; her lips, though, were pursed, as if in anger over a betrayal.

When she was dead, the women left, and I sat next to my mother

until the sun shot light through the window in front of us. Two
men came to take away her body, but first they had to uncurl my fingers from her *corte*.

The guerrillas also killed Mayor Gualim, and they probably would have killed Lieutenant Rubio but, alerted, he had driven to the military base in Cobán. By the time he and thirty soldiers returned, the guerrillas were gone. Lieutenant Rubio questioned my sisters, and they told him that my father had charged the guerrillas, all five of them, trying to protect my mother and the rest of us, but they had gunned him down as he was strangling one and kicking another.

Lieutenant Rubio repeated the story around town, and it was all my father needed to become a hero. My mother was buried next to him, and the priest said three words about her: "She loved him."

When all the mourners had gone—even my sisters, who had clung to the cross above my father's grave as if it were an extension of his body—I sat beside my mother. I imagined her telling me stories, her voice as warm and soft as the rain that fell. I knew I could speak to her now, could tell her anything. But, as always, I didn't need to.

Three weeks later, my sister Florinda married Lieutenant Rubio. They slept in my mother and father's room, the entrance to which Lieutenant Rubio fortified by replacing the wood door with a metal one. "The guerrillas will need a tank to get me out of bed," he announced.

I turned sixteen, an occasion only my mother would have remembered.

One morning, I left money for Florinda in her skirt while she was bathing, and that night I heard her tell Lieutenant Rubio, "The strangest thing happened. I found twenty quetzales in my pocket." Lieutenant Rubio laughed and said, "A gift from God." The next morning, I did the same thing; and that afternoon, as she was washing clothes, Florinda mentioned it to Lieutenant Rubio. Lieutenant Rubio didn't laugh this time but said, "You either forgot or . . ."

He stopped, a worried look on his face, and Florinda asked, "What's wrong?"

"No, I was thinking . . . ," Lieutenant Rubio said.

"What?"

"It could be the guerrillas," Lieutenant Rubio said, and he explained that he'd heard that the guerrillas sometimes notified their future victims. It was a psychological game they played. A friend of his, another lieutenant, had received a cardboard heart anonymously every Sunday for six straight Sundays, and on the seventh Sunday a guerrilla shot him in the market as he was buying apples.

I didn't leave Florinda any more money.

At night I saw boys and girls my age standing out of reach of the streetlights, huddled in shadowed embraces, their arms so positioned as to make it hard to determine which arm was his and which hers. It was a game I played, divining which body part was whose, but this game, I knew, was only a pretense to project myself into the mind and heart of one of those mysterious, huddled figures. My thoughts on these occasions did not befit an idiot angel.

To have a girlfriend, I would have had to sacrifice my silence. In those unions in the shadows, I heard words and had no doubt that they were as important as the embraces and kisses. But my silence was my gold. So I walked down the long main street in town, peering into the shadows, and at the end of the street I sighed to the stars.

One night, though, I kept walking, past the *municipalidad* and park, past the uninhabited house decorated with political slogans from an election years earlier. I walked past the basketball court and down the hill, past the Caminos Rurales complex, where a dog barked at me before a woman called his name, and past the coffee fields, the plants looking in the moonlight like silver skirts. I walked all the way to San Cristóbal, where I knew, from listening at my father's meetings, that there was a whorehouse.

It was a wood building that used to be an elementary school. The word "Second" was still visible above one of the doors. A tall woman with hair on her chin greeted me at the gate and led me to a red-lighted room with three tables. A man sat at one table, slumped in his chair, eyes closed. Four beer bottles stood in front of him. I sat at another table.

"A beer or straight to business?" the woman asked.

I said nothing.

"A beer then," she said, and she brought me one.

I let the bottle sit in front of me like a candle.

A thin girl with small lips painted bright red stepped into the room and sat at my table. Although she wore a blue dress, she was *indígena*; I could tell by the way she spoke Spanish, flatly, as if she'd had to memorize the words: "I'm Dolores. I think you're cute. I haven't seen you before, have I? Don't you like your beer? Want to treat a girl? Yes?" She took the beer and had a sip. "Thank you. You're kind. How nice. You're cute. May I?" She took another sip, and another, and before long, the beer was finished.

"There aren't many people here, the day before market. Every-one's getting ready whatever it is they're going to sell. Tomorrow they'll have money. And they'll spend it."

She smiled. "You don't talk much. Don't like to talk? That's okay. That's fine. Another beer, or are you ready?" She smiled. "You're ready?"

She took my hand. She led me out of the red-lighted room, into the courtyard, and then into a smaller room with a school desk, a chair, and a bed. I sat in the chair, she sat on the bed.

"Here," she said, tapping a place next to her. "Sit here."

I sat next to her.

"There," she said. "Much better." She kissed me on the cheek. Then on the lips. Then the cheek again. The lips again.

"What would you like?"

I said nothing.

"You don't talk, do you? Well, I'll talk."

And she talked a long time. I must have heard a thousand lies. Finally she said, "Well, what would you like? Anything?"

I pulled a fifty-quetzal bill from my trousers and handed it to her.

"Well, that's a lot," she said, "for nothing." She smiled. "But thank you."

I got up to leave. I had opened the door and stepped out when I turned back to her. The false brightness had drained from her face and she was eyeing the fifty-quetzal bill oddly, as if she didn't trust it. When she saw me looking at her, the brightness returned to her face, but I had seen her unguarded and she knew it.

The next night the three tables were occupied, so I stood in the corner. The tall woman with the hair on her chin brought me a beer and I handed it to the first woman who came up to me, although I didn't follow her to her room. I shook off another woman before Dolores approached me. "You again," she said, smiling her false smile. "Buy me a drink?"

She drank the beer and then took my hand and led me to her room.

I sat next to her on the bed.

"How are you tonight?" she asked, her smile resolute. "You liked it so much last night that you're back again? You sure must have had fun."

"Okay," she said, after a while. "Will you talk tonight? I'm really not used to talking so much."

"Well," she said after more silence, and I sensed her annoyance, despite her smile. "I told you most of what I have to tell last night. Of course," she said, almost in a whisper, "I don't remember all I told you." She kissed me on the cheek, the lips, the lips hard, and she pushed her tongue into my mouth and I let it slide between my teeth and flick against the insides of my cheeks.

"What?" she said, almost angry. "What do you want? Well? Come on, what is it?"

I handed her a fifty-quetzal bill and stood. Before leaving, I looked at her. She was ready. She was smiling.

"You pay well," she said. "Too much. You know, the rate is ten quetzales. But thank you."

I didn't leave just then. I wanted to see if I could outlast her smile.

"Come again tomorrow?" she said, and then her smile fell briefly, as if an unpleasant thought had struck her.

The next night I waited a long time at a table and I saw Dolores go with two men; I shook off every woman who approached me. The tall woman with the hair on her chin asked, "Don't you like the other girls?" It was almost morning when Dolores finally came to take my hand and lead me to her room.

"What?" she said, and there was no smile. "I feel sick, I'm sick of this. I've got this terrible mess inside of me." She grabbed a towel

and pushed it under her dress and wiped. She threw the towel to
the far side of the room.

"What is it? You come here to say nothing? Well, what do you
want? This is too hard. Come on, let's do it."

She grabbed me and pushed me onto the bed and straddled me.
"Come on, isn't this what you're here for? Isn't it?"

I nodded.

She smiled, not her false seductive smile but a smile of triumph.
"You are?" she said. "You are. Well."

My mute admission seemed to stem her anger. She got off me
and I sat up. "Well," she said again and kissed me on the mouth.

"Well?" she said. "If you'd like, we can do it."

I paid her fifty quetzales and left without looking at her.

I saw Dolores talking with the tall woman. Dolores was shaking
her head. The tall woman walked up to me. "Wouldn't you like
another girl tonight?" I waited. Dolores shrugged and came from
behind the tall woman and took my hand. She let go of it as soon
as we were out of the tall woman's sight.

She opened the door and walked into the room and sat on the
bed, leaving me standing. "I'm tired of you," she said. "You're like
a priest. Well, I don't go to church. I tell you honestly: I don't like
you. I hate you even. You come here like some kind of angel. What
are you? A freak?"

"Talk!" she shouted. "Talk, you devil!" She started crying. I sat
down next to her.

"I was born dead," I said.

My response stopped her tears. She looked at me, her eyes open
in fear or interest. I was startled at myself, and afraid. I paid her fifty
quetzales and walked quickly into the night. I'd given myself up,
surrendered my secret. I was distraught. But at the same time I felt
exhilarated; my heart thumped, my lungs filled with the sweet scent
of roses from a nearby trellis.

I thought about staying away. Dolores would forget I'd spoken,
and I could reclaim my secret. But although I felt nervous—terri-

fied of what my life would be with speech—I was excited, and I wanted to reveal everything, all I'd heard, seen, and done.

The next night I arrived early, and Dolores took my hand and led me to a room. We sat together on the bed. She said nothing, smiling.

"I was born dead," I said, and I told her about the dream my mother had before I breathed. "I understood I was different from everyone. I knew I had a kind of power. Because people believed I was an idiot, I heard what they said, saw what they did, as if I wasn't there."

I told her about my father's meetings and the people who'd been killed, about how, because I wasn't supposed to be alive, I felt no obligation to them, no obligation to God. "I could have warned them, I could have told them to run away, but instead I took their money."

She asked about the money, about how much I had. And what did I do with all the money? I explained that I didn't do much at all with it. "I give some to you," I said. "I used to give some to my mother."

After I explained the rest—about the guerrillas, about my mother's death—Dolores sighed, as if tiring of my story, and said, "I don't know much about God. But I remember hearing, well, we all hear, that God is love. And you say you don't obey God, but you did, kind of, didn't you? You did love her?"

I paid her and left, but not before crying, another secret lost.

I waited the next night until it was almost dawn. When Dolores still hadn't come, I walked out the door. The tall woman with the hair on her chin followed me.

"I wasn't lying," the woman said. "Dolores isn't here. She's dead." I stopped. "I couldn't tell you in there. All the men would hear." I stared hard at her. "It's true," she said. "She gave some man a disease and he didn't appreciate it, and he came last night, late, and shot her. He was very angry. You'd think these men would learn to expect certain dangers, but . . . well, I couldn't tell you in there. I mean, if the men found out a girl had a disease, well . . ." She must have read something in my face, or thought she did, because she continued gently, "I know you liked Dolores. But these things happen. It happened last year too, right around this time. It's not what you'd call unusual." She paused. "Anyway," she said, smiling, "I know you won't tell anyone. Dolores told me about you. You don't talk."

I walked back to town in the growing light. When I reached the park, I ascended the stairs of the raised platform and grabbed hold of the railing. I leaned my body over it, as I'd seen Mayor Gualim and other politicians do during their campaigns, and made as if to speak. A crowd gathered: women on their way to market carrying *mandarinas* and onions, men who'd been waiting for a bus in front of the *municipalidad*. It was as if they were anticipating another miracle. But I could only have delivered the opposite: curses against the cruelty of it all, the pain. And they'd heard this before—heard it from their own mouths. There was no miracle in rage.

I waited until their curiosity gave way to the practical: the bus came, the market called. I watched them disperse, and then I left the platform. As I walked down the street to my room, listening to the babble coming from *tiendas*, I knew I would never speak again.

My silence was the only thing I could never lose.

Three days later, Lieutenant Rubio was shot dead in the market. He was buying apples. Florinda sobbed on the floor of her room, my two other sisters kneeling beside her. Later, after Florinda's tears had stopped, they all grew terrified, wondering if the guerrillas would come for us. But they must have known what my mother knew—that the guerrillas ignored women and imbeciles—because when night came, their fears gave way to exhaustion. Lying in Florinda's bed, holding on to each other, they slept.

I stayed up and watched the dawn, wondering if God had ever stopped the sun before it rose over the horizon, stopped it dead. And if so, had it risen on its own, a sun not meant to be born but somehow born? And if so, was the day still God's?

KATHRYN CHETKOVICH

The World with
My Mother Still in It

*Kathryn Chetkovich lives in Boulder Creek, California. Her stories have
appeared in various literary journals and anthologies, including the*
Georgia Review, New England Review, ZYZZYVA, Threepenny Review,
and Best American Short Stories 1998. *Her story collection* Friendly Fire
*was a finalist for the PEN Center USA West 1999 Literary Award in Fiction.
She is currently working on short plays and a screenplay.*

*"This is a book that's genuine fun to read thanks in part to the comic vision
that gives these stories a memorable charm. The humor in* Friendly Fire
*springs more from keen observation than situation. It's a complex humor
that seems absolutely natural to the predominantly youthful voices of these
narrators; yet, beneath the quips, there's a wisdom that prevents the
youthfulness from ever seeming callow and a sense of understated sentiment
that's all the more affecting for its comic guise."*
STUART DYBEK, 1998

My parents and I are drinking watery Tom Collinses and talking
over the sound of *Sixty Minutes*. Several pills are scattered near the
corner of my father's place mat, and he occasionally reaches down
to rub his leg, which has been cramping and giving him trouble
lately.

My mother, who used to manage sit-down dinners for forty,
brings out a bowl of snacks made from various breakfast cereals
tossed with seasoning salt. It's a recipe she's clipped from one
of the health-and-longevity magazines my father subscribes to in
her name.

"Well," my father accuses me, "you look good. How's Steven?"

"He's fine." I told Steven he did not have to come along with me

38

tonight—a test he failed by taking me at my word and staying home

to listen to the game on the radio. "You look good, too." I hear myself talking in what Steven calls my Donna Reed voice. "Both of you."

My father tilts his head toward my mother. "She's the one," he says. "The constitution of a horse." He rubs his fingers over his knee in a slow circle.

My mother rolls her eyes. "Oh, I know!" she says. "You'll never guess who we heard from today."

I look from one to the other. My father's attention is back on the television. "Who?"

"Ray!"

"*My* Ray?" My mother has the unnerving habit of keeping in touch with my old boyfriends, and I turn around suddenly, half expecting him to come walking through the swinging kitchen door. When he and Anna got married, Steven and I went to the wedding, but that must be four years ago now, and we've fallen out of touch.

"Wasn't he the one that totaled your car?" My father keeps my exes straight with these Homeric epithets. The two-timing one. The one who always called collect.

"For the millionth time, Dad. That was not his fault. He was rear-ended."

My father waves this information away. "As I recall, he didn't pay you a cent for your troubles."

"Dad, it wasn't his *fault*. Besides, the other person's insurance paid for everything."

"Good thing." My father sniffs and turns back to the television.

I look at the clock. I've been here half an hour.

"Anyway," my mother says, "he and his wife just had a baby. We got the announcement in the mail today."

For a moment I have that strange, startled feeling you get when you're staring at the phone and it suddenly rings. "That's great," I hear myself say. "Great."

Steven and I talk about children sometimes, but talking seems to be our version of actually having them. I can't exactly say I want them, but as the youngest in my family, with no children of my

40

The

World

with My

Mother

Still

in It

own, I do sometimes feel like the caboose, hurtling forward and facing backward, watching the empty track behind me run off and disappear through all that open, dusty landscape.

"Poor Ray. I'm sure he has absolutely no idea," my mother says. My father, with his motto "Expect the worst and you won't be disappointed," is considered the cynic in the family; but it's my mother, that realist, who always puts temporary happiness in a long-term context. "I thought I'd get them something," she says to me now. "Do you want to go in on something with me?"

"She let him walk away from a wrecked car—isn't that enough?" My father, clearly enjoying himself, scoops up a handful of the little cereal pillows.

By eight, dinner is over and the dishes are almost done. One of my parents' regular programs is about to come on, and my father hovers in the kitchen doorway, working a toothpick around in his mouth and glancing at the clock. My mother finishes wiping the counters and says "O-kay" with the exhaling satisfaction of someone crossing the last chore off a list. She unties her apron, which she's had on since I arrived, and disappears into the pantry.

My father steps over and pulls a couple of folded twenty-dollar bills from his pocket. "Here," he says, holding them toward me. "For gas."

"Dad, you don't need to do that," I say, but he holds the money there, pointed at my heart, and I take it.

My mother returns with a bag of oatmeal cookies in one hand and a small jar in the other.

"Steven likes these fancy mustards, doesn't he?" she says.

From the front door they watch me walk out to the car. "Tell Steven to come along next time," my mother calls out.

"Not if he's working," my father adds. "You tell him if he has to work, we understand." After the years I spent with film students and drummers between bands, my father still can't quite believe I married a man with a job.

Outside the light is just beginning to fade, and the air is still soft and warm. I drive home with the windows rolled down to let in the summer evening: the smell of watered concrete, chlorine from someone's pool, a sudden sweet blossom my father, an unlikely gardener, would know the name of. I wish for things without knowing what they are.

At home Steven is lying on the couch in the darkening room, listening to the game. His head and feet, in socks that are wearing at the heel, are propped on the arms of the couch. On the radio the Giants' middle reliever gives up a double, and a run scores.

I have trouble for a second recognizing this as the life I have chosen, but then Steven moves over to make room for me on the couch. He takes my hand and asks me how I'm doing.

A walk, then a single, and then the manager takes what announcers always refer to as that long, slow trip to the mound. I can feel the length of Steven's body next to mine. I rest my hand on his thigh.

Soon it's almost completely dark except for the tiny red lights on the stereo receiver. I suddenly remember that it was Ray who taught me the boy's pleasure of listening to a game in the dark, and I later taught it to Steven.

In the darkness Steven's body is a kind of palimpsest on which I can make out the faint erased marks of the few important ones who came before. Ray was the first of these, so he became the prototype for all the handsome preoccupied men I fell in love with after—the ones who, when we were out, would pull me close and kiss me on the forehead while they looked over my head at something down the street.

A year or so after we broke up, I saw Ray at a party that we had both gone to alone. I was still so young that I even thought of myself as young; I remember a feeling I had then, that the cement of my life had not even been poured, much less begun to set. A couple of hours into the party, when I saw Ray go into the bathroom, I slipped in after him.

He hesitated for a moment, then stepped over to the toilet and unzipped his pants. Later that night we ended up back at his apartment and made that familiar, distracted love once more, but it was the ease of sitting on the bathroom counter while he peed, not the sex, that reminded me of my heart by breaking it.

"I've had a hard time getting over you," he said, playing with my hair in the darkness of his bedroom. "I hope to God you don't intend to put us both through that again."

42

The
World
with My
Mother
Still
in It

That seems to be my special gift, getting men to throw me the keys on condition that I won't take them anywhere.

"My arm's asleep," Steven says, pulling it from under my neck. It's the eighth inning, and the game is now comfortably out of reach; it's just a matter of nailing the last pieces of the loss into place.

"Ray and his wife just had a baby," I say into the darkness, and Steven, God love him, says, "Ray who?"

I lock my eyes on the back of my mother's flowered overblouse as we tack our way toward the baby department. I get dizzy and fatigued if I step off the linoleum trail in department stores, but my mother bushwhacks her way through that dense landscape of fabric with her usual sense of direction, empty sleeves swinging in her wake.

"It's not too late for you, you know," she says, shuffling expertly through the tiny outfits on the sale rack. "This is cute"—she checks a price tag—"well, not *that* cute." She moves to another rack.

"Oh, Mom." I squeeze a grunting pig and a quacking duck in conversation. I'm doing what I always do when I go shopping with my mother—waiting for her to make up our mind.

"I'm just talking," she says. "I'm not saying anything."

I've never told my mother about the abortion I had with Ray, and this moment among the pastels and friendly animals at Macy's suddenly seems as close to telling her as I am likely to get. But it's like spotting the exit for a place you've always meant to go while you're on the freeway headed somewhere else.

"He always seemed like a lost soul," my mother says cheerfully. "Maybe fatherhood will bring him back to earth."

We finally settle on a bright-yellow outfit and a cow with big black stitches for eyelashes. On our way back across the store we pull up at a table piled with sweaters and my mother tries to buy me one.

"Or would you rather have something else?" she says, when I look at them without picking one up. "A skirt, maybe?"

I can see where this is going, so I set the shopping bag down to pick up a sweater, and when I reach down again for the handles, the cow's harlequin face is looking up at me from its nest of tissue paper. For a strange, mixed-up moment, I imagine my mother snapping Ray's new daughter into her little yellow playsuit while my father stands a few feet away, making funny noises and congratulating himself on getting the baby to smile.

We buy the sweater and cross the mall to a coffee place my mother likes. After we sit down she leans across the table conspiratorially. "That man over there goes to my church. His wife died last year."

Even sitting down, the man looks unsteady; he stirs his coffee with a badly shaking hand. He looks like someone you would hate to be behind on the road.

"Is he okay?" I say.

"What do you mean?"

I shrug. "He seems old."

"He's younger than your father."

Before we leave, my mother gets up to go to the rest room. On the way, she stops at the old man's table. He starts to get up but she touches his shoulder lightly and he sinks back down. He gestures to the chair across from him, and my mother smiles but gestures back to me. He takes her hand in both of his. If something were to happen to my father, I find myself thinking, this guy would be standing in line. The word *stepfather* jumps incongruously into my mind.

Finally my mother heads down the hallway to the rest rooms and I get up to pay the check. The cashier, a dark-haired beauty, is busy flirting with the young man piloting the espresso machine.

"Excuse me," I say.

"Sure," she says, taking the slip without looking at me. She has rings on six or seven fingers, and her eyes are outlined in black. I feel a brief stab of regret that when I was the age to wear that look myself, I was convinced that makeup and too much jewelry were tools of the patriarchy.

After I pay, I move toward the door to wait for my mother. Outside, in the filtered light of the mall, kids stand around with their arms crossed and women wheel by with their strollers. A few minutes later, when my mother still has not appeared, I turn back toward the tables to look for her.

The old man is gone and there is my mother, standing at the mouth of the hallway, searching the room of tables. When she does

44

The

World

with My

Mother

Still

in It

not step forward but just stands there, holding her purse in both hands, I realize she's lost.

"Mom! Mom!" I hurry toward her. I can see her start to smile at the sound of my voice. When she spots me, her shoulders drop in relief.

"That was the strangest thing," she says as soon as I reach her, picking the moment up and putting it carefully in the past. "I just got completely turned around when I came out of the ladies' room, I guess."

"Are you okay?"

"Oh yes, I'm fine. You know how that is when everything suddenly looks unfamiliar."

I do not say what I am thinking. Neither does she. I move both shopping bags to one side and take hold of her hand with my free one. Once we get outside she gives my hand a squeeze and lets go.

"I'm not going to say anything to Dad about that, and I don't want you to either," she says.

"About what?"

"Right," she says.

We're crossing the hot parking lot toward the car. After the banners and fountains and piped-in music of the mall, the asphalt and glare outside seem like part of an essential, biblical landscape. The stiff twine handles of the shopping bags cut into my fingers. The coffee and sugar have made me jumpy. My feet are hot, and I feel tired and cranky. I can sense my mother, that peculiar love of my life, starting to slip off one edge of the world, and the children I am not going to have, those cherubic monsters, slipping off the other.

"Almost there," my mother says as the car comes into view. "We're almost there."

Oceanic Hotel, Nice

Tereze Glück grew up in Woodmere, Long Island, and now lives in New York City. In 1993 she was awarded a grant from the National Endowment for the Arts, and she has been a fellow at the Virginia Center for the Creative Arts, Ragdale, the Ucross Foundation, and Djerassi. Her stories have appeared in numerous magazines, including the Antioch Review, Fiction, Epoch, Story, Columbia, North American Review, Gettysburg Review, *and others.*

"May You Live in Interesting Times *displays Tereze Glück's tender, compassionate heart and her gorgeous ear for the rhythm and rhyme of prose. It is a sensual, haunting book.*"
ETHAN CANIN, 1995

Nicholas said, "I must have a cigarette."

Said is not exactly accurate, since he could hardly speak. It was, I think, a matter of strength, or lack of it—he just did not have the strength to use his voice. He whispered, kind of. To hear him I had to lean over, so that my ear was near his mouth. I hated this. His breath was warm and sour-smelling. I was as squeamish as a startled cat that starts at any sound, and slinks away, its body low to the ground, as if it thinks no one can see it. I thought germs were coming towards me on his breath—viruses like rain. His breath was hot, and also moist. I hated everything.

"The Chapel," Nicholas said.

"The Chapel?"

"I must have a cigarette," he said.

I looked at him dumbly.

"My pants," he said. All of this in that half-whisper.

"What?" I said.

He tried to gesture. He could not gesture any better than he   45

could speak. This gesture consisted of a raised forefinger. I tried to
follow some logical line of direction. I turned around and saw the
closet, and a pair of sweatpants shoved onto the shelf.

Surely, I said to myself, surely he does not expect me to put these
on him? Because it was clear he could not put them on himself. He
could not so much as lift his arm, never mind his leg.

I got the sweatpants down from the closet. "I'll get a nurse," I
said. This seemed a little shameful. But I was more relieved than
ashamed.

I turned my back while they pulled the sweatpants over his legs.
His legs were—you know. As thin as everything you remember—
the prisoners of war at Andersonville, those famous photographs,
or the survivors at the concentration camps. I am not exaggerating.
I am not making one of those venal comparisons—you know, this
or that is like the Holocaust. I am simply describing his legs, and
the best description is in these images. There was almost nothing
left of his legs. They were bones with skin pulled over them. There
was no calf to speak of.

"Can you put him in the wheelchair?" I said to the nurse. I was
thinking, Bless these people, I can't believe they do what they do. I
was as nervous as a cat. I wanted just to get out of there. The whole
place smelled of illness with an overlay of sour-sweet camouflage.
Hospitals don't smell spanking clean—of Clorox, or laundry, or
bright bleached things—they smell of illness and the effort to mask
it. The smell can make you sick. When I am in a hospital I try not
to breathe too deeply.

"My sweater," Nicholas said.

The sweater was on a chair. I was as afraid of the sweater as I was
of him. The sweater was dirty, with stains on it that maybe were
food and maybe were blood as well. The sweater was matted. Under
my fingers the sweater felt like old foul things dried and caked over.
Nicholas's whole apartment was like that, until one Saturday Gwen
and I just went to clean it up. We went to Woolworth's and bought
every cleaning supply you could think of and rubber gloves. I said,
"I'd just like to *hose* this place down." Gwen says I repeated this
many times during the course of that day. We went there when we

thought Nicholas was in Paris, only it turned out he wasn't in Paris at all, he was in the hospital, but we didn't know that. He did make it to Paris, apparently, but he collapsed there, or had a seizure, or something, and was taken to the hospital in Paris and the next day was somehow put on an airplane for New York and was met at the airport by some friends, not us, other friends, and was taken to a hospital in New York. That was last fall, and it was spring now; that was a different hospital stay, a different episode, although when I think back on it, it may be more accurate to say that it was just the beginning of a long episode which seemed to be shaping up to be, well, his last. Since then he never really got back home for more than a few days before landing in the hospital again.

To put the sweater on him I had to touch his arm, which made me feel faint.

"Oh dear," I said to him. "I'm afraid I'm no caretaker." I smiled. I got one arm in an armhole and somehow managed to get the sweater behind him and his other arm in. I felt faint again—I mean exactly that, as if I would faint. I lectured myself. If it's awful to be *near* this, I said, imagine what it's like to *be* this. But in truth this meant nothing to me—my whole body replied, But I am *not* this! This is *not* happening to me and I'm glad it's not! This was said in protest. This was physical health resenting the tyranny of illness. This was one self encountering the fact that it was not in fact another self. This was me being imperial.

Still the sweater got on him somehow. The sick feeling in my stomach did not go away. Now we had to get him into the wheelchair. All this had taken, fifteen, twenty minutes. All this for a cigarette.

A cigarette, of course, was pretty much all that was left to him.

I went out to the nurse's station. "Could somebody put Mr. Rhodes in a wheelchair please?"

"Where you taking him?" a young man said.

"To the Chapel," I said.

The nurses had a discussion about who would do it. The one who was on duty was eating a sandwich. "It's my lunch hour," she said. Another one said, "That's all right, you eat, I'll do it." This impressed me. This was the kind of helpful behavior we are led to believe has died out, but imagine, here it was, and right in the heart of New York City.

There was some discussion between the nurse and the young male nurse about how to best get Nicholas out of the bed and into the wheelchair. As experienced as they were, they were still perplexed. Finally they swung Nicholas's legs from the bed so that his feet dangled over the side of the bed. Then they lifted his shoulders and swung his body kind of sideways. I'm not sure what they did next; I think I turned and walked out into the hall. When I turned back around he was already in the chair. His face was gaunt and exhausted. He looked to me like one of those portraits of Christ, where Christ can't hold up his head, and his head leans to one side, and his entire body is limp with suffering. The male nurse came up to us. "Now Mr. Rhodes," he said. "No little side trips, you hear? No little side stops for a cigarette or anything like that." Then he turned to me, as if neither of us could hear what was addressed to the other. "You take him to the Chapel and that's it," he said. "No little side trips for cigarettes. Okay?"

I stared dumbly at the young man. "Well," I said.

"No cigarettes," he said. "This is a no-smoking hospital."

"Look," I said. "You be the one to tell him, not me."

He knelt and spoke to Nicholas. "No cigarettes Mr. Rhodes, you got that? This is a no-smoking hospital and that's the rule. It's not fair to other patients."

Then he turned back to me. He seemed to want some kind of answer, which was difficult, because I never could lie, not even small lies about unimportant things. I hung my head like an errant child. Then I looked up at him. I had the feeling that I had a kind of pleading look on my face. "Look," I said. "What difference does it make if he smokes or not? For God's sake, it's his only pleasure. Can't he just have a cigarette? Who does it hurt?"

The male nurse looked at me. "I sympathize," he said. "Believe me, I'm a smoker myself. But those are the rules."

I shook my head. I was trying to work myself up to the required lie.

"Look," the man said. "Just don't tell me. That's all. Just don't
tell me."

"Which way's the Chapel?" I said, looking him in the eye.

It took a few minutes to get down to the Chapel. I wasn't very
spry with a wheelchair. Nicholas's feet kept dragging, and he didn't
have the strength to lift them onto the footrests of the wheelchair,
and I didn't want to touch them. Every now and then I'd stop and
try to lift his feet anyway, which made me shudder. All this time I
was just thinking what a bad person I was to not even want to touch
his feet, but there it was—I just didn't, it made me shudder, and
that's that. He had on those thin stretch foam slippers they give you
in hospitals, and the slippers kept coming off his heels, so that they
hung from his toes. I'd stop the wheelchair and squat down and try
to pull the slippers on without actually having to touch his skin, and
then I'd try to lift his legs by just holding on to the slippers. In fact
I did not succeed, not with the slippers or the footrest, and we'd
wheel along and I'd hear his feet dragging along the floor.

Just as we got to the Chapel a man came in with a woman and a
child. The man had an IV hooked up to him and wore the blue robe
of the hospital. He had bandages around his head. He sat down in
the back with the woman and the child. "Fuck," said Nicholas. Of
all the things he had said to me today this was the clearest.

"I'm sure they won't stay long," I said. After all, it wasn't as if *he*
wanted a cigarette, which could take some time if you wanted to
enjoy a few. He was only here to talk to God, presumably, and let's
face it, conversations with God are pretty one-sided and after the
first few minutes all you do is start to repeat yourself. I figure I'm as
qualified to speak about this as the next fellow. I talked to God endlessly and I was always saying the same thing. I read a lot of self-
help books which explained to me that I was doing the wrong kind
of praying, which I had always somehow known, my idea of a prayer
being to *really really really* beg God for whatever it was I wanted.
When I didn't get it, which I never did, I always thought it was
because I hadn't wanted it hard enough and the thing to do was
want it *more*. As dialogues with God go, I'd have to admit that mine

were pretty primitive, not to mention missing the point, so it wasn't altogether surprising that my prayers were never answered.

Although maybe they were answered only who could decipher the answer? Which was always the problem with God in the first place.

After a few minutes, the man in the Chapel got up and left, followed by his IV rigging, the woman and the child. "Thank bloody God," Nicholas said. He tried to get his cigarettes but he really couldn't move his arm, so I got them for him, gingerly, the way I'd put his slippers back on his feet. The sweater was, frankly, a mess. God knows what was on that sweater. I hated to think what was on that sweater.

I had some reasons to shudder in the matter of the sweater. Last fall my friend Gwen and I had gone to Nicholas's apartment to clean it up. It was so foul, so dirty, I couldn't bear to go there. When Nicholas and I would make a date, he'd say, "Meet me at my apartment and we'll have a little drink," and finally I said to him, "Nicholas, I just can't go to your apartment any more." This may sound extreme but then, his apartment was something extreme. So we would meet in restaurants.

All this was before he was in the hospital, when he could still get around some, could still go out to a restaurant for dinner. He was planning a trip to Paris—in retrospect this seems sheer madness, he was so ill, but he had got as far as he had got precisely by imagining trips to Paris and then *taking* them, God damn it. For some time he'd been living mostly on will, and it wasn't a half-bad program at that. So he went to Paris, and Gwen and I decided to clean his apartment while he was gone as a surprise for him. Really I did it for myself because the apartment just made me so outright sick I couldn't stand it. I just wanted to clean the God damned thing. I just wanted to *hose* the God-damned place down. A good hosing down was exactly what it needed. I don't want to elaborate, but that apartment was thick with things you wouldn't believe—caked blood on the mouthpiece of the telephone and on the sheets, and thick layers of oozy substances that had dried. Some of them were food and some of them, well, weren't. The sheets were filled with cigarette holes with charred edges. Gwen said, It's amazing he

never set fire to himself.

We put on rubber gloves and just went at it. Our original plan was to hire someone to do it and we'd just kind of oversee the task, and in fact we did hire someone, but when she started in cleaning Gwen and I looked at each other and just pitched in. Gwen said later, when we were having a drink and congratulating ourselves, Well we couldn't exactly just stand there and watch her clean. In the end it took three of us all day and we didn't even finish at that. The woman we hired, whose name was Marilyn and who was very kind, something you could just tell about her right off, cleaned the kitchen and the bathroom, and Gwen and I did the living room and the bedroom. There was a little study and in fact we never even got to the study and to tell the truth, one day was enough. One day could make you feel like a saint, which we did.

We found two dead mice under a fine mahogany table in the living room.

Also, we threw out all the bedclothes.

So I had some reason to be fearful of the sweater. But everything I was doing was something I hated, so I just grimaced and did this as well—put my hand in the pocket of his sweater and got his cigarettes. I took one out and put it between his lips.

"Water," Nicholas said.

"What about water?" I said.

"Get some water. For the ashes," he said.

"But I don't have a cup or anything. Where do I get water?"

"Go look for a kitchen or something."

"Look you can just tip your ashes onto the carpet. They're good for the carpet." I remembered how, when we were in college, everyone always used to say that. Everyone used to drop their ashes onto the carpet and rub them into the carpet with their feet and shrug and say, "It's good for the carpet."

But he was insistent so I left him there, with the organ and the pews and the stained glass windows, and went to find a water fountain, and a cup to put the water in. I found the fountain but no cup. I kept wandering until I saw some people in uniforms—orderlies, maybe, something like that—and I stopped them and said "Excuse

me, where can I get a cup? Is there a kitchen on this floor or something?" but they just shrugged and said no, there wasn't. When I'd
been gone a few minutes I thought I just better get back to Nicholas. He'd just have to use the floor, that was all.

So I went back to the Chapel. He was still there, slumped in his
wheelchair. I'd been half-afraid I'd find him on the floor.

"I couldn't find a cup anywhere," I said. "Just use the floor. It's
good for the carpet."

"What about the stub?" he said.

There was a fire exit right near us, that opened onto an alley-like
affair. "The fire exit," I said. Then I got half-afraid I'd put the stub
out and get myself locked out in the alley. I had a whole, instant
daydream about this—like something out of the old Alfred Hitchcock Television Hour they used to show on Sunday nights when I
was growing up—I'd be locked out on this landing that didn't go
anywhere, and Nicholas would be in his wheelchair, unable to open
the door, unable to call out for help.

"Matches," Nicholas whispered.

I looked in the cigarette box, and fished around again in the
pocket of his sweater, and then the other pocket. There were no
matches.

"Nicholas, there are no matches," I said. I felt oddly relieved, as
if fate had taken over and it was all out of my hands. Everything
would be over more quickly now, if he couldn't have his cigarette,
and then I'd be able to get out of there. Get out of there and go
home, and wash my hands, and have a hot bath.

"Oh God," Nicholas said. "Can't you go find matches?" he said.

"But who could I ask?" I said. "You're not supposed to be
smoking."

"Look," I said. "I think we just better forget the cigarette thing."

I wheeled him out of the Chapel and down the hall toward the
elevator. It was all the way at the other end of the floor, so it took
a few minutes. Nicholas's feet dragged along the floor, and his slippers kept slipping off his heels. Every now and then I stopped and
tried to put them back on and tried to put his feet up on the footrest, but I wasn't doing any better than I'd done before.

We waited for the elevator. Hospital elevators always seem to take forever, and this one was.

When it came, it had a lot of people in it, and they had to move to make room for the wheelchair. I wheeled Nicholas in and he said to a man next to him, almost as clearly as he'd said the word "Fuck" earlier when he saw the man in the Chapel, "Excuse me but do you have any matches?" The man put his hand in his pocket and like a magician pulled out a book of matches. I just laughed and laughed.

So we rode back down in the elevator and went back to the Chapel. "God damn it Nicholas," I said, laughing. "Nothing like a little motivation." This was why he was still alive at all.

We went through the whole thing again. I got the cigarettes out of his pocket, and put one between his dried cracked lips, and lit a match. He managed to hold the cigarette in his hands, holding onto it as if it were something that could support his weight, something he could lean against. But he couldn't tip his ashes. When the ash got long, I'd take the cigarette and tap it, and the ashes fell onto the floor, and I rubbed them into the carpet with my foot.

When it was time to put out the stub I opened the fire door, and I had my daydream again. I was careful to hold the door open when I ground out the stub on the cement.

Then we did it all again.

All in all Nicholas smoked three cigarettes. He sighed. "I haven't had a cigarette in four days," he said. Not since his last visitor.

After the third cigarette I said I had to go. I took him back upstairs and the nurses took him out of the wheelchair and put him back into the bed. We said good-bye and I rode the elevator down to the main lobby. I was walking out the door to the street and there was a woman walking out the door right beside me, and I said to her, "I hate hospitals, I just hate them. If anything ever happens to me I swear I'll just *die* before I end up in one of these places." I was outright shuddering. She looked at me as if I were very strange. "Really?" she said.

I walked up Seventh Avenue and stopped at Barney's. I spent an hour there, and I bought something expensive. I was trying to get the hospital out of my head, and its smell off my skin. I was trying

to replace the hospital with aesthetic pleasure, expense, silk, perfume, gold jewelry, fine linen.

We had some fine old times together, Nicholas and I. We found
each other very funny, very clever. We made each other laugh and
were pleased with ourselves. Also we both liked good things—fine
meals, good champagne, expensive clothes. We had some extraordinary meals, and not just in New York. We had them in Rome, and
in Positano and Capri, and a couple of years later in Paris. We were
once at a famous restaurant in Rome, although I forget its name
even if it was famous. Nicholas would remember its name. He knew
the names of all the best restaurants in Rome and Paris. It was early
evening and we were sitting outdoors among a long row of tables.
We were feeling very jolly, very witty. We were with a couple of
other people, so we made a lively group. Someone said something,
it doesn't matter what, and we all laughed loudly. A man at the table
behind us said, Well you'd *think* they could keep their *voices* down.
He was with a boyfriend, that much was clear. They were Ameri-
cans. We laughed again, over something else, and the man said, very
uppity-like, directly to us this time, Could you *please* keep your
voices down? We just shrugged and he said Hmph, you could at
least be *polite*. Nicholas was smoking a cigarette and he turned
around and smiled and said, "Oh, but we couldn't *possibly*."

That was when he had money, before he had to pay all his money
to his doctors and for medicine. He was independently wealthy, he
had always been a rich boy, so of course he had no insurance. What
was there to be afraid of in those days? He got some venereal dis-
eases, which was just par for the course, his course anyway, and he
got an inconvenient abscess which ended up restricting his sex life
somewhat, but why did he have to worry about insurance? He was
young and essentially healthy and rich, and even more than that, he
was talented. He wrote two books and published them to some fine
reviews. So when he got sick he had to use all his money for his
treatments. Then he had no more money so he went on welfare and
was a ward of the state. Even then we kept going out to good restaurants. He had an apartment in Paris, from the days when he was
rich, and got some money from renting it. He didn't get enough to
live on, never mind enough to pay for his medicines, but he got

some, and what he got he used for dinners out, when he could still go out.

The last time we had dinner together was in the fall, just before the trip to Paris when Gwen and I cleaned his apartment. I met him at his apartment even though I hated going there. I wouldn't have a drink, though. This bothered him but it wasn't just the disease, it was the filth in the apartment. I told him this outright. I wasn't about to lie to him. Maybe I should have, but then, I couldn't even lie to an orderly in a hospital about a cigarette.

His apartment was on the third floor of a townhouse, and there was no elevator. I went down the stairs first. I didn't help him because it was easier for him to hold on to the bannister than to me. He could hardly walk. The disease had done something to his feet, I wasn't sure what. He had neuropathy, although I'm not sure if that's what made for the difficulty in walking. In any case he could no longer walk very well. He was very skinny and weak. I waited at the bottom of the stairs. Every now and then he'd curse. We went down the front stoop to the sidewalk. Nicholas held on to the railing of the stone steps while I hailed a cab. He started toward the curb, to the cab, but when he walked he would trip over his feet— one foot would somehow end up a little in front of the other, so that when he took the next step his foot would be in his way. He tripped and grabbed hold of the railing, which was still within reach. "Fuck," he said. I went to help him, and put my arm through his, but I was shuddering.

It took us so long to get to the restaurant that when we got there, they had given our table away. I'd booked a table in the smoking section of course, so Nicholas could smoke, but they had to seat us in non-smoking. Every time he wanted a cigarette he had to go over to the bar. It took him forever to walk to the bar, so I spent a lot of the dinner sitting alone at the table, waiting for him.

The food was good; I remember. A restaurant critic was at a table nearby. Various people whispered her name and glanced over at her table. Nicholas and I sat next to a very nice young man and woman. I don't know if they were a couple or if they were just friends. We fell into conversation with them and it turned out her brother had died of AIDS. She was very friendly, very forthcoming. In fact when

Nicholas wanted a cigarette she walked with him to the bar. She was being much nicer to him than I was. For me this was the beginning of the decline—I think of it that way—in which his presence, formerly a pleasure, had become a burden. *He* hadn't given up but it seemed that *I* had.

We weren't making clever conversation any more. We were trying, but trying only made it worse. There is something truly awful about bravery, I find. It makes you kind of weak in the stomach. Give me misery any day. At least it's honest.

Nicholas's teeth had fallen out long ago. He'd had false teeth made, but they were a problem. They were one of the reasons we'd been so late for dinner and had lost our table. It took him a long time to put them in. While I waited for him in the living room of his apartment, I could hear him cursing in the bathroom while he tried to put his teeth in. I guess they weren't very comfortable, because it wasn't easy for him to eat. I was sitting across from him, at this wonderful restaurant, where the food was inventive and elaborately presented, so I couldn't help but see him, the gingerish, painstaking way he'd eat. He would drool a little, bits of food would fall down his chin. He still made a great ritual of offering me a taste of his food, and sometimes I would take a little from his plate before he began to eat, and I always gave him some of mine to taste, but in fact I had come to hate the ritual, its insistence, its provocation and denial. He was doing something for himself with this ritual—making claim to some normalcy, and making a statement—but I was reduced to audience, a functionary of his gesture. I tried to hold up my end, but I was minding more and more, and the fact is I was no good at dissembling.

That night, when I sat looking across the table at him, I kept thinking: Let me out of here, let me out of here.

I just wanted to run away.

I was as miserable as a sick cat. I could hardly make myself smile.

I took him home, and he held my arm as we walked toward his front stoop. I turned to look at him while he was talking and I said, "Nicholas, you're bleeding." His mouth was bleeding. He stopped and found a handkerchief and held it to his mouth.

I took him upstairs and got a cab for myself. When I got in the cab I saw that there was blood on my sleeve. I sat with my arm held

away from me, as far as I could get it. I was shuddering as if I could shake it off—I mean the arm, or the blood. Shuddering was getting to be my main mode, at least so far as Nicholas was concerned.

When I got to my apartment I found a pair of rubber gloves under the sink and I put them on. I took my coat off and hung it on the door of the closet, away from anything else. I went into my daughter's room. The room was dark and she was asleep. "You took sex education, didn't you?" I said in a loud whisper. There is something about the dark that makes us whisper, even when it's our intention to wake somebody up.

She bolted up in the bed. "What?" she said.

"You took sex education, right?"

"Why?" she said.

"I got Nicholas's blood on my coat," I said. "I can't get sick from that, can I? I mean—you took sex education; you'd know, right?"

"Mother, I need to sleep," she said.

In the morning I took the coat to the cleaners, and I've worn it often since then. I say that as if to acquit myself of something— some mean and furtive criminal act, such as fear.

Shortly after that Nicholas left for Paris and Gwen and I went down to clean his apartment, only of course he wasn't in Paris very long at all, and at the time Gwen and I were cleaning his apartment he was already in St. Vincent's Hospital, only no one had told us. Eventually I located him, and went to see him in the hospital, where he said to me, "I must have a cigarette."

I would say my decline was complete by then.

After the hospital, when I got to Barney's, I smelled the perfumes, and looked over the china and glassware, and I even tried on some expensive clothing I knew I would never buy. I tried on a black dress made out of the same fabric they use for tuxedos, and I was looking at myself in the mirror. I just stood there and stared at myself. I stared and I said to myself, "You have no compassion." This was uttered coolly, just a cool assessment, an objective remark as neutral as a comment about the color of my eyes or the length of my hair. It was just a fact, like any other fact—trees, sky, concrete, illness, death. In the mirror, through the fine fabric of the black dress, it was as if I could see a burned-out center in the middle of my body, where a heart used to beat; and even this failed to move me. Upon reflection this is not so surprising; for, what was left to be moved?

I did not buy the black dress. It was too expensive, and in any case I had no place to wear it. I went back down to the main floor and bought a lemony perfume called "Oceanic Hotel Nice." The bottle had an art deco picture on it, in bright blue and a mustard yellow, of a boulevard with a palm tree and the facade of a hotel. It could very well be Nice. I'd been there once, some years ago. It was raining when we were there, and we did not stay for long, but I bought a tin of olive oil, for which Nice was famous if I am not mistaken. I still have it, somewhere in the back of a kitchen shelf, unopened I expect. I'm like that—I buy things and then I forget to use them. But I wear this perfume all the time; it's my offering. Of course Nicholas would have preferred a cigarette, but I don't get downtown often.

Nothing

Ann Harleman is the author of the 1996 novel Bitter Lake. *Her awards include Guggenheim and Rockefeller fellowships, two Rhode Island State Arts Council grants, and the PEN Syndicated Fiction Award. She is on the faculties of Brown University and the Rhode Island School of Design.*

"Nothing is quite predictable as Ann Harleman's delicately rendered stories take gentle, surprising turns."
FRANCINE PROSE, 1993

They must have been waiting all afternoon for someone like me to come along. Sitting in the narrow lane between a low bungalow with a green-painted porch and Bethel Baptist Church. Hot; at loose ends under that loud sky. Three of them had their back against the stone wall of the church, legs in cutoff jeans stretched out in front of them, while the fourth, a few feet away, drew pictures in the cindery dust. The back of his undershirt, cropped raggedly just above his waist, showed a large grey patch of sweat. He kept his head bent close to the ground and drew with his index finger. The watchers snickered. The artist wet his finger again, leaving a thin crust of dirt on his lower lip. He added a few more strokes. He smiled down at the ground, then up into the painfully blue sky.

The sun shone straight down into the alley. They all grinned and punched each other and one of them pulled a joint out of his jeans pocket. They squatted in the dirt, sucking fiercely when the joint came to them and squinting past each other. The forward set of their shoulders said, Men's Business.

That was when I came along, driving slowly back from the doctor's with my sad news. Big silver Volvo waiting for the light to change. Must have a/c, all them windows up. Silly bitch can't see the fuckin light's busted.

One minute I was studying the little church, following its squat lines and thinking, as I always did when I passed it, about the people who'd built it—what they dreamed about and who they loved and how they punished their children. The next minute I was thrown sideways. My shoulder hit the side of the door; then I bounced the other way. The stick shift banged my knee.

Two on the right side, two on the left, they rocked the car back and forth, side to side. They moved with the absorbed, purposeful elegance of dancers. Absurdly, there came to my mind for an instant the face of the first boy I ever dated, so intent on me that once he walked right through my screen door. The muscles stood out in their shoulders and upper arms, dark skin almost purple. On their faces was the ferocious tenderness of a mother who rocks her squalling baby.

I never drove in the city without locking the doors. They couldn't get in; but I couldn't get out. I couldn't put the car in gear and drive forward. What if I ran over them, parts of them? I was caught. What if, as Daniel and I had so hoped, I *had* been pregnant? I know the uterus curves around the fetus like a hand holding an apple; but I could see it, little shrimp fetus—little imaginary child—brutally sloshing, rocking as I was rocking in the belly of the Volvo. The air in front of me filled with little black dots, like the veil on a hat. I felt for the seat-belt buckle, couldn't find it. I leaned to my right and put my head down.

The rocking stopped. When I sat up, there was a face in the side window, surprisingly young, a child's face almost: nose splayed against the glass, five pads of fingers pressing on either side. His eyes were two or three inches from my face. A child's eyes. I rocked on the edge of them. Brown; no, blue; no, brown and blue. I pulled my eyes away.

I saw my chance then. The group's fine, feverish concentration had broken. The three other boys had moved around in front of the car and they were dancing. They jerked and jumped and banged on the fenders. As if it belonged to someone else, I watched my foot find the clutch. My hand grabbed the gearshift and shoved it into reverse.

The car shot away, scattering boys in its wake. Naked arms and

legs seemed to fly out from their bodies. I punched the switch, and
all the windows in the car came down with a soft collective thud.
The block blurred past in one long, hot breath—stone church the
color of dried blood, spindly leaning porches, catalpa trees with yel-
lowed leaves limp as old newspapers. At the Dairy Mart on the corner, with its plate glass held together by a huge spidery asterisk of
masking tape, I backed left. I took the long way home.

When Daniel looked up from stirring the chicken curry to ask
what had happened to me, eyes crinkling with concern, I told him,
nothing. When he asked what the doctor had found, I told him.
Nothing.

That night I dreamed of it, the rocking, the face flat against the
glass. I woke with a wordless shout. Warm, wet air clung to my bare
arms and legs. I could hear the sound of crickets through the open
windows. Above us the skylight was empty, a square of grey-washed
darkness; the moon had drifted out of it like a boat untied.

Kath? What is it? Daniel half-whispered.

I had a dream.

What about?

No, I said. In the dense heat wrapping us, I shivered.

Daniel's hand in my damp hair smelled like coriander. For a second I thought we would make love, we would try again, as we had
so often; but he only began to untangle the long cord of his radio
earplug, which had wrapped itself around my shoulder.

Do you want anything?

No, I whispered. Nothing.

He fitted the plug into his ear.

They had been bronze, those child-eyes, the color of muddy
water in sunlight. Close up, the ragged rim of blue around the pupil
was like the spark when you touch hands with someone on a cold
day—that small soft explosion of surprise.

Coming into Rio Harbor

Elizabeth Harris has written two novels: Hazel's House, *a finalist in the Pirates' Alley Faulkner Society competition, and* The Looks Thief. *She teaches fiction writing at the University of Texas in the undergraduate and graduate programs (in the English Department and in the Michener Center for Writers). Since winning the John Simmons Short Fiction Award, she has married and taken on the care of her ninety-three-year-old father.*

"The Ant Generator *includes an impressive variety of stories, which have in common long, meditative narrative movements and a bemused awareness of the uncertain frontiers between the quotidian and the dreamlike.*"
MARILYNNE ROBINSON, 1991

After we got home and called the police, we sat in the room they called the library drinking gin and trying to get hold of ourselves, while the light dimmed out of the room little by little. The room was full of expensive replicas of antique lamps, but we didn't turn any of them on, and the last things I could see in the room before it went dark were the gold frame on Augustus John's portrait of Goedele hanging over the fireplace and the white flowers in the red-and-white twenties dress she was painted in. Julian called her the Love of My Life. She'd been dead for thirty years. The time Lottie told me this, I said Julian would have to have a love of his life.

"Yes," Lottie said in her staccato way, "if not her, then someone else. And she would have to be dead."

"And painted by Augustus John, and hanging over some beautiful mantelpiece."

"Or maybe her heart preserved in formaldehyde," Lottie said, "in crystal. Waterford. Or her whole self, like Lenin." We laughed.

But afterwards Lottie said more thoughtfully, "It is easy, is it not, to love the dead? And yet, he does love her, or he believes he does."

IN MEMORIAM—Hamill, Frankie, d. 17 April 1972, five years
ago today (suddenly, as the result of an explosion). Gone but *Elizabeth*
not forgotten. Our dead live on in our ideals. *Harris*

> We will not give up
> That for which you died.
> In Jesus' name, Mother-in-law and Family.

(*Londonderry News*, 18 April 1977)

Lottie had lived with him for three years, ready to leave him for half that time. "He is a monster," she said once: but this is the way Lottie talks. "And yet, there is something about him. Why do you think I am still here? It is not only because I do not want to spend all my days in some office. There are other men with money."

When I met her, she was sprawled out on a light-colored hearthrug in a black dress in the drawing room of a less remote Irish country house. I was the visiting American, invited by slight acquaintance, gawking. Very chic, very European, she looked Greek, had lived in Greece for years; her first husband had been a Greek. In fact, she was German—a remote cousin of Heinrich Himmler ("Well, it's not my fault!" she said). She told me all this in our first conversation. How near the end of war her father, who was a commercial butcher, had resigned from the Nazi party and been drafted into the army and sent to the Russian front, where he was killed. How her sisters had emigrated to the States, and she'd once lived in New York for a year herself. We were friends immediately. "Oh, you must come north for Christmas!" she said, and she meant it. Julian said, "Oh, yes, do." He smiled, his lips pressed together. Maybe sixty years old, maybe forty pounds overweight, he sat tightly on a small straight chair in a black three-piece suit, with the waistcoat cut very high over the tie. That same evening, we also met Mick Jagger. I didn't recognize him. I said, "Oh, and what do you do?" He said, "I'm a rock and roll singer." He had on a Mickey Mouse T-shirt and a diamond.

"Well," the woman said, "'twas the only place I could find, but as you see, it's not good. There's no place for the children to play except in the street, with the soldiers walking up and down. And although the building was put up only four years ago, there's big chunks of plaster falling, and down the hall is always overflowing, and of course, the two wee rooms is not enough for the nine of us.

"After I pay the rent and the electric, I have usually about four pounds left for the week. With that I buy usually bread, margarine, tea, sugar, the powdered milk, and some eggs. Sometimes I buy cabbage and a small bit of bacon instead of the eggs. When Brian was working and, of course, we had more—not a great deal, but a bit more—I would do the shopping every day. And in those days I would sometimes buy rashers and potatoes and things. But now I usually go right out and spend the money on bread all at once, so that we will have it.

"It's a bad dream I have at times—that the children will starve. This way, I give the children a slice in the morning and two slices for tea, except sometimes towards the end of the week there's only one slice for tea. We always eat up the eggs right away, and if I let the children drink any of the powdered milk, we'd have none for the tea half the week.

"Ach, I don't know. Things couldn't go on the way they were. One side of the community had all the jobs and the other side had none. Brian worked with those people, and he always said that they were the best people in the world. I just don't know what it is. I guess they've never gotten close enough to us. They regard us as monsters.

"I couldn't say. You mean, do they think that if we have a bit more, it's the less for them? The dear Lord knows we've all little enough."

(A.-L. Mahier, Women of the World, 1977)

Tourists among the rich, we were intrigued at how Julian had come by his wealth, or appearance of wealth, as it seemed now mostly to be. "Oh, people gave him money," Lottie said as we drove past his wintering green fields. "He acts as if he had inherited stacks and stacks of money, but he has got this all," she waved her hand, "by simply assuming that he deserves it."

She turned into the drive and the grocery sacks shifted across the back seat. Out there in the country, miles from everything, we had to cross the border to shop. It was the Wednesday before Christmas, and the next Sunday the grocer's where we had been was blown up. They were after somebody who lived upstairs, we heard. From the bridge, where we waited in the inevitable rain while Welsh soldiers checked IDs, we could see the steel beams of what had been the custom house drawn up at one corner in the shape of a flame.

"A sort of con-man, then," I said.

"Oh, no," she said. "People gave to him because they loved him. Look at me if you doubt that."

She kept the great house for him, managed the farm—in New York, she had managed a medium-sized hotel. They were breeding cattle, but he took no interest in it; she and the farm man did everything. And she shopped and cooked and cleaned, had people over—Julian's social acquaintances, who had become her own—or gave parties for them. She was introduced around the county as his companion.

"And they all think they know," she said. "Isn't it funny?"

They were not lovers. "Oh, I think it stopped around six months after I got here. I don't care who knows. It had been all right, not great, but you see I was so much in love with him I didn't care, and then one night he said, 'Get the clothes brush,' and he started beating me with it, and I said no, and he said, 'Well, I have to have something more,' and I said, 'Well, not that, because it hurts and I don't like it.'

"And that was it," she said. "Except for one time, I think."

The house was one of those square eighteenth-century jobs you used to see all over Ireland with the roof caved in, which was the way Julian had bought it. He had fixed it up with his third wife's money. There were gilt birds at the tops of the rainspouts—also floodlights he'd put in just the year before, Lottie said, for security.

"Julian is no different from many others," Lottie said, "and in his charm as well. He had nothing to start with and he was nobody in particular."

Perhaps that was part of our fascination with him, that he had once been as we were. And yet, we did not think we would've done what he had to get where he was.

"I have heard him say, 'My father spent everything he had to send me to school at Rugby.' Because for them, that is everything." She waved her hand in the pigskin glove. "They were rather ordinary upper-middle class English people.

"His father had some kind of successful and, you know, what they regard as more or less acceptable business—the wine trade, or something—but there was no aristocracy at all. Except the Portuguese great-grandfather. You will notice that is the only one of his relatives he ever talks about." This was the great-grandfather who had received a peerage and an estate from the emperor and empress of Brazil for helping restore them to the throne of Portugal.

Lottie drove slowly up the rough farm drive, her gloved hands loosely on the wheel of the Mini. "I think it was some famous old London queen—though Julian was not that way—who got him into it, what we would call now the international jet set—a man who was in love with Julian when he was young. He was terribly good-looking, you know. He was in a movie, I do not think a very good one.

"All his wives had money, and the duchess who was his mistress, whom he still calls his friend, once gave him forty thousand pounds to invest in something. Of course, he later sold out of it for I don't know how many times as much.

"And Goedele, of course," the love of his life who killed herself in Rio de Janeiro, "left him everything. Not that she had much by then."

From the kitchen steps the dogs ran out at the car.

"Go on! Get out of the way! Oh, yes, that is true. He has her silver. I have seen it in the vault in London. Of course, whatever he had once, he is going broke from the boat."

The boat was the yacht he was building to sail to Brazil in the summer. "He will have a hundred-thousand-pound mortgage on it before he is through," Lottie said. "I don't know why they give it to him. He says, 'I must have it,' and they give it to him. He is quite mad; he does not care about his debts. You have to realize . . . ," Lottie stopped. "Oh, these people: it is all a matter of class."

Now reptilian armored cars rumble through the streets.
Barbed wire and road blocks bar every roadway into the bomb-
devastated ghost town of the city center. Troops in blackface
patrol the neighborhood like a jungle of a foreign land.

(Jordan Bonaparte, "In Londonderry,
Tragedy Touches a Man of Peace," *Life*, August 18, 1972)

From where we sat in the car, we could see fields just across the
river, in Northern Ireland, and far mountains in the distance. The
engine ticked, cooling in the quiet. In a moment we would unpack
the car, carry groceries inside. What happened to Goedele, I wanted
to know.

"Oh, it is quite a story," Lottie said, turning her square shoulders, her high-boned olive face to me. "She was the wife of some
East Prussian nobleman who sent her to Berlin when the Russians
advanced, and stayed behind. 'My house, my furniture, my art collections. Without these things, my life would not be my life.' He
was captured and died in a concentration camp. He was much older
than she was. It is all in her memoirs. There is a copy in the library.
Then she met Julian in Berlin after the war. He was a naval attaché,
still a young man; she was a middle-aged woman.

"They had gone to Rio together; one wonders how, as neither of
them had any money. Apparently it was quite the place after the
war, and perhaps he meant to take her to where he, too, had preten-
sions of aristocracy. They had a quarrel. He went out. When he
came back she was dead, in the hotel room, of sleeping pills. Who
knows why? But, you know, he said to me quite recently, and he
does not talk about her, she had lived through so much already. Life
as she had known it was over. I think she is on his mind nowadays.
Perhaps it is the trip to Rio, or this other war."

This other war was never very far away. Locking the garage, Lottie said, "We never used to lock things up, but since Gordon was
killed last Christmas . . . In his car, with a bullet in his head. They
found him the next day. A very prominent businessman. Not involved in politics. Insofar as anybody is not."

Out there in the country, with the wind blowing, the silence of
the house was loud, and Julian sat away downstairs in his study over

plans for his yacht all day and sometimes all night. Lottie lowered her voice in the kitchen, "They should kill him, you know." She was taking groceries out of the sacks, still wearing her coat and gloves. "You are shocked, but they should kill all of the ones like him, strictly speaking. If anybody was running this war properly, which they are not."

They buried Agnes McAnoy, 62, widow and mother of three, in Belfast last week. And Molly McAleavy, 57, mother of eleven. And Marie Bennett, 42, mother of seven. And Arthur Penn, 33, father of three. And Elizabeth Carson, 64, whose husband Willy lost an arm. Pathetic lines of mourners wept after the requiem at the Catholic Church of St. Matthew, half a mile from where the attackers had tossed a bomb into the crowded Strand Bar in East Belfast.

(*Time*, April 28, 1975)

The rest, all Protestants, were then gunned down in a withering hail of automatic fire. Ten died instantly. At week's end the badly wounded survivor remained in serious condition at a nearby hospital. The killings are believed to have been carried out in retaliation for the assassination the previous night of five Catholics.

(*Time*, January 19, 1976)

All Julian seemed interested in was the yacht—the yacht and the Atlantic crossing to Rio that he was going to make as soon as it was finished. He had lived there for a while, after the war: his second wife had been a Brazilian girl.

"She was very rich and very young," Lottie said, "and he spent all her money and divorced her." They had been divorced for sixteen years. He was still friendly with her, though. "He has to be," Lottie said. "He owes her alimony he has never paid."

She showed up for Christmas, too. She telephoned from London, where she lived, two days before. On the telephone in the hall, Julian made a face. "Why yes, Lina," he said, "do come. That would be lovely."

Afterwards he said, as if to himself, "It won't be so bad having her, with the others." The others were me and a gray man, an old friend of Julian's who was the descendant of a famous British mili- tary hero.

"Ah, it's just like old times again," Lina said, coming in the front door with her chin in the air, though she had never lived in that house. She was a plain-looking, middle-aged woman with a wide nose and red-dyed hair.

Lottie and I wanted to sympathize with her for what Julian had done to her. "She works at a travel agency," Lottie said. "She has to. She has nothing."

She did seem to have a lot of clothes. She kept changing into different outfits several times a day. She cried over her Christmas present from Julian ("Oh, darling," she said to him). It was a book about cats, which Lottie had bought "because I am sure he has not thought of her."

We all met at meals in the dining room, where the wallpaper was supposed to represent Brazil: Julian had had it printed up from eighteenth-century plates in the Victorian and Albert Museum. On one wall black-booted conquistadores discharged a volley from blunderbusses at naked brown Indians fitting arrows into bows behind brilliant green palm fronds; on another, white-shirted overseers with whips stood over black slaves cutting cane. A jaguar crouched in the jungle under a boa constrictor, while gauchos in red neckerchiefs twirled lassos on the pampas and the mountains towered lavender round blue Rio Harbor.

Julian and the gray man discussed British military history. When Lina mentioned her psychoanalysis, everybody looked away, and she talked about her cats instead.

She stayed for three days, until she and Julian had a fight in the middle of the night, and he drove her to Belfast airport at four o'clock one morning.

"Like everyone else," says shipyard worker John Bleakley, "we stay at home at night with our own kind and don't answer the door."

(*Time*, September 11, 1972)

For the last few weeks, we rarely saw Julian except at mealtimes. He would come up from the study, where he sat all day at his desk in front of the framed proclamation of thanks from the emperor and empress of Brazil to his great-grandfather. There he busied himself with minor decisions about the yacht.

That midday he paused, abstracted, in the doorway of the dining room, his face the color of the burgundy he drank afternoons and evenings, his mind still on what he had been thinking about. He had on a pair of old woolen suit trousers with a small hole above the knee and a raveling sweater. You could see he had once been good-looking; he still acted like a man who is good-looking. "But I think he has stopped caring about it," Lottie said another time. "It is a matter of habit."

We had been standing in the dining room waiting for him. He looked from one of us to the other and said, "Do you think the bottom color should be painted only up to the waterline, or eighteen inches above it?"

Lottie made a noise with her mouth and did not say anything.

At the sideboard, Julian uncorked a bottle of wine. He had small hands, with the little fingers so curved they looked almost deformed. "Always have green glasses for white wine," he said to nobody in particular.

When he had sat down at the table and surveyed what was offered, he raised an eyebrow. "Omelet. Don't much like eggs myself. They eat a lot of eggs in this country."

"The price of meat!" said Lottie, who tried to run the household economically.

"They eat a lot of eggs in this country," he repeated, picking up his fork. "They like 'em."

The meal was not much different from any other we three had shared alone. Julian made an effort at polite conversation but seemed bored by it. We talked, as we often had, about politics and the war, which he believed to be a manifestation of the inherent savagery of the Irish. Towards the end of the meal we were talking about salmon fishing rights on the river: there had just been something about that on the TV news.

"They want to make extra money," he said, "and poaching is

easier than working at whatever it is they do. It's as simple as that."
He began to peel a banana with a knife and fork. He regarded the
ability to do this as a test of civilized table manners.

"But there is no work for them," Lottie said. "How are they to
support their families?"

"If they'd stop blowing up businesses, there'd be work." ("There
was *never* work!" Lottie said. "That is why—")

"And why should they have families at all?" Julian said.

Lottie made some gesture to indicate that this was too silly a
question to reply to. "He calls himself a liberal," she said to me
privately, after some earlier one of these discussions.

"Well, of course," he went on, "I understand that they *will* have
families. But why should they? You've seen their wretched children.

"Look here," he said, as if to set things straight on the subject
once and for all. "The salmon fishing rights have been awarded by
government contract to the company, and anyone else who fishes
the river for salmon is stealing. They ought to put armed men out
there. That would stop it, provide work, too. Except, of course, you
couldn't hire one of them who wouldn't sell out to his friends."

"What is the matter with you?" Lottie said. "One would think,
to listen to you, that you had no sense at all!"

Julian merely gave her an amused glance and ate his banana with
knife and fork. But afterwards, as if he thought this would placate
her, he said, "My dear, I wonder if you would come downstairs
this afternoon and give me your opinion about some things on the
yacht."

"The yacht! The yacht!" she raved. "If I hear one more thing
about that yacht, I shall lose my mind, like you!" By the time she
was through with this, though, she seemed to have used up her
anger.

"You're tired," he said kindly.

She admitted she hadn't slept well the night before. "Take a
nap," he said.

"If I take a nap I won't sleep tonight either," she grumbled.

"Mm. Don't sleep much myself these days." He mused briefly.

"I'll tell you. Why don't we all go for a drive?" He looked from
her to me, me to her.

We didn't say anything; she and I had driven all over the North and West of Ireland together and thought the roads belonged to us. We did not especially want to spend the afternoon driving around with him.

To me, he said, "Have you seen Grianan Aileach?" This was an ancient ring fort that he knew I wanted to see.

"I've seen it a hundred times," Lottie said.

"Oh, but Debra wants to see it," he said. "We must go to Grianan Aileach." And so we went out that afternoon, by his choice and because of who we all were.

In the last chapter the man identified pseudonymously as Peter McHare makes the following confession: "When, according to our orders, we arrived at the house, I remembered being there once as a boy. The man bred dogs on the side, and my father or one of his friends had gone there twenty years before concerning the purchase of a dog.

"When Michael told him he was under arrest and we had orders to bring him to trial, the prisoner said (or words to this effect), 'Then if I'm to be tried in a court of law, you'll not mind if I ring up my lawyer.'

"Michael said that was regrettably not possible, that under the new order full legal process would be restored, but the exigencies of war made such impossible now.

"We took him away under the eyes of his wife and child. The prisoner was tried by military tribunal and, as the major shareholder in Harmon Dee, Ltd., Linenweavers, found guilty of having for many years consumed the people's substance.

"Asked if he had anything to say for himself the prisoner said that he had lived according to the order of things as he found them, and that it had not occurred to him to think that he did wrong. The prisoner was known about the neighborhood for a good-tempered man and an honest breeder of Irish wolfhounds, and his reputation was brought out in his defense.

"He was sentenced to death by firing squad, and we were

ordered to carry out the sentence, the trial taking approxi-
mately ten minutes.

"After the kerchief was around his eyes, he was given the
opportunity to say whatever he had to say, and these are his
exact words: 'I wish to convey my love to my wife Charlotte
and to our son and daughter; I beg pardon of all whom I have
offended; and I commend my soul to its Maker.'

"The order being given, the execution was carried out. Our
men standing by were affected by the prisoner's behavior,
and, it may be to put heart into the rest of us, the officer second in command said that though shocking things might be
done to improve the people's lot, he would do them himself,
since shocking things had always been done and, like as not,
for bad reasons or no reasons at all.

"Exactly how they fixed on that man, out of many they
might have chosen, I couldn't say."

("Review: *Peter McHare's Confession*," *Lately*,

7 August 1976)

Julian was particularly courteous and attentive, opening the car
doors for us, seeing us in. He was handsome in a sheepskin coat
with the collar turned up: his profile was still fine, above the chin.
He drove north along the river and then on up into the mountains,
being charming, pointing out things in the landscape with slight
gestures. At every farm a black-and-white dog ran out at the car or
sat watching us go by. At one farm the dog lay on top of a tall stone
pillar.

"It's the same dog," Julian said. "Don't you think? How does he
get from one place to the next so fast?"

The climbing road grew rough and finally ended. Above, on
the summit, the round fort sat like a fez. We got out, climbed towards it, and went in the narrow passage through the thick unmor-
tared wall. Inside, paper trash had been blown around a large grassy
circle open to the sky. We climbed on up the ancient stacked-stone
staircase that ran, narrow but utterly solid, around the inside of
the wall.

"How they fit these stones together," Lottie said, "to last so long!"

"Sixth century," Julian said, "or seventh."

The wind at the top blew strong. "Warm enough?" Julian said. "Lottie? Debra?"

The lesser mountains, blue where we looked up from the farm, were brown to look down on, with white roads snaking around them. Lough Swilly lay on one side, Lough Foyle on the other.

"This is where the flight of the earls took place," Julian said. "When Queen Elizabeth the First finally subdued the country. They drove them up this far, and down there from some harbor on Lough Swilly they took ship for Spain. The remnants of their aristocracy."

Over from Limavady, the pink smoke from the plastics factory spread out across a small patch of sky.

"There was still some history left when this thing was built," he mused. "Still some civilization to come. The English brought everything worthwhile to Ireland she ever had. Now it's falling apart."

Lottie said, "What's falling apart? Nothing's falling apart."

"Well, what do you call it?" He stretched his chin up and looked down at her. "People being murdered in their beds. The Bogside taking over."

And so the delusory peace was broken, but the outing seemed to be over, anyway. We had seen what there was to see. Julian went down the hill apart from us, having done his polite duty.

Back in the car, he slumped over the wheel and let us climb in by ourselves. Before he started the car, he said to Lottie, "You will look over those plans with me now, won't you?"

She sent me back a glance that said, "You see? He only did that so I will do what he wanted to begin with."

Early in October a number of women, whose husbands and sons were among the internees, broke down the outer defenses of Long Kesh, surged into the compound and burned several buildings.

(A. Boyd, "Imprisonment Without Trial," *Nation*, November 30, 1974)

The valley where we came down was flat but with scattered clumps of trees. So it was possible to drive, as we did, around a tight curve and come suddenly on something we had had no warning of in advance. There, at one of the British Army checkpoints that had been empty all spring, a blue car was parked crosswise, blocking the road.

"Oh, my God," Lottie said.

Two men in the back seat watched us over their shoulders without moving. Julian put the Bentley in reverse, but already there was another car blocking the road behind us.

"Where the *hell* did they come from?" Lottie whispered.

Julian said, "I always meant to put the revolver in the car."

And it's just as everyone says: you don't believe these things will happen to you—at most, to someone you know slightly. After the first flooding physical sensation of terror, my first thought was, they shouldn't kill me, I'm a foreigner. Then I thought, except that I will have seen them. Afterwards, Lottie said she thought exactly the same things.

The driver from the car behind us got out and walked towards us, while another man was still struggling to get out. All of this seemed to happen very slowly, but there was nothing we could do. Then there were two men walking towards us, and I saw that the man who had struggled to get out of the car wore the right sleeve of his raincoat empty. He has lost an arm, I thought at first; then I saw he held it inside the raincoat, which he had buttoned up over something large.

When the driver, who was a young man, got up close enough to look at Julian, he said, "It's not him." He wore an old suit jacket that he kept his right hand in the pocket of.

He put his face right up to the open window on Julian's side. He had straight shiny clean brown hair. "This is not the man," he said again.

The man with the bulky raincoat came up to the car and laughed in a funny way. "It is not. No, of course it is not." He was older and very Irish-looking, and he had the creases in his face of a man who smiled a lot, but he looked worried and irritated then.

The younger man called to the car up ahead, "This is not the man." Two men got out and came towards us, spare, hardfaced countrymen carrying unconcealed automatic rifles, which they pointed at us the rest of the time.

And then, when Lottie and I had tensely begun to hope, Julian said, "Tell your friends to get their car off the road."

Lottie drew a hissing breath through her teeth, and the older man, who seemed to be in charge, looked at Julian and turned away from the car. ("Will you shut *up*?" Lottie whispered to Julian.) He smiled at her coldly with his lips pressed together.

"It's the Bentley," one of the riflemen called back.

"As if there's not more than one Bentley in the county," the older man muttered, but not loud.

Julian stuck his head out the window and said to the two with the rifles, "Get your car off the road."

The older man in charge turned back towards Julian and asked in a casual sort of way, "And who might you be?"

"I am Julian Powell-deBarros of Foyle House," he said, "and you are blocking a public road."

The older man seemed to have a tic around the eyes that Julian's saying this set off. His face twitched, and he turned away again. The other men had drawn together in a little group, and he went to join them. They eyed us and seemed to argue. ("You have got us all killed!" Lottie whispered to Julian.)

After a few minutes, the group broke up and all four men came towards us, the two with the automatic rifles in the lead this time. One of them said to Julian, "Aye, you'll do."

The older man gestured ridiculously with the thing he had been holding buttoned up inside his raincoat, and the muzzle of a large weapon stuck out. "Now, if you'll just come quietly with us."

"Bandits!" Julian said, but he got out of the car.

"Now, Miss," the man leaned on the car and put his head up to the window, "you drive."

Later Lottie said to me, "They feel very secure. These things are never prosecuted. Everyone is afraid."

She slid over into the driver's seat and looked at the man. "Let him go with us," she pleaded. "He's half-mad. He's not responsible." The man looked away into the distance and his face twitched.

"Of course I'm responsible," Julian said; it was not clear who he was speaking to. "And so are these men, all of them."

The man looked back into the car. "Now, ladies, you'd best drive straight home," he said. Then the road ahead was open, and Lottie put the car in gear.

The last look we had of Julian, he was standing there very erect, smiling a little with satisfaction, as if at least it was all happening the way he knew it should be.

We drove back to the house and called the police, where Lottie was a long time making them understand what had happened.

> I have hated God's enemies with a perfect hate.
> (The Rev. Ian Paisley)

We huddled in the cold library waiting for the police, who would not be able to do anything, clutching the heavy square glasses. At first Lottie had busied herself with ice cubes, the ice bucket, as if for some ordinary social visit; then she said, "What am I doing?" and we just sat.

"It is frightening," she said at one point, "when things happen after you have said they should."

We felt, too, the guilt of being alive.

"Maybe they'll let him go," I said, though I didn't believe it, "or he'll get away. Maybe they'll demand ransom."

"No," Lottie said.

After a while, she said, "He was the one who wanted to go out."

Later she said, "And always, he must act the master."

Then we were silent for a long time, while the room got dark.

After I couldn't even see her sitting at the other end of the long tweed sofa, she said in a different tone, "I suppose he does not mind much—did not. Would even prefer it to a heart attack. When I first knew him, he used to say that when he was old he was going to live at the Ritz in London, have a room on the Green Park side, and never go out at all, make people come and visit him if they wanted to see him. But it had been a long time even then since he had the money to do a thing like that."

She was silent again, and we sat on in that eerie evening feeling of an empty house where the lights have not yet been turned on. Minutes passed, five, ten.

She burst out: "He says, 'Civilization is on the decline everywhere,' but he is, was, talking about himself. He had only his fifty-nine-year-old collapsing body and his life in the grand style, which is a what-do-you-call-it—completely out of date in the modern world. I do not think there was anything for him beyond the yacht and the trip to Rio."

Then she was quiet again.

In the end she said, "You know what it was about him that attracted me, long after I ceased to care for him in other ways? It was that he believed in himself. It's like he used to say to me sometimes, grab hold of me and say to me—even in these last months when we've meant very little to each other—'I love you, I need you, you know that, don't you?'

"And it wasn't true. Not the way you or I would think of love. But it was true to him. Whatever rot he talked, whatever wrong he did, he never questioned. He believed that it was right."

I said whoever heard of such a thing.

"Oh, well, yes, of course," she said, "and especially the people around here."

"Not us?" I said.

She said, "That is different."

"I suppose they all think that."

"Then they are wrong!" she said, and we laughed, from the strain, and got up and turned on the lights.

Gladys Knows

Since winning the Iowa Prize, Jim Henry has finished his master's degree in English at Cleveland State University and taught for one semester at Oberlin College (an experience that taught him that he was not a teacher); he now works as an instructional designer at an on-line education company in Chicago. He continues to write fiction and has been working on a play.

"There is present a small speck of Donald Barthelme's alacrity, so that we often see through the narrator's eye during a moment of amused irritation. [Henry's] characters struggle with private dreams and demons and with public versus private realities. . . . [I]t's difficult not to feel uneasily, and perhaps a bit exhilaratingly, implicated."

ANN BEATTIE, 1997

ONE

Gladys curses her mother under her breath as she pushes a lawn mower across the grass. Eddie, her brother, always makes such straight lines, and yet to do so seems impossible.

The heat is unbearable and Gladys has a hangover.

She needs a cigarette—badly. At the end of every line she stops, sweating, and surveys the strip she's just mowed, invariably finding that she has wavered. Every time. Looking back over the half yard she's done it looks like it was cut by a drunk, a madman, a retard.

Gladys laughs to herself. The grass will need to be emptied soon, before another line is done. Her bra strap is giving her a rash.

In the backyard the Capp twins are digging in the pile of topsoil left by the nursery the weekend before. Gladys sighs, thinking that it'll have to be loaded into the wheelbarrow and spread around the yard into all the various beds her mother dug last weekend with one of the men from the Raw Deal, the bar her father had owned. His name was Jaime and he smoked cigars and worked with no shirt on. He was one of the many men that had been coming over lately.

Like most of them, lately, he was *not* one of the men from the funeral. This is Gladys' main frame of reference with the men that come over for her mother: ones she remembers from the funeral, and ones she doesn't.

Gladys dumps the grass clippings and heads over to see what the Capp twins are doing in the dirt. They are secretive little boys about ten years old who live two houses down. They never dress alike and hate to be thought of as special because of their twinness.

She asks them what they are doing, bent over and smiling her biggest smile. The boys twist their heads up to look at her, squinting into the sun.

"Mind your own business, Barf-bag!" one of them says and they snicker and go back to their digging.

Back in the front yard Gladys is again appalled at her inability to cut even one straight line. The mailman drives by and honks at her as she stands with her hands on her hips regarding her massacre. Billy Walker from up the street walks by—a mess of greasy hair, torn jeans, and nose rings—sucking on a Popsicle and stops to stare at her staring at the grass.

"It's a matter of where you look," he says, coming across the lawn. "If you look directly in front of you as you go, you'll never cut in a straight line. You've got to look to the end of the yard and navigate yourself there."

Gladys tells Billy to fuck off and he shakes his head as if to laugh, the Popsicle stifling any noise. Gladys despises Billy Walker, even though they once had ended up practically fucking out in the woods after a bottle of gin.

"I'm just trying to pass on the wisdom of the suburban sages. Grass cutting is an art, my little Gladys." He grins, knowingly. He begins again, "Like fellatio, it only *seems* easy. Doing it right requires skill."

Gladys says nothing.

The fellatio remark sets her heart pounding. Billy must know that she and Maddox—one of Billy's good friends and Gladys' boyfriend—had a fight last night because Maddox wanted to come in her mouth. She wouldn't let him, though, because she knew he'd screwed Emma after the bonfire the week before. It ended up being a big scene; bigger than it needed to be anyway, and Maddox had almost hit her. He must've told Billy all about it.

Gladys imagines with disgust the conversation *that* must've been.

She glares at Billy, who takes the Popsicle out of his mouth and then shoves it back in . . . takes it out . . . shoves it back in . . . out . . . in. A disgusting leer creeps across his pimply face and then he turns to leave, rolling his head back and cackling.

Gladys reattaches the bag to the side of the lawn mower and pulls the starter. It takes her a couple of strenuous tugs but finally it starts and she turns back to face the yard. She takes a deep breath and then remembers she'd meant to smoke a cigarette after dumping the clippings, but that "Barf-bag" remark from the Capp twins made her forget.

TWO

At dinner Gladys sits in silence while her brother asks their mother if he can bring his new girlfriend over to watch a movie on the VCR.

Mrs. Laker sniffs her peas and says it is a strange time of the year for canned peas. Eddie asks again about his girlfriend, would it be all right if she came over and they watched a movie. "All right?" she says, dramatically arching her eyebrows, pursing her great, painted lips. "All right!? What, so I suppose you can fuck her on the couch. I know what you kids do. Little swine."

Gladys watches Eddie's face recoil from the encounter. She wonders what he expects. It is best not to even mention girlfriends or boyfriends to their mother. The thing to do is to just bring them over and let her make her scene and then have it done with. Once she's done with that you can rely on her to disappear into her room for a good long cry.

Although, lately, she's been calling the Raw Deal; "For company," as she says, "a widow needs that now and then." This is her new thing. Any time of the day or night these men come banging into the house, usually drunk, and they just go right up to her room. Sometimes they stop on their way out and smile at Gladys. Some of them she knows, most she doesn't.

"Well, so I guess it'll be okay then?" Eddie says.

Gladys wonders why he persists.

"Okay? Okay? Since when does anything have to be okay with me around here? Since when has anybody in this house given a good goddamn what I have to say about anything? Bring her over. Screw on the kitchen table for all I care."

Gladys gets dessert from the freezer after dinner. It's some ice cream and cookies her mother mixed together in a fit of inspiration that afternoon after Gladys finished the yard. She'd found her mother in the kitchen in a baggy pair of gym shorts and a white V-necked T-shirt with no bra, sitting at the table in front of a two-gallon jug of vanilla ice cream and two open packs of Oreos. She was mixing them together in a small Rubbermaid bucket. "What would be better?" she said, her eyes thrilled, her hands a sticky mess. "Try and think of one thing better than ice cream and Oreos together," she said. "Just one." Then she went back to mixing it all together with wild abandon.

Gladys was picking up some Oreo wrappings when a man came out of the living room in his underwear. He was holding a basketball tightly to his chest. "Shit," he said. He bounced the basketball once. Gladys glared at him and her mother sucked on her fingers, turning from one to the other. The man bounced the basketball one more time and turned and left.

Eddie whistles as he does the dishes and Gladys dries. She wants to ask him how he always gets the lines so straight when he cuts the grass. Upstairs their mother is singing "High Hopes" at the top of her lungs while rearranging furniture. After dinner she said that it was time to shake up her life with a little redecorating.

"Do you suppose someday she'll just drop dead?" Eddie asks as he rinses the soap out of an ice-cream dish.

Gladys doesn't understand. Everyone drops dead.

"I mean, do you think she'll just run out of energy some day and just stop, like a toy that runs out of batteries or something like that?"

Gladys says she supposes so.

"I picture it sometimes. She'll be going on a rampage, or moving some furniture, or, I don't know, something, one of her *things*, and then she'll just stop, stand straight up, smile once . . . and then just fall down dead. Just like that. It'll all be over."

Gladys is about to tell her brother that he is dreaming, that in the real world people don't just disappear, they linger, they annoy, they take their time exiting. And it's almost never on cue. But then her mother appears, leaping down the steps. She comes bounding into the kitchen, singing, "everyone knows an ant . . . can't . . . move a rubber tree plant . . . but he's got high hopes, he's got high hopes."

She starts dancing around the kitchen table, one hand on her hip, one arched over her head, spinning herself like a music box ballerina. "He's got high apple pie in the sky hopes." Finally she sits down—collapses, really—at the table and sighs a tremendous sigh that leaves her limp and crumpled.

She breathes heavily a few times, pushing the hair from her face. Finally she speaks. "I hate this fucking world," she says, and starts crying, "I hate it more than either of you could ever imagine." Eddie slowly turns the water off—"More than you could imagine in your wildest dreams"—leaving the house in absolute silence.

He and Gladys slowly walk toward their mother, slumped in the chair. As they inch their way across the soiled linoleum, looking back and forth at each other, just as they approach her, she bites her lower lip, lifts her head and says, "Is there any more ice cream?"

THREE

Maddox picks Gladys up in his father's Cadillac. He is all dressed up and has a flower in his lapel and a corsage in a box.

Gladys is surprised, shows it.

"We're going ballroom dancing," he says, pulling out of the driveway.

Ballroom dancing?

"That's right, m'lady, ballroom dancing."

Gladys doesn't know how to ballroom dance.

"There's nothing to it. Besides, the man leads."

Gladys is wearing jeans.

"Fear not."

They get onto the highway and Maddox pulls out a tape and pops it into the stereo. His father's Cadillac has a great stereo system with speakers all over the place and a graphic equalizer built into the dash. (His father is a lawyer and the local judge.) The tape is opera, which at first makes Gladys laugh, but then she sits and listens to it, a soprano with piano accompaniment, and she feels herself relax.

It starts to rain and the drops have a hypnotic effect as she stretches out in the vast American expanse of front seat. She hugs herself into the velour upholstered seat and marvels at the feeling of flight the car offers.

Maddox lights a joint and hands it to her. She inhales deeply and feels the warmth of it in her head. He turns the music up and the car seems to speed up with it. She looks out the window and sees that they are weaving through traffic like magic, like a video game. Lights fly by to the left and to the right, cars part in anticipation of them. It looks as effortless as a walk in the park, and yet they are in two tons of steel and glass.

This feeling of wellness stays with Gladys through most of the joint—through three arias, the beauty of which brings tears to her eyes, makes her spine tingle in a way that reminds her of coming. She feels herself gliding through an unreality as pure as light, as soft as a dream. Even the rhythm of her breathing is harmonious and magical.

Air tastes like sugar, her blood pulses through her veins like the clearest of crystal streams. Her hair feels like silk. The world speeds by like a light show. The world has *become* a light show, as harmless and distant as a laser light show at a planetarium.

She looks over at Maddox and feels a tremendous love for him. She wishes she had let him come in her mouth—he gets such a charge out of it. So what if she couldn't figure out why it mattered *where* he came, if it was *in* or *out* or *on* or *behind* or, who cared,

really. The things we let distract us, she thinks, the things we let
ourselves be derailed by! She'd let him come in her mouth, she
thinks, staring enraptured at him, on Main Street at noon if it
would make him happy.

She stares at the side of his face, lit by the halogen street lamps, and her heart pounds for him. The world is perfectly tuned, spinning just as it should. Precisely right. Why had they fought? Just go with it, she thinks, just let it be.

FOUR

But, then, slowly at first, the old familiar anxiety creeps up on her. (She knew it would happen. For months now pot had been making her paranoid.) Suddenly, the shrill screaming voice of the singer begins to grate on every nerve in her body, she feels seasick from the motion of the speeding car. She sees her entire life as one long perilous journey leading up to this one incomprehensibly senseless moment, speeding like lunatics toward a "ball" of some sort— whoever heard of a "ball"?

It is absolutely obvious to her: this is how she will die. It all makes the most perfect sense. Every minute of her long and tortured existence has been leading to this one moment. Her entire history reveals itself to her; it spreads back behind her like a thin, winding path barricaded on each side by tall, sheer walls precluding deviation of any sort. Her death is upon her, her fate is sealed, as it always had been. What a fool she'd been not to know it!

Her body tightens into a knot. She can barely breathe. She pulls her limbs into herself desperately gasping for air.

A scream builds inside her. She feels it starting as a tiny, shrill plea in the bottoms of her feet. And then it builds. And it builds. By the time it has reached her knees it has become a screech, then it becomes an operatic howl, a desperate guttural cry, a tremendous scathing wail, an inhuman, no a *super*human fantastic scream.

She feels it leaving her mouth against her will, it seems to shatter the interior of the car as it comes, bursting forth. A lifetime's worth of suppressed screams, all of them at once, every scream she never dared scream all her life long, looses itself upon the interior of Maddox's father's speeding Cadillac.

There are immediate results.

Maddox himself picks up the howl, like a contagion. He somehow loses control of the car in the course of his own screaming. Suddenly they are spinning in the rain, the car is spinning uncontrollably across the four-lane highway. They scream and scream. Death is imminent and now both of them know it, so they scream some more. All around them events slow unnaturally.

It was like watching yourself on TV, they will both recount later, *it was like watching a movie.*

They spin to a stop in the grass between the highway's north and south sides. They are unhurt. The car is undamaged. They are out of breath.

"Jesus Fucking Christ," Maddox says, "what the hell was that scream for?"

Gladys can barely open her mouth.

"Jesus Fucking Christ. I think I shit my pants." He is gasping desperately, his eyes so wide it looks to Gladys like they might jump out of his head. "This suit is a rental!"

Gladys notices a foul odor.

FIVE

The Ballroom, a rented party hall really, is decorated with crepe paper and balloons. A spinning mirrored ball hangs from the ceiling. Punch is served by old ladies in taffeta gowns. Maddox and Gladys are the only people under twenty in the entire ballroom. They are the only people under forty, under fifty. It turns out it is an event the police department has put on to raise money for an animal shelter. Maddox's father, as the local judge, got tickets but at the last minute couldn't go because of diarrhea. (Maddox hadn't shit his pants after all.)

Gladys refuses to dance most of the night. She stands in a corner and watches Maddox go from one person to the next, shaking

hands, patting shoulders, flirting with old ladies. He will be a politician someday, she thinks. Good family connections, good looks,
broad shoulders.

He says he is going to study political science, then law. "I'm a
good catch," he told her one night in the back of his car. Gladys
was staring off into space, winding and unwinding her bra strap
around her middle finger.

Gladys wasn't aware of having cast a line.

SIX

A woman named Chartreuse eventually takes it upon herself to talk
to Gladys. It is late and the crowd has thinned out. The band looks
bored.

Gladys notices the saxophonist checking his watch. A woman in
the corner opposite Gladys, with a crowd of leering men encircling
her, is drunkenly trying to recount the Ten Commandments. "Thou
shalt not covet . . ." she keeps saying and then giggling.

Chartreuse comes over and shakes Gladys' hand through a white
glove. "How do you do?" she asks.

Gladys nods unconvincingly. They introduce themselves and
then Chartreuse tells her that she knew her father many years before. "He used to date my Maggie," she says. "This was before he
met your mother, of course. He was on the football team. Did you
know that?"

Gladys knows.

"Of course you would. He was a fine young man. Very polite,
well dressed. Like men were back then. He and my Maggie used
to go to the drive-in, to the raceway, picnics. That sort of thing. A
very innocent time. Seems almost comical now." Chartreuse looks
thoughtfully skyward and continues, "I saw a boy yesterday walking
down the street with a red Mohawk and rings pierced through his
cheeks."

Gladys smiles. That is Jimmy; an actual suburban heroin user.

Chartreuse shrieks. "My God! Heroin? Really?"

Gladys nods, pleased to have shocked this annoying woman.

"He *injects* heroin? With *needles?*"

Gladys laughs.

"Here in Province? Well, you see what I mean. It was a different world not so many years ago. Your father was a good man."

Gladys thinks about her father, the man that took Chartreuse's Maggie to the drive-in and on picnics. She sees them living in slow motion and soft focus, in a world lit like a douche commercial.

"How long's it been now?" Chartreuse asks, fidgeting as people do, Gladys has learned, when asking about the dead.

"Three years," Gladys says, imagining the spinning pages of a calendar flying off into empty black space.

"To lose someone in a murder is an awful thing. I can't begin to understand what your family must've gone through. And to think it was for, what—what did they get?"

"Forty-six dollars," Gladys recites. People usually act as if it would somehow make sense (or be at least in accordance with their view of the world) if her father's killers had at least stolen some serious money before shooting him squarely in the head, twice. As if a higher figure would allow them a better night's sleep as they fooled themselves into believing that the world makes anything even closely resembling sense.

"Forty-six dollars. Hmmh."

Gladys spots Maddox waving to her from a circle of policemen. When he catches her eye he motions for her to come over. Relieved, she tells Chartreuse her boyfriend beckons.

She looks over toward Maddox and says, very impressed, "Maddox Haines, very good. A girl could do worse."

Gladys shows surprise.

Chartreuse stands up and dusts off her gown. "I always make it a point to tell the young that everything changes. They always seem so sure it won't. That they already know everything. But things change, my dear. Soon much of what you think and feel will be just a memory, a hazy memory. You'll have trouble remembering what it was that you feel so passionately now. About everything."

Gladys has nothing to say.

Chartreuse goes on, patting Gladys' shoulder and smiling broadly. "Many people are crushed by life, a woman my age has seen a lot of people utterly deflated by it," she says. "We shouldn't judge

them, though it seems easy. I knew your mother too. She was actually friends with my Maggie at one time. This is a small town."

Gladys imagines its smallness, pretends she is looking at it from above, all the aluminum houses sitting on square plots of green, her yard with its crooked lines.

"To my mind," Chartreuse continues, "that we can even go on, at times, is a miracle. Truly. Up there with walking on water and all that rubbish. That we even find the strength to just go on."

SEVEN

On the way home Maddox teasingly complains that the wife of a politician is supposed to be sociable. "Mix!" he tells her, "Even if you think everybody's an asshole, it's still better to talk to an asshole than to just sit by yourself."

In her defense Gladys says she'd had a lovely talk with Chartreuse.

"She's a nut."

They listen to opera again but don't smoke any pot. When they pass where they'd spun out Gladys feels a chill in her chest. She puts her hand on Maddox's thigh, asks to lie down, she just wants to lie down.

"Whatever," he says.

Gladys moves the armrest and lays her head across the seat onto his thigh. She watches the sky stream past through the windshield and thinks again of flight. She tries to make herself feel the sensation like before, the feeling of everything going smoothly, of the universe being in order. Her head spins, however, and she has to close her eyes.

She turns on her side and strokes Maddox's calf. At home her mother will have some man over. Eddie'll be with his new girlfriend watching one of his super-violent movies. Maybe that is the universe being in order, she thinks. Maybe the universe has no choice but to be in order. Maybe we have a faulty conception of what order is; if we just looked differently and expected something else, not necessarily something less, we'd be okay. She shifts herself a little bit, trying to imagine this new way of looking at things, trying to imagine a Gladys who knows, and yet isn't affected. Maddox begins stroking her hair and fidgeting slightly on the seat. He delicately traces a finger along the line of her jaw and beside her other cheek Gladys feels Maddox getting erect.

Stealing Trees

Since winning the 1997 John Simmons Short Fiction Award, Lisa Lenzo has written a novella, Flying Off the Edge of the World, *and a memoir,* The Shadows of Sparrows.

"In this collection we are offered more of a landscape than a map, yet its interlocking pieces gradually form a whole that seems greater than the sum of its parts. In some way, it would seem we've all walked there."
ANN BEATTIE, 1997

We started stealing trees after the elms were dead and gone, when the city planted a twig in front of Frank's house. The twig had no branches and no leaves. It was as thin as a car antenna. From Frank's front stoop at dusk it was invisible.

So Frank and I started driving around at night and stealing thicker, bigger saplings, ones with branches and lots of leaves. We'd dig them up from the better neighborhoods in northwest Detroit, dump them into the trunk of Frank's Fairlane, and replant them on Frank's front lawn.

Frank refused to call what we did stealing; he was always correcting me: "Tree relocation, Stanley. The 57 Farrand Street Tree Relocation Project."

We could plant the trees at Frank's house because Frank's mother didn't live there and Frank's father never noticed what we did. Mr. Chimek played cello with the Detroit Symphony, and when he wasn't in concert he was upstairs in one of his rooms, either practicing music or listening to it. Occasionally he'd wander downstairs and fry himself some eggs, then go back up without turning the burner off. I can still picture him leaving the house for a concert: dressed in his black suit, white hair springing out of place, walking past the trees without turning his head. I lived five blocks over from

91

Frank, and since my mother never passed by the Chimeks' house, she never saw our accumulating collection of stolen trees.

I suggested to Frank that we stop stealing trees after we'd bagged and replanted half a dozen. But Frank pointed out that stealing trees was less degenerate than setting tires on fire and rolling them down the ramp of the underground parking lot at Farrand and Woodward, something we used to do all the time in junior high. And by relocating lots of trees onto his front lawn, Frank said, and sneaking a few onto the lawns of our neighbors, we were helping to restore our city's reputation and name: "Highland Park, City of Trees."

We used to watch for the signs with these words—stamped in a circle around a tree silhouette—when we were little kids coming home from Detroit; crossing over the Highland Park border, we'd shout, "*Now* we're in Highland Park!"

In those days, the elms formed a ceiling of leaves a hundred feet up from Highland Park's streets. I didn't notice the leaves over my head as I grew older any more than people notice the ceilings of their houses. But when I was a little kid I used to look up past all the space to where the layers of green began and watch the breeze stirring the leaves and imagine myself up there.

Ten years later, there wasn't a branch or leaf left in all of Highland Park's sky, but the signs were still standing. We watched for them on our way home from stealing trees, and though we still spoke out when we crossed over the border, our voices were quieter and our emphasis had changed. Most of the time we'd be smoking a joint or a pipe. "Now we're in *High*land Park," we'd say. "City of *Stolen* Trees," I'd sometimes add.

"Relocated trees, Stanley," Frank would insist.

Daytimes that summer, Frank and I worked at the rag factory at Woodward and Cortland, cutting up new rags and washing and drying old ones for the guys at Chrysler. Evenings we played basketball with Frank's neighbors, usually quitting when it got dark, but when we felt like it playing on into the night using the light Frank had rigged on his garage. (The guys we played with said Frank should turn the light off and just use himself as a bulb, he was so pale blond—white hair, moon-white skin—that he almost glowed in the dark. They didn't comment on my whiteness, except

for once when I was sunburned, and Dwight Bates fouled me and I cried out, and Dwight said he thought all the tender white people had moved out of Highland Park.)

Besides stealing trees and playing ball, another thing we did that summer at night was sit around while Carol Baker cornrowed Frank's head. Cornrowing was big then, but just among black people. This was before Bo Derek.

I'd sit on Frank's porch and watch Carol working through Frank's hair and listen to her fuss and scold and threaten to slap Frank if he didn't hold still. As Carol got close to finishing, she'd swear she'd never braid such a fine-haired jumpity fool ever again. But Carol braided Frank every week all that summer, and whenever she went to slap him, her palm landed so lightly it was more like a stroke. Frank would reach up and take hold of Carol's hand, and Carol would pull away and threaten Frank some more. Frank just smiled and fingered his braids. He liked being fussed over, and the tight, close, pale braids kept his hair out of his face, which was perfect for playing basketball, and for stealing trees.

In August of that summer, Frank's father had a heart attack and died. Frank and I found him on the floor of his practice room with his tiger-necked cello lying beside him. My mom said Frank could come live with us for a year (we had one year of high school to go), but Frank wanted to stay where he was. He'd lived in that house all his life.

Two weeks after Mr. Chimek's funeral, Frank decided that we should steal a tree from downtown. He had seen its picture in the paper next to an article about the new Blue Cross building. The tree stood out in the foreground of the picture, a dome-shaped, leafy maple. So far we had stolen only locusts and oaks, the main kinds of trees being planted back then. The maple looked almost too big to steal, but we decided to check it out in person.

First we smoked some marijuana. Then we drove downtown. The maple looked even better in real life. Its hundreds of leaves were perfect and huge, and it looked as if its branches had been set in their upward, outward curves with a whole lot of planning and expertise. But there were too many cops cruising around down there—they never gave us a clean opening. At two o'clock in the morning we got on the Chrysler Expressway again, lit another pipe, and headed north, back toward Highland Park.

We hadn't gone a mile when Frank spotted the tree of heaven on the freeway slope. Later, planting the tree on his lawn, Frank said, "I've thought of another name for our project: the Otto Chimek Memorial Grove." But when he first saw the tree of heaven, Frank didn't mention his father, he didn't say anything at all—he just pulled over onto the shoulder and looked at me with his high, shining eyes.

"What are you doing?" I said.

Frank pointed at the tree.

"What?" I said. "You want *that* tree?"

It wasn't the best-looking tree even from the car. Just your typical ghetto tree that grows anywhere at all, but mostly in vacant lots and from between sidewalk cracks. Not the kind of tree that anyone plants, let alone steals. I looked at it, branches angling downward like palm fronds, then at the green sign hanging from the freeway overpass just ahead: MACK ½ MILE. On our trips between downtown and Highland Park, we had seen the sign plenty of times, but we hadn't even thought of stopping here before. This was a part of the city where black people didn't stop unless they knew someone who lived here, and white people didn't stop here at all.

The tree was growing close enough to the overpass that if a car crossed overhead we could hide below, and if a car came down the freeway we could scramble up on top of the overpass. I tried not to think about what we would do if cars came by both places at the same time.

Frank pulled on the hood of his black sweatshirt and tucked handfuls of his long braids inside the hood until none of the dozens of plaits showed. I pulled on my black baseball cap. Then we got out of the Fairlane and started up the grassy slope.

Old, dry litter cracked like glass under our feet. I looked at the overpass to my left and felt like I was on another planet. All my life I'd seen freeway embankments and overpasses, but never from this angle, the overpass at eye level, the embankment slanting under our feet, nothing between the overpass and us, nothing between the grass and us, but the cool night air. Standing on that hill made the

whole world seem tipped and slanted—it seemed like the world had been set on its edge.

I spread the garbage bag beside the tree. Frank pushed the shovel in to its hilt eight times, cutting a circle around the skinny trunk. He had just got the roots separated into their own private clump when we heard a raggedy car in the distance, up on street level.

Suddenly it seemed a bad idea to duck under the overpass. It came to me that every movie that ended badly had people getting wasted in closed-in, concrete places. Frank and I glanced at each other. Then he ditched the shovel and I dropped the bag, and we ran the rest of the way up the slope and jumped out on the service drive and started walking along it as if we had not just run up there from the expressway canyon.

Soon we heard the raggedy car, or at least a raggedy car, approaching from behind us. We forced our breathing slow, tried to loosen our legs and our shoulders. The car drew closer, and then alongside us. We turned our heads toward the car but kept walking. The driver, black as the car's upholstery, leaned his head out the window. "Can you please tell us how to get to the corner of Russell and Pearl?" he asked, his voice a perfect imitation of a prissy white man's. Four or five others inside the car laughed. All of them were black. At least one was a girl.

Frank smiled in the direction of the carload of people, trying to act as if he were relaxed enough to think their joking funny. He kept walking. I kept step with him, wondering where we were going. We were getting farther from our car.

"You boys lost?" someone from the back seat said.

"No," Frank said.

"Oh yeah?" the driver said, sounding black this time, "You sure *look* lost." More laughter came from the others.

Frank glanced at the driver. "Yeah, I know we do," he admitted, just the right amount of blackness creeping into his voice—enough to let them hear that he was not a total outsider, but not so much that he seemed to be making any sort of claim. We still kept walking, but we didn't say anything more. It was better to say too little than to say something wrong.

"Where you boys from?" the driver asked.

This time Frank didn't answer.

I steadied my breathing. "Highland Park," I said carefully, trying to sound offhand and matter-of-fact, as if I didn't expect my answer to boost their opinion of us.

The girl shrilled something wordless from the back seat.

"Highland Park!" the driver said. "They let you boys stay in Highland Park?"

"For now, I guess," I said.

The driver eyed me more closely. Then he laughed, almost a friendly laugh, his lips breaking wide. He looked to be about twenty years old. He was wearing a light brown shirt zipped open at the throat. "And where you going later, man, when you got to move?"

"I don't know—*Romulus*, or somewhere," I said, with true dejection at the prospect. I'd never seen Romulus, but I had it pictured as rows of dirty white shoebox houses that collapsed when the jets flew overhead.

"*Romulus*," someone from the back seat said. "Where the fuck is *Romulus?*"

"I know where Romulus is," the driver said. He jabbed his finger in the air. "Shit, you got to move, man, don't move to Romulus. The whites out there so mean they don't even like whites."

"If I was white," the man in the passenger seat said, "I'd move to Grosse Pointe, Bloomfield Hills, somethin' like that."

"If you was white," one of the men in the back seat said. "Listen to the nigger: 'If I was white.'"

The three in the back seat laughed loudly and easily. I let myself smile but kept my own crazy laughter down in my belly.

"I got one other question to ask you," the driver said. The laughter stopped. I could feel all the ground I thought we'd gained slipping away from us. "Why was you digging up that tree?"

The trouble that had been floating around grew bigger and clearer, pressed at the quiet. My vision started shrinking inward. I couldn't focus, I could hardly see. I didn't look at Frank or at the driver or anywhere.

"I know there's plenty of them raggedy trees in Highland Park," the driver said. "So what I want to know is, what do two white boys from Highland Park want with a tree that's as common there as

dirt? I mean, that tree is as common in Highland Park as niggers are, am I right?"

"We've been digging up all kinds of trees, from northwest Detroit, mostly, and planting them in front of his house," I said, glancing at Frank. Frank was looking down at the pavement.

"You boys really are lost," the driver said. "This is not northwest Detroit."

Frank kept on looking down. I couldn't see his eyes. Frank! I thought. Do something! Save us! Frank had a way of winning people over to him, sometimes without saying a word. Too bad this wasn't a carload of old people or women or girls. But even among the guys at school Frank was well liked, for a white person.

I thought of letting the men in the car know that Frank's father had just died. I thought of letting on somehow that he'd died just last week, just last night. But as soon as I thought of it, I knew it would be a mistake to bring up that subject at all.

"I don't think you boys really are from Highland Park," the driver said. "I think you're from one of them suburbs where they let the raggedy white folks live. Taylor, maybe. Or Romulus."

I thought of ways to refute this—name all the streets in Highland Park, show the eraser-burn tattoos our sixth-grade classmates had rubbed into our shoulders, at our request. But I thought that eraser-burn tattoos might be a Highland Park black thing rather than a black thing in general, and Frank's and my tattoos wouldn't have shown up that well anyway in the dark, being white on white.

In fourth grade, when our school was just about half black, the black kids in our class made plans to build a spaceship and fly to the moon, blowing up the earth as they left. They talked about it one day while the teacher was out of the room, said they wouldn't save a thing on earth except the people they took with them, and started calling off the passenger list. They named all the black kids in the room, and then one of them said, "And Frank Chimek." "Yeah!" another boy said, "Frank Chimek is cool." After talking it over a little, they added my name, too—Frank and I were the only two white people on earth they thought deserved to be saved.

But of course I couldn't say this to those men in the car. I

thought of all the times I'd wanted to convince someone of something—convince a girl that I was the guy for her, or a teacher that
my excuse was really real, or some guys who wanted to beat me that
I didn't deserve to be beaten.

The driver said something about taking us back to the tree.

A deep voice from the back seat called out, "What you going to
do with 'em, blood, lynch 'em?" The whole group laughed hys-
terically. I couldn't help smiling, though it felt like the smile of a
crazy man.

"Let's lynch them *and* that sorry-ass tree," another voice from
the back said. "Hang 'em all three from the overpass."

The driver waited until the laughter died. "I don't like white boys
stealing niggers' trees," he said, "no matter how sorry the trees is,
or the boys. Y'all move over and make room for these boys."

There was movement inside the car. A door clicked open. I jerked
as if the click had come from a knife or a gun, and I guess Frank
must have moved too. "Wait! Wait!" someone screeched. It was the
girl. She scrambled forward so that her wide face and thick, round
arms leaned over the front seat. "Take off your hood," she said to
Frank.

Frank looked up from the street with that distant expression
people and dogs wear just before they get beaten. "Fool!" the girl
said, slapping at someone in the back seat. "Don't be pulling on
me. Take off your hood," she repeated.

Frank looked at the driver.

"Go on," he said.

Frank untied the string and pushed the hood back, and his blond
braids unfolded and fell all around him.

"I knew it!" the girl crowed. "They told me white folks couldn't
do their hair like that, but I knew y'all could, I knew it. Come
here—let me see."

Frank didn't move. He just stood there with his braids lying in
lines against his scalp, snaking down around his shoulders, practically glowing in the dark.

"Damn, boy," the driver said, "did you get dunked in a tub of
bleach?"

"Maybe he's an albino," the girl said. "Maybe he's really black." She and the man sitting in the passenger seat started arguing.

"C'mon, woman, a white black man? Give me a break."

"I saw a black albino once, man, in my social studies book. It was a purely white black man."

"Girl, you're talkin' about an Oreo."

"I'm talkin' about an albino—don't you know what an albino is?"

"Why don't y'all stop talking stupid?" the driver said. "The man is obviously white."

"For real," the deep-voiced man agreed, "he's some kind of white freak."

"Naw," another man from the back said, "he just wants to be black."

"Is that it, man?" the driver said to Frank. "Do you wish you was black?" Everyone in the car looked at Frank.

Frank lifted his head, his blond braids tilting back, and looked at all the faces looking at him. "Right now I do," he said simply, his face serious but hardly afraid, a hint of pleasure at his joke showing around his mouth and in his eyes.

The men in the car laughed suddenly, with surprise. "Right now I do," one of them repeated, and everyone laughed harder, with the deep-voiced man saying "No shit! No shit!" over and over between the laughter of the others.

When the laughter finally stopped, there was a floating sort of pause, like when you're standing on a teeter-totter with both ends off the ground. The driver said something to the others that I didn't quite hear—"Let's go" or "Let them go." Then he turned back to Frank. "I don't know why in hell you want that tree, man," he said, "but if you still want it, go on and take it—then take your crazy asses back home to Highland Park or wherever it is you're from before you run into some mean niggers or the police. And next time you want to steal a tree, go on out to Grosse Pointe or Bloomfield Hills and steal yourself a nice *white* tree, something like a *pine* tree, all right?"

"All right," Frank said.

The driver shook his head. The car rumbled off. Frank and I

walked, fast, back to the freeway slope and lifted the tree of heaven into the garbage bag. Then we walked down the slanting ground holding the bagged tree between us, checking the wide, gray freeway for cars.

The huge overpasses on either side were suspended at our level. We were leaning back against the pull of the slope, taking big strides. It felt like we were traveling between planets, like we were walking down from the sky. It felt like we were aliens—aliens in both worlds. But at least the world we were heading toward was home.

RENÉE MANFREDI

Where Love Leaves Us

*Renée Manfredi is an associate professor of English at the University of
Alaska in Fairbanks. She has recently completed a new novel,* Wild Geese,
*and is at work on a second collection of stories and a book of nonfiction
essays about life in Alaska. A screenplay and a third novel are
also in the early stages.*

*"Renée Manfredi's stories—mostly of fathers and daughters—are intense,
even harrowing. But they're written with the calm assurance of
someone who knows she has a subject and a story to tell."*
FRANCINE PROSE, 1993

All around the fountain are tiny blue lights that cast shadows the
color of twilight on the sculpted lovers in the center. The form of
them changes with distance; up close their embrace is the tryst of
all great passion: part despair, part delight, part unifying mystery.
From my bedroom window or roof—where I sometimes sit and
work on my photograph albums—the shape of the sculpture is not
human at all, but something like a terrible, dark fish that heard a
fatal note in the air and rose to it.

Bruno and I stand in the backyard the third evening I am home,
and he holds me in mock imitation of them, laughing as he always
does, though the figures are as familiar to him as I am. We were in
love the summer we were both eighteen, but have since been able
to stay lovers the way some people remain friends after the romance ends.

"So? Why are you here *this* time?" He backs me into the fountain
so that my spine is pressed hard against the cement base. I pull him
toward me and bend backwards so that my hair is immersed in the
water. With his tongue, he traces the trail of water running down
my neck.

"I've come home because, believe it or not, she asked me," I say, meaning my mother, C.D. Since being on my own, I have been home for six extended visits within seven years, the principal reasons being that I was between schools or jobs and not in love. I am a disgrace, according to C.D.—"twenty-five years old and still transitory"—but am not dissuaded from returning even after I came home last summer, after giving up my research assistantship, to find that I no longer had a bedroom. C.D. had redecorated it into a sewing room, complete with a large work table and a new French teal carpet the fallen needles in which I had to pick out of my soles every evening. She finally conceded and moved in the daybed from the guest room.

"I don't know what you want," she said last summer. I was sitting on the floor surrounded by romance novels—I indulge when I am on the rebound—and Butterick patterns. She leaned against the doorway in her nightgown, her cold-creamed face making her look like some sort of displaced mime. "They pay for your tuition, they give you a stipend. There are some people who would kill for that."

I said I didn't know what I wanted either, but what I *didn't* want or need was work that required me to assist in burning lab animals with a blow torch in order to experiment with skin grafting. My work is in genetics and I am opposed to vivisection for any and all purposes. She said, "You think you can get through life as a functional human being and not do certain things because they're contrary to your beliefs?" I said that I wasn't as concerned with getting through life functionally as I was with just getting through it.

Bruno puts his hand inside my shirt and leans into me. I turn my head and watch my hair floating in tendrils around my head, undulating gently like uncoiled roots. Bruno says something to me which I feel as a vibration in his chest against mine. He laughs and grabs my elbows, pulls me up so quickly that my hair drags my head back. The novelty buttons on his jacket jab my breasts. Mr. Ed (mouth open in mid-sentence) decorates one side of his collar, a day-glo green one with a black X that reads, "You are here," the other. I look at him, marveling as I always do at the physical beauty of this man—the way the last of the sun makes his skin and hair the color of autumn, the full mouth with its Botticelli lips, a sweet roof for the cleft in his chin which tempts my tongue. I succumb. I've Renée had many men and have been in and out of love dozens, maybe Manfredi hundreds, of times, but with Bruno I can never resist. The body has a memory of its own, remembering what has long been white ash in the mind.

"Lena love," he says, running the words together. For as long as I've known him he's called me this, his tongue gliding over the L's and held by the O's, looped and fastened. *Lenalove.*

"And it's good to see you," he says, squeezing the water out of my hair. "So why did the ice lady ask you back?"

Bruno has called C.D. this since we were in high school and she wouldn't let him in our house because he had a "reputation"— rumors of drug use (true) and petty theft (untrue). I think C.D. secretly fears Bruno because he is not *contained*; energy in all its forms is sexual and C.D. holds tight in her skin.

"Why else? She missed me."

He laughs and covers my ear lobe with his mouth. "Me, too."

"The ice lady has her reasons, I'm sure. Maybe it's just loneliness." Since my father died two years ago, C.D. has become less impatient with my visits home, but I do not deceive myself: if company is all she wanted, then she asked me only because my sisters declined. I do not mind. I am between semesters, but not schools or jobs, and this gives me the upper hand: sustained criticism of my lifestyle or attitude and I'm back in Chicago. Her life is threadbare, mine is full. I have love (Bruno here, a young biologist back in Illinois), which insulates, grounds me.

I turn to look at Bruno. He has moved to his motorcycle and is rolling a joint from the stash he keeps in the compartment under the seat. He glances at me then up at the house. C.D.'s form is silhouetted in the window, her body shaped in a half moon as she bends over the sewing machine. She spends hours there, though what she's working on she does not say or leave lying around for me to see.

"Do you think that's the only reason she asked you here?" Bruno says, lighting the cigarette.

"What? What reason?"

"Loneliness. Maybe she's into the reconciliation thing. Maybe she feels guilty."

"C.D. never feels guilty. And for what anyway?"

He shrugs. I take the joint from him and inhale, feel the smoke deep in my lungs. I straddle the seat behind him and hang on, waiting for the beautiful terror to come as it always does when I am high: the feeling that my skin will not hold me. "Drive."

He hands the joint over his shoulder to me and starts up the engine. I finish it off, the waves of the drug in my body numbing my limbs, making me feel buoyant and set to music. Bruno speeds down the highway, the emptiness of the road a void broken only by the headlight.

We stop at a clearing bordered by woods on three sides. Bruno spreads his jacket for me next to a fallen log, and I lie with my back against it, pulling him toward me so that I am anchored on both sides. I trace the line of his throat with my index finger. There is a certain tautness about the skin, as if the bones there push the words down before he can speak them. Bruno's words—always *chosen*— have a certain luster to them which stays with me and becomes my own, like pearls worn directly against the skin.

"What is it?"

He looks down at me. "What do you mean?"

I pull his jacket around my shoulders and lie on top of him so that he cannot avoid my eyes.

"Lena," he says, voice trailing off. *Love*, the crickets supply in answer. He reaches into the pocket of the jacket and takes out his cigarettes. I hold the lighter in front of his face, the glare causing his pupils to constrict, drawing expression into pinpoints. I toss the lighter aside and run my hand through his hair, pressing in on the scalp until his skull resists. "Tell me."

He gathers my wrists together in one hand. "What are you talking about?" He pries my fist open and kisses my palm. "Lena," he says, laughing. "You never were a good *substance abuser*. You always get paranoid. Remember the time when . . ." He draws me into reverie then to himself, our bodies melded as one shape. *Now now*—words I repeat for their sound.

C.D. has displaced or rearranged everything that is familiar: she has left me with a bed and a bureau which I've filled with what I've brought, but my father's walnut desk—which took three of us to move on my last visit home—is back downstairs in his study.

Above her sewing machine the bookcase, save for two shelves, is filled with sewing paraphernalia. I make my way around scraps of fabric, using some as bookmarks: a wisp of Chantilly lace marks my place in *The Lives of a Cell*; a strip of blackwatch plaid in *The Origin of Species*. I keep what I own stacked beside me, reading every morning, exams and the search for a thesis topic looming. Symbiosis and its role in synchronicity comes to me as a potential topic as I finish the Lewis Thomas books and work my way through psychobiology and animal studies. I am fascinated by whales, their intelligence and communication through water vibrations that make rhythm a language. I read in one book that echolocation is to hearing what X-ray vision is to sight. And to a lesser extent, I am fascinated by the emotion of dolphins and seals. The mother seal mourns, *wails*, for the baby as she watches the hunters club it; the more beautiful the fur the more vigorous the blows. I saw on a Sunday morning nature show the mother seal's actual *tears* as she watched her baby being bludgeoned. She crawled toward the killers as they dragged it away. And then the stilling of her body, the motionlessness that comes with knowledge and surprise: where in this larger world, this land to which she doesn't belong, are the danger warnings the water and its rhythm provided? Danger creeps stealthily on the earth, cruelty leaves no tracks. But of course I'm anthropomorphizing, knowing even as I do that lesser mammals haven't the capacity for any pain that is not physical: the brain is underdeveloped, the cerebral cortex and frontal lobes crude.

The sun is not yet fully risen. I crawl out onto the roof with my photograph albums and loose pictures I want to affix. The air is cool, the light indefinite.

I spread out the photographs before me, grouping them according to dominant expression, postures, rather than chronological time. Most are of my father. He was a fine-looking man, and in each picture he is the subject, the center always, upstaging all others so that comparatively they are nothing more than negatives of themselves. My father's expressions were never duplicated. In the hundreds of photographs I have of him, each one is subtly different—a testimony to his originality, genius: everything before and behind his eyes was forever new, though his three chief expressions were delight, despair, and surprise. The caption beneath one: "C.D., C.D., and Lena at eight." Both with the same initials (Carolyn Diana Healy, Charles Daniel Hayduke), the family joke is that my mother married him so she wouldn't have to change the monograms on her (L. L. Bean) sweaters or bath towels. In the photograph before me, my father (expression delight) holds me and leans against a rock wall at the beach. C.D. is herself an appendage. My sisters, two sitting at his feet and one behind him, are clusters of shadows. That was the summer we found out he had multiple sclerosis. In the photograph, all but my father hold the news on their faces.

C.D. and my sisters, unlike me, were afraid of the water, so my father and I together began and ended our days with the water and the sun. Arising just before dawn, we would stand at the shoreline and wait for the light to join the ocean with the sky at the horizon. ("Hear it *sizzle*; the morning, Lena, inhales.") We would wade in and he'd lift me when the water reached my neck, sleep still clinging to me like the early fog that hung over the water, my mouth tasting salt as we rose and fell with the rhythmic pulse of the waves. There was a church cemetery nearby, and from certain angles we could see the headstones that jutted from the grassy hillside. He'd look in that direction when the bells rang (whole notes resonating), tightening his grip on me as we waited for the last peal so he could ask, "How many dead people do you think are in that cemetery? (pause) They're all dead." Laughter cresting with the waves. And in the end, when the disease had weighted and paralyzed him, the water let us borrow time, the buoyancy making his body obey, the salt giving back what was rightfully his. The night I awoke to find him sitting by my bed, finger poised over the wheelchair's control panel, I did not need to ask. Into the night I took him, the air thick with the scent of fish, stopping at the water's edge where I helped him from his chair onto the sand. On his elbows he crawled, dragging his body as I pushed him from behind until we were fully immersed

and I could steady him. "Nothing like a little reverse evolution,"
he said, laughing. I held him, bouncing gently, his body light as a
child's, the delicate freckles on his scalp where his hair had parted
making him seem somehow so vulnerable that I kissed him there.
We felt ourselves being carried out, the current pulling us further
away from shore, his wheelchair (seat of judgment) a tiny, forgotten
anchor. "It wouldn't be so bad, would it, Love?" he said. "To be
carried away, give yourself over to it, and just let the water wear you
down." Three months later when I saw him in that hospital bed,
body shrunken and tangled with tubes and machines that parodied
the rhythms of life, this fine man who had lived, *loved*, and could
heal others but not himself, I thought, Oh, I should have, should
have let the water have us both where your last expression (and
mine too) would have been one of delight and not surprise.

I gather up the photographs along with some maps and bro-
chures that belonged to him. One is a pamphlet about the ruins of
Pompeii—a place he always longed to visit but never did. Only
when a thing is in ruins does it move toward importance, he said
once. True, I know now: the instant a lover leaves is when he gains
my respect. Love is born only out of wreckage.

I spend all afternoon on the roof waiting for Bruno, my body
molten and languid in the hot sun, ideas flickering but not taking
hold: eugenics, ancestral memory, and especially the possibility of
learning in utero. I've read studies of geniuses made before birth
simply by the pregnant woman reading aloud—particularly lyric
poetry, since that is heard as much with the nerves as with the ears.

C.D. climbs out onto the roof as I look through the stacks of
photographs and drink a peanut Coke (five shelled and roasted nuts
in cola with ice, my father's "cure" for a hangover). Head to toe,
she is dressed in a shade of blue formaldehyde would be if it could
be projected visually: the palest hue of it, sick and cloying. She is
wearing my shoes. She sits beside me and tosses aside the photographs without so much as a glance. "Well," she says, running her
hand through her hair, the shell pink nails—my polish—catching
the light as they sift beneath the dark (silken) strands.

"Yes?"

"Look, Lena . . ."

She watches as I stir the Coke with my finger, the skin of the peanuts sticking to the ice cubes. "Yes?"

"I've been dating someone. I thought you'd want to know."

"Yes. Well." I should have guessed this. Her self-possession lately, the air of languid fullness that could have come only from a lover. It is the precise reason I require so many men.

"I borrowed your shoes. I'd nothing to match this skirt." She smooths the pleats and picks at imaginary threads. "I made this one without a pattern," she says, lifting the skirt above her knees and examining the hem. The veins in her legs are visible through the damp, blue stockings and the nylon smells faintly of lilac. I look away and sift through the stack of photographs. Here's one that dates back to the early 1900s. It is of my grandfather as a little boy, wearing short pants and suspenders, sitting among a flock of geese, some in half-wing. I've kept it because his expression is replicated in my father: a look of fleeting delight with something dark just about to cross the features, the pale light in the eyes as though nothing precisely is *there*.

C.D.'s sandaled foot is in front of me and I slip a photograph of my father beneath her toes. She glances down at it. It's the one taken in London, at a medical conference. He is standing with a group of doctors, including a striking female physician with hair the color of firelight. C.D. draws in the corners of her pink-frosted mouth. "What are you trying to tell me?"

I picked this snapshot arbitrarily, but C.D. reads meaning into the smallest gestures. "If you have something to say, say it." She hands the photograph to me and takes off her shoes. "You think it's wrong of me to be seeing someone so soon?"

No. Two and a half years: time enough for both bodies to grow cold. I say, "Don't you think that's a remarkable picture of Daddy? It's my favorite of his bewilderment expressions. That's all I meant."

She nods, eyebrows arched. "He was a fine and courteous man."

We stare at the fountain—I always turn it on at midday—a fine spray of water misting our faces when the wind shifts. "What I wanted to tell you is that I'm going out for the day and to ask you

if you would join us for dinner next week. Here. You're welcome to
invite Bruno."

"You're kidding? Since when is Bruno welcome?"

"I've misjudged that boy. I think he cares deeply for you."

How do you know? I want to ask, but she stands to go. I lie back on the roof and close my eyes, trying to cool my over-heated brain.

A little later, I hear C.D.'s laughter, the sound of her (my) high heels clicking on the pavement, a car horn. I lean over the edge. That's not a car, that's a love story: a '57 Chevy convertible so well kept that it might be this year's newest model. C.D.'s friend looks good: blond, like Bruno, with nice forearms: muscular and well-proportioned. Bruno's forearms are the only part of him I don't love: they appear underslung, too short for his large hands. C.D.'s friend says something to her then bends her head toward him and kisses her hair.

By early evening she still has not returned. I spend hours in my room searching through my books for a possible thesis topic, but nothing is yielded. My prospectus is due in the department in ten days, which gives me about a week to come up with something, allowing time for the mail. I weigh the possibilities of microbiology, the genetic transmission of antibodies for the germs that live in the air. Or DNA and its role in speech, voice patterns: do we choose certain words, use certain inflections because we are genetically predisposed to them? And, by extension, what influence does voice tonality and modulation exert over others?

When I can stand the solitude and frustration no longer I call Bruno. A short time later he climbs in through the window as I am reading my father's *Physician's Desk Reference* and pamphlets on illicit drugs. Bruno straddles the chair backwards and grins idiotically, trying to make me look up and laugh.

"Marijuana in large quantities can cause impotence," I say, reading the side effects/contraindications column. "Be careful of the cannabis, Love."

He jumps up and dives onto the bed, scatters books to the floor. "I've got a little tucked away," he says, lifting my skirt and resting his head on my stomach. I pull him up by the hair. He smiles and rolls off the bed. It is twilight and the room darkens in golden shadows. Wreathed and muted in this light, objects seem indefinite, the dust motes in the beams falling across the carpet like cells that no longer hold. Bruno walks around the room picking up buttons and pattern pieces from C.D.'s sewing table.

"Let's go somewhere," I say.

"Well, Love, I'm not exactly dressed for fine dining," he says, holding a long pattern sheet against the front of his pants. "Perfect size twelve." I smile at him in the mirror. His hair is gold in the last of the sun.

"Bruno Bruno Bruno," I say, and think: what good is willpower when it's up against a boy with a headful of light?

"Yes, my little love biscuit," he says.

I rest my chin on his shoulder and look at our reflections. "You have the strangest place in my heart."

"Hey, now, you're not going Hallmark on me, are you?"

"No chance," I say.

He turns, his eyes filling with me as I undress and walk to where C.D. keeps a tin of mismatched buttons. I place a whole row of them down the front of me, my skin making them stick with its own sweaty heat.

"Lena," he whispers. With his tongue, he lifts the button I've placed in the valley of my throat then works his way downward, until I am entirely unfastened, ready to step out of my skin.

Later, we drive to the old barn at the edge of town where we first made love back in high school. We have used every part of it, including on top of the feed chute. It is in the middle of nowhere, surrounded by nothing except overgrown grass and shrubbery. There is no indication where the house might have—*must* have—stood. The mystery of it is what attracts us: what kind of people or force destroys the house and farm and leaves its repository? We speculate: the barn is magical, hundreds, thousands, of years old, the wood kept supple and durable by the love that still lingers within. Often, as we lay in the hayloft (light through the high window muted and oblique no matter what time of day), we've invented stories. Illicit affairs at midnight, two young lovers (Anna and Jacob), one of whom is married but unloved anywhere but

here. They make love in front of the stable, the scent of hay and the
darkness closing in on them, wondering themselves as the stillness
is broken now and then by the stamp of a hoof against the hard
earth, how many people before them have done the same thing?
They might remark on how the animals link them to the future, the
silent knowledge in velvet eyes looking on, passed on infinitely,
threading through time. Here the story becomes irresolute: passion
a given, the point of contention between us is always the fate of
the lovers themselves. I would have the young woman, Anna, fall
through the ice while skating on the lake. Though her body was
used as a woman's should be, she would be driven by something
unspeakable to risk moving to the center of the ice. Her weight
does not hold. There is a crack beneath her and then the January
water shocks against her, freezing forever what is finally clear (and
fatal). Sometimes I have her young lover plagued by grief the rest
of his days, his spirit murky and sluggish; often I have him assist in
her death: it is he who chases her to the center and looks on as she
falls through.

Bruno always imagines them to be outlaws hiding out, innocent
except for the crime of love. His imagination always stops there,
and he is given over to physicality: what the man feels inside the
woman, the things she does to him—physical and spiritual—that
make it as though they share just one skin.

The clandestine air, the solidity of the walls here, sometimes
make me so restless that even passion is no good: Tell me you love
me, I'll say to Bruno, but he just holds me and laughs, says, "Lena
love, what is love anyway, but something only the body can speak?"

Bruno lights a joint and passes it to me. "I really shouldn't. It
keeps me awake. C.D. will be at the sewing machine early, and I
won't get any sleep."

"Where *is* the ice lady tonight?"

"Out for the day, night, who knows."

"Is she seeing someone? I've seen her around town with some
guy."

"Why didn't you tell me before? Why didn't you ever say
anything?"

He shrugs. "You never asked, exactly. What's the big deal, anyway? The ice lady found someone who'll risk the thaw. And as for you, my little furnace," he says, and moves on top of me.

The straw murmurs beneath us. I grab tightly to Bruno when I feel myself spiraling, weightless, my voice small.

"Lena Lena Lena." His body tightens against me.

The proof, Love, is what we're left with in the end—phrase that comes to me as I stare up through the high window. And now finding my own rhythm: "Say it. Say it."

"Lena *love*."

In my father's study I work on my thesis outline: ancestral memory and its role in genetic differentiation among human beings. If (I assert) DNA can subject the body to genetically rare mutations, why not a certain chemical retention in brain composition that allows memories to be inherited? Subheadings: the strongest emotions (love, fear, and jealousy) may, when incremental and repetitive, embed pathways in the brain that alter its genetic structure so that the same alteration, and thus the emotions and memories that go with it, are inherited from one generation to another.

It's a stretch—more in the realm of poetry than hard science—but it seems to be more applicable than my whale studies.

C.D. taps on the door then walks in, perfume a wave that announces her before I even look up.

"Well. How do I look?"

I glance at her. She is wearing a black satin skirt and a red jacket with sequins that catch and refract the light like little mirrors. Her lips are crimson.

"Very magnetic, C.D."

"You like it? I wasn't sure. I didn't want to appear too eager, if you know what I mean. I had to borrow another pair of your shoes."

I look around the side of the desk: the Saturday night black pumps with the sling-back straps. I smile, remembering. Ice lady, if those shoes could talk, they would direct you to the finest pair of wingtips in Chicago where they stood, toe to toe, in a phone booth at midnight.

There is a softness to her face, a certain way the clothes move easily with her body—as if her lover himself had arranged the folds—that causes something to catch in my throat. She sits. Behind her a photograph of my father smiles over her shoulder. If you could see her now, I say to him silently, love would turn the air to salt, the body obeying once more.

"C.D., you look lovely."

She smiles and leans her elbows on the desk, "It's been a while, you know," she says, and runs her finger along my glass of peanut Coke.

I watch her hands. "Been a while for what?"

"Well, since I've given a dinner party." She sips the drink.

"Anyway, it's not a dinner party. It's just me and Bruno and your friend."

She nods, touches the cold glass to her forehead and cheeks. "Will you help me, though?"

"With?"

"With keeping conversation lively. You always did have more social skills than I."

She looks past me as I look at her, tugging at one of the pearl earrings that were a gift from my father. Her expression is flat, concealing intention.

Just enough light is left for us to see our reflections in the sliding glass doors in my father's study. C.D. and I watch, our images melded in the glass, as Bruno, holding a bouquet of flowers, pauses beside the fountain and speaks to C.D.'s guest (lover? boyfriend?). There is a space of pinkish light between their bodies, the upper half of the sculpture to the left of them like a dark, clutching arm.

"Oh, he is attractive, isn't he?"

I find her eyes in the glass, but can't tell who she's looking at. (One hand placed on each image, what would I feel? One like dry ice, the other a fragrant warmth: I grow cold, I fear.)

Bruno steps in first and across his face: surprise. "C.D., you look wonderful." He hands her the flowers and his expression softens into appreciation.

C.D. smiles back and turns, brings the stranger into our circle. "Bruno you've already met," she says, touching his shoulder. "And this is Lena."

He takes my hand and smiles. "Your mother tells me you're going to be a biologist."

He is of medium height, his body sinewy and compact in just the way I like best.

"Geneticist," I say.

The stranger, Richard, I learn over dessert, is a systems analyst and was introduced to C.D. by a friend of hers who was dating him at the time. He has that air of presence and purpose that most women find irresistible. He says little and is content, it seems, to watch C.D. as she speaks. He keeps her wine glass full, and smiles at me when she says something clever as if to say, Isn't she a rare thing? Who could capture her in words? And she: something that stepped out of a painting, skin white as ermine, jewels at her ears and the valley of her throat, and, as any woman in love will, attracting all eyes.

The candlelight flickers across the table, the flame held in the surface of the dark wood. I look at Bruno, cover his hand with mine, and think: there is no reason why we couldn't rediscover love. He glances from C.D. to me with a detached smile. Back then, at eighteen, love began as a hallucination we shared. We'd dropped acid in a corner stable of our barn. It was my second time, and he talked me through it, suggested images so that my fear would not cause nightcrawlers with the heads of bats to devour my flesh as I watched, as happened six months earlier.

"Now we are in a field of flowers," he said, and I saw them: crimson and purple peonies that grew bigger and fuller as I ran until they were as big as moons and flat as water lilies. The air caught in my lungs, thin and sharp, my legs stems that tore as I ran. Bruno (himself, yet *not* himself) caught me, held me, teeth flashing white, hands touching my breasts and thighs; something I could watch but not feel as I lay weighted in the straw, the night half-lidded as a turtle's eye. I said, "Am I *here*, or am I *there*?" Two of me, disjoined. "Everywhere and nowhere, Love." Solitude blanched the grass, a white pocket in which we spun, wrestled. His words, held within

the white light, trickled into colors: Prisms of topaz and ruby resting on my eyelids, mouth. The air a canvas, I had but to breathe.

I turn to look at Bruno now, his face in profile. I want suddenly
to put my lips to the delicate blue vein threaded over the bridge of
his nose, to feel the pulse over the cool bone. He does not notice
me. C.D., effusive and shimmering with all those sequins, draws
him to herself. *Ice Lady, you had us all fooled*. She turns to look at
me suddenly. Bruno and the stranger follow her gaze.

"You don't have much to say tonight, Lena."

I shrug. "Sorry," I say, but she holds my stare. "Is this a citation
from the Conversation Police?"

Bruno and Richard laugh. I look down and pull toward myself all
the candles on the table. (*Now*, Bruno, where am I?)

So, it'll be late: I have half a dozen prospective topics, some as
detailed as sixteen pages, lying in piles on my father's desk. I can
no longer work in my bedroom: C.D. is in a fever, patterns, fabric
everywhere, working until midnight sometimes like some Penelope
weaving, unweaving, afraid to finish. I grow restless, my body an
inertia that even Bruno fails to move.

What do you own, Lena? Words in my head, voice an amalgam-
ation of many.

I have given, have I not? My body suspended in countless nights,
betraying me only once: the time I thought I had found it with a
beautiful man from my biology class. Glances exchanged over mi-
croscopes for months, my hands forgetting what to do when I felt
his eyes on me, though I'd done hundreds of dissections. And his
surprised laughter when I cried after he split open the frog's belly
and the purplish black eggs burst through the skin. And later, his
breath on my neck, angry and shallow because that time I *couldn't*.
"I don't know what bitches like you want," he said. Love—that
time I was sure it was real—making the body tighten in fear of
losing what only it can give.

But now, Lena, what do you own?

Nothing. But emptiness is a kind of phenomenon.

And love?

Something I whipped into white heat with words.

Symbiosis and synchronicity; eugenics; ancestral memory; none of these will do. I write a note instead to my thesis advisor, making excuses for what I don't yet have.

C.D. knocks on the door then walks in. She is holding a hair-permanent kit and tiny pink and gray curlers. "I know you're busy, Lena, but Richard is taking me out tonight and look," she says, holding out a strand of limp hair. "Would you mind?"

I shake my head no, and we go outside—the odor of the solution lingers in the house for days otherwise. She opens a folding chair then sits, handing me curlers and comb. It has been years since I've worked on her hair. There are silver strands beginning at the crown, but otherwise it is as dark as mine (and as soft). I work the comb through it, neither of us speaking. My father's funeral was the last time we had any sort of physical contact. A slight shock goes through me as I stare down the part in her hair.

"So," she says after a few minutes. "What did you think of Richard?"

I thread a strand of hair through a curler and roll it as close to her scalp as I can get it, tightening, tightening. "I could see the attraction there."

"I think I'm in love with him. I haven't felt this way in twenty years. That's a little too tight. I don't want kinkiness," she says, touching the one I've just rolled.

"Twenty years?" The teeth of the comb glint silver in the sun.

"Well, you know what I mean. I'd just forgotten how it *feels*."

"How does it feel?" I rest my hand on her head. I can feel the vibrations of her speech, then her laughter, through her skull.

"Oh, Lena, *you*. You who've had so many boyfriends."

I finish the rows at the back of her head, alternating pink rollers with gray so the curls will vary in size.

"Easy, easy. My scalp is sensitive." She straightens her back and reaches around to where my hand is.

"So how *does* it feel, C.D.?"

She takes the question rhetorically and laughs again. "Something about younger men . . . they're always so *ready*. I don't mean physically. I mean a certain generosity of spirit. Richard is only three years younger than I am, but it makes a difference." She turns her

head slightly, catches my eye out of the corner of hers. "You know,
over the years I've watched you bring a parade of young men
through the house . . . well, envy can take the form of disapproval,
can't it? And Bruno . . ."

"What about Bruno?" I pick up the bottle of permanent solution
and pull off the tab at the nozzle.

C.D., smelling the odor of the apple pectin, turns around to
look. "Not too much of that. It makes the curls set in stiff."

"What about Bruno?"

"Oh, well, you two. He's a fine young man, Lena. I've just recently begun to see that."

I squeeze the bottle in even rows, carefully soaking each curl.

"I thought maybe the four of us could go on a picnic or something this weekend. Do you have much work to do?"

"Why all of a sudden are you so interested in Bruno?"

She turns abruptly. "How much of that are you using?" she says,
looking at the bottle in my hand.

"Will you just turn around and relax, please? I've done this a hundred times. I know what I'm doing. You're making *me* nervous, for
Chrissake."

"Well. You don't have to curse."

"I asked you why you're so interested in Bruno."

"Well, because you and Bruno keep me young. Young ideas."

I empty the rest of the bottle on her head and open the second.
"What does that mean exactly?"

"What I mean is, I've *learned* from you, Lena."

I stare down at the rows of curls twisted around the rollers like
tiny, precise waves. "You used me."

"What? What did you say?"

My vision blurs. "I said you *used* me. Is that why you asked me
home? That's it, isn't it? Of course. You figure you're a little rusty
in the romance department so you'd ask the slut home and observe.
She's fucked hundreds. *She* must know what men want."

"Lena!"

"But you're no better. All those times, all I ever wanted was
someone to love me. I thought if I could find at least one person to
love me then I wouldn't just be some hunk of ice spinning through

space. God knows I had no example from you. You stopped loving him the moment he got sick. And *now*, now you think you can just imitate the way I dress, my mannerisms, and know what I know?"

"My God, I didn't mean . . . didn't know."

My fingers tighten around the middle of the bottle. Curls at the crown glisten, gullies between them filling and overflowing toward her temples.

She jumps up, making little sounds in her throat. "It's in my eyes! It's running into my eyes." She closes them tightly, acid forming a gummy seal. I take her arm and lead her to the fountain.

"It's burning. I can feel it burning right through the tissue."

I push her head into the water. "Open your eyes. Open them. The water will flush out the poison."

"You did that on purpose," she says, gasping. "You poured that into my eyes deliberately." She holds the towel to her face and sinks to the earth, cheek pressed against the cement base of the fountain. She looks up at me, the weariness of age now on her face. Her eyes are red slits, already swollen and heavy as a blossom. *Receive now the dispensation of my knowledge.*

I walk a straight path to the house feeling light as an ash in the wind.

Upstairs in the hallway, where it has again become an ordinary table, is the sewing machine, leaves folded over, a flat surface out of which the vase of Bruno's flowers rise. My bedroom door is closed. I nudge it open with my foot.

Words rush up and die in my throat. C.D. has clothed the room—bedspread, curtains, vanity skirt—in matching dark blue fabric with a tiny beige print. The bed meets the window, the print of the spread rising, cresting at the pillows and splitting in two where the curtains are parted with eyelet, the pink light between opening out to the sky. My legs will not hold. I sink to the floor, feeling each bone in my spine against the door frame, and am freezing cold suddenly despite the midsummer heat.

What is love but something only the body can speak?

Out of the corner of my eye I see her form. I turn. Her hair is in waves now, released from the curlers. She sits in the corner opposite me, the surprise still on her face and now mirrored in my own.

"I just wanted to give you something. I just wanted you to feel welcome again. That's all."

We watch as the last of the twilight sinks behind the mountains. Shapes disappear in the dark. The night is broken by the steady rhythm of her hair dripping onto the carpet: the sound of a thaw. The sound of a seal's tears after the hunters have come.

SUSAN ONTHANK MATES

Ambulance

*Susan Onthank Mates is a physician and the former director of the Rhode
Island State Tuberculosis Clinic. She attended Juilliard, Yale, and the
Albert Einstein College of Medicine. She has been on the faculty of Brown
University in Medicine and Biochemistry (research) and has won a number
of competitions and awards including youth soloist with the San Francisco
Symphony, NIH Clinical Investigator Award, the AAUW Recognition
Award for Young Scholars, and a Pushcart Prize. Her stories are performed
as plays, anthologized, and taught in colleges and medical schools.
She lives in Rhode Island with her husband and children.*

*"Glowing, intelligent stories, generously encompassing. Complex people
finding themselves at their moral crossroads."*
JOY WILLIAMS, 1994

I was putting my feet up with the evening shift nurse on the
women's ward. Marie was a practical nurse; this was the old Lincoln
Hospital in the south Bronx, and the city only paid for registered
nurses on the day shift. Not that the patients weren't in completely
capable hands with Marie. She was a sharp Jamaican duststorm of a
woman, tiny, wiry, and astoundingly energetic. Most evenings, the
ward hopped like a nightclub with one demented act; she sang, she
scolded, she exhorted, she divulged. She was an efficient pied piper,
sucking those sick people right out of themselves, away from broken linoleum and army-green cloth partitions and the disinfected
stench of the open ward. On Marie's shift, the junkies were so
entertained they even gave up their usual pastime of knocking the
roaches off the curtains.

Anyway, that evening things were quiet on the ward. Marie and I
had finished the chores, tucked everyone in, and sat down to rest

our feet and talk. I was sweating in the heat of the New York night, but she was starchy and crisp as usual. Marie's voice was as quick and precise as her body. She spoke in a patois recitative, accompanied by the whirr of the fan, the flies buzzing, and the chanting. Always the chanting. Marie called them her singers, the ones who went to their death not groaning, not screaming, but singing, coaxing death with a monody of "gates, gates, gates in the sky," or "wash the baby, the baby, Oh Lord, the baby," or "cooking, scrubbing, cooking, scrubbing." The three old women were placed one on each end of the ward and one in the middle. Marie always prepared them for the night by smoothing their pillows and straightening their sheets, as if they were still aware. And they just kept on crooning their way into death, putting the rest of us to sleep.

Marie was talking about her son. "That one, my Jamey, he's a smart one." She laughed. "He put himself in law school, oh my. He's gonna be something. He always was a crackerjack."

"Is he married?"

"Oh sure, and the first little one on the way. Imagine me a grandmama."

"Marie, don't you have another son?"

"Yeah honey, I do."

"What does he do?"

"I don't know. I haven't seen him now, two years it will be. I lost him young." She sat absolutely still.

"Lost him to what, if you don't mind my asking?"

"Lost him to the streets. Jamey, though, now you should have seen him in high school. Wasn't he the sharp one!" and she was moving again.

There was a tendency in the south Bronx to describe the place as a living thing, a sort of monster, a filthy maw of burned-out buildings that chewed up children and spat them out broken, lost. I didn't ask any more about the other son.

In that silence, the paging began. It started innocently. Just the chief of the emergency room wanted for an emergency. Nothing much to wonder about. Then the senior house surgeon to the emergency room. Then the security personnel to the emergency room. Then all the senior doctors still in the hospital to the emergency room.

Then, "All doctors to the emergency room, stat, all doctors to the emergency room, stat." The page operator spoke with a peculiar nasal urgency.

I jumped off my chair and looked at Marie.

"Not you, honey, you're a medical student."

"But what's going on down there?"

"Whatever it is, you best stay here. You'll be the only kind of doctor we got up here now." She readjusted her legs on the chair.

Then the page sounded again, "All medical students to the emergency room, stat, all medical students to the emergency room, stat."

This time I tore down the hall, my short white coat flying. There was no safe place to leave things at Lincoln, so when you came for overnight duty, you brought everything in your pockets. All medical students bulged with the tuberous accretions of their status. Coins, notebooks, ophthalmoscope, pens, syringes, and tampax came jumping out of my pockets as I rounded the stairwell. I clutched my pockets and tried to glide. As I came down the last hall, I could hear the emergency room. Something was definitely going on there. Solo yells and screams peaked over a general chaotic chorus, like some experimental war requiem. I charged into the waiting room and stopped dead.

The strict rows of wooden chairs had been overturned, kicked out of the way. The middle of the room was a twitching mass of muscle and skin, with a pause provided here and there by a knife blade, a chain, an ice pick. I had seen knife fights in the waiting room before, but the scale of this one was staggering. There must have been fifty kids in studded leather jackets going at each other. Several policemen were dubbing with staccato bashes. In the corner, an isolated security guard was wrenching a gun from a boy. The boy's jacket had "Death Lords" spelled across the back in a rhinestone arc. On the floor were two dumps of doctors and nurses trying to resuscitate bleeding bodies. Oblivious to the chaos around

them, they were moving through their routines; pumping chests,
starting intravenous lines, calling to each other.

The audience to all this was the arriving relatives and girl friends,
some in torn jeans, some in cheap but businesslike suits, some
dressed for a night on the town. They were crying and reaching
from the sidelines; now and then a woman's high wail sang out as
she saw a son fall. The girls were paired on the floor, their spike
heels and ankle chains coiled in vicious duos, green nails ripping
faces as they tried to unroot each other's acrylic hair.

I stood paralyzed by the entrance. One of the guards spotted me
there and forcefully gesticulated that I should go across the waiting
room and into the treatment area of the emergency room. Without
thinking, I plunged through the spectacle and found myself in the
treatment area.

Here, things were much the same, except that there were more
bodies lying flat with people working on them, and fewer still upright, causing damage.

"Here, hold this!" A surgical intern pushed my hand over a man's
neck. I let the pressure slack a second while I stepped closer. A hot
shower of blood sprayed over me, soaking into my whites, splatter-
ing my face. I pushed harder and it stopped. I angled around the
other people cutting and stitching and pumping and breathing, and
managed to wipe my glasses. Out of the corner of my eye, I saw the
knife coming and stepped aside as a pale boy with a bloodstained
T-shirt erupted through the crowd.

"Gonna finish the job, you son-of-a-bitch!" He staggered back.
Somebody tripped him; he fell on the tile floor and didn't get up
again.

An arm brushed my shoulder. I turned with a jump to see the
chief resident on duty that night. He was shouting something at
me. I grabbed a nearby hand and pressed it on the neck wound,
then followed the chief.

He shouted, "Medical student?"

I nodded.

"Need you to ride an ambulance. Supposed to send an M.D., but
we can't spare any. You'll have to go. Go out to the bay, we'll bring
the patient."

The night air was a shock—dark, cool, and quiet. An ambulance sat there, back doors open, ready to receive. The driver leaned out, an unremarkable man. He pulled the pipe out of his mouth.

"You the doc?"

"Yes."

He nodded contentedly and disappeared again into the dark.

"Hey, medical student!" Two emergency room nurses were wheeling out a stretcher. A still form lay on it, gleaming in the night. I walked over.

"Here's the papers, you'll have to bag him." She handed me the bag. I had never used one before. I squeezed it as she had, forcing the air down the tube into his lungs. She turned to walk away.

"But where are we going and what am I supposed to do?"

"Keep him alive if you can." She turned back into the emergency room.

By this time, the other nurse and an orderly had lifted the stretcher into the ambulance and rolled the patient onto the narrow cot attached to one side. I was moving with them, trying to squeeze the bag in a kind of breathing-dance. I had never paid much attention to breathing before.

They closed the doors and I was alone in the back. In the dim light of the emergency lamp, the frail papers of the temporary chart were almost unreadable. Slowly I made out the writing. He was "unknown male," and we were going to Jacobi Hospital for neurosurgery. He had a bullet in his head.

I looked down at him. He was eighteen or twenty, motionless aside from my breathing. His face was serene, as if lost in the deep sleep of childhood. There, frozen forever, the sweet four year old, the clever eight year old, the awkward twelve year old. The top of his head was bandaged, but there was no other mark on the smooth skin of his body. I wondered what his name was.

The ambulance started, the siren went on with a deafening wail, and we shot out of the hospital bay. The violence of the ride surprised me; I was barely able to keep my balance as we swung onto the Bronx River Parkway. I did my best to keep squeezing the bag as we swerved through the dense traffic, but I was frightened. The light inside the ambulance flickered with each maneuver, as if with a faulty connection. As we roared shrieking off the Parkway and onto Fordham Road, disaster struck. A car cut in front of us, and the ambulance driver veered suddenly, accelerating around it. I went flying across the back and landed with a crack against the glass of the rear doors. I wasn't looking, but I saw it anyway, the Bronx River churning in the moonlight below the doors. The water foamed ominously over fierce rocks, figments of the dimming moon. I turned to look for the boy (I called him Angelo). He had slid off his cot and onto the floor, sprinkled with nickels and dimes from my coat. Underneath the glitter he was turning dusky blue.

I screamed for the driver, but nothing could be heard over the noise of the siren. We were hurtling relentlessly toward Jacobi. Panicked, I straightened his body and smoothed the pillow under his head.

I forced a sudden, rational calm. Think. You can reason this out. He's turning blue because he doesn't have enough air. Give him air. I tried to squeeze the bag harder. Nothing moved. So. The tube is blocked. I looked at the tube. It had been pulled out when he fell, and the end was stuck in his mouth. If the tube isn't in the lungs, the air isn't going there. How am I going to get air to his lungs? Oh Angelo, stay alive. Mouth-to-mouth resuscitation. I'll just keep it up until we get there. I yanked the tube completely out and pulled back his jaw. We were still sliding back and forth along the floor of the ambulance as it jerked and turned, accelerated and stopped. OK. I learned this. I can do this. I did it.

I didn't notice that we were there until they opened the back doors, flooding the ambulance with the neon lights of Jacobi's emergency room. The light hurt my eyes, and I didn't dare stop breathing. I just stayed where I was, breathing into Angelo's mouth. I heard a woman bellow "Anesthesia," and, a minute later, someone tore me away from him.

"My, what a picture you look!" One of the emergency room nurses pulled me out of the ambulance. "We hear you had a real gang war down there at Lincoln!"

I nodded, still dazed. My mouth was coming out of numbness into bruised stinging. I touched my tongue to my lips, feeling their swollen strangeness. Angelo was being taken off by the trauma team.

"Here, you go get a cup of coffee, Bobby here will wait for you, won't you Bobby," she looked up at the driver. He nodded calmly, pulling on his pipe.

I went in, and the medical students assigned to Jacobi drifted around, trapped by my bloodied whites like small animals frozen in the headlights of an oncoming car. They made nonchalant conversation about trauma and gang war and other things we didn't understand. I barely heard them, the roaring darkness filling my ears as if I had crossed from another world and wasn't quite back into this one.

When I tried to go to the cafeteria, one of the aides stopped me. "You look disgusting with all that blood all over you. You can't go round people like that."

I looked at her. I needed a cup of coffee. I had no change of clothes with me. But in the well-lit hospital corridor, I knew I was inappropriate, wearing so much blood.

I went back out to the ambulance and climbed in the front.

The driver started the engine. "Got some coffee?"

"No," I said.

"Ah," he nodded, "people are like that."

We rode back quietly, smoothly. When we pulled up to Lincoln, he said, "I got another call. I'll just let you off." I slid off the seat and jumped to the ground.

"Thanks," I said. I looked up at his face, obscure in the dark of the cab. "Doesn't it bother you, ferrying people back and forth, night after night?"

He must not have heard me, because he didn't answer. Instead, the ambulance took off, swallowed again by the night, leaving me standing there alone.

The next morning I stopped by Jacobi on the way to Lincoln. There was no sign of "unknown male" on the neurosurgical ward or in the recovery room. I asked at the admitting office. They couldn't find him either. The clerk was busy, but she told me that usually, when they disappear like that, it means they died before they could get properly admitted.

When I got to Lincoln, the head nurse on days stopped me in the hall. She was an old friend of Marie's.

"So I hear you rode the ambulance last night." She was a large woman, and she looked down at me without smiling.

"Yes."

"Folks at Jacobi tell me you were giving that boy mouth-to-mouth when you got there. That's a good way to get all sorts of disease." She paused for a minute, as if she were going to say something more, then turned to go. "Remind me to teach you how to use the ambubag sometime."

Something of what I was feeling must have shown on my face, because she suddenly frowned and grabbed me by the shoulders. "Do you think you should have saved him? Who do you think you are? Better than you tried to save that boy's life, not just in one minute in the end, but year after year after year, and you some white girl gonna come down here and make everything all right in a few minutes?" She herself was shaking now. She pushed by me and ran down the hall.

I saw Marie later that night, as I came on the ward to order insulin for a diabetic. She was smoothing down the pillow for one of the chanters, the one with breast cancer. The old woman was out of her mind and didn't notice, but Marie was smoothing her pillow and pulling up her blanket anyway. I walked up to her.

"Anything else you need before I go to dinner?" I didn't look at her.

"I heard about you riding the ambulance with that boy that got shot."

"Yeah, well I didn't do much for him, did I?" I tried to turn away before she could say anything more, but she was too fast for me.

She fumbled in her pocket and pulled out some dog-eared Polaroids. "Here, let me show you something. My new grandbaby, just born last night. Isn't she beautiful?"

She smiled like the moon breaking loose on a cloudy night.

The End of Romance

John McNally's collection Troublemakers *was chosen for Book Sense 76, a list of recommended books by independent booksellers across the country. He has edited two anthologies:* High Infidelity: Short Stories about Adultery *and* The Student Body: Short Stories about College Students and Professors. *McNally has won a James Michener Fellowship, a Djerassi Fellowship from the Wisconsin Institute for Creative Writing, and a scholarship from the Bread Loaf Writers' Conference. "The End of Romance," included here, won both the* Sonora Review Short Fiction Award *and the* Mari Sandoz Award.

*"*Troublemakers *is, on every page, in every sentence, simultaneously laugh-out-loud funny and absolutely heartbreaking. John McNally's work will remind you of the greatest stories you ever heard from your best friend, or your long-lost cousin, or the improbable barroom genius you end up next to at the end of the night, except they're even better: vivid and moving and eloquent and full of the kind of moral weight that reminds you what stories are for. He has things to tell, and he does so, beautifully."*
ELIZABETH MCCRACKEN, 2000

Squeaky Fromme came to Roger Wood in the night, in a dream, and when he awoke, Roger could still feel the weight of Squeaky, a whisper in his head coaxing him back to sleep. She had orange eyelashes, difficult to see in direct light. Her hair was naturally curly and red, her nose thin. She was covered in freckles, too—across her face, along her back, up and down her sun-blistered arms and legs. She told Roger how much she liked him. She baked hash brownies for him, mushroom pie, and cookies laced with LSD. She spoke incessantly about Charlie Manson, her savior. *You've got to meet him*, she kept saying, and each time she said so, Roger nodded.

Roger awoke alone in bed. It was true then: his wife had left him.

He didn't have the slightest idea where she'd gone or how long
she'd be there. She'd given no indication, only a general sense that
she was disgusted enough to leave him for good.

It had happened last night, on Christmas Eve, Tracy pacing the
living room and reciting what struck Roger as a well-rehearsed list
of complaints, "things," she called them, *things* she couldn't live
with anymore: the way Roger left his half-empty Coke cans all over
the house; his relentless diet of red meat; his unwillingness to try
Chinese food; his toenails, always in need of clipping; the way he
combed his thin hair to the side instead of straight back; how he
never tucked in his shirts except at work; how the balance of their
checking account was always a mystery; his refusal to throw away
socks with holes or briefs once the elastic had gone bad; the way he
looked at people when they spoke to him, as if they were speaking
Zulu; the way he filled the sink with warm water, dish soap, and
filthy dishes, then left everything to soak, apparently forgetting it
all, never touching any of it again, the water turning gray while
water-logged hunks of tomato, spaghetti, or green beans floated to
the surface; the fact that he wore his T-shirt when they made love.
The fact, it seemed to Roger, that he existed.

After she had gone away for the night, Roger stood in the bathroom, peering into the medicine chest, lifting smoky, orangish
brown cylinders of pills and shaking them. He found Tracy's Valium
and took four, chasing them down with a coffee mug full of Hun-
garian port. On the couch, flat on his back, he watched CNN, the
same news stories repeating over and over, hour after hour: Libya
building a chemical weapons factory; Israel bearing down on protesters; Squeaky Fromme escaping from the women's prison in Al-
derson, West Virginia. When he couldn't stomach it anymore, the
yawn of sleep becoming too strong, he hit the remote and dragged
himself to the bedroom. He slid open a drawer where Tracy kept
her underclothes, swept everything to one side, and picked up her
diaphragm case. He opened the pink box and removed the diaphragm, and for a good minute he stared at the orb, holding it up
and turning it this way and that in the light as if it were the Hope

diamond or a lunar rock, and not the stiff, rubber sperm-catcher that it was. At least she hadn't taken the diaphragm with her, he thought. He was, for the time being, safe.

That night, Roger dreamed about Squeaky Fromme—the Squeaky of his childhood, the way she had looked back in the late 1960s. And in his dream, she was taking Roger around the ranch, introducing him one by one to the Family—Linda Kasabian, Leslie Van Houten, Patricia Krenwinkle, and Susan Atkins—women who touched him with their warm palms while Squeaky whispered into his ear, *You've got to meet him. You've got to meet Charlie*. Even in deep sleep, Roger knew she meant Charlie Manson—a man she trusted with her life, the man she honestly believed was Jesus Christ.

Zach and June charged the Christmas tree, searching for their presents. They shook each box carefully, then violently shredded away the wrapping paper. Neither noticed that their mother was gone—or *if* they noticed, they didn't say anything. Each time Zach opened one of the presents he had asked for, he glanced back over his shoulder and smiled at his father; June, on the other hand, looked sullen, searching for something that wasn't there, a gift Roger had forgotten or didn't know she wanted. He kept waiting for her to smile at him, as Zach had, but she continued searching, no longer shaking boxes, merely peeling away the paper before moving on to the next gift.

Groggy, hungover, Roger stared blankly at a crumpled pattern of Santa Clauses, each one returning the stare and waving at him. He shifted his focus to a hangnail jutting from his thumb. Too tired to get up and find the clippers, he decided to pull on it. He yanked it twice, his eyes beginning to tear up, but the hangnail remained. It pointed now at an even more dangerous angle. He pushed the wound back together and said, "Don t forget to check your stockings, kids."

Then Tracy came home. She pulled her Mustang into the drive, and the kids stopped what they were doing. They could see her through the large living room window. She was revving the engine too hard, her car disappearing in swirls of exhaust; and with one final rev—her foot evidently pressed all the way down on the accel-

erator—she cut the ignition.

"Sweetie," Roger said when the front door creaked open.

Tracy walked over to him slowly, cautiously, as though he were a small but dangerous rodent. She said, "I'm back." Wads of wrapping paper surrounded her feet. Her hair was flat on one side. "For the time being," she added.

"Mom!" Zach yelled. "Look at this!" He lifted a high-powered squirt gun the length of his leg above his head; but June was already running away, back upstairs, pulling her hair and screaming, unable, Roger thought, to weigh this day against all the others, to accept the promise of failure, especially today, on Christmas morning.

On the day that Squeaky Fromme was apprehended by the authorities and returned to the penitentiary, Tracy told Roger that she was going to start spending more time with the women she worked with.

"The girls," Tracy called them, though *which* girls, Roger didn't know. The women from the PTA? The women she volunteered with at the Salvation Army?

"I need my own life," she said.

Roger watched the headlights of Tracy's car illuminate the semi-dark living room, then swirl along the wall as she backed out of the drive. Roger got off the couch, walked into the bedroom, and opened the second drawer of their clothes chest. He pushed aside abandoned panties and hose crumpled into a ball of static cling. He slid everything from one side of the drawer to the other.

Had she moved it?

He checked the other drawers, pulling everything out and throwing it onto the floor. He jerked the drawers one by one from the chest and shook them, even after each drawer proved to be empty. Roger rubbed his face, then scratched it hard. It was gone. Tracy had taken the diaphragm with her.

Sitting on the edge of the bed, Roger stared at the naked drawers piled on the floor. That was all he could stand to do—stare, remain motionless, lose himself to inertia—but then he became aware that his shirt was moving. It was *twitching*. *Odd*, he thought. He watched it closely, listening, finally deducing the cause: his heart, beating. It was pounding harder than he thought possible for so little movement. And then he heard a clicking noise. At first he thought it was a bird tapping on his bedroom window, until he noticed a rhythm to it, a pattern, how it clicked only between the beats of his heart. It was getting harder to breathe, and the clicking got louder: it was, he realized, the sound of his windpipe opening and closing.

Roger felt as though his heart had floated up to his neck and lodged itself, cutting off his breath. He was certain he would die if he didn't stand up at that moment, so he did. With his children asleep upstairs, he left the house. He walked for several blocks, losing track not only of time but direction as well, just moving, moving, until, at long last, a wave of exhaustion swept over him, and when he got home, he cleaned the bedroom and put everything back to how it had been. He took four Valium and lay in bed thinking, *It's nothing, nothing at all*, but hoping he would fall asleep long before his wife came back home and slipped into bed beside him.

Roger ate breakfast and thought of Squeaky Fromme coming to him on Christmas Eve: her droopy eyelids, the downward curl of her mouth, the way she tilted her head back and off to the side when she smiled.

He decided not to say anything to Tracy about the diaphragm. If she was, in fact, having an affair, he would find out soon enough. If she wasn't, why make false accusations? Why bring it up? Instead, he sat at the table and pulled on his hangnail—that same hangnail—though the pain had sharpened since Christmas, and a red blotch had begun to form around the point where the hangnail intersected with his thumb.

"What's wrong?" Tracy asked.

"Hangnail," Roger said.

"Don't pick at it," she said. "You should get the clippers."

Roger shrugged. He opened a fat paperback and carefully examined the *chilling 64 pages of photos!* in the middle. Then he flipped back to the front of the book and read aloud the only words on the first page: *The story you are about to read will scare the hell out of you.*

"Yikes," Tracy said. She was chopping onions on the cutting board, her eyes beginning to water. "What're you reading?"

"*Helter Skelter*," Roger said. He'd found a copy at the Paperback Trader on Spruce, the front cover torn off, the pages wavy and bloated from having been submerged in water. A flooded basement, Roger thought. Or perhaps someone had fallen asleep in the tub, dropping the paperback into a warm bubble bath in December.

"Is it any good?" Tracy asked.

"I don't know yet," Roger said, then he held the book toward her and said, "Look. It's bloated."

The next time he glanced up from reading, he saw his kids, Zach and June, sitting in the living room, watching cartoons. They seemed startlingly taller and older since the last time he'd really looked at them. They spent a lot of time in their bedrooms, or they were outside, pedaling their bikes at dangerously high speeds, heading nowhere. They were like cats, disappearing for what seemed like weeks at a time, then showing up just when you'd begun to think they'd been hit by a car or taken in by strangers. Though maybe, in truth, they were around more than Roger realized, and somehow—he wasn't sure how this was possible—he'd simply overlooked them, much as he'd quit noticing certain pieces of furniture or clothes he never wore anymore. He considered joining them on the floor, sprawling out in front of the TV as he had when he was ten years old. Back then, the television set was always on the blink—rolling, fuzzy images; only one antenna, bent and wrapped in aluminum foil; needle-nose pliers resting on top for turning the channels. That was 1969, and Roger would stare intently for hours at the images flickering across the screen, his brain compensating for the slow flip, the greenish tint, and the blurry heads, until what he saw became as clear as life: bald women with carvings on their foreheads, sitting every night in groups of four, five, or six. They were the Manson girls, camping out on the corner of Temple and Broadway, in front of the Hall of Justice.

Roger's mother had watched the news religiously, absorbed by the relentless details, always sitting in her recliner in front of the

Motorola, feet propped up, a cigarette resting in the ashtray or between her fingers. Whenever Roger spoke, she shushed him.

"Shhhhh," she said. "Listen."

After the news, later in the night, they watched *Rowan and Mar-
tin's Laugh-In*, though Roger's mother didn't think *Laugh-In* was
all that funny. Instead, she talked about those poor bald girls on the
corner.

"It takes a lot of dedication," she said, "to take a pocketknife
and carve something on your forehead. You've got to be careful,
Roger."

Night after night, they watched the vigil, and Roger began playing a game: pretending the Manson girls were speaking directly to
him—that somehow they, too, could see him as he saw them. And
what they told him was that Charlie was Jesus Christ, that the murder trial was Charlie's crucifixion. They warned Roger of Judgment
Day, which was near, just around the corner.

Roger's mother had read a magazine article about the X's they'd
put on their foreheads—how the girls had used knives the first
time, but when the scar tissue began to fade, they branded themselves instead, heating the side of a screwdriver, then pressing it
firmly into their skin.

"Could you imagine!" his mother said. Then she lifted her purse
and rifled around inside for a pack of cigarettes. Chainsmoking,
leaning back in her recliner, she began developing theories about
each of the girls, and she had decided that it was Squeaky who'd
been hurt the most by what was happening to Charlie, that she was
the girl who most needed *"real* love," as Roger's mother put it,
"real affection," that it was Squeaky who had been drawn deepest
into Manson's spell, his ruse.

"Poor Squeaky," she said, and Roger nodded.

Roger played with his Hot Wheels for hours at a time. He created
towns and mountain valleys out of a half-dozen pillows and the
blankets on his bed, and he used the names he'd heard so often to
give life to the characters who drove his little cars. Manson owned a
fire truck. Leslie Van Houten and Patricia Krenwinkle shared a forest green Ferrari. For Susan Atkins, a cement truck. But Roger gave

Squeaky a junkyard of cars to choose from, whatever she wanted: a
Corvette, an ambulance, a Rolls Royce.

In school, during recess, Roger stayed at the edge of the black-
top, off to the side, and he watched the girls play in groups of four,
five, or six. Hopscotch, mostly. Or jump rope. Certain boys could
tease the girls and get away with it. They could step into a game,
ruin it, then lure the girls back toward them again, and the girls
would no longer be angry. They spoke with their eyes, these boys.
They understood the give and take of play and danger. Roger
wasn't one of those boys. It took Roger years to come to grips with
the fact that he would never be one of these boys, that he was incapable of that sort of control. With boys like that, there was another force at work—a spirit or a demon—another presence altogether invading their souls.

At night, in bed, as Roger inched his way into sleep, he began
seeing girls with large, smooth heads moving closer and closer,
surrounding him at the corner of the playground, their skin tinted
green and fuzzy like TV static, all of them holding hands and circling Roger, chanting, "*Charlie, Charlie.*"

And now the dreams were coming back, years later, and what
Roger saw in his sleep were women, not girls. They lured him with
drugs and food and sex; and on a particularly cold night in January,
Susan Atkins came to Roger, rubbing herself against him, brushing
her lips gently across the lobe of an ear, whispering, always whispering; and even in sleep Roger knew that she was the worst, the one
who had done the unthinkable. But here, alone, just the two of
them, Roger could let it slide. She was rubbing herself against
him, and Roger knew his weakness—the weakness of all men, it
seemed—and though Roger knew full well what Susan had done,
it didn't make a difference. He was willing, for the moment, to give
her the benefit of the doubt.

Roger Wood worked for UPS, picking up and delivering packages.
He drove a huge, solar-heated, chocolate-colored truck. Lately,
while driving across town, he pretended that he was behind the
wheel of Manson's famous VW Van. The van had been spray-

painted black, and Manson drove it up and down the California highways, picking up hippies along the way, luring them back to Death Valley, to the Spahn Movie Ranch, where the Family lived, took drugs, had sex, and drove dune buggies. The year 1968 struck Roger as the sort of moment in history that happened only once to a nation—a country's adolescence—and for awhile, Charlie Manson reaped its rewards. Charlie'd had it all. Roger couldn't even begin to imagine what having it all would feel like. The Ford administration loomed over his own adolescence. Then Carter and disco.

Often, while working, Roger saw hitchhikers standing near the exit ramps—young men mostly, or middle-aged drifters. Today, though, while on his way to a Radio Shack delivery, Roger noticed a woman at the side of the road, her feet sunk all the way into the snow, so he eased his truck onto the shoulder. He got out, walked to the passenger's side, and opened the truck's door. She was tall and gawky, much younger than he'd thought at first glance. She told him that her radiator had blown out. Her car, she said, was at least a mile back. Roger shut the door for her, the way he might if they had been dating, going home after a long dinner in a nice restaurant.

Merging back onto the highway, Roger said, "There's not a pay phone for another five miles."

"I know," the woman said, and that was the end of their conversation.

The silence made Roger's head feel extraordinarily heavy. The longer he kept silent, the harder it was to speak. What would Manson have said? Would he have offered a joint? A snort of coke? A hit of acid? Would he've told her about the ranch? Would he have mentioned the Family in passing, gauging her interest? Sooner or later, sex would have come up—but those days were long gone. You had to be careful now. You had to watch what you said to strangers.

Roger listened for signs of his kids moving around upstairs, but he heard nothing. They had gone to bed or were silently roughhousing, the way they did some nights. Roger couldn't remember the last time he'd actually been up there. For all he knew, they'd switched bedrooms or drilled holes in their walls.

While brushing his teeth, he opened the medicine chest, and to

his surprise, Tracy's diaphragm case was inside, wedged between cinnamon floss and Mercurochrome. For the first time in weeks he felt the pressure that had been building in the center of his chest lift. It was possible he'd been imagining things, that he'd been jumping to hasty conclusions. He pulled the case out and shook it, though shaking wasn't necessary: it was empty. This was a code, and Roger knew all too well what it meant, that Tracy was waiting for him to come to bed.

He slid in next to her and whispered her name: *Tracy.* She was facing a window, her back to him, the crook of her arm blocking her face. Touching her thigh, Roger said her name again, louder than he meant to: "Tracy!"

"Don't shout at me," she said. She looked over her shoulder at him and said, "What?"

Roger smiled, but Tracy looked away. "Not tonight," she said. "I'm beat."

"What do you mean, *not tonight?*"

"I mean, *not tonight.* What else does *not tonight* mean?"

Roger's throat tightened. He kept his voice even and said, "Were you in the mood *earlier?*"

Tracy rolled onto her stomach and said, "Not particularly. No."

Roger had a sudden and violent impulse: to reach up inside her, touch the diaphragm he knew was there, and say, *What's this?* But the impulse passed, and Roger, exhausted by the probability of his wife's deception, turned over and tried willing himself to sleep.

That night Roger had what he thought was a dream, that he called his boss, Lou Delahanty, in the dead of night. He needed to talk to the man, a matter that couldn't wait until morning, so he reached over and dialed the number. Fifteen rings later, Lou's wife answered.

It's Roger, he said, whispering into the mouthpiece. *Can I speak to Lou?*

Mrs. Delahanty said, *Who is this? It's late. Do you know what time it is?*

No, I don't.

It's four in the morning, she said. *Lou's still asleep. Who did you say you were?*

Roger.

Roger who?

Roger Wood.

Well, she said. *I'm not going to wake up my husband, Roger Wood. You can talk to him in the morning.*

My wife, Roger said.

What did you say?

I think my wife is having an affair, Roger said. *I think she's cheating on me.*

Mrs. Delahanty didn't respond. Then Roger began crying. He felt utterly helpless, whispering to a woman he didn't know, asking to speak to his boss, a man he *barely* knew. But he had to tell *someone;* he'd been holding it inside, hoping it wasn't true, *I'm sorry*, Roger said, and he returned the phone to the cradle.

Roger carefully backed his truck down into the sloped loading dock at the Dutch Boy warehouse. The dock had been designed for tractor trailers, not delivery trucks, which meant Roger would do a lot of lifting, handing one box at a time to a man standing high above him on the dock who, in turn, would hand it to another man, and so on, each box passed fireman-style until it reached a plywood desk where a teenager smoking a cigarette took inventory. Roger made deliveries all over Platte County and beyond, and he recognized the faces from loading dock to loading dock, but the men rarely appeared to remember him, and their conversations on the dock seemed impenetrable.

When he was fourteen, the year Squeaky Fromme tried assassinating President Ford, Roger became painfully conscious of his shyness around certain girls—so shy, he was incapable of speaking, of meeting their eyes. What he felt was a sort of helpless paralysis. Silently, he made up dialogues, hours of conversations that would never take place. Once in awhile he caught himself mumbling, hidden thoughts accidentally seeping through his mouth, given a voice. He hated himself for this, and now he hated how he felt around these men at the loading dock, strangers he'd seen every week for the past two years.

On his break, in the Sam's Club parking lot, he thumbed through *Helter Skelter*, but all he could concentrate on were the smudged photos, and of those photos, only those of women who'd come to visit him in the night: Squeaky, Linda, Leslie, Patricia, and Susan.

After lunch, Mr. Delahanty called Roger into his office.

"Have a seat, Rog," he said.

The boss, who was at least twenty years older than Roger and bald except for the mouse gray fringe around his head, examined the surface of his desk, as if searching for flaws, then touched his nose gently with his forefinger and thumb. The office was tidy. Hanging on his walls were several framed photos, and in each one, Delahanty was either holding up a fish or planting his foot onto the side of a large, dead animal. He touched his nose again and said, "Someone told me you've been picking up hitchhikers."

"Just one," Roger said.

"Company policy." Delahanty shook his head. "Company policy prohibits a driver to pick up hitchhikers."

Roger nodded.

"You should know better."

"You're right," Roger said. "I'm sorry."

"Don't let it happen again."

"It won't," Roger said.

Delahanty sighed. "Look," he said. He pinched his nose, then rubbed his palm across his desk as though fanning a deck of cards. He said, "I'm going to ask you straight out. Are you feeling okay?"

"Sure."

"You've got vacation time coming if you need it."

"What?" Roger said. "Have I done something wrong?"

Delahanty squinted at Roger, rubbing a large, moist palm over his smooth head. He couldn't keep his hands still. It was as if they had brains of their own, each hand attempting to conduct a life separate from Delahanty.

"You called my house four o'clock this morning," he said. "You spoke to my wife."

Roger shook his head, but he knew it was true.

"Now *Roger* . . ."

"It wasn't me," Roger said. "Why would I call your wife? Sounds like a prank."

Delahanty said, "Hmmmm. A prank. That's odd. Who would call my house pretending to be you, then tell my wife that *your* wife is having an affair? Don't you think that's odd?"

"My wife *isn't* having an affair," Roger said, but hearing himself say out loud what he'd been silently suspecting nearly broke him down right there in Delahanty's office. All along he'd thought he was in control, but now, for the first time in his life, he felt as if anything, anything at all, were possible. "If she was having an affair," Roger said, "I would know."

"Okay. All right," Delahanty said. "But no more hitchhikers. I mean, Jesus Christ, what were you trying to do, get the company sued?"

"No, sir," Roger said. "I'm sorry. I love this job."

And though he meant what he said, he was sorry he'd said it. Delahanty smiled, then laughed. He pounded his desk a few times with his fist and said, "That's a good one, Rog. For a second, you had me fooled." He rubbed his palms together and said, "Know what? You're a funny man when you want to be."

Without asking for permission, Roger took the rest of the afternoon off. At home, he found Tracy lying across the couch, asleep. She was wearing a sweatshirt he'd never seen before. *Chicago Black-hawks*, it said. Roger sat down across from her, leaned forward, and stared at her. He stared for nearly an hour, until the image of the Blackhawk Indian faded into a fuzzy swirl of abstract black-and-red streaks.

"I didn't know you liked hockey," he finally said.

Tracy opened her eyes, and when she saw Roger, she took a quick breath. "You scared me. When did you get home? What time is it?"

"I didn't know you liked hockey."

"What are you talking about?"

Roger pulled at his hangnail. His thumb had become infected,

the skin surrounding the sore inflamed, almost too tender to touch.
He yanked on it again, hard, ripping it almost free, but not quite.

"Don't do that," Tracy said.

"Why not?"

"You're making it worse."

"You should talk," Roger said.

"What's that supposed to mean?"

Roger said, "I didn't know you liked hockey."

"Jesus Christ!" Tracy yelled. "What are you talking about?"

He pointed at her sweatshirt.

"*This*?" she said. "I bought it at the Salvation Army two days ago. So what? It's a sweatshirt. It keeps me warm. I *don't* like hockey. In fact, I *hate* hockey."

Roger glared at Tracy for a moment, then stood and left the house. Coatless, he headed for downtown, a two-mile walk. The temperature had dipped well below zero, and his ears were throbbing as though someone had popped him several times about the head with their palms.

At the side of the road, Roger looked up and pointed at a low-flying airplane. The plane was so low, its shadow overtook a school bus, two pedestrians, and a pet store. Briefly, Roger himself was caught in the shade, then a blast of sunlight hit him again, and it was at this moment that he noticed his arm and his finger, the fact that he was pointing. He looked around, but no one had noticed, or if they'd noticed, they didn't care.

Roger walked quickly to a bar called the Jack O'Lantern for a drink. It was early afternoon. Except for the bartender, Roger was alone. He kept nodding without meaning to, thinking about Tracy and nodding. When he saw himself in the mirror, he quit moving his head and tried erasing all of his thoughts, but his wife kept returning. She'd come to him wearing another man's sweatshirt, eyes dark from long, sleepless nights, her diaphragm sealed-up inside her. His chest began to hurt, a distinct pain, as though someone were actually chewing on his heart. She was killing him. It was that simple.

Roger watched the bartender dunk dirty glasses into soapy gray

water, his sleeves rolled to his biceps. He let himself get lost in the
rhythm of the dunk, the hypnotic movements of a bartender in the
middle of a lazy, shadowy afternoon. His mind began to drift, and
eventually Tracy floated away.

Six hours later, Roger was halfway across town, leaning against
the bar at Papa's, drunk, a plastic cup half full of beer in his right
hand. He kept squeezing too hard, creasing the cup. Papa's was
packed with bikers and paraplegics, its usual potpourri of clientele.
Whenever Roger got drunk, he was amazed at how his mind simply
traveled—certain French words he'd learned in high school, long
forgotten, mysteriously returning (*l'oiseau, une parapluie*); graffiti
he'd once seen in a public restroom somewhere in Virginia (*I'll
crank your head for fun*); October, the first cold snap, seeing Tracy's
breath in the church parking lot after the wedding.

The floor in Papa's was sticky. Pickled eggs lay piled in a dusty jar
next to the cash register. Pool balls rolled from its coin-operated
trough to the cave at the end of the table. The world of the bar
had become Roger's world. He returned, again and again, to a
single phrase: *the most graphic moment of your indiscretion*. It was
an image, a flash that caused his windpipe to contract, his throat to
click.

A man playing pool leaned into Roger and said, "I used to play
better pool before I got shot in the head."

Roger nodded, and the man sank four striped balls in quick
succession.

People pushed against Roger, trying to flag down the bartender,
momentarily crushing him. And then the crowd parted, as if the bar
itself were yawning, a gulf starting at the center of Papa's to where
Roger stood, and beyond. At the center of that gulf was a midget,
too drunk to climb onto his barstool, and a man in a wheelchair.
The man in the wheelchair gripped his armrests and began pushing
himself up, attempting to stand. Once on his feet, balanced, he let
go of the chair. He took two careful steps toward the midget, placed
his hands beneath the midget's pudgy arms, then, grunting, lifted
him onto the barstool. Everyone had become silent, watching, mes-
merized. And Roger was certain in that instant that God was trying
to talk to him, that a man rising from his wheelchair to lift a mid-

get onto a barstool was a message, a clue, and Roger started crying
right there, in the middle of Papa's, because he couldn't fathom
what the message meant, but he knew if he could interpret it, he
would understand why all of this was happening to him, and then
maybe, just maybe, Tracy would stop having an affair and everything would return to normal.

"Roger," Tracy said. She nudged him. "Roger."

"What?"

"Are you okay?"

"I'm fine," he said.

"You were talking in your sleep."

"Was I?" He yawned and said, "I've been having strange
dreams."

"Like what?" Tracy said.

"You could call them religious, I suppose."

"How so?"

"The Second Coming of Christ," Roger said. "He comes to
Death Valley, and they crucify him."

There was a moment of silence. Then Tracy said, "I've been having odd dreams, too."

"Oh yeah?" Roger said. "Odd how?"

"They're about you."

"Me?" Roger said. "What's so odd about that?"

"You're following me around town. You're trying to kill me."

"Really." Roger wanted to comfort her, but he couldn't think of
anything comforting to say.

Tracy was smiling. Her dark mood had lifted. It was, as they say,
an odd turn of events. But Roger had gone out of his way today,
planning every move, hoping for just such a turn.

"This *is* romantic," Tracy said, "but why won't you tell me where
we're going?"

"Because," Roger said. "I told you already. It's a surprise." He
tried smiling, too, but Tracy was looking out the passenger-side
window now, watching the scenery flick by.

"How much longer?"

"Not much," Roger said. "Half an hour. Maybe less."

They'd been driving for three hours. Roger had come home from work early, called the baby-sitter, then ordered Chinese. He washed last night's dishes. He clipped his toenails. After dinner, he asked Tracy to help him dress his thumb. While Roger applied the Neosporin, Tracy prepared the sterile gauze and surgical tape. She kissed his bandaged wound and said, "I think we should see a marriage counselor."

"Sure," Roger said. "That's a good idea." But Roger knew the truth: they would never go to a marriage counselor. It was over between them.

That night, when they pulled into Athens, Ohio, Tracy said, "What time is it? The baby-sitter's going to kill us, don't you think? What time did you tell her we'd be back?"

Roger ignored her. He followed the directions he'd been given over the phone. He was good at that sort of thing. It was his job, after all—finding places he'd never before been, locating them in a timely manner. They parked and walked across campus to a movie theater in the student union. Roger had spent two weeks placing phone calls to theaters, and when nothing panned out, he called the distributor and found the closest showing. Ohio University. It was Phi Beta Kappa's Cult Movie Night, and they were screening *Valley of the Dolls*. One night only.

"Hmmmmm," Tracy said. "*Valley of the Dolls.* Isn't this supposed to be a terrible movie?"

"The worst," Roger said. He pointed at the movie poster and said, "Look, though. Sharon Tate." Then he led her into the dark theater.

He knew he couldn't explain it to her, none of it. There was no place to begin, so all he could do was hold her hand, maybe squeeze it for reassurance; and as the lights dimmed even more, and as the first reel of the movie began to play, Roger whispered into Tracy's ear, "I'm sorry."

The movie, as promised, was awful. The acting, the script, the soundtrack—all of it. Though buried under the film's surface was Sharon Tate's future. And Roger Wood knew what Sharon Tate didn't: that soon she would be pregnant. That she would carry the

child for eight and three-quarters months. That one night, for no
good reason except random bad luck, she would be stabbed sixteen
times. In the heart, the lungs, the liver. That a woman named Susan
Atkins would taste Sharon's blood, just out of curiosity.

"Are you okay?" Roger asked.

"Shhhhhh," Tracy said. "Watch the movie."

Roger shut his eyes. He saw himself as he had been in the dream, holding Squeaky's hand, a chain of five women and one man, all of them skipping like children. They were going to see Charlie. And Charlie would welcome them, welcome Roger, probably hug him and offer food. After supper they would smoke a joint and drop acid; and sooner or later, the women would move closer to Roger, ruffle his hair, and tell him to loosen up. And all of this sounded good, the days and nights slipping pleasantly by, months, maybe years. But Roger knew this sort of freedom—the freedom to do whatever you please—came with a price; and as he stepped into Manson's arms, accepting his grasp, he let go of Tracy's hand. It was a compromise. But that's how it was, wasn't it? There would always be compromises. And the price of such freedom, Roger knew, was darkness.

Igloo among Palms

Rod Val Moore's work has appeared in a number of literary magazines. His Iowa Award–winning collection of short stories, Igloo among Palms, *was reprinted in paperback by the Hinterlands Press. He continues to live in Los Angeles with his wife and son and to teach at Los Angeles Valley College. He has recently taught courses in the M.F.A. program at the Los Angeles campus of Antioch University. Currently he is at work on a novel set in southern California in the 1930s.*

"Oh, these are wonderful stories. Every one boundlessly inventive, unexpected, engrossing, edgy, and kind—their unsettled characters wandering, in all earnestness, full-tilt through the unhealthy environment of now."

JOY WILLIAMS, 1994

If for no other reason than to get out of the house, Tod said yes he would do it, he would volunteer for the emergency dry ice delivery job.

"Are you sure, Toddy?" asked Ike, his big brother, owner of the ice business. He looked up from where he was crawling on hands and knees with a smelly can of malt liquor in one hand and a bug-spray aerosol in the other, showering poison on a poor red and black beetle as it battled its way ever more slowly across the linoleum. At that point it was already one in the morning.

"I'm sure," groaned Tod. He was a tall boy and stood up slowly, painfully, like a stork that unfolds itself to fly.

Then Ike went through the details of the job: that it was only the Junior Boy Supermarket in Rosetta and that they needed a delivery PDQ because one of the long freezers had gone down, and Juventino the regular driver wouldn't work at night, and if they didn't get the dry ice in there before long, Junior Boy was going to lose

an inventory of frozen confections to the tune of two thousand
dollars or thereabouts.

Not that the dry ice would keep Tod cool as he drove through
the night heat. The only way it would air-condition the car, Ike told
him, was if you kept the windows rolled up, and, if you kept the
windows rolled up, you'd die of carbon dioxide poisoning.

"Because that's all dry ice is," he went on, though Tod already
knew the facts and understood perfectly, from living with Ike,
how dry ice is nothing more than carbon dioxide gas that's been
squeezed into a chamber so pressurized that it solidifies into white
smoky blocks that burn your fingers, if you touch them, just as
badly as would red-hot burners on a stove.

"But why don't I just take the truck," Tod asked, "and put the
dry ice in the back, in the bed of the truck?"

"Because you can't," said his brother, who tried every day, usually without success, to get Tod to help out with the business.
"Truck's broke down. That leaves the Carluxe, Toddy. But Junior
Boy only needs six hundred pounds, and we'll be able to get some
of that in the trunk and the rest in the back seat."

The Carluxe was an old vermilion-colored Imperial, fantastically
large, that had been in the family for years. It was Tod, as a verbally
precocious child, who had named it first the Car Deluxe and later
simply the Carluxe.

The brothers moved swiftly after the details had been worked out
and they had the car loaded and ready to drive in a few minutes.
Then Tod took hold of the wheel, inched backward down the driveway, hit the gas, and soon was unchained and over the speed limit,
finally and maybe forever on his own. It felt good to be going, not
because of the favor he was doing his brother, but because of the
feeling of going and going. Going to be getting gone. Yet by the
time he could really open it up on the late-night highway, he was
disappointed to find that out there the heat in the fields was as unbearable as the air-conditioned cold at Ike's house, and that the
smell of dark green crops and their dust of malathion was as smoth-
ering as Ike's sour malt liquor. There was no moon out, and between Giza Beach and Rosetta there were no landmarks, no street-

lights or billboards, just the narrow asphalt that extended like a dreary dark canal between acres of carrots on the left and strips of dark alfalfa on the right.

"Not the scenic route," Tod shouted over the radio, already as bored as he always knew he would be in the ice business. But the boredom for some reason sparked him and strengthened his determination to try to please his older brother for once, try to make this an outstanding delivery, the greatest delivery in the history of dry ice. Not as proof, of course, of wanting to get in on the business, but more as a silent apology for never having any intention to.

Immediately Tod relaxed, and then felt sleepy. To stay awake he drove with one hand down, on the bottom of the chrome and bakelite steering wheel, and one hand up, poised near his cheek, to sometimes slap himself rhythmically and lightly in time to the tinny rock and roll, in this way keeping himself half-awake enough to wonder if maybe when he got back from the delivery he could get up the nerve to tell Ike he was moving out. Occasionally he would glance in the rearview mirror at the six carefully arranged blocks of dry ice, all tightly wrapped in thick brown butcher paper and bound with scratchy twine, all still giving off their thin and slightly poisonous fog, like old cardboard suitcases leaking ghosts.

He thought, It is at least ninety holy degrees, and it's hours since the sun went down.

He thought, It's going to be hard to stay awake for half an hour, and I should try singing or reciting poetry or *something*. And he switched off the radio.

Try humming something when you're drowsy on the road, he recalled being told, and tried it, but his tuneless voice broke off by itself and he thought, I am like that red and black beetle on the linoleum and the dry ice is the bug spray Ike is using to get me.

Later there were thousands of dead leaves blowing across the road in front of him, round and noisy as rocks, sometimes spinning into whorls that lost themselves beneath his advancing headlights. The road was spookily empty for miles. Then, with the suddenness of a dream, a creature materialized out of the darkness. It was a lone

hitchhiker, a man with eyes lit up like a startled deer, and he appeared at the far perimeter of Tod's headlights a hundred yards
ahead, at the side of the highway, his legs whipped and circled by
the stream of leaves.

Tod didn't know what to do. He couldn't say to himself, I should
stop, or I'd better not stop. He checked his digital watch and saw
that it was six minutes after two. Giza Beach was only five miles
behind, and the car was already pushing through the heavy sea-level
air at eighty miles per hour. Still lost in thought, Tod drove right
past the gesturing figure at the side of the road. Then he did hit
the brakes, but tentatively tapped the gas again, tapped the brakes,
swallowed, then veered the Imperial rightward so that its tires
crunched down onto the shoulder and the speedometer needle
dropped to between five and ten miles per hour.

There was a strange thing with the hitchhiker. Somehow he must
have run ahead—though how anyone could have moved so fast
Tod could never understand—because suddenly there he was in the
headlights again, windmilling his arms, and Tod had to swerve to
avoid an accident and even then thought that at the last moment he
must have clipped him because when the Imperial finally scraped to
a complete stop and Tod took a look in the rearview mirror the man
was getting up from the dirt and staring at his palms.

"I'm okay, I'm okay," he shouted.

It was a bespectacled and bearded man, and he stood for a moment at the back of the car, grinning, his glasses and his teeth now
lit up bright red, like safety reflectors, from the brake lights.

Tod was amazed to find his heart beating fast. But then the hitchhiker jerked open the passenger door, flopped down beside Tod,
leaned so close that their shoulders grazed, and tossed his daypack
in back with the ice—and then it occurred to Tod that the guy was
all right, that despite the long dirty hair and beard, the baseball cap,
the eyeglasses secured in the back by an athlete's elastic, the hitchhiker's face somehow did not say I am that psychopath that has chosen to kill you, but said I am a harmless nobody, I am guileless and
guiltless, I am more frightened of you right now than you probably
are of me.

"You know what?" gasped the hitchhiker. "You didn't hit me. It was close, but no cigar. In fact, just the opposite. You rescued me. You know that you're a saint, don't you? A fucking *saint*. You know that? You are one holy fucking savior in one man's hour of need."

"Been waiting a long time then?" Tod asked, uncomfortable with the gratitude, frowning as he maneuvered the car smoothly out onto the highway and slowly regained speed.

"Not that long, my man. What I mean is, being picked up on a night like this—hot as the hobs of hell, as they say—by someone carrying a load of ice in a classy old red Imperial. Far fucking out."

This hitchhiker, thought Tod, is from somewhere not around here, but beyond that he couldn't place the gliding, somewhat over-salivated accent, or quite know what to make of the comment about the ice except to know for sure that the guy could not have known about the ice when he put his thumb out for a ride.

"We call it the Carluxe," smiled Tod, experiencing a peace that sometimes came over him when preparing to speak of things he knew to be indisputable and true. "And this kind of ice, dry ice, won't cool us off much. It's pure carbon dioxide. It's got to be enclosed to work, you see, to get things cold, and we've got to keep our windows down or we'll choke on the stuff. That's why I can't turn on the air conditioner."

"You know I only thumb rides at night, to stay out of the god-damn heat," continued the hitchhiker, showing no sign of having understood about the ice. "During the day I sleep. Somewhere in the shade if I can. You know, in somebody's barn or even out in the fields. Even then it's hard to sleep. Wish I had me an igloo made out of that dry ice, though, when I try to go to sleep tomorrow."

Tod let it go. It wasn't worth explaining twice. There was a silence while Tod sniffed at an herbal scent of Chapstick or throat lozenges that had come in the car with the hitchhiker.

"Originally, I am from Texas," announced the vagabond seriously, staring ahead at the highway and pronouncing the words very carefully, as if unveiling the week's winning lottery numbers. "And my name is Luther. Do you know that I've been doing this for years, living on a few dollars at a time? And I *mean* a few dollars too. Five

here, ten there. Now I'm aiming myself at my girlfriend and I feel
like—" And he sang the next part. "—a horny leetle monkey goin'
back to its leetle monkey tree."

Then they rode for a mile, two miles.

"I know that feeling," said Tod, nodding in so approving a way that the lie felt very truthful, and very wise.

Two more miles.

"So," smiled Tod, trying to keep the talk alive, afraid to ask Luther what it was he meant when he said he'd been doing *this* for years. What was *this*? But then asking it.

"So what is it you do, Luther, while you're waiting for rides?"

That was Luther's button. That was exactly the question that Luther seemed to have been waiting for. He drew himself up like a Texas senator and then spoke, and recounted in some detail how he marched along the side of the road each night, listening to the insect music of the huge agribusiness landscape, taking a few vegetables from the fucked-up margins of the fields, turning to stick his thumb out whenever headlights came into view, using the silence between cars to ruminate at length on subjects such as the danger of malathion and other insecticides to farm workers, the decline of the small family farmer, the reports of guerrilla war in Mexico. Tod found out, then, that Luther was the kind of person, so unlike himself, who could talk and talk, who could spring from thought to thought, fact to fact—that Luther was the kind who would lean close to share little secrets, to talk on and on with a cold monotone persistence which sent strange shivers through Tod's knees and thighs and made him press harder and harder on the Imperial's accelerator pedal. The one thing that Tod kept thinking about was Luther's strange way of leaning close to whisper but not speaking in Tod's ear, instead just staring straight ahead at the highway, cramping one arm to run his fingers through his Chapstick-scented beard, finally taking off his complicated glasses and wearily covering his eyes with his hands but still talking and talking with his vaguely persuasive Texas accent and his way of stretching out his body on the seat straight as a board, even with his hand over his eyes, only to fumble idly with something, a set of keys perhaps, in his front blue jeans pocket.

The other thing that Tod kept thinking about was that talking to the hitchhiker was like conducting an interview but without having to ask questions. Luther provided the questions and then the answers. "Are the Mexicans going to start a war up here too, maybe in Sonora?" he asked. "No," he answered, "even though this is Zapata country, the agrarian reform is stronger here." And so on.

But Tod could not keep up with Luther's talk show. It had turned into something about aggression and cowardice and what Luther almost shouted about the "inevitability of one class dominating the other," and Tod suspended his attention after awhile in order to focus more sharply on himself and on the highway with its endless hyphenation and giant dreamy green exit signs on the periphery of everything. Sleepily, he decided he would like to tell the hitchhiker—if the hitchhiker were anyone but Luther—some story of his own. But there was no story to be told there and then. For the first time Tod wished he did work at his brother's ice plant, among the Mexicans, because there, he thought, there must be some of the storytelling and class struggle that seemed now to be missing from his life.

But then Tod's thoughts blurred, his eyelids grew heavy as nickels. He dozed off for a fraction of a second and his head fell through space for a moment, hurtled down toward his breast until a reflex, full of adrenaline and panic, snapped it back up straight.

"Did you know," he blurted, realizing that the hitchhiker had been silent a long time, staring out the window, and hadn't noticed his fleeting snooze, "that all these carrot fields out there used to be a dry lake bed? Do you know where the largest dry lake bed in the world is? Do you know where they get the gas to make dry ice?"

Then, when there was no reply, just Luther's herbal odor lingering for a moment in the air, Tod cleared some part of his mind and told what little more he knew about the ice plant. He explained to Luther about the enormous cold room, and about how the ice cubes and the ice blocks were manufactured, how they made the wet ice clear as diamonds, not milky or white like refrigerator ice. And he somewhat clumsily described how they concocted the dry ice—a wonderful substance that exists on the border between solid and gas—and how dry ice is used for more than just the

spooky effect in punch bowls and rock concerts but also is important in a variety of industrial processes that in turn drive the national economy.

Then Tod's stream of unadorned truth broke off, and before he
could go any further, before he could move forward to a story that
he thought he could make up about the ice plant, he felt utterly
empty, just plain out of mental fuel. He could see that Luther
the vagabond had changed again—except that this time he was
stretched out straight, his hand in his pocket, all in all looking much
larger and stranger than when he had first clambered into the car.
He had done something to his hair, taken off his baseball cap and
used a girl's barrette to arrange it in a wild bun atop his head, and
in the interior gloom of the Imperial he looked to Tod like some
kind of monstrous bearded businesswoman.

"What did you say the name—" began Luther, finally moving
and gesturing again, taking his hand out of his pants pocket to daub
deftly at his lips with his balm. "What did you say the name of your
ice company was?"

"I'm not sure I did say. But anyway it's not my ice company. I
don't even work there. It's my brother's ice company and sometimes I do him some big favor. Tonight I'm delivering this dry ice
to Rosetta. The Mexicans don't work at night. But the day of the
explosion—the big explosion—I was just minding the office for a
few minutes while everyone was out on delivery."

Tod felt a tiny choke in his throat, as if he were about to cry. The
lie had been told, and was unforgivable. Now, what would be his
punishment? But only a long silence followed. What explosion, Luther was supposed to say. What big explosion? But Luther was busy
with the window on his side, trying to roll it down, discovering with
a whistle that it was already down all the way, and then thrusting his
head far out into the darkness, as if he were trying to get as far away
as he could from the claustrophobia of the cab, or, Tod couldn't
help thinking, from the claustrophobia of sin.

With a fluid twist of his whole body, Luther drew his head back
in. His face was flushed with the late night heat, but it appeared to
Tod that he had not gone back to his initial good humor or entertaining pedantry. In fact, it looked as if he had breathed in with the

farm air a new and unexplainable power. His ponytail had come undone, his nostrils flared, and he sat erect in the cab, like a man wearing a spinal brace, his hair spitting out behind him in the breeze. Then Tod saw that his passenger was fiddling with something, tossing something from one hand to the other.

"Wow," said Tod, barely able to get the words out, but not afraid. "That's a knife."

It wasn't a regular hunting or pocketknife, but looked like something more primitive, something out of a movie about lost tribes. Its handle had the soft brown look of deer antler, and the blade looked viciously sharp, not made of steel but of something more elemental, like obsidian.

"Picked this up in the jungles of Co-Sta-Ree-Co," drawled Luther.

"Blade's as hard and sharp as diamonds. Want me to write a message on your windshield?"

Tod could see, now that Luther held the thing up close to his eyes, that it was in fact a plain fake, molded out of tin and plastic, more likely to have come from a tourist shop in Mexilindo than a jungle.

So this is one chink in the armor, thought Tod. He felt good about that, and he sat up straight at the wheel.

"Be careful with that thing," he said. "Luther, don't do anything to this car, all right? My brother's going to check for every new little scratch when I get back home."

"But," said Luther, flipping the knife back and forth again between his hands, "this here's no ordinary knife. This knife was used for surgery among the Indians down there. It cuts without tearing, cures without blood. I can stick it into anything I want without opening a wound. Watch this!"

And with that Luther suddenly seized the knife in his right hand and plunged it with all his strength into an expanse of white upholstery just an inch from Tod's shoulder. But before Tod could move or speak in outrage, he heard Luther's cackling laugh and saw the joke—it was one of those knives that kids play with, the kind where the blade retracts inside the handle on a spring and makes a pretty good illusion of penetration.

Still enjoying his prank, Luther reached behind him and put the
knife away in an outside pocket of his daypack, then turned to face
his driver with a grin Tod could feel burning into him without his
turning to look.

"Luther, you gave me a scare," sighed Tod, not wanting to laugh, not wanting to approve of such lunacy. But when he stole a glance, Luther was sullen again, staring into his lap, biting his lip, then slipping a finger into his pocket, producing another barrette with which he regathered his ponytail.

"Let me out of here," Luther said quietly, succinctly.

"Why?" cried Tod, alarmed. "Why do you want to get out here in the middle of nowhere?" Then he laughed, condescendingly. "I'm not a murderer, you know. And you couldn't have picked a worse spot, I'm afraid."

"Don't be afraid, man," said Luther, speaking evenly, pleasantly. "Just let me out, this is where I want to get out."

"But hey," replied Tod, not wanting to seem concerned but at the same time reaching with one foot into the darkness beneath the steering wheel and braking the Imperial to a crawl. "This isn't any-where. It's still a few miles to Rosetta. Let me drive you into town and find a good spot for you to hitch."

But even while he spoke Tod felt secretly relieved, and pulled off the road and finally braked to a complete stop in a swirl of trash. For some reason he turned off his headlights. A moment later Luther had sprung out of the car, had taken a few steps down the ink-dark road, then dashed back to talk to Tod again through the open window.

"Thank you," he breathed, as if having resolved some interior struggle. "I'm okay. You go on to Rosetta. I think I prefer to walk from here, see if some fucker comes along who's maybe going far-ther than you are."

"Well," hesitated Tod, "if you're sure. Okee doke. At any rate, thanks for the company."

Then the hitchhiker's face, strangely bloated and sad, withdrew a bit but stayed framed in the window for a moment as if on a tele-vision screen, with eyes so puppyish and soft in the darkness that Tod suddenly realized that Luther was really as handsome under the beard as a soap-opera star. Then the face disappeared, and Tod pulled back onto the highway, and drove on.

There followed several miles of unrelieved boredom.

"I'll stop at Eskimo's," said Tod, and when he saw the yellow and white sign of the twenty-four-hour franchise, he started thinking hard about the chocolate shake that he knew would calm his nerves and give him that extra boost he needed to finish the dry ice job.

The parking lot was empty, but he pulled in carefully between two of the fishbone parking lines farthest from the door of the restaurant. He was thinking so hard about the shake that he had almost put the episode of the hitchhiker out of his mind, and so it was with a wrench of astonishment and sorrow that he noticed that Luther had forgotten his green daypack. There it was, still nestled among the misty ice blocks, a remnant of the vagabond, a sliver that he couldn't get out of his finger. The thing to do, he considered, was to dump the thing in the garbage and get on to the market.

Or leave it in the parking lot where Luther might find it?

It was just then that he saw the girl. She was tiny and bright, a Tinkerbelle, maybe fourteen years old, or fifteen. She appeared to him first through the rear window of the Imperial, but distant, a little figure far across the parking lot, standing at the entrance to the restaurant. She was wearing a white and yellow cap that from where he sat looked like a giant fried egg, and she was holding open the restaurant door from the inside and calling out to him.

"I was just thinking of closing," he could barely hear her shout at him, in a crackling but immediately appealing voice. "Did you want something to eat here or to go?"

"I thought—" he cried back after a second, after he had scrambled out of the car and stood up on the door ledge to get a better look at her. "I thought all Eskimo's were open twenty-four hours."

"Yeah, I know," she yelled, and started walking across the parking lot toward him. "It's just that I'm working alone tonight. I've been cooped up in there for more hours than I care to think about and I was thinking about saying screw the customers—excuse me, of course I don't mean you—and, you know, sneaking out."

She stopped about ten feet away and Tod saw that her cap was

supposed to look not like an egg but like a daisy. "But come on if
you'd like," she smiled.

Then, because of the daypack, Tod faced a decision. He could
drive back and try to find the hitchhiker, or he could go in and eat
and assume that the hitchhiker might find his way to Eskimo's and
recognize the Carluxe.

"OK," said the girl, taking some steps backward. "I hereby take
your silence to mean no. OK? We're closed. Sorry we missed you.
Come back and see us again soon."

"No, no," said Tod, suddenly fishing out the daypack, slinging it
over one shoulder, and taking a few steps toward her. "I want a
Polar Bear Burger," he lied, feeling less hungry than before. There
was a thin sharp smell of cattle manure in the air, almost like a mist,
and he remembered the big Rosetta feedlots. "I want fries and I
want a chocolate shake. To go. I'll eat it in my car, and then you can
close up."

But she was already on her way back to the restaurant and he
had to run to slip inside the automatic glass door as it closed just
behind her.

Inside the restaurant everything was as bright as noon in the basin, but compared to the outside heat, absurdly cold, and all the
walls and tables and chairs were covered in crisp, phosphorescent
tones of yellow, white, and green. No customers in sight. After
a few minutes the girl brought the food, not packaged to go, to
Tod's table and then, to his surprise, sat down across from him and
watched quietly while he ate.

At first he concentrated on the food. He was interested to find,
upon unfastening the Styrofoam clamshell that he expected to contain his sandwich, a pile of steaming, garlicky shrimp. But he said
nothing, made no complaint. The rest of the food was as he had
ordered: a tall round waxy cup, with its charge of chocolate shake,
too thick to sip through the clear plastic straw. There, too, was the
order of fries, cut in half-moon shapes that reminded him, when
they spilled out of their bag on the bright table in the bright green
light, more of lime wedges than potatoes.

The girl's face, as he ate, followed his movements, and was so bright and round that it distracted him. But, he thought to himself as he jostled the last bit of shake into his mouth and shot a glance over the edge of the cup, she is not especially attractive. Her face is round and smooth, he thought, but she is not a beautiful girl, she could not be hired as a model. For one thing she didn't have enough hair; instead of cascading to her shoulders or streaming out like ripples of summer wheat, her locks hung straight and limp beneath her hat, like Luther's. She had brought the food to him wearing, suddenly, an oversized school jacket decorated not with athletic letters but with several little enameled pins that he decided must be academic awards, and now he noticed her habit, whenever she lay her arms on the table, of clenching her fists and drawing them just inside the frayed sleeves, two instant amputations. That's not becoming, he said to himself, and also he didn't like her eyes, which were small and black, eyelashes done with mascara in a way, he thought, that made them look more like a pair of black stitches in her face than eyes.

"Why is it always so unbearably cold in here?" she said out loud suddenly, wrapping her handless arms around her ribs. She shook her head no and leaned forward when she spoke.

"You're asking me?" snorted Tod, toying with his final french fry, not looking up.

"It's the manager, he keeps the air-conditioner controls under lock and key, so we can't set the temperature to something a little more realistic. He says the tourists like it this way. But guess what?"

"What?"

"They complain to me about it all the time."

She shook her head no and leaned forward again, and Tod realized that this was a kind of tic with her, her odd way of speaking. He thought it gave her conversation a strange quality of conspiracy, and he tried to chew quietly as she talked because he wanted to hear every word. Then, when she was quiet for a long time, he swallowed and spoke. "And you can't open the doors to warm things up," he suggested, "because of the feedlots."

"Very true. It isn't surprising that customers don't want to think about feedlots too much when they're inhaling their ground beef. But now we'll talk about *your* interesting job."

"What makes you think I've got an interesting job? Or that there
is such a thing?"

"I don't know. You have an interesting job because you strike me
as mature enough for an interesting job. Either that or you go to
college at India Basin, where I go, or up in Santa Sierra. Or even in
Brahma. You grew up here on the lake. You work during the sum-
mers and live with your parents."

Tod ate his last fry, then began carefully and idly to fold the
greasy cardboard shell that read "french fries" in murderously red
letters.

"Hey," he said. "How can you just slip out, like you said you were
going to? Doesn't the manager come around to check on you?"

"He comes every morning at five—he's very predictable. I know
how to get back just in time and make it look like I've been here.
But—hey yourself—I really do want to know about your job."

He paused, then lied. She had said his job must be interesting,
and Tod lied only to keep from shattering the atmosphere which he
felt all around them and which he knew her flattery had made.

"My brother and I run an ice factory. We inherited it from our
dad. That's my job. I mostly do the delivery side of the business."

"Do you really have ice in that car? Why doesn't it melt?"

"The way they—we—wrap it up with paper, it melts very slowly.
But besides that it's dry ice."

"Do you have a boss? Is he like mine?"

"It's my brother."

"Your brother is your boss?"

"No. You don't get it. We run the business together. He's more
like my partner. But he takes care of the plant, and I make the
deliveries."

Tod was watching the girl as he spoke, wondering what her name
was, but it seemed too late already to ask. Her face, he kept thinking, was so round. Nice and round. Round like an Eskimo's.

"All right," she said, frowning, shaking. "Now for the hardest
question. What kind of contraband are you carrying in the bag?"

But the bag, Luther's daypack, was something Tod had already
forgotten about, and for a moment he was startled and couldn't
imagine what she was talking about.

"Oh that," he finally shrugged. "That's a funny story. I picked up a hitchhiker on the way here and he forgot it in my truck."

"But that's too good to be true!" the girl screeched. The frown was broken, and she laughed and clapped her hands, then held her hands in front of her nose like a closed book while Tod stirred uncomfortably on his plastic bench seat. "Do you realize," she smiled, "who you picked up?"

"No idea," he mumbled, half-expecting her to say that it was her fiancé or her boyfriend and thus break the spell.

"The vanishing hitchhiker, that's who. You don't know the story? All right, the story goes like this. You're driving late one night on Highway 7, say, and you pick up a solitary figure at the side of the road. He introduces himself, you introduce yourself, you proceed to have a nice conversation. Maybe he makes cryptic remarks about a car crash, maybe he doesn't. At any rate you let him off, only to discover later that he's left something in your car, maybe a wallet, maybe a DAYPACK. Anyway, it has to be something with his address in it. You find the address, notice it's in a nearby town, and drive over the next day to return the forgotten item. Except the hitchhiker doesn't answer the doorbell, it's his wife or his mother. You tell her the story and all the while she's looking at you like you're crazy or she's just seen a ghost. 'But that's impossible,' she says. 'Our Herbert died in an auto accident a year ago yesterday.' 'Where exactly was the accident?' you ask, an icy hand laying hold of your heart. 'Why, right out on Highway 7,' she says, 'JUST OUT-SIDE OF GIZA BEACH.'"

Tod was unimpressed. "This was not one of your ghost hitchhikers," he said. "Besides, he wasn't from around here, he was from Texas."

"Oh," the girl snapped, impatient, drawing her hands even farther into her sleeves. "You don't get it, do you? The next thing I was going to say is, let's look inside his daypack, for an address, go look up the poor fellow's family."

"My story's more interesting than that, because it's a true story." At the same time that he spoke Tod was comparing Luther and the girl, thinking how much he had been getting to like her, how much

more he would rather tell her some more stories. Maybe the one
about the ammonia leak, just to get things started. Then he would
settle back and listen to her for a while, and maybe, he thought,
learn a thousand things from her, let her be his real teacher. But
then she had spoiled things by talking about ghosts.

On the other hand. What if her story were true?

Meanwhile the girl was grimacing and biting the knuckle of her
index finger in such a way that it had turned red and white and
shiny, like a gnawed bone. "Listen," she said. "I wonder. Well I
wonder if you could do me a favor while you're here."

Tod hesitated. Suddenly he had run out of words, suddenly he
was dull and nervous and feeling the dryness of the air conditioner
in his sinuses, and he daubed at his nostril with his finger, and it
came away with a perfect little bead of blood. In the silence he
started thinking about making love to the girl, about what it would
be like. He pictured her, for some reason, wearing a black bra, like
tough high school girls wear, and wondered if it would be the kind
that undid in the front or the back. Then he had a terrible image of
himself trying to penetrate her, but with a penis that retracted with
every thrust, like Luther's knife.

"I wonder if you could do me a big favor," repeated the girl,
leaning forward across the table and opening her miniature, all-
black eyes as wide as they could go.

"What favor?"

"I'd really like to get out for a while. But now it's gotten so late.
I wonder if you could stay here in case the manager comes along.
Could you? If he comes in while I'm gone, just say that I had to go
around to the bathroom. Then come outside to the date garden and
whistle or something. Will you?"

"There's a date garden?"

"Yeah. You didn't know? We're surrounded by palm trees here,
it's nice. You didn't see the palms? This is the old Vern-Lee Gardens. This used to be Vern-Lee's Date Shack before they turned it
into an Eskimo's. Anyway, when you came that's just where I was
heading, I mean, into the garden. Every night I try to get out and

take a long walk out there—it's really pretty great at night. Kind of spooky, you know? If I don't get to do it I just about don't make it to the end of my shift. Will you do it? Will you cover for me?"

Tod could hardly wait for her to stop talking, he was so prepared with his answer. "Yes," he said intently, leaning a little toward her. "Yes."

"I don't know. Are you sure? Maybe I'll get you in trouble with your job? Are you sure your ice won't melt?"

"It won't melt. Anyway, what if I told you it wasn't ice after all, that I'd been lying about everything? That what I have in the back of the car isn't ice, but the body of that hitchhiker, that I've killed him and brought him here to bury in the date garden?"

The girl looked upset for a moment and then she broke into a great round Eskimo grin.

"That's better," she laughed. "That's great. When I get back we'll check that daypack of yours and get the family address."

"OK. See you."

And she was gone, dancing out into the night, leaving a puff of feedlot air behind her as the glass door closed without a sound. Tod stretched his legs out on the bench, leaned back against the softness of Luther's pack, and then, serenely, trustingly, fell asleep.

The first thing he realized when he woke up was that he was still alone in Eskimo's, and the second thing he realized was that the sun was starting to come up, and that there was a piece of paper on the table that hadn't been there before and that it was in fact a letter meant for him.

Dear customer (ice delivery man)

Thanks again for being here while I went out. I did come back a few minutes later to ask you something but you were asleep. What I wanted to ask was can Luther and I borrow your car, but didn't want to wake you up so took your keys anyway and promise we'll be very careful with your fine car and your ice and just be gone a short while. Sorry I kidded you about Luther. That business about the vanishing hitch-hiker was just my stupid joke. The minute you walked in I knew you had given Luther a ride because I recognized his green daypack. Luther is, as I guess you can figure out, really my boyfriend, and I guess he kidded you too when he told you he doesn't live around here. The real reason I had to leave you alone was to meet him. Don't worry we'll be back before sunrise and before customers start showing up. Yours, the Eskimo's girl (Janine).

Still slow with sleep and recoiling from the gritty, shrimpy taste in his teeth, Tod rose, stuffed the letter in a pocket, and swung Luther's daypack onto his right shoulder. When he stumbled out into the parking lot he found the predawn wind not just free of heat and feedlot misery, but full, for just a moment, of a strange winter sweetness and coolness. He gladly breathed it in, like a diver who comes up from holding his breath too long, and as he breathed, and even as the coolness disappeared and was replaced by the familiar suffocation, his eyes cleared and he felt the creases relax a little in his face, even in his clothes. The first thing he looked for in the rising light was the date garden, and when he turned instinctively in the direction of the refreshing wind, he saw for the first time the tall feathery outlines of palm fronds silhouetted against the gray sky, already alive with the sound of tiny, nervous birds who hid themselves high up in the deep black-green of the foliage. There, he said to himself, is my oasis, and he had taken several long, unimaginably buoyant steps toward the trees when he was brought up short by the belated realization that what the letter said was true, that Ike's car, the vermilion Carluxe, was gone.

Tod hissed. I'm not responsible for this, he thought, I'm not to blame, no one can blame me for this. I kept Luther from wrecking the car before but this loss is a result of something insane, something I can't control. Suddenly he sat down hard on the asphalt, his back turned to the dates, facing the glaring yellow light of Eskimo's. I'll wait for them here, he thought, and play it cool. Nevertheless, he couldn't help bringing his hand down hard on the black asphalt, holding back a sob, spitting out something. Then, acting on a different impulse, he jumped up, wheeled around, and set out for the date garden.

Tod realized it must be one of the old gardens that had been planted decades ago, back when there was some odd idea that the valley could become the date-growing capital of the world, could surpass the ancient cultivations of India and Egypt. For a while, his brother had told him, the harvests were impressive and the soft heavy dates were superior quality, and there was a lot of excitement and planning. But soon most of the trees had succumbed to a mysterious tree rot and died, aliens from another desert, unable to adapt. Years later a few diminished groves remained in the valley, some providing fruit for curious tourists, others, like this one, neglected, losing their sweet crop every year to the lucky birds. Tod, for one, had never paid much attention to the orchards, never even eaten the good sweet dates at harvest time. Now, as he walked down the corridors formed by the smooth silver trunks and could watch the sun just emerging at the end of the perpendicular corridors to his left, Tod felt larger than life, like a holy man in some cathedral of Islam, wading thoughtfully through the thick grass that grew between the marblelike columns, falling to his knees once to examine the bright drops of dew and tiny yellow flowers that turned out to be not flowers but tiny yellow pinfeathers the date birds were shedding from above. The thin, sweet breeze that he had swallowed in the parking lot now came to him again. Then it was gone, and the sun was above the horizon and it was miserably hot. He stood up and the birds he had heard before had begun to flutter more noisily, as if agitated by the heat, pitching and scratching at one another loudly, battling for perches in the jungle of fronds twenty or thirty feet above his head. Shifting Luther's daypack on his shoulder, Tod veered sideways into a new long row of trees—and then thought he caught a glimpse of red quite far away, a shade of reddish orange that made him think that it had to be his brother's car.

Tod moved cautiously to his right, and there in fact it was, the Carluxe, only now it was directly ahead of him, in full view, parked in sunlight, windows rolled up tight, grass shivering around the hubcaps. He stepped slowly toward it, dull with fear, following the wounds in the grass left by the tires. Now he could feel absolutely no further pleasure in the burning morning. The sun, though only an inch above the horizon, had already begun to scorch the tops of

his bare forearms and fill his throat, as on every summer day in the
basin, with the taste of syrup, of yellow solar expectorant.

There was no farther to go. He could reach forward and pull
open the passenger door if he wanted, but he hesitated. He did try
to open the door, but it was locked. Then, running a hand along
the long strip of cool chrome trim, he walked slowly around the
whole circumference of the Imperial, idly swallowing down the heat
like soda pop, finding all the doors locked tight.

Not that he could see in. It was all opaque because the dry ice, in
its slow disintegration, had filled the whole interior of the car with
fog. Tod considered the fog, and decided on two likely explanations
for it. One was that Luther and Janine were nearby—he pictured
them rolling together in a patch of sweet grass—and had left the
windows rolled up when they left the car.

The other possibility was that the couple—the two, he kept thinking, who had lied to him were still in the car. If they were in the car—
and Tod considered this possibility with a stab of satisfaction, followed by a flood of melancholy—they were dead, asphyxiated.
Slowly, composedly, he considered how he might get inside the car
and free them, revive them, and he even rummaged for a second in
the daypack, hoping to find some kind of tool or wire. But of course
the only thing that he came up with was the toy knife, which was
useless. Maybe, he thought, staring again, taking a step backward,
maybe Janine and Luther had really believed that they might flee
the wretched heat by rolling up the windows and letting the ice air-
condition their love. But it was dry ice, as he was sure he had told
one or both of them, again and again, and it was truly cold, colder
than cold, but poison.

Out of the Girls' Room and into the Night

Out of the Girls' Room and into the Night *was reprinted by Anchor Books, in a somewhat slimmed down version, in the fall of 2000. A novel,* The Good People of New York, *was published in May 2001, and a collaborative project—a book of stories, recipes, and collages Nissen has done with Erin Ergenbright—will be published in the spring of 2002. Nissen is still living happily in Iowa City.*

"These stories abound in a rich life, holding sad, awkward, edgy contemporaneity in their generous embrace. They do not soothe or forgive or reassure; they love the creature as it is. There is great originality and great freedom in Thisbe Nissen's approach to her subject, a kind of classicism in her lucid and compassionate interest in the ways of this present world."
MARILYNNE ROBINSON, 1999

Silver Tarkington went on a blind date to the Chilton School senior prom with a boy named Barry Gorda, who was the best friend of Jarrett, who was the boyfriend of Fernanda Albion, who was the daughter of the family friends with whom Silver happened to be staying for that particular weekend in June. Silver had to fly in from Houston for an early freshman orientation at NYU that coincided with the weekend of Fernanda's prom, and when Silver learned that Fernanda was finding her a date for said prom she was less than thrilled. She'd suffered through her own prom back in Texas a few weeks earlier and couldn't muster an ounce of enthusiasm at the prospect of slogging through another one. Besides, she'd broken the heel of one dyed-to-match pump and lost the other somewhere between the booming Houston country club and the sandtrap just past the third tee, where she'd smoked a joint with Cyril Houser

while her own date puked peach schnapps into an azalea bush across
the fairway. Plus, the fact that Fernanda had to import a girl from
two thousand miles away to be Barry Gorda's prom date didn't exactly recommend him as a real winner. Nonetheless, Silver bought
a fresh pair of hose, borrowed some shoes, raked on the requisite
mascara, and squeezed herself back into the shimmery-sage snip of
a dress that had seemed quite reckless and inspired back in Houston
but here at a New York dance club amidst a group of eighteen year
olds who appeared to be dressed less for a prom than for a haute
couture funeral, she felt sort of like an oxidized Statue of Liberty:
a trifle absurd and worse for wear.

Barry Gorda threw big parties when his folks left for weekends in
the Hamptons, had love handles that bulged over his cummerbund,
and was known affectionately as the Cheese.

"The *Cheese*?" Silver whispered to Fernanda. They were at their
table watching Barry jog out onto the dance floor to entertain
a group of break-dancing white boys who clustered around him
chanting "CHEESE. CHEESE. CHEESE. CHEESE."

"Barry *Gouda*," Fernanda explained from beneath a well-arched
eyebrow.

"Clever," said Silver flatly.

"Oh, they're quite a creative bunch, our boys."

Silver gave a little snort. She and Fernanda—estranged since age
nine when the Albions had moved from Houston to Manhattan—
were hitting it off again famously. Markedly less impressive was Jarrett, Fernanda's boyfriend of three years who made Silver think of
a St. Bernard in tails. He was headed for Tulane in the fall, Fernanda
for Hampshire College, and Silver figured any attempt to do a long-
distance thing would last about three days before Fernanda hooked
up with some multiply-pierced multimedia performance artist and
sent Jarrett running to the Louisiana Tri-Delts for consolation.

"And what's the Cheese doing with himself next year?" Silver
asked.

"Last I heard, moving to Amsterdam."

"Where prostitution's legal?"

"Drugs too," Fernanda added.

"Lovely."

168

*Out
of the
Girls'
Room
and into
the Night*

Fernanda's voice was suddenly less confident. She faced Silver. "Do you totally hate me for setting you two up?"

Silver smiled reassuringly. "Please just don't phrase it that way— it sounds like you thought we'd really hit it off."

"Well he certainly seems to have taken a liking to you," Fernanda teased, but it was quite plainly and painfully the truth of the situation.

"I'm sure I've done something in my life to warrant a little penance," Silver said. "I'm thinking of this date as a sort of community service."

"OK," Fernanda said suddenly, her tone abruptly new, and she reached out and laid her hand on Silver's forearm. Her face washed over in a sort of eerie film. "Don't turn around, OK? Just sit there and pretend we're having a normal conversation."

"We're not?" Silver asked.

"What?" Fernanda's gaze was distant, but like she was trying to demonstrate to someone far away that she was focused very intently on Silver. Silver didn't turn around. She had the distinct sense that Fernanda might slap her if she tried. "Approaching from behind you," Fernanda said, "is someone we'd like to see spend as little time at our table as possible. If you think of anything that'll get me, or him, out of here, do it. Ready, two, one, we have touch-down."

Something had indeed landed beside Silver in Barry Gorda's empty chair. It spoke as if to announce itself: "Fernanda Albion."

Silver looked him straight on. "I thought *she* was Fernanda Albion?" she said, forking a thumb toward her friend. The guy didn't seem to notice or care.

"Smith Parker Hewitt," Fernanda said, stony as anything, drawn out and slow.

"What's that, a law firm?" Silver clucked, to no discernible response.

"Silver Tarkington," Fernanda said, lifting her chin in Silver's general direction.

"Is this *The Name Game*?" Silver said.

"You don't go to Chilton do you?" asked the man. He had a nice retro-looking shirt under his tux jacket. He looked old, maybe forty, and was not handsome but attractive. A sort of Neanderthal John F. Kennedy.

"Is it required that we all answer questions with questions?" Silver asked.

"That depends on what game we're playing, doesn't it?" he answered, still staring straight at Fernanda.

"Oh, OK, I get it," Silver said. "It's like Kazaam, right? You can't look at the person you're talking to?"

Suddenly Mr. Ape-Kennedy snapped out of whatever trance he'd been in, scooped a handful of peanuts from a dish on the table, and turned to Silver, all chatty-casual and peanut-popping smiles. Fernanda leaned toward Silver, yet spoke in a voice that anyone could hear. "Mr. Hewitt teaches Science at Chilton."

"Please," he said, extending a hand to Silver, "call me Smith."

Fernanda clapped her hand over both of Silver's and with extraordinary insistence held them to the table. "Call him Mr. Hewitt," she said. "Don't take any chances."

"It's so hard, really," Mr. Hewitt said at Silver, as though they'd been exchanging confidences all evening. "Even during social time," he swept a hand vaguely at the dancing crowd, "the students still insist on enforcing that dichotomy, reinscribing the gap between teacher and student, putting us at a surname's distance."

Fernanda snorted and recrossed her legs. "As if," she said, just as Jarrett lumbered up behind her. It was like she could smell him coming—not surprising, Silver could too: Polo cologne and tequila shots sucked back in a bathroom stall—and Fernanda practically jumped on him as he slid into the chair beside her. It was more affection than she'd shown him all night, and he slurped at her gratefully, like a long-neglected housepet.

"And you are . . . ?" Mr. Smith Parker Hewitt asked Silver.

"Confused," she said.

"You're a teenager," he funnelled another handful of peanuts into his mouth. "What do you expect?"

Silver pulled at a curl of her hair and inspected it for split ends.

"Confused?" Mr. Hewitt waved his hand right in front of her face, like a hypnotist checking to see how far under his patient had gone.

170

Out

of the

Girls'

Room

and into

the Night

"Silver," she said.

"What?"

"Silver," she said again.

"Hi ho," he said. "What is this, word association?"

"My name," she told him.

"Silver?"

She nodded once, put out a hand to say, *enough, OK?*

Mr. Hewitt, to his credit, moved graciously on. "Here with . . . ?" he cued.

Silver turned toward the dance floor to point out her date and raised her hand at the exact moment that Barry Gorda happened to finish a floor spin and look up to see if Silver had caught his killer move. Mistaking her raised hand as a signal to *him*, he climbed to his feet, gave a little nod to the guys (*my woman calls*), and made his way toward the table.

"The Cheese?" Mr. Hewitt said with an unmistakable note of amusement.

"Blind date," Silver said, wishing she could lie well enough to pull off being madly in love with Barry Gorda. She couldn't. "I'm a friend of Fernanda's," she explained, at which they both turned again to Fernanda, who was thoroughly engrossed in picking the strawberries off an extra piece of shortcake at the table and looked like she'd forgotten completely that she was at her senior prom. She had the air of someone standing naked before an open refrigerator at 3 A.M. nibbling leftovers. Mr. Hewitt had the distinct air of someone who'd rolled out of bed behind her.

Barry arrived at the table frazzled to find his seat occupied by a Chemistry teacher and hovered awkwardly behind Silver and Mr. Hewitt. He said, "Hi," but no one was paying attention, so he just kept on standing there doing a little stationary sway-dance, trying to figure out how to reclaim his rightful place at the table. He flicked out his left hand and knocked Mr. Hewitt on the shoulder. "They didn't give you peanuts at the chaperones' table, Mr. H?"

Mr. Hewitt glanced up at Barry, seemingly unaware that he was eating peanuts at all. "Huh?" he said.

The song in the air ended, *Red Red Wine* giving way to a differ-

ent beat which Barry's body seemed to recognize. With his right
hand he knocked Silver on the shoulder like he was a pinball flipper.
"Wanna dance?" he asked, twitching toward the crowd.

Silver seized the moment. She yanked Fernanda's arm. "Hey, you guys, Barry wants us all to come dance." Barry pulled Silver from her chair; Silver, Fernanda; Fernanda grabbed Jarrett; and they flew onto the dance floor like a little chain of cartoon animals, airborne as a kite tail in their haste. Mr. Hewitt was left to his salted peanuts.

Everyone was dancing; Billy Idol roused even the most defiantly sedate promster. The four squeezed into the crowd and made a tight circle which felt to Silver like a doubles boxing match since someone had obviously tipped the boys off that if all dance techniques failed, they could do Rocky moves and no one would know the difference. Silver tried not to look at Barry or Jarrett, feigning instead what she hoped looked like a sort of music-infused trance, her energy concentrated in a white-girl overbite to let the world know she'd been transported by the song, but really, it was just not the kind of music that would inspire such blissed-out possession, and when Barry and Jarrett and the few hundred other sweaty teenagers joined in on the musical bridges like depraved football fans screaming "HEY HEY WHAT GET LAID GET FUCKED," it was simply impossible for Silver to maintain any sort of detached oblivion to the scene around her. It was all beginning to feel like her worst nightmare of a frat party—every reason she was getting the fuck out of Texas and coming to New York, where things were supposed to be different but, apparently, were not. Silver wanted *off* the dance floor.

Amid the frenzied, bouncing mob, Silver tried to catch Fernanda's eye but kept catching Barry's instead and then having to pretend she hadn't. Finally she just stepped across the circle and put her face to Fernanda's ear. "Bathroom," she shouted and then got mopped in the face by a carwash of thick, drenched-with-sweat hair as Fernanda nodded *yes* and stole Silver away from the crowd.

The ladies' room was not much roomier. A scantily ventilated cave crammed full of girls in bad dresses, it was the hang-out spot of the uncool, the dateless, and the dowdy, and it seemed to Silver

172

*Out
of the
Girls'
Room
and into
the Night*

that it was probably the place she most belonged at this entire affair: in the bathroom she saw the first outfits all night that bore even the tiniest twinge of color. These wallpaper girls were friendly, at least, smiling *hey* to Fernanda and introducing themselves to Silver right off the bat, like they were welcoming her into the clubhouse. Silver and Fernanda found a spot at the corner sink by the towel dispenser, and Fernanda pulled out a handful of paper towels and started blotting her face. Silver stuck her wrists under the faucet, looked in the mirror at Fernanda behind her, and wondered if it would be tactless to just demand an explanation about Mr. Hewitt. Fernanda read her thoughts.

"Oh," she said. "So Mr. . . ." and then she waved her hand to say, *yes I mean Hewitt, but there are too many ears here so I'll not use his name*. Silver turned off the water and Fernanda handed her a wad of fresh towels. "Jesus," Fernanda sighed, "it all goes so far back," and her voice was low, so Silver moved in closer to hear as Fernanda hoisted herself up to sit on the bank of sinks. "OK," she said again, "so I've been totally hot for him since like eighth grade. We had him for Life Science, or whatever you learn in eighth grade, and, I mean, you saw him—he's such a little hottie." Fernanda scowled then, as if it just made her crazy to admit how damned attractive she found him. "And I know everyone has the crush-on-the-teacher thing, whatever, but it wasn't like that. There was a *thing* with us. *Between* us, you know? We flirted. But not like teacher-and-student flirting, you know?" And though Silver wasn't sure she did know how else exactly a Neanderthal science teacher might flirt with a thirteen year old, she nodded anyway.

Fernanda lowered her voice conspiratorially. "Anyway, it goes on like that forever, Jarrett and whatever other guys in my life notwithstanding. And of course it gets more intense, you know, as time goes on, as I get older. It's like: once you've slept with *someone*, then the idea of sleeping with another someone just isn't such a big deal. And then once I'd slept with a couple people, you know, it was just like, OK, I want to sleep with Mr. Hewitt. Which is what it's all been about with him since fucking eighth grade."

Silver did a heavy-lidded blink, trying to convey shock. "You didn't."

"Ugh—I did." Fernanda's face broke in a guilty smile. "Three

weeks ago," she confided, like this was gossip about someone else
she was spreading, not her own life turning into tabloid before her
very eyes. "Barry had a party. Jarrett was away with his folks at some
family wedding something. Smith—Mr. Hewitt—he lives like a
block away from Barry." Silver must have looked kind of revolted
then, because all of a sudden Fernanda started trying to justify everything. "He's not total skeeze," she said. "It's not like he comes
to high school parties on a regular basis."

Silver was skeptical.

"No, no, I swear. He doesn't even come to Barry's ever. He just
came that night. He knew Jarrett was away."

Silver was barely hearing the details at this point; her brain was
still trying to make its way around the original fact. When she spoke
she could read her own lips in the mirror behind Fernanda's head.
"You slept with your Chemistry teacher."

"Ugh," Fernanda grunted, like she'd heard all the admonish-
ments before. "I know, I know, I know . . . But the thing is that
that's not it."

"What *else* did you do?" Silver said, unable to imagine at that
moment what else one *could* do.

"It's not what we *did*," Fernanda said, and Silver's relief was
nearly palpable. "It's just, he won't leave it there, you know? You'd
think it would be the other way around," Fernanda went on, "older
guy fucks younger girl and then blows her off while she gets stupid
and moony and decides she's in love, and he's the one, and yadda
yadda yadda. And, you know: whatever. It was fine. It was sex.
Whatever. But him—he's totally *gone*." Fernanda paused, as if to
let that sink in, but Silver didn't want to infer anything about what
"gone" meant until Fernanda clarified her terms. There were a lot
of ways one could interpret "gone." The whole thing was a bad TV
movie. Definitely one set in Texas.

"He calls my house," Fernanda said. "I had to tell my folks I was
on the fucking *prom committee* and he was the advisor! He leaves
letters in my locker, and they're all like: he's in love with me, he
wants to be with me, I shouldn't go away to college . . ."

"He said that?" Silver asked, incredulous.

174

*Out
of the
Girls'
Room
and into
the Night*

"In so many words," Fernanda said. "And it's like *he's* reassuring *me*—like I'm going to think he's bailing and he wants me to know that he's seriously in love with me. Like this is all completely his *real life*." She paused, almost out of breath. "I mean, what do I *do* with that?" she asked, and it was an earnest question, like she thought Silver might actually have a response.

The bathroom door swung open again with a blast of music that made Silver feel like she'd had a wad of cotton yanked out of her ears. "*. . . like no one else, ooh, ooh, she drives me crazy, I can't help myself, ooh, ooh . . .*" Some girl on her way into the bathroom had stopped in the threshold talking to someone in the hall, the door propped open on her taffeta hip. Suddenly Fernanda's expression went tight, eyes narrowed to charcoal slits. Outside, Mr. Hewitt stood with one shoulder resting lightly against the opposite wall, ostensibly engaged in conversation with the girl in the doorway, but his stare was trained directly past her and into the bathroom. Fernanda shook out her hair, gave him the cool angle of her profile, threw back her head and laughed and Silver thought: what you *do* is stop doing *that*.

In the mirror behind Fernanda, Silver could see the row of toilet stalls, a steady stream of girls in black trotting in and out, the metal hinge doors swinging open and shut, all of it flipping past like a game you can't quite stay on top of, a round of Three-Card Monty where everything's moving far too fast. And these girls—all of them, with their sly come-hither stares, their *you want me you come get me* looks, or that dead-on frozen glare that says *in your dreams, asshole*—they turn away then, out of the girls' room and into the night, and what they know, or don't know—and maybe that's the crux and the tragedy of it all right there—is that they may be saying *you piece of shit bastard you think you can fuck me*. But at the same time, they're saying *I'll let you*. In the same breath they're saying *you can*.

Free Writing

Sondra Spatt Olsen lives in New York City, where all her fiction takes place. Her stories have appeared in the Antioch Review, Iowa Review, Southwest Review, Indiana Review, Pleiades, Lilith, *and* Witness. *Since 1991 she has completed two story collections and a comic novel.*

"These stories describe with humor and illusionless generosity the urgency and volatility of our passions and the baffling constraints of the relationship within which our passions are expressed. They are alert to the embarrassments people seldom confess to, the tendency of emotion to attach itself to totally inappropriate objects, the shameless inconstancy of self-love."

MARILYNNE ROBINSON, 1991

September 28

What am I doing here, trapped in a grammar class? It would be worse if I weren't the teacher. Students bent over your ragged notebook paper, do you know who you are, and where we are going? Free writing means writing whatever comes into your head. Don't let those pencils slip off your damp little scraps. Don't stop; don't think. If you get blocked, just repeat the same words till you break through.

Free writing will set your creative juices flowing. That's what Mildred, Director of Composition, said. And even if it doesn't, it takes up ten minutes of this interminable remedial hour. Wastes ten minutes, that's what I say, me, Fortune's free-writing fool—eleven years of experience teaching my guts out, but not the Director of Composition, no, not me. Many are called but few are chosen. We also serve who only sit here till ten o'clock at night in this windowless building. Teaching the Unteachable. Reaching the Unreachable. It's OK if you really want to do it. But I don't really want to do it.

Must keep busy scribbling, though. Theme paper, smooth, white, available at any stationery store. It's the third night of the term, for god's sake, and how many students made it to a stationery store? Two out of twenty. My brain cells are popping one by one, and if I find free writing hard, how are you faring, poor bastards?

May Mildred be smashed with heavy thesauruses, smitten with semicolons, crushed by colons. If I get the chance, I'll wring her shallow chicken's neck. False, smug, self-righteous, hypocritical. Oh for a stream of icicles freezing her face! Oh dull housewife with a duplicating machine! She brags like a horse. She's teaching Romantic Poetry tonight in this very building, upstairs where there are snot-green industrial carpets, very chic, while I labor in a bare room, formerly an animal laboratory, drain in the middle of the floor, air conditioning booming off the formica like Victoria Falls.

I fancy I hear Mildred's grating voice through the ceiling, shredding the Odes. Faint melodies are sweet but those unheard are sweeter. I fast, I faint, I die, I try. If you don't like my harmonica, don't blow it. If you don't like my harmonica, don't blow it.

Stop this nonsensical parody of the only world the world has ever known. Get on with your class, Miss Thirty-Two-Year-Old Free Writer. Start the semicolons rolling.

September 30

Now, ladies and gentlemen, ten minutes ago I was crying in the toilet of the East Science Facility. Would that interest you if you knew it? Spinster schoolteacher, tough old birdy, meets long-lost lover in dim corridors of the East Science Facility. Almost knocks him over, in fact, since she, always buxom, has gotten very tubby in her loneliness and frustration, and he, always on the small side, has gotten weedy thin in whatever sick situation he's creating nowadays. Separation obviously isn't good for either of these birds, but after two years do they fall into each other's arms and cuddle, crying, "Well-met, well-met," all hugs and kisses and echoes of old ecstasies?

No, sirs and mesdames, they are cold. "How are you, Ivor?" Cold, cold. "Teaching one course while working on your dissertation?" Fine, good. Still working on your bloody dissertation. Too much screwing; one's vital juices stop flowing. (You told me *I* was preventing you from finishing your dissertation, dog, remember?)

"You, Helaine? Still working on your novel?" Sure, pal, would you like to see it? I've got it here in my back pocket. Just dash it off by candlelight after teaching four overcrowded composition courses. A chapter a day keeps the doctor away. Beats masturbation.

Do we exchange confidences? Relive old frolics? Review lusty quarrels and juicy brawls? No, we chat coldly. You look as distinguished as ever, Ivor. Do you still wear tattered underwear? Still shower with a cap on, like a girl? Still thrash around in your bed like a sardine? Publish essays in the *Pisspot Review*?

Perhaps you saw me crying, sisters. Through the mile-wide crack in the toilet door. I was in the cubicle that locks, sobbing into the corrugated toilet paper. I saw you, Charlene, standing in the spot of peril by the mirror (miraculous gray hair detector), getting cracked by the door each time it opened. You gave me a searching anthropologist's look. Some tribes would rather be seen peeing than crying. I pretended to have a heavy cold, my stiff upper lip like a handball court.

Oh Ivor, why didn't you just put your hand on my cheek and say, "There, there, old duck. If you lose some weight, you can hold out another fifty years?" Or why didn't I just silently kiss your hand?

We want to be happy, but how are we going to do it? My class wants to be happy, but how are they going to do it? We want to be loved, but how are we going to do it?

These questions ask themselves.

October 5

Awake, sluggards! Cast off your multiple choice exams. Throw your textbooks out the window. (But there are no windows here—no matter.) Anoint yourselves with salad oil. Put on your royal bathrobes; the feast of meaningless mistakes is about to begin.

How I wish I had a little cookie to nibble on, meanwhile. To compose myself as I compose. Make little announcements. See all those sleeping, swaying heads bounce up.

"Class, I'm taking next week off to be with my lover. We're locking ourselves in the slop closet with a twelve-pack.

"I'm planning to set myself afire. Forget about the theme paper. Please bring unleaded gasoline.

"No, better, I'm planning to set your assignments afire. If you want the ashes, you must give me a stamped, self-addressed envelope by Thursday night."

Peter Heinz is absent tonight. Peter Heinz is absent; so is José Pereirra and John Incremona. I don't think you can pass the course, young man. Why not, sir or madame? Because you're stupid.

Where is my plagiarist? There he is, slumped in the back row under the coats. A weedy blond. Butter wouldn't melt the scoundrel. Did he think that I'd believe those fine, sensitive moments occurred in *his* childhood? And that sublime final image, the blue rubber ball disappearing into the cloudless sky never to be seen again. A bit of poetry in English 1.5. David Gold with the golden hair. A long history of thievery, I'll wager. Absent from the first impromptu essay, clever dog, and planning to be absent from all future impromptus. A strong, solid style, a little better than Orwell's. A maniac's handwriting. Absurd technical errors (like missing capitals) unimaginatively sprinkled here and there. I'll track this plagiarist down if it's the last thing I do. Catch him inky-fingered. Nail him at the Xerox. I will not be tricked by a stripling. I'll try Orwell first. Haunt the libraries. Leave no stack unturned.

"How pleasant it is at the end of the day / No follies to have to repent / But reflect on the past and be able to say / My time has been properly spent."

October 7

Full Professor, step right in; take a seat in the back. My guardian and my observer, observe me, yes. An amazing display of talent— no relaxation but lots of nervous tension and anxiety to make you feel at home. I'd strip myself naked for you, Stranger, but how will you get it in your Evaluation Report?

"We generally do ten minutes of free writing right at the start to let the creative juices flow, heh, heh, heh."

Such tact! Such wit! Fly with me to the blackboard and see how we go. The true thrill—grade a paper with me. Watch me stalk sentence fragments, pounce on wordy constructions, disport myself

among awkward tenses, linger on those everloving concrete details.
I want to caution you about one thing, however. I always put ob-
servers on my Death List.

He looks pretty bored, my keen observer, lolling in the back row,
playing with his pencil. No learning takes place here, Buster. Why
don't you try an auto school?

October 14

Walking to school from the bus stop today—unspeakable happiness. I floated! I sang! And why?

Because David Gold is alive. He walks, he talks, he exists on this
planet. He is sitting before me now, holding his head in his hands,
not free writing a bit. All I can see is a grubby green sleeve and some
golden hair.

Dear boy. You are my booster cable. I thought my heart had gone
dead long ago, but for good or bad, you recharged it for me.

It was his turn for a conference. He sat sideways by my desk, with
his lanky legs folded twice over, staring at the blackboard. He had
been late; he didn't seem to be listening. I couldn't mention his
plagiarism until I had some evidence, and in my frustration I let my
contempt show too plainly.

"Losing that rubber ball must have left a big hole in your life,"
said I scornfully. "Do you always omit capital letters at the beginning of sentences, or do you do it just for me? Have you ever
thought of attending Handwriting School?"

He looked straight at me for the first time, flushing, and one
bright tear rolled out of one eye. At that moment the rest of the
class came piling into the room. "I'll talk to you about this later," I
said, turning toward the others. "We're going to write impromptu
tonight," I told them impulsively.

They shrank back with well-known groaning noises. "It's not
fair. . . ." "Why didn't you tell us?"

"Then it wouldn't be impromptu." I smiled encouragingly.

"Don't be afraid. It's only one paragraph." Only your native language. I hurriedly wrote a topic on the board.

Meanwhile David moved back to his seat, turned his plastic chair
around to the wall, tucked his head down to his chest, and sat in

that furious hidden posture until I called for their work. All the while I sat there, watching him, half-suspecting his paper was going to be blank.

As soon as the classroom was safely cleared, I plucked his impromptu from the pile. One and a half closely scribbled sheets. Describe a concrete object concretely. Almost impossible for a remedial student. I was a sadist to assign it.

David described his Harley-Davidson so crisply I could see it shining before me on the sidewalk. (Still no capitals, but editors can always fix up that sort of thing.) I thought—perhaps he had this magnificent paragraph up his sleeve, would have written about motorcycles no matter what the topic. Perhaps he had assorted plagiarisms stuffed in all the pockets of his jeans. Then I remembered the single rolling tear and his scarlet, vulnerable face, the fury in his hunched-over neck. I read the paragraph again, savoring it. I felt an unfamiliar yet well-known stirring in my chest. (All great things are clichés.) I felt joy swelling up, or perhaps it was pain. Felt something, anyway, instead of dead. I remembered the last time I felt my heart move. I was sitting in the front seat of Ivor's car, parked for a long time in the snow. "You don't seem to understand. I'll put it more plainly," he said. "I don't want to see you anymore."

I will purify myself for David's sake. I will better my life. David Gold exists. For no other reason, I rejoice.

October 19

A class of five. Five little blackbirds sitting on a branch. My brilliant one is not among them.

George, your work has not been good. Achilles, your work has not been good. Everyone else, your work has not been good.

Nobody's work is any good. Except for my darling.

I had today:

2 cups coffee with real milk
1 toast with diet butter
1 midget bagel with peanut butter
1 cup Bran Buds with skim milk
1 roast beef sandwich with lettuce & tomato & a cup of tea

That's not too much. A penitential menu. When I come home, I
will have:

   1 cup decaffeinated coffee with real milk
   1 piece of deskinned chicken, broiled

That will truly be delicious. That's not asking too much. Who am
I to ask too much?

He has a girlfriend. How could I have not noticed it? She waits
for him every Tuesday and Thursday evening right outside in the
hallway beside the elevator. She is short, size three, I'd say, young
and nondescript. When he emerges, she falls comfortably into place
at his side like his hunting dog, and the elevator closes slowly upon
them. They never speak. They are shy. Their utterances are too sig-
nificant for the general public. She is a deaf mute. How will I ever
know what the answer is? Why do I want to know in the first place?

They are probably necking in the backseat of a car right now, her
head pillowed on his grammar. No, I am hopelessly outdated. They
are screwing.

I am glad he has a girlfriend. I am glad he is screwing.

Face it, Helaine. Don't be a fraud. It's not just that he is a fine
student with a good mind whom I will be glad to recommend for
the Nobel Prize. Not that he's shy and humiliated and at my mercy.
He also has rosy skin and long muscular legs in tight pants. He is a
beautiful, desirable young man. And I desire him.

October 21

All you can eat and doughnuts, too. A steaming cup of hot coffee
and a cracker. A bowl of chili, reddening your mouth. Plenty of
fresh milk and cookies. Sesame crackers and small kegs of beer.
Tree-ripened pears with russet flecks on them. Cider and doughnuts. Hot tomato soup with six oyster crackers tumbling on the
surface. A bacon, lettuce, and tomato sandwich crunching crisp, especially the lettuce. No soggy greens, please. Two mugs of fresh
coffee with cream. A peppermint stick ice cream cone. Twelve cinnamon buns with jelly inside. A hogshead of cream cheese, one-half
pound smoked Scotch salmon, and two dozen bagels. Chilled cav-
iar, black ripe Greek olives. Dainty little cucumber sandwiches with

the crusts cut off. Rum mulled with cider. A barrel of pickled herring with fresh onion curls. Carrot sticks as a refreshment. Cold Heineken beer, oysters, beets with pickles, a bit of salami and cold tongue on fresh bakery rolls with onion and a quarter pound of sweet butter. Freshly scrambled eggs and toast and a very tiny little bit of ketchup. I give up all of these for you, my chicken.

October 26

I can't help thinking someone is out to get me.

Could it be me? Am I out to get me?

This time I arranged our conference better. Little seminar room not used at this hour. Thirty minutes before class time so we won't be interrupted. I have emptied my papers on the table to give the little cell a homier look. I have muted the air conditioning. I have put his last essay with a big red A in magic marker on top of the pile. Everything to put him at his ease.

He is not at his ease. He does have a pleasant sweet odor about him, which I can't quite place. He has crossed his legs more gracefully this time, but he's still looking at me as though I'm about to take a bite from his rosy flesh. He thinks I am a meat-eating dinosaur—ferocious Tyrannosaurus rex—when I am really a shy, lovesick Brontosaurus—huge vegetarian with a marshmallow heart.

"You are a talented writer," I begin. "What are you doing in this remedial class?"

"I failed the proficiency exam. Do you think I'm taking this class for fun?" He is still angry with me. He speaks in a thin, waspish, bratty young man's voice. "I failed it three times, if you want to know."

I try not to be insulted. I hate English 1.5, too, so why should I be insulted? Am I teaching it for fun? "You must get terrifically nervous, then," I say kindly.

"I don't know."

"Well, there must be something on your mind when you take the exam."

" I think it's because my mother works here."

Oh, I think. I visualize the refugee daughter of a great philosopher, scrubbing floors in the library. Blond braids pinned upon aris-

tocratic head. All hopes pinned on her son. "Does your mother
expect you to do very well? Is that why you're nervous?"

"*You* know my mother. She teaches in this department." A petu-
lant smile tweaks his mouth for an instant before he drops his dy-
namite. "Mildred Gold." Director of Composition. Administrator
of proficiency exams.

The son of Mildred. In a flash I understand everything. Omis-
sion of capital letters is, after all, a reasonable act for the son of
Mildred. He does pretty much what he wants. Revenge is his rea-
son for living. Does poorly in school because it irritates her. Is lazy.
Has gotten everything he's ever wanted. Psychologically unsteady.
Poor boy.

Also oddly, in the same flash I understand something about myself. Humiliation is the root of the attraction, but it's *my* humiliation, not his. Humiliating for a grown woman to care about a boy.
And now that I know whose boy it is . . . I feel self-disgust oozing up.

He lives in the home of my enemy. Empties her garbage. Shovels
the snow on her front walk. Walks her poodle. I've lost all respect
for myself. How can I care for the fetcher and carrier of Mildred's
petty household domain? Her bootblack.

He was once a speck in her ovaries; he passed down through her
birth canal, squeezing her bladder. She wiped his baby ass for him,
and he vomited over her when he was sick. These sordid custodial
details notwithstanding, he now has the power to hurt me, that is,
I now love him desperately. I am helpless and angry, but my fine old
poker face does not betray me. From outside I appear calm and be-
neficent, not even very much surprised.

"It must be hard for you to study a subject your mother teaches,
in a program she directs. Why don't you switch to another school?"

"She won't allow it. It's inconvenient."

"What about your father?"

"My stepfather. He does whatever she wants. She's a very powerful woman."

Admiring (spurious) smile on both our faces. Mildred. What do
I really know about her? She is always rallying others to her causes.
Collecting money for the Big Chairman's wedding present (third
marriage, why bother?). Appeals and posters clutter her office.

Sauvez les Trésors de la Nubie. Rettet die Schatze aus Nubien. Salvad los Tresoros de Nubia. Prevent new coal gasification plants in Navajo Territory. Save our Football Field. Ban the Bomb. Robert Frost's sappy face beams over her shoulder. None of this good work seems native to her. Everything's a front. She works hard to seem good-natured. Her hostile, stupid eyes twinkle from behind her aviator frames. For some reason, she hates me.

"I could speak to her about it. You really don't belong in a remedial class. You must know it."

He gives me a blank look. A marble-eyed look of elegant Greek statues. Antinoüs, the Emperor's favorite, whom I also fell for once at Olympia.

"Of course, I'm very glad to have you in my class," I say warmly. "I like brilliant people."

Whatever made me think he was diffident? He accepts my declaration with bland indifference. His royal due. "I was thinking of going out west," he remarks.

"Next summer?"

"Next month."

"Oh, please, David. Don't do anything precipitously."

"I'm going by motorcycle. If I go, I have to do it before it's too cold."

"Does your mother know about this?"

He gives me an "Are you kidding?" look.

"How are you doing in your other courses?"

He looks pleased. Glad I asked. "I'm failing two, math and sociology, and an A-plus so far in the other, in Ivor Braun's class. He wants me to major in Comparative Literature. And I don't know about your class."

"C," I say, just to shake his self-image a little. Exactly like Ivor to give out A-pluses at midterm, then let you down hard at the end with a B. Did the same to me once. "You deserve an A, David, for content and general style, and an F, of course, for punctuation. But if you sat down for twenty minutes and read your grammar book . . . Why didn't your mother tell me about your problem? I see her every day."

"She wants me to be independent."

"I'll bet."

I say it out loud, sarcastically. He doesn't flinch. He doesn't blush. His eyes are green and filled with contact lenses. I hate to mention how long his eyelashes are.

"Don't speak to her about it, please," he says seriously. "Just pass me. That's all I need."

"How old are you, David?"

"Twenty-one." He grins, ashamed.

"So old?" Only eleven years between us. Dr. Johnson's wife was at least twenty years older. He was inconsolable when she died, but kept right on writing his dictionary.

"I dropped out once before, when I was in high school." He leans forward a little, as if telling a secret. I'm enjoying his lovely fragrance. "My mother got me a job with Scribner's, as an office boy."

I think more about Mildred, what it must be like to live under her benevolent direction. I can't imagine what it must be like.

Mildred wears a lot of makeup. She articulates poorly. One of her mimeographed notices began, "Due to a lack of examination booklets. . . ." I guess you could say she is vulgar for an academic or academic for a vulgarian. She takes a housewifely interest in paper clips, envelopes, and exam books. She is the chatelaine of the supply closet.

At the end of each semester, Mildred collects a set of essays from one student, chosen at random from each class. They must be submitted in a lightweight, soft-covered binder with metal fasteners. She reads through the papers and makes some trenchant comment. Last term mine said, "Fine!" The semester before that, there was no exclamation point, so I guess I've improved. A few years ago, I taught Creative Writing, which I rather enjoyed, but Mildred thinks I do better with Composition. "We need good people in Remediation," she said good-naturedly. She likes to be chummy. When I stopped seeing Ivor, she said, "I see you've stopped seeing Ivor." When I lost the office key, she said, "Do try and be more careful with this one. I know you're an artist and have published a book, and all that, but . . ."

It's 9:30. The class is looking at me a little bit cross-eyed; they're tired of writing. David is smiling at me from way back there, flirtatiously peeking at me from under his hands. It's a kind of sweet blackmailing smile, a buddylike smile, most unsuitable for student-teacher relationships. I know you know I'm a gem, that smile says. I've revealed my true identity, like Billy Batson. What are you going to do for me now?

I will close up shop. One final thought occurs to me: the ultimate humiliation. That pleasant, sweet odor I liked so much was, oh help, bubblegum.

October 28

Tonight an unusual show: Ivor and David together. Standing together at the front of the lunchroom, they canceled out each other's good looks. Ivor, of course, seemed much older; next to David's bright head his gray hairs suddenly stuck out stiffly, like brush bristles. He seemed worn, stained, as though seen through a muddy filter. David, on the other hand, without Ivor's authority, looked white and pasty, like a pie taken out of the oven too soon.

I had a clear view but couldn't hear at all. They seemed to be speaking pleasantly enough, but urgently. Why were they all standing up? This was no passing chatter. At one point David thrust out his hands in the incongruous shrug of a Yiddish peddler. He couldn't account for something. What the hell was it? I was torn by curiosity but kept flicking my eyes back and forth mock-casually and, desperate to see, purposely blocked my vision with my upthrust coffee cup. It occurred to me, as it often does, that someone else in the lunchroom might be watching me. I determined to betray nothing to the unknown watcher but felt on reflection that I must look like a frantic bunny, my head swiveling, eyes swimming, my mouth still chewing wildly my already swallowed food. But of course there was no one looking and nothing to be seen.

Oh yes, I forgot to mention that David's girl was present throughout the colloquy, standing silently at his elbow. She impressed me as usual as being very short (She always seems only to come up to David's elbow. His elbow stands out in these scenes), very dowdy, and vaguely nice. Naturally I never focus on her, as my eyes are engaged elsewhere. I would not recognize her alone.

When the conversation, which took about three minutes, was over, David and the girl walked briskly out of the lunchroom. Now something strange happened, which I have read about in books but never experienced before. Either David put his arm around her as she trotted along at his elbow or else he didn't. I, an alert type, watching with the fixed seriousness of a U.N. observer, am uncertain. Perhaps they flowed along so smoothly, so adhesively that it looked as though they were connected by an arm, and I seized on this false dramatic detail to remember. Or perhaps there was an arm, and even as I looked at it (this is what I have read about in books), I was unwilling to see it.

November 4

I am not even on campus. I am on Main Street in front of the public library, at least three miles away, when I hear the zoom of a motorcycle. The chances that this will be David are 7,000 to 1, but these days I am thrown into a frenzy by the sight of any motorcycle. It's the ambiguous figure of the helmeted, goggled rider that throws me—the masked rider of the plains. This time the figure I imagine is David *is* David. It must be, because the rider in back is Mildred.

The bike pulls up to the curb for a moment, and she hops off, spry as you please in her denim pantsuit. She's a pretty high kicker for a woman her age; you have to give her credit. Goes to the health club three times a week and steams herself to a pulp. Takes yoga, too. I saw her chuffing away in the lunchroom once, noisily demonstrating how to expel poisonous, used-up air from the lungs. She sent a little poisonous stream my way.

As David roars off, I try melting back against the library wall, but she's spotted me. She hails me excitedly. I wonder whether to bring up David's problems, but, as usual, subtlety is not a requisite with Mildred.

"Well, are you going to pass him?" she asks.

"Mildred," I say diffidently. "Why don't you send your son to another school? It can't be good for him to study under your shadow, so to speak."

Her powerful carbon-arc eyes shoot me a furious look through her glasses, but her mouth continues smiling benevolently. "He's not failing, is he?"

"Mildred," I begin again, "I won't fail him unless he forces me to do it. The trouble is—he's stopped doing his assignments. How can I pass him if he doesn't write anything?"

"Well, I thought if anybody could handle him, you could, Helaine. I can't make him write. I haven't been able to make him do anything since he was toilet trained." She laughs raucously. "What he does and when he does it are a mystery to me. He has his own apartment over the garage. He has his own transportation, his own stereo. You don't know what it's like to have a teenage son these days."

"If David doesn't like college work, maybe he should just be cut loose. He's not really a teenager anymore, is he?"

Mildred is really furious with me now. Or is she in pain? Her face has creased badly in a spasm of some emotion; it's hard for me to tell.

"We've tried that already. He quit a good job in publishing to work at a soda fountain."

The image of David in the guise of a soda jerk is as painful to me as it is to Mildred, but for different reasons. Perhaps he has waited on me in a comic-book cap, and I've thought him negligible.

"Helaine, Davey is beyond my control. That's what I'm trying to tell you. How will he get along without his diploma? He can't stay in my garage forever. And he used to be such a bright, cheerful kid." Mildred's voice is breaking. She is actually weeping, her eyes glazed over. She is metamorphosing before my eyes from department tyrant to bereaved parent, and I resent it. Dammit, Mildred, stop sniveling. Stalin worried about his teenagers, too, perhaps.

November 9

He did not come for our conference tonight. He did not give me any assignments. He entered the room all tousled, rain-bedraggled, his jeans soaked up to the knee. Perhaps he'd been stuck on the highway. "David," I called out cheerfully. "You look as though you waded to class." He stalked past my desk, avoiding my eyes.

I rather expected it. Screw you, he's saying. You claim to be my admirer and friend. Prove it. Pass me no matter what I do. Fail me, and I'll go west. Go ahead, wreck my academic career.

I had a fantasy about him the other night. A daydream, that is, I was controlling it. I dreamed he came to my apartment for tea. I dusted especially for him. I bought two cakes from the Dumas Pâtisserie, and I took my Tabriz carpet out of hock.

He brought grass, special high-quality Acapulco Gold, and we sat on the carpet, sharing a joint. In my dream he wore a fuzzy woolen sweater of an unusual orange, something pumpkinlike but more pleasant. All colors were sharp because of the imaginary grass, and I felt myself leaning imperceptibly toward him, till I felt the sweater fuzz against my bare neck. We were listening to Chopin, *Valse Brilliante.*

You think this was prelude to an erotic fantasy? He stroked my neck, I slowly unbuttoned my blouse, my nipples popped out, he unzipped his pants. You are wrong, quite wrong. You know me very little. In my dream I never forgot he was David. In my dream we simply sat in a deep passionate calm; Artur Rubinstein was doing all the work. Then David said solemnly, "Thank you, Helaine, for a very happy moment. Don't get up; stay with the music." He left the package of grass on the table and went away, and I never saw him again.

November 16

He is absent again. He is not here tonight. He is absent again. He is not here tonight.

Freewriting freewriting freewriting because I'm so afraid. I have to hold my face together.

She came in, the girl, just now while I was writing, and said, "Here are David Gold's assignments. He's sorry they're so late."

I stare at her. "Where is David?"

"He said please excuse the handwriting. He was nervous; he had to write them on his wedding day."

"His wedding day!"

She giggles. "We were married this morning at City Hall and tomorrow, if he finishes his paper for Comp. Lit., we're going to California." She giggles again, a cheerful young girl.

I stare at her harder. She looks wholesome, a nice friendly face, too nice for him. She's wearing a useful gray jumper. She should be wearing alençon lace with a bouquet of stephanotis and sweet peas. From the back of a motorcycle she hurls her bouquet.

I hold the envelope steadily in my hand. "You're going by motorcycle?"

"No, by plane. His mother gave us the tickets as a wedding present. We were going to go at Christmas, but we decided not to wait."

The people in the front row have stopped writing and are looking at us curiously. Up till now I have never let anyone, not even my observer, interrupt my free writing.

"Now that he is up to date . . ." She has a soft voice. Her enunciation is very good. "David wants to know, can you please give him an Incomplete grade? We'll be back next semester."

The result of this question is that I begin shaking from the waist down at my desk, as if I have palsy. My legs are trembling so violently, I have to keep shuffling my feet, as though something unpleasant has stuck to my shoes. I can also feel myself blushing, but to my astonishment, the girl doesn't notice a thing. Of course. The desk has a little skirt around it for modesty's sake.

"Why doesn't David come and ask me himself?"

"He can't. He's writing this paper for Comp. Lit. And I think he's embarrassed."

Now that I look at her, I recognize her from the front desk of the library. She has checked me out many times. I wish to say, "It is highly irregular to give the grade of Incomplete except in cases of serious illness or a death in the family," but the words seem like bullets, and I can't mouth them. Instead I put the envelope in my briefcase, and I nod, smiling. I clear my throat, I croak a little, I say, "Have a good time." As she exits, smiling, I see she is taller than I had thought. I still don't know her name.

This happened one minute ago. I already feel a little remote from it. I am planning to resume my normal life. My mouth has already frozen back to its normal shape. My legs have stopped trembling. No one could tell how I feel.

How I wish I could start all over again as a tadpole. Something small swimming around in a sea. Something squirreling along.

I don't know what to do. I don't know what to say. I don't know where to go. The door is blank. The wall is blind. The floor has a drain.

The mouse lurks in the pantry. Garbage roots in the backyard. Birds fly in the circular sky.

Don't relax for a minute. Make sure you sleep at night. Give a knock if you exist. No knock if you don't. Nod your head if you can breathe. Forget me. Forget me not.

November 18

Another opening, another show.

Another opening, another show. Another opening, another show.

Another opening, another show. Another opening, another show.

Another opening, another show. Another opening. Another show.

The Oracle

*Elizabeth Oness directs marketing and developing for Sutton Hoo Press, a
literary fine press. Her stories have received numerous honors including an
O. Henry Prize and a Nelson Algren Award. She is at work on a novel.*

"Elizabeth Oness's Articles of Faith *has a strange and amazing range: her
work is impressive for what it risks, and even more for what it achieves. . . .
Oness is a tremendous and heartfelt and gutsy writer."*
ELIZABETH MCCRACKEN, 2000

I'd been home, out of college, only a few hours; I hadn't even un-
packed the car, when my mother told me that she had met someone. He's a dentist, she said, and he's been saved.

"Saved from what?" I opened the refrigerator to survey its contents. Whenever I came home from school, the abundance of her
refrigerator amazed me. At school, the staples in our refrigerator
were ketchup, mustard, and beer.

"Saved?" I prompted her.

"Philip, don't be smart," she said.

"No, really, what brand of Christian is he?"

"Oh, I know it doesn't matter to you. But he told me about it
on our first date, how everything's changed for him, how he gets
along with his ex-wife now, and how he really feels like he's helping
people, much more than fixing their teeth." She smiled a little as
she repeated his happiness.

I had noticed a difference in her at graduation, but I thought it was
relief that I'd made it through college unscathed. She seemed more
relaxed, less precise. She no longer moved things and straightened
them when she talked, a habit she picked up, or maybe I only noticed
it, the year my father died. After the first months of mourning I
waited for her to break out of herself, to become less restrained, but

she continued in much the same way. She was a pretty woman with a

small, square jaw, and long brown hair just starting to turn gray. Every year she asked if she should cut it, and every year I said no.

"Mom, I think you're in love," I said.

"Oh, I'm not," she smiled as she denied it, then set the plate she was holding back in the dishwasher.

"You don't even know if you're loading or unloading." I took the clean plate from the rack. "So he's divorced. Does he have kids?"

"He has a fourteen-year-old daughter who's just started to live with him again," she said. "And he's having a cookout tomorrow. He asked if you'd come, he wants to meet you."

Whenever she was flustered, my mother inspected some insignificant object as if its stillness would steady her. She examined the calendar on the kitchen wall as if it were new. I walked over and hugged her; she felt smaller, her rib cage like a brittle basket. I squeezed her lightly and released her. She looked up at me, reassured, and smiled.

The following night, on the way to his house, I tried to get her to describe Hal. She blushed and said I would meet him myself. It was strange to see my mother fidgety over a man. As far as I knew, in the years since my father's death, she had never even been out on a date. Of course her friends encouraged her to get out more, meet someone else, but she always refused. This devotion to the memory of my father was antiquated, probably even wrong, but my mother would not be pressed about things she didn't want to do. She had the ability to summon a formality that kept people from pressing her further. We drove through a wooded development, winding down smoothly paved roads with those peculiarly feminine suburban names: Natalie Court, Caroline Lane. We finally stopped in front of a large, modern house. Wind chimes hung from a Japanese maple in the yard. A slender window divided the house; starting by the front door, it rose up to the second story. Hal opened the door before my mother had a chance to knock.

"Hello, Deirdre." He kissed her on the cheek and turned to me.

"Philip, it's a pleasure. I've heard a lot about you." He shook my hand firmly. It was a humid day, but Hal seemed freshly scrubbed, as if he'd just stepped out of the shower. His light crewcut was edged with gray; his blue eyes were pale-lashed, rimless. A large gap separated his two front teeth. No wonder he was a dentist.

We walked through the house, which shone with polished wood floors and sleek, modern furniture, and into the kitchen, where the back wall, almost entirely glass, looked onto a lush backyard. Hal guided my mother through the doors, placing his palm against the small of her back. His fingers were short and thick. Peasant hands, my father would have called them. He started to lead us down to a small group of people standing around the grill when a young woman, dressed entirely in black, walked over.

"Philip, this is my daughter Megan," Hal said.

It didn't seem possible she was only fourteen. I was careful with my eyes; I tried to stare only at her face.

She smiled briefly and brushed her hair from her cheek. A clutter of black plastic bracelets and silver chains slid down her arm.

"Philip just graduated from University of Virginia," Hal told her.

"How impressive." She wrinkled her nose at me.

Hal looked uncomfortable.

"Deirdre, you look nice." Megan kissed the air near my mother's cheek. Her lips puckered, then relaxed into their fullness. It wasn't your usual fourteen-year-old gesture. I later came to associate those airy kisses with girls I'd known in college—when I ran into them many years later. Women I'd never touched would greet me with that pressure on the arm, a softness aimed at my ear.

"Would anyone like a drink?" Megan asked.

"I'd love a beer," I said.

Megan went into the house and my mother and Hal joined the group at the grill. I lingered awkwardly, waiting for Megan. She returned with two tall-neck beers and nodded at our parents.

"Well, what do you think?" she asked.

"About what?"

"About them." She gazed at me, unblinking. She had light gray eyes, darker near the pupils. She seemed to be deciding if I was playing dumb. "They really like each other," she said. "My father keeps hinting they might get married."

"I just got back yesterday." I wanted to defend my ignorance.

"I'm trying to take it all in." Then cautiously I said, "My mother
says your dad's been saved."

She snorted and looked across the lawn at Hal, who was talking to his friends, one arm gesturing, the other around my mother's shoulders. Megan took a long drink of beer. I wondered if he let her drink or if she was just showing off.

"Yeah, he's been saved all right," she said.

"What about you, have you been saved?"

"Hell no," Megan laughed.

"What do you believe in?"

"Oh, I don't know." She twisted up her mouth, chewing on the inside of her cheek. Her hesitation made her seem closer to her age.

"What do you believe in?" she asked.

"Elliott's," I said.

"What?"

"Elliott's Apple Juice. It has little quotations written on the inside of the caps."

She shook her head.

"I meditate for an hour every morning before I choose my first bottle." I leaned closer, lowered my voice. "I believe in the cosmic synchronicity of my choosing a particular quotation. I live every day by the wisdom inside a bottle cap—unless I drink two bottles; then I have to change my whole philosophy in the middle of the day."

She laughed, then looked at me sideways to make sure I was kidding.

"It's as good a thing to believe in as any, I suppose." She looked out over the yard. She was one of those girls who tried to look bad, but couldn't really pull it off. Her hair was cut in bangs and fell just below her ears, a stylish cap of dark hair that showed off her long neck. She affected the attitude of a streetwise flapper, but her face gave her away. Her cheeks were slightly round, childlike; she had a sprinkling of freckles. Megan. It was hard to be tough with a name like that. Her black T-shirt, cut wide and ragged around the neck and cropped along the bottom, ended a few inches below her breasts and stayed out there, not tucked into anything. I wanted to slide my hand up underneath it.

"I have to make a phone call." She turned abruptly and walked toward the house.

My mother introduced me to the other guests. We listened to a tall woman with waving arms tell an elaborate story that turned out to be a movie plot. A man in camouflage pants talked to Hal about target practice and a new rifle he'd bought. I ate food as it was handed to me. I was aware of the dark smell of charcoal, Megan's bare shoulders, scents of dark and light circulating through the blue evening. Hal worked his way around to my mother and me.

"So you had a chance to talk to Meg?" he asked.

"Yes," I said. "She seems quite grown up."

Hal looked at me hard, trying to decide what I meant.

"I hear you did well at school, magna cum laude. Maybe you can encourage Megan. She's bright, but she doesn't apply herself."

I nodded and tried to look understanding. He was reminding me of her youth. I was afraid whatever I said would be wrong.

Later, as my mother prepared to leave, I watched Hal draw her over to him, circling his arm around her waist, so that both of them could wish his friends good-bye.

"Did you have a good time?" Megan's question startled me.

"Not exactly my type of party," I said.

"What is your type of party?" Her voice was low, flirtatious.

"I don't know." I stumbled, afraid her father would hear her tone if not her words.

"Well, I'm sure we'll be seeing each other again." She looked at me, wide-eyed, from under her bangs.

Washington, D.C., was a tropical city in the summer. The sky could threaten rain all day, and after it finally poured, the air was still thick and hot. I spent that summer working on my résumé, studying the classifieds, and meeting with alumni who worked for companies I might be interested in. I felt like I was moving into a borderless cloud. I drank apple juice, hoping for clues to my future. In my cap one day:

> There is only one success—to be able to spend your life in your own way.
>
> —Christopher Morley

I had no idea what my own way was. I went out at night with

friends who were in the same postgraduation haze. I read the *Washington Post* completely, every morning, as if one day I would find in its pages the exact thing I was meant to do. I thought about Megan almost constantly. I tried not to. I thought about her when I woke early in the summer heat, filled with the shadows of my dreams. I thought about her at night, too: her mouth, the way she put a bottle to her lips. I tried to imagine living in the same house with her. I imagined her getting out of the shower, walking past my room in a towel, wet.

My mother occasionally asked about girls I'd gone out with at college, but her questions were random; she might have been asking about a professor, or a difficult course I'd taken. I assumed she didn't want to know anything too specific, my answers might embarrass her, so she ironed my shirts and asked about my interviews, which weren't real interviews at all, but a series of talks with men who had established specific places for themselves in the world. I looked forward to weekends, when I wouldn't have to answer her questions; but when I woke up alone, sunlight filling my room, the house silent below me, it seemed that Hal had everything in that glassed-in house several miles away: he and my mother eating brunch in the kitchen, Megan upstairs sleeping late. I imagined her face, flushed with sleep and creased a little from the pillow, her smooth hair awry. I wanted her before she put on her grown-up edginess; I imagined her arms around my neck, how she would curl her long legs around mine. I tried to picture exactly what she looked like under those flimsy clothes, and I lay in bed for what seemed like hours, wondering whether she was a virgin or not. I fantasized until I exhausted myself. Then I slept, and when I woke, I tried to think of how I would distract myself for the rest of the day.

One Saturday morning my mother called from Hal's and asked me to dinner. I'd just gotten up and I stood in the kitchen, listening to her on the phone while I waited for the coffee to finish dripping. It was strange to be invited to another man's house by my mother. Driving over that night, I thought about Hal; my opinion of him shifted slightly each time we met. That night he seemed confident, self-sufficient, but there was an odd difference between him and my

mother, as if they were the right and left shoes of a slightly mismatched pair. Hal insisted on cooking, as if his kitchen wasn't my
mother's territory yet. When he moved around the table serving us, I
watched his reflection in the large window. He was substantial,
squarely built—each of his polo shirts was the exact same tightness
across his chest—but he seemed like a pasty shadow superimposed
over my memory of my father, a dark, transparent man of air.

Megan hurried into the kitchen and grabbed an apple off the
counter. She wore a short black skirt, high-topped sneakers, and a
long T-shirt. She moved as if she hadn't grown into her body yet.

"What's the hurry?" Hal asked.

"I told you, I'm going to the movies with Jill."

Hal stopped for a moment, holding a dripping spoon above
a pan.

"I asked you last week. It's *Gone with the Wind*." Megan's tone
was highly reasonable, as if she were talking to a child. "We went
through the whole thing about how it's a long movie, remember?"

Hal smiled, but his tolerance seemed strained.

"What about dinner?"

"Mmm, lasagna. Save some for me. Don't let Philip eat it all."
She grinned at me and hurried out the door.

At home that night, I sat in front of the television, flipped
through all the channels twice, and turned it off. I tried to remind
myself what I'd learned about women in the past few years. I found
that the girls who dressed most wildly, who seemed so sure of their
looks, often wanted talk more than sex. Of course you could never
be sure, but it was the straight ones, those preppie girls in button-
down shirts who seemed a little awkward, shy even—those were the
ones who had their diaphragm in their purse.

"So has Hal decided what he thinks of me?"

My mother and I were sitting in the kitchen. I'd made dinner,
spaghetti with clam sauce, because she seemed tired and I'd had
another long week that added up to nothing. My mother managed
a print shop in Bethesda. They did stationery, fliers, advertisements;
it was not a bad job, but it was hectic at times. The owner kept
saying he was going to retire and leave my mother in charge.

I bought a bottle of wine for dinner, although my mother didn't

usually drink. I poured a glass for each of us, and when she gestured
for me to stop at a small amount, I kept pouring. I missed this hour
at school, sitting on the porch with a few beers, grumbling about
professors, telling stories or lies, and watching the sun go down over
the Blue Ridge Mountains.

"I need a new dress for church on Sunday," she said.

"You're going to church?"

"I've been going for a few weeks." She twirled her spaghetti on
a spoon and took a large bite.

"What's it like?"

"It's fine."

"It's church, of course it's fine. What's it *like*?"

"Well, it's a regular service, but everyone seems very sincere. It's
a little embarrassing. When they pray they sort of raise their hands
in the air." She showed me, raising one arm, then the other almost
shyly, her open palms in a gesture of supplication. "Sometimes,"
my mother started to giggle, "they only raise one hand, like asking
to be called on in class."

"Does Hal do that?"

"No," she said, relieved. "But it's strange. Sometimes I wonder
if there's something wrong with me. I don't feel anything." She
smiled a little, lightened by her admission, and tapped her glass for
more wine. She had made two completely uncharacteristic gestures,
the raising of her palms, tapping her glass for wine. The unnatural
movements made her seem younger, confiding.

"The thing is," she hesitated, "it's important to Hal, he wishes
I were more interested. I don't mind going, but . . ." her voice
trailed off.

"But what?"

"I guess if I were more involved, he would be more sure of me,
somehow. Of course he's never said it like that, but . . ."

I looked out the window. The sky was pale behind the trees. "If
he really loved you, he'd want you either way," I said.

"I suppose." She sighed and picked up her plate.

The next morning my mother announced that she and Megan
were going shopping. "You and Megan?"

"Hal said he'd buy her some clothes if she'd get something that wasn't black."

When Hal's car pulled in the driveway, I picked up the newspaper as if I hadn't been waiting. My mother answered the door, and I heard her and Hal making plans for later on. Megan's shoes clicked across the kitchen floor. I listened to her opening up the cabinets and getting something to drink. When my mother went to get her purse, Megan came in and sat down next to me.

"So you and my mother are going shopping?" I put the paper down.

"My father set it up, he wants us to be friends." She said it evenly, as a statement of fact. When she looked around the room, I thought how small our house seemed. She leaned back and stretched, looking up at the ceiling. I wanted to run my finger along the tendon at the back of her knee.

"But I do like your mother, she's a good person, innocent in a way."

"Innocent?"

"She always believes the best about people."

It surprised me, her saying this. It was true. My mother always had a theory to account for someone's bad behavior. Serial killers, rapists, thieves, she believed that, given enough time, a person's goodness would ultimately rise to the surface. I'd never known whether to call it optimism or foolishness.

When they left, the house seemed drained. I picked up a novel and put it down. The oak wall clock ticked louder, almost faster, as if it might rattle the china in the cabinet below.

My mother returned with a whole outfit—a skirt and blouse made of pale brown cloth with brightly colored threads running through it. A loose-fitting vest went over the top.

"They're wonderful for you." Megan grinned and held them up against my mother.

"Do you think your father will like them?" My mother touched the cloth with her forefinger.

"He'll like anything you wear." Megan's voice was encouraging. She took a soft purple belt from the bag and playfully dropped it over my mother's head. "What about you?" I asked.

"He said he'd pay for whatever I wanted as long as it wasn't black and it didn't show my navel." She pulled out a pale green shirt made out of silky cotton. "It's kapok, it's made out of milkweed—the way it hangs is terrific." She stared at me, daring me to imagine her in it, then held it up, turning it around. "Backless. It looks great on."

Then, finished with me, she hugged my mother and thanked her for being so sweet, for taking her shopping.

A few days later my mother asked me to have dinner with her and Hal. She asked in a careful way that hinted it was important.

"Is Megan coming, too?"

"I don't think so," she said.

"She likes you." I remembered Megan hugging my mother.

"The divorce was hard on her. Hal's had a little trouble with her, but they seem to be working it out. It was a big step for her to move in with him."

"What kind of trouble?" I asked.

"Oh, that's not for me to say."

"Mom, if you're going to start, I wish you'd finish."

"I only said it's been a bit difficult."

My mother could be annoyingly proper. She didn't gossip. What had Megan done? Drugs? Possibly. Gotten pregnant? Too young. Well, not technically. I went round and round in my head. Imagining the possibilities made me jealous.

When Hal came to pick us up for dinner, Megan wasn't with him. He opened the car door for my mother, touching her arm as she got in. I slid into the backseat, watched the blur of fast-food restaurants and chain stores as Hal maneuvered down Rockville Pike, neatly cutting through traffic, a few aggravated horns honking behind him. When we climbed out of the car, heat rose up off the pavement, matching the heat in my head. Inside the restaurant, nets and fake sea memorabilia were strung along the walls. The smell of fish and melted butter made me hungry. Hal asked about the job hunt. I recited my growing list of dead ends.

"Well, it's hard to know what you want to do. I didn't decide to be a dentist right out of college."

"What did you do when you graduated?" I asked.

"I went to California, surfed for a while, then I went to Alaska. I had this romantic notion about working there, but the emptiness drove me crazy, so I came back and joined the service. I knew they'd pay me to train me."

"Why did you choose being a dentist?" I asked.

"I was good with my hands. I could talk to people, and I figured if you have to work, you might as well make money."

I liked his honesty if not his reasoning. Over the meal we talked about work and school. He mentioned shooting, and I asked a few questions about skeet shooting. It seemed that I'd been having the same conversation for weeks. Finally, Hal took a drink of water and aligned his silverware next to his plate.

"I just want you to know that I love your mother very much. She's a rare woman. I also want to tell you that I've come to God in the past few years. He's the center of my life. I know that each person comes to Him in their own way, and I don't ever want you to feel that I'm pushing you when I express my feelings about the Lord."

I couldn't look at my mother. His honesty was painful. I felt myself blush.

"Well, I appreciate you talking to me," I said.

"I also want you to know that you're always welcome at the house. Don't worry if it takes you a while to find the job you want. I know you're a real self-starter. Be picky about that first job." He took my mother's hand and squeezed it.

"Thank you."

I reached for my wine glass. It was empty and I lifted it up, feeling that Hal's words called for some comment, but I had nothing to say. I felt the silence as my arm came down. There was only a single glass of wine left and I didn't want to pour it for myself. Hal did it for me.

"And Megan looks up to you. Don't worry if she acts smart. She has a little growing up to do."

"She's a lovely girl," I said, feeling myself redden.

The waitress returned with coffee, and our conversation floated back to the surface.

I woke the next morning knowing that Megan was out of the
question. I had to stop thinking about her. Finding a job so I could
afford my own apartment was the only way out. At eleven o'clock I
had an appointment at the World Bank with the father of an old
roommate. Getting ready to leave, I looked myself over in the mirror and felt better. I would get a job and get my own place. I bought
an apple juice when I got off the Metro, and my bottle cap confirmed me:

For he who has no concentration, there is no tranquillity.
—Bhagavad Gita

I was shown into an office that looked like a private library. The
walls were filled with bookcases, oil paintings, and photos of Paul's
father shaking hands with important people. A set of golf clubs
rested in the corner. Paul's father gestured toward a leather armchair.
A secretary appeared in the doorway to ask if I wanted coffee. When
she shut the door behind her, the hum of air-conditioning sealed us
in. After looking at my résumé and asking a few questions, he let me
know that my background was mediocre, that studying French
meant practically nothing. I should have studied Spanish, German,
Japanese, or Russian, those were the important languages. I listened
to his polite advice and excused myself as quickly as I could.

Down on the sidewalk, I watched the people hurrying by and I
wondered how it was that they all had something specific to do. A
bicycle messenger wove down the sidewalk and through the standing traffic; pedestrians flattened themselves against solid objects and
glared in his wake. I took off my tie. I was wet through to the back
of my suit. At the entrance to the Metro, a man with no legs was
propped up on a cardboard square. He held out a paper cup, and I
glared at him and stepped onto the moving staircase.

When I walked in the front door, the house seemed small. I
looked at the photographs of me growing up, my mother and father; they seemed at once familiar and generic. The house was still.
I went to take a shower, to wash the morning off, and when I got
out, the phone was ringing.

"Hi, Philip. Is your mom there?" It was Megan.

"She's at work. Do you want me to give her a message?" I didn't want to let her off the phone yet.

"No." She was quiet for a moment, then her voice picked up. "Well, I guess you had the God talk last night."

"Well, there wasn't a whole lot of discussion."

Megan giggled. "Look, do you feel like going into the city, just walking around or something? I want to get out of the house."

"Sure." I said it before thinking.

"Great. Come by in about half an hour, okay?"

I tucked the towel around my waist and went to get dressed.

"So what did he say last night?"

We were driving toward D.C. without a specific destination. I was aware of being in the same small space with her. She leaned against the car door, her knees tipped toward me. "Come on, what did he say?" she asked again.

"He said that he loved my mother a lot, and he talked about how important church was, all that." I was too embarrassed to repeat the words he'd used.

"That's all?" she asked.

Megan directed me as we got closer to the city: turn here, go left up there. It was funny the way she ordered me around. We parked in Adams Morgan, an old Hispanic neighborhood now gentrified with restaurants, record shops, and bars.

"I'm starved," Megan said. "I know a Mexican place that's cheap, and they make terrific margaritas."

She led me down the shopping street into a seedy part of town. A runny-eyed woman shared a stoop and a bottle with two men. On the corner, a check-cashing store was crowded. The restaurant was empty except for a Mexican family in the corner. The dim quiet was soothing; we were hidden from the daily world. Megan explained how she'd found the restaurant, but I didn't always pay attention to her words. I watched her mouth, her long fingers, ten perfect crimson dots at the tips. The icy lime and salt blended in my mouth, became warm in my stomach. Megan ate slowly, fishing around in the salsa for bits of tomato.

"I can't wait to go to college," she said. "No one around to watch what you do."

"Is it better living with your father?"

"Dad's weird, Mom's weird, it's kind of a trade-off." She stirred her drink, wiping salt down into the slush.

"How did your dad die?" she asked.

The question surprised me.

"He had cancer. One of the kinds you're supposed to survive."

"How old were you?"

"Thirteen."

"It's a rough age to have that happen," she said.

I laughed out loud. Her expression shifted from concern to anger.

"What?" she demanded.

"Rough age, as if you're the voice of experience."

"You don't have to be any special age to know things." She stared at me and sat back in her chair. Then she looked off at the mural on the wall. The slight roundness under her chin trembled.

"I'm sorry."

She crossed her arms and looked away. "Never mind," she said. "Maybe we should go."

"I really am sorry."

"Then pay." She leaned over the table and pushed the check toward me.

We left and walked into the late afternoon sun. I wanted to touch her, to cup my hand around the nape of her neck. We strolled down the shopping street, and, as we stopped to look at some of the more bizarre store windows, I felt her anger ease.

On Columbia Road we turned west and sat down near a playground at the top of the hill.

"Do you think being saved has really changed him?" I felt philosophical; drinking sometimes made me think about God.

We looked out over the playground. The sky was pink and orange behind the apartment buildings that bordered the park. Two chubby little boys started to fight over a plastic tractor.

"He's changed all right, but he had to. He got caught. And he's sorry." Her voice was bitter.

"He got caught?"

She paused, weighing something.

"He needs to make something out of everything. He couldn't have all the ruckus and just go on his merry way. He had to do something positive." She sneered when she said "positive."

"Positive?"

"Yeah." She kicked her foot against the wall. "Jerk. Once I got a really good report card—all A's except one B. My dad has always been real big on grades, and I was so excited that I went over to his office right after school, which is something I never did. The waiting room was empty, so I went back to where the offices were, and no one was there. I started to feel scared, everything was so quiet. His office door was closed, but I heard sounds of moving behind it, so I walked up to the door to knock on it, and then I heard a woman's voice, little sounds, then not-so-little sounds. They got faster and louder, and I just stood there, listening. Finally they stopped and I heard my father's voice and a woman giggle and I just turned around and left."

"How old were you?"

"Eleven, twelve, I guess."

"You didn't tell anyone?"

"No, my mother found out some other way."

My stomach felt as if I'd hit a sudden bump in the road. I thought about my mother, wondered if he would do that to her.

"So when all this got found out, that's when he got saved?"

Megan nodded.

She put her arm around my waist. Then she leaned against me and I slid my hand down her arm, smoothed her hair.

"I'm sorry," I said.

"You had nothing to do with it." She sounded mad, as if she were going to cry.

"I just mean I'm sorry it happened."

"Well, things happen all the time. I still think my father's a jerk. And I hate all this Christian shit. I know the reason for it."

"But you said you think he's really changed."

"I think he has. That's why I'm mad, too, because he feels all

better now, and I still feel like a kid standing outside his door with
my stupid report card, listening to him fuck his hygienist."

Our arms were still around each other and I was suddenly aware
of my limbs, as if I were singing in public and I had to decide what
to do with myself. I held her lightly, unsure of what to say. Two
teenage girls with bright shopping bags walked by, and I imagined Megan at twelve—standing outside a door, her face pale and
freckled under the fluorescent lights, listening to her father and his
nurse. I rubbed her arm, but she ignored me and stared out over
the playground. I bent to kiss her shoulder, she turned and studied
me, then she slid her arms up around my neck and kissed me, a little
shyly at first, then not shyly at all. We stayed like that for a long time,
talking and kissing until dark.

When I walked in the door, my mother was watching TV with
the lights out. Usually she read, curled up in a chair with her feet
underneath her. The blue light deepened the lines in her face. A
burst of canned laughter spilled out of the television. She asked
how my interview went, and at first I couldn't remember what
she was talking about. Then I remembered that morning and
started to explain why it was lousy. Even in the dark I saw she wasn't
listening, so when I said I met a friend for dinner, the lie came
easily.

"Are you okay?" I asked.

"I suppose." Her voice was low.

"Did you and Hal have a fight?"

"I wouldn't call it a fight," she said. "I don't feel like talking
about it now."

She forced a smile. I wanted to help her, but I was too full of
Megan. When I kissed my mother's hair and said good night, she
didn't move.

"Do you want me to turn off the TV?" I offered.

"No," she said.

I touched her arm and left her in front of the television.

I stretched out on my bed and thought about Megan, the way
she tasted, the small sounds she made. I wondered what Hal had

told my mother. I would have to say something to her, and I dreaded it.

The next day I was afraid that Megan would retreat into her prickly self, but when I called her, she suggested that we meet. Before we could arrange it Hal must have walked into the room, because her voice changed and she hung up.

The whole week was a series of interrupted phone calls and aborted plans. I couldn't pick her up because Hal's office was adjacent to his house and my car would be recognized. There were no buses in her neighborhood. I started to hate the suburbs.

I told myself that I'd talk to my mother after I saw Megan again. I put it off because I couldn't think of a way to say what I knew. Finally, one Thursday night, my mother came home early from dinner with Hal. She sat down in the kitchen and pulled off her shoes.

"Mom, did Hal tell you about his marriage, his divorce, and all that?" I tried to sound casual.

"Yes, he did." She was sorting through the mail, placing it in small piles on the table. The definiteness of her answer surprised me.

"What did he say?"

"That's between us, don't you think?"

I stood by the bulletin board, poking a large plastic tack in and out, making a circle of tiny, dark holes.

"Well, you've seemed kind of upset. I thought it might be something to do with that."

She looked up at me surprised.

"His first marriage has nothing to do with it. He's a much different person now, anyway."

Her words startled me, *much different now*.

"Is there anything I can do?" I didn't know what else to say.

"No, Philip," she smiled, weary. "It's really between us."

I stuck the tack into the wood molding and decided to go for a drive.

The following night Megan called after I'd come home from having dinner with some friends. She sounded as if she'd been crying.

"What happened?"

"My friend Barry was in a car accident."

"Is he alive?"

"He's in a coma."

"Do you want me to come over?"

"Yes."

"Where's your dad?" I asked.

"Out with your mother."

On the way to her house, it occurred to me that Barry might be an old boyfriend. I switched off the radio and rolled down my window. The night air was cool as I drove past the dense woods. Her front door was unlocked, and I let myself in. Megan was on the phone with another friend of Barry's.

When she got off the phone, she seemed calm, as if she had settled some question. Without saying a word she went to the refrigerator and poured two large glasses of wine. She wore the backless shirt she'd bought with my mother; the fabric fell in a deep loop that showed the curve of her waist, the indentation of her backbone, all the way down to the small of her back. She padded down the hall and I followed her long legs, shadowed in the dark. We lay down on her bed and I let her talk about what happened until she started to cry again. My heart was beating quickly, out of rhythm with her sorrow. I slid my hand up under her shirt and touched her very slowly and softly. She moved against me when I put my mouth to her breasts. I was afraid to ask my question, so I touched her and waited. When she unbuttoned my shirt, reached for my pants, I knew it would be all right, and the rest of our clothes came off quickly, awkwardly.

I looked down at her face, the slope of her shoulders, her flattened breasts pale in the half-dark. Her mouth was open but she made no sound. She moved with me, but her motions seemed more a mirror of mine than her own. I slid my arms up under her knees. Her body was pliant, but she was somewhere far away, somewhere only in herself. I waited as long as I could before letting go.

Afterward, dozing, everything inside me settled into place. Then I heard voices in the living room, my mother and Hal. I started awake, sweating. I strained to hear what they were saying. What if they found me here? Then I remembered my car in the driveway.

They already knew. My stomach felt like it was being squeezed by a cold hand. I heard Hal's voice, loud and angry in the living room and I looked at the clock by Megan's bed—1:35. Megan lifted her head from the pillow and heard them. She cursed under her breath.

We lay still for a moment, then she threw back the covers and got out of bed.

"What are you—"

She took the chair from her desk and placed it under the doorknob.

"I don't want him bursting in here," she said.

The air ticked behind my thoughts. I thought of Hal talking about target practice; I wondered if he had a gun.

"He is going to kill me," I said.

"No, he's not. Besides, it's nothing he hasn't done himself."

I couldn't see her eyes in the dark, but her voice was bitter and calm.

We lay still. Hal was shouting in the living room, and then my mother's voice was raised back, something I hadn't heard in years. The front door slammed. I wondered if she'd take the car. Blood pounded in my ears. If she took the car and left me here, Hal would kill me. I was sure of it. I felt for my jeans on the floor and rattled my pockets. I had the keys.

Then my mother's voice again:

"Take me home."

"Drive your son's car home."

Her voice lowered. She must have told him there were no keys in it, reasoning with him.

Finally, they left. We lay still, listening, making sure they were gone. The house creaked. Outside, the trill of crickets and peepers shifted into high gear.

"What will he do to you?" I asked.

"He'll be furious, but he won't *do* anything." Her voice was quiet and defiant. "I'll just tell him I haven't been saved yet."

"You're not afraid of being left alone?"

"No, but you should go."

I tried to dress quickly in the dark, but my fingers felt stiff and uncoordinated.

Megan didn't dress. She got up with me and took the chair from underneath the doorknob. We stood by the door, and I slid my hands down her back, wanting to feel what I had an hour ago, but I was too nervous and shaky to feel her smoothness under my hands.

"I'll call you later in the morning."

"Okay, you better go," she said.

I hurried out to the car, keys in hand. It stalled once and my heart started to pound again, but it caught the second time and I pulled out of the driveway.

When I got home, my mother was waiting. She stood by the kitchen table; the part in her hair was crooked, her eyes were bright.

"You had to do it, didn't you?" she shouted.

"Mom, I wasn't trying to—"

"It really was the last straw, do you know that? The last straw, to come back to Hal's house and realize that you two are in bed together."

My mother focused on me as if I looked different than I had that morning.

"She's just trying to get at Hal. She doesn't care about you. I hope you know that. She's a confused young woman. She'd sleep with almost anyone if she thought it would hurt him."

My mother's mouth was dark, rectangular, as her shouted words floated out. I leaned against the doorjamb and looked past her; I couldn't see outside through the kitchen light's reflection. I remembered Megan's calm defiance, her efficiency as she set that chair under the doorknob, as if it were something she had practiced. I felt the connection of everything I wanted to believe was separate— Hal gently guiding my mother through a door, Megan moving underneath me in the dark. My mother stopped to catch her breath and her features settled back into what I knew.

House Fires

Nancy Reisman's fiction has appeared in Tin House, Five Points,
New England Review, Kenyon Review, Glimmer Train, *and other journals.*
She has received fellowships from the NEA, the Fine Arts Work Center in
Provincetown, and the Wisconsin Institute for Creative Writing, and she
holds an M.F.A. from the University of Massachusetts-Amherst. She
currently teaches creative writing at the University of Florida.

"Individuals and generations are interwoven in these stories, intricately
and delicately, as if to persuade the reader that innumerable threads
of mystery and surprise are worked into the closest fabric of intimacy
and familiarity. There is a rapt respect for human singularity
in the writing that readers will be grateful to share."
MARILYNNE ROBINSON, 1999

When Randi died, my family went haywire: one by one we shorted
out. My father, a dignified cardiologist, took to drinking and bellig-
erence. My mother's mannered calm gave way to hysteria. I became
pale and inept and forgot how to hold conversations.

My sister was killed at night by fire; afterward, the indigo black sky
seemed intolerable. Ordinary flames left us stricken and obsessed.
Her last minutes seemed a vast unlit space I could neither penetrate nor ignore. In my attempts to comprehend them, I went as far
as lowering my fingers over lit matches and holding my breath. I
ended up writing Randi secret notes, which I left crumpled in the
kitchen trash. *Wake up and jump out a window. Do this scene over*
again, some way I can see it: a rescue, a sprained ankle, momentary
coughing, an embrace on the street, in the light of fire engines. Here,
steady yourself. Let me wrap your ankle. I will bring you blankets.
Within weeks I took to dressing in Randi's old clothes, castoff
sweaters, worn jeans, dresses from her past: some of them held

traces of her crushed-lilac scent. I'd wear them until my mother

made me take them off, or until there was nothing of Randi left
in them.

The house Randi lived in was a two-family in New Haven I saw
only once, after the fire; the surviving structure was roofless, open
along the western side, char and ash and air where Randi's room
had been. Left over were objects from storage: books she didn't
use, an olive raincoat, camping equipment, all smoke damaged. The
fire was caused by faulty wiring and fanned by high winds, the sort
of thing you'd never anticipate. Imagine, for example, your life
is rising, the proof is everywhere, at your Ivy League law review,
in your lovemaking, in the mirror. Certainty crests, crests again.
You work impossibly hard and sleep heavily, sleep through the first
scent of smoke. When do you realize you are trapped in sheets of
flame?

Her voice burned. Her intellect burned. I don't know what to say
about her soul. Randi's body reminded me of certain sea pebbles:
white, smooth, perfectly separate. That night she was sleeping, a
woman wrapped in quilts, a woman turned inward, a self on a bed.
No one reported hearing her—no cries, no calls. Did she, at the
end, remain asleep? Did she wake to the knowledge of fire and
nothing else, not even herself?

That winter I became unsure of my skin: it seemed too thin and
insubstantial to contain me. At night I felt a sudden panic and
imagined spilling out into the dark air, slipping beneath the sound
of stray sirens, dissipating. Near my parents' house a local diner
burned, and I stayed at the window biting my nails and watching
the sky grow chalky. I couldn't ignore the ways fire annihilates: the
objects that steady us—landmarks, banisters, familiar walls—disappear or char down to remnants. An address no longer counts; a
phone number drops away. Proof of the past vanishes and the infra-
structure of our days collapses into chaos. It is pure loss, and yet,
coming upon someone else's fire, we pull over to the side of the
road, stand in the street, stare from the top of the hill at the gorgeous and terrible flames. In some living room the family photos

are seared off the wall; outside the house we *stand back, stand back* but can't leave.

On the worst nights I crept downstairs to my parents' dark family room and turned on late movies: *Stella Dallas, Splendor in the Grass, Shampoo*. I would watch anything. At first I fell into film because of the story lines, but it also seemed a world impervious to fire. Even celluloid, which can so easily shrivel from heat—a sudden melting on screen, burns blooming over a city street or hotel lobby or a woman's bewildered face—seemed salvageable. The image curls away into brown arcs and blank space; the film breaks; the projectionist snaps off the machine. But wait, and the film begins again, skipping a few lines of dialogue, losing a gesture. The damaged reel will be replaced by a new, flawless print. Finally, somewhere, there was recourse.

Eventually, I studied film; now on my insomniac nights I read theory. I return to Bazin, who wrote in the aftermath of World War II and, nevertheless, insisted on unity. He thought that film's promise and purpose was to elucidate the real, to reveal the patterns already before us, and he believed that unity of space and time were paramount. So he relied on long shots: if a scene includes a man and a woman in a room, the camera should give us a clear view of both the characters and the space, all within a frame. No jump cuts, no breaks in time. When the scene is whole, we witness the simultaneous body language, the woman stirring her coffee as the man stares into his lap, the man leaning forward as the woman says his name, the thickness of the oak table dividing them, the strange juxtaposition of their tensed bodies and troubled faces against extravagant floral wallpaper. How small they appear stumbling down a hill in the snow; how terribly close in the hospital elevator they must take together. Each shot reveals the shifts in power. I like this idea; I am drawn to Bazin's faith. But is wholeness itself illusory? So often I see things in pieces.

Picture, for example, my mother the months after Randi died, a forty-eight-year-old woman weeping into her coffee, weeping into the houseplants, slamming doors when contradicted, then weeping behind one or another slammed door. Every evening after six, she'd

prepare an impressive dinner none of us could eat. You could film her for minutes at a distance, a woman alone in an immaculate kitchen, snapping green beans and fishing Kleenex from her pocket, then calling, "Dinner everyone," as if there were ten of us. Or you could abandon Bazin's principle and film her face in close-up, film the lined hands, the manicured nails, elaborate rings and traces of arthritis, fingers breaking and breaking the beans, and then cut to a shot of my father pretending to work but actually drawing squares on a notepad. Watch my father refill his Glenlivet, see in close-up the heavy lines beneath the eyes, a single twitch at the corner of his mouth, and hear my mother's voice, "Dinner everyone." Or you could view the plush empty rooms of the house, one after another, then cut to my father's face, his sip of scotch. Cut to me, disheveled, on the floor of the living room, thumbing the classifieds without looking at them, headphones over my ears. Hear the sound of those snapping beans. Cut to my mother's face, then to the wintry lawn, "Dinner everyone."

I hear my father's voice swim out of the dark. Beyond the window blue snow accumulates over the college lawns. It is Vermont. It is December. His voice seems to emanate from the band of falling snow rather than the phone line; we are nearly mutes. He almost chokes on my name but then repeats it, breathlessly, "Amy," over the miles of cable between Boston and Bennington, across the 5 A.M. blue dark. He says that Randi was in a fire. What do you mean? I say.

She was in it. She didn't get out.

My mouth tastes of metal and the night flattens into slabs of light and dark, the snow into two-dimensional flecks. I brush my hair. I dial the busline, write a schedule on a drugstore receipt, dress myself in a sweater and leggings, find matching shoes. In dawn light I board a bus that travels past fields of snow and stripped silver trees, stopping in tiny towns along the Connecticut River valley. Two seats away from me, a woman hums songs from West Side Story, and once the driver stops to tell a man in the back to put out his cigarette. The air becomes increasingly white as we drive and the daylight thickens. All the way down the highway snow falls, small frenzied flakes that seem never to end.

In New Haven we held hands. My parents seemed crushed and ancient, and our gaits dropped off to a shuffle. On the grounds of Yale the three of us walked in a row, hand-in-hand: sometimes I was on the outside to the left and sometimes I was in the middle. At a restaurant table my father touched my hand, then clasped my mother's, then knotted his own together while a waiter brought us coffee and plates of eggs we ignored. At the funeral in Newton, my parents held hands at the graveside, and when I stepped back, away from the rest of the mourners, they appeared to be at the very edge of the grave, heads bowed; a gust of wind could have knocked them in. They were gripping each other's hands and didn't sway or lean or turn, becoming in that moment a still shot of snow-flecked hair, shoulders in overcoats, almost trembling, a small bridge of hands. Aunt Natalie shepherded me from the funeral parlor to the graveside to my parents' house and into a chair; she held my hand, and later other relatives and friends would take one hand or the other and hold it, sometimes purposefully, sometimes almost absently, as they sat with plates in their laps and spooned up mild foods, offering me pieces of bagel or sliced cucumbers. The Orthodox women on my father's side of the family wore dark velvet hats with delicate brims; their warm, soap-scented hands stroked my stubby, nail-bitten fingers. It was as if in all this handholding we would find the missing hands or reconstruct them somehow.

My thirteen-year-old cousin, Ellen, held my hand to tug me away from the living room, to tell me that Randi had explained sex to her. "She was the best," Ellen said. "She knew everything. I wish she weren't dead." All at once, Ellen burst into tears and clung onto me, crying into my navy dress. We swayed in the kitchen for several minutes, Ellen's soft animal sounds rising, my silence wrapping and wrapping them. I kissed Ellen on the forehead and watched the weather arrive in the backyard. Then Aunt Natalie found us and helped me upstairs to nap.

After a week of visits from relatives and friends, gifts of coffee-

cakes and casseroles and pots of soup, everyone disappeared. There
were the three of us. For a few weeks I kept an eye on my mother,
who sometimes needed help getting dressed. The king-sized bed
dwarfed her; she would lie on the right side, the quilt gathered
around her, propping her head just enough to see me pull blouses
and pants out of her closet and wave them in the air before her. She
would shake her head at one outfit, shake her head at another, eventually shrug at something. I'd turn on the shower for her and get
the temperature right. I'd wait until she was done and hand her a
towel. By then she was ready to be on her own. "Okay, doll," she'd
say, and then I would falter. I did have projects to work on: I had
taken incompletes in all my fall classes but could hardly think about
the sociology of militarism or the French subjunctive. In truth, I
could hardly think. I watched my late movies, got up in time for
Good Morning America, and napped during the day. To occupy myself, I often folded laundry.

My father went back to work almost immediately. I thought it
was because in his office there were people he could save. Or because he didn't know what else to do. He claimed that, since he'd
cosigned all of Randi's law school loans, he couldn't afford a longer
leave. No one believed him. One of my father's partners, Barry
Levitz, suggested that my parents leave the country. "Take a real
vacation," Barry said. "Go to the Azores. Go to France." This was
something my mother wanted and my father resisted. A week before my spring semester was to begin in Vermont, she pulled me
aside and asked me to go with them to Paris. It seemed an unsavory
idea. And shouldn't I try school? "I can't go now," I said. "I don't
have a passport."

"We can't go without you," my mother said. "We couldn't leave
you here alone."

"You should go," I said. "Eat pastry. Go to the Louvre. I'll be
okay."

My mother pursed her lips and gave me a once-over: I'd been
wearing a bathrobe for two days.

"I'll call you in Paris," I said. "Anyway, I have to go back to
school."

"We'll talk later," she said.

But no one went anywhere.

If I were to film that first month, I would want to focus on small gestures, small sounds, a sort of bewildered scratching against the largeness of the space around us, the largeness of each day. But for how long would that work on the screen? There ought to be narrative development, but of what sort, and how should it be filmed?

The following months in Newton, we all had a propensity for breaking things. Bright drinks fell to the floor. Lamps sat too close to the edges of tables. The patio door slammed too hard, breaking a spring. "Nuts," my mother would say. Picture, then, a shot of a hand knocking backwards into a juice glass, the glass shattering, bright orange spilling over the white linoleum floor.

"Shut up," my father says. "Just shut up." This at dinner, while my mother and I grasp at conversation about the unexpected pigeons at the birdfeeder or the recipe for stuffed cabbage or what is at the Newton Cinema. A faint pinkness creeps up through his cheeks and forehead, over his balding scalp. He is not drunk. He is a man I've never met before. My mother bites the inside of her cheek: she holds firmly to the belief that dinner conversation is both a right and an obligation. Silence at the table is uncivilized. She stares at the roast potatoes and julienned carrots on her plate and says, as if he were a child, "Abe, you don't have to eat with us tonight."

One night, he grunts and stays. One night, he takes his plate off to the study. My mother is utterly white and gray, her skin more drawn, the pale blue of her eyes washed out, her jawline rigid. Her conversation with me becomes even more tenuous, bits of chaff thrown into the air. *I bought apples today. The gas man will be here Thursday morning. Buddy Stern is getting married again.* The scene repeats itself until my mother just shakes her head, tears up, and drops whatever line of conversation she's started. I stay catatonic through dessert.

Would it be more cinematic to hear the voice, the low shout, "shut up," and cut to me alone, an hour later, striking a match, my index finger racing through the flame? What does it mean to pair my father's voice with that action? To follow it with shots of my mother's sudden entrance into my room, her hard slap across my face, the gash made with the edge of her ring, my right cheek slowly welling blood?

We are both stunned, my mother and I. Her mouth shapes a perfect, cerise-lipsticked O. My face stings as she pulls me into the bathroom and jams my burned fingertip under the cold water. Red bruises form on my wrist where she grips it. "Don't you ever," she says. In the mirror I see her glance at the cut on my cheek. Neither one of us touches it.

Later the shock wears off. One day I try on Randi's blue satin prom dress, pour myself some Glenlivet, and lounge in Randi's room, reading my mother's back issues of *National Geographic* and sifting through photographs of Randi's old boyfriends and high school triumphs: Randi at a diving meet arrowing into a pool; Randi and Alex Goldman waving from a ski lift; Randi in a black strapless dress, drinking a Bud. I find Randi at eighteen in an emerald green sweatshirt, thick amber hair cut to shoulder length, head tipped onto Bob D'Amato's shoulder. She is the cat with the canary, and sexy, brainy Bob D'Amato wraps both arms around her, his teeth astonishingly white. My mother walks into the room, colors at the sight of me, and slaps me on both cheeks. Neither one of us is surprised. I say nothing. I take off the dress in front of her, rehang it in Randi's closet, and slip on my jeans and sweatshirt.

A week later, when I mistakenly set the table for four, my mother slaps me again and I mechanically clear the fourth place. My father lifts his head from the stack of mail he is sorting. "Marian." He shakes his head ever so slightly. Then they are both stock still, staring at each other. They don't notice my exit from the room.

How would an audience's view change if I cut back and forth between the slaps and the wailing I hear late at night from my parents' room, or between the slaps and the latest instances of my mother's social decline—her skittishness in supermarkets and clothing stores, her new awkwardness with friends? Would it be more accurate? Or too overt, too manipulative? Montage can be tricky and coercive, which is why advertisers and other propagandists embrace it. But the wailing is important.

Most mornings, even then, my mother kissed me and smoothed my hair.

My father, on the other hand, could not easily greet me. He rose in the morning for work, he left the house, he called my mother once in the afternoon, he returned at six and secluded himself. Perhaps that is when he wept. He shouted when his brooding was interrupted. *Get out of here.* I crumbled; Randi was the one who could shout back. And yelling was not part of our relationship: when I was small, one stern look would keep me in line. So I began to move stealthily when he was home, slipping past him into empty rooms, avoiding him in the hallway, though this could backfire. *What's the matter with you, are you a mouse?*

Appease, I thought, appease. I left ridiculous notes in his briefcase—*Have a good day!*—along with packages of Fig Newtons or oatmeal bars or peanut butter cups. During a break in the cold weather I washed his car. He acknowledged nothing. In previous years I would have found a thank-you note on my dresser; he might have taken me to lunch. It's true that his solicitude had always coexisted with a controlled bluster, an arrogance I'd witnessed from the sidelines of medical meetings and in unsatisfactory restaurants. But he'd always responded to appeasement, to the phrase "I see your point," to the free drink sent by the manager. And always he was protective of my mother, of Randi, of me. We were beautiful, he said, we were smart, we were angels. Especially Randi.

It's vacation. We are in Maine. I am picking blueberries with my mother, and my father and Randi are on the dock, fishing. Randi must be about nine. I am seven. I watch my father tug at her ponytail; she grins up at him, then reels in a sunfish big enough to keep. My father holds the hooked fish in the air, where it flops about. He and Randi grin and grin. She is slick as an eel in her green one-piece. I stuff my mouth with blueberries.

"Hey," my mother says. "Save those."

I open my hand and offer her several half-crushed berries. She relents and eats a few, but moves the bucket out of my reach and

hands me a Styrofoam cup to use for picking. When I look out toward the dock again, Randi is holding up the now-dead fish and
waving it in the direction of my mother. My mother stands up and
waves back. "Great," she yells. "Marvelous."

Fantasy 1: I happen to be in New Haven and arrive at the scene
of the fire in time to pull Randi out alive. Everyone is stunned by
my courage and skill, even the fire squad. Randi and I hug each
other and cry. Before I can berate her for being in that house, on
that night, for being asleep too long, for exposing me to endless
wrath and sorrow, she apologizes. She also apologizes for ever calling me an airhead.

Fantasy 2: Randi's house goes up in flames, but she escapes unscathed. This moment of threat and escape—the sirens, the flames,
the coldness of the night—shakes Randi enough that she sheds a
layer of arrogance. She begins calling me long distance and sending
gifts through the mail. She tells me how lucky she feels to be my
sister.

Fantasy 3: I am the one who escapes the fire. Randi rescues me,
takes me to a good hotel, and stays up until I fall asleep. The next
day, everything is fine. She gives me her favorite sweater and we
order room service.

Fantasy 4: I am the one who escapes the fire. I do it without
Randi's help. She is amazed at my bravery and luck. She admits to
her friends that she underestimated me. "She was always sweet,"
Randi says, "but I thought she was hapless. Was I ever wrong." After that she wants us to take vacations together. "Let's go where
you want," she says.

Fantasy 5: There is no fire.

I thought about the fish in Maine. I thought I was dying. In the
bathroom I would read the label on my father's package of razor
blades and assess the blueness of the veins in my wrists. Then I
would sit on the white tile floor, weep, and wait for the weeping
to recede into a distanced calm. It was then I felt Randi's absence

in its cleanest form: an endless, zero-gravity drifting, a world of lonely air.

Contemplating the razor blade left me oddly belligerent. I'd leave matchbooks around the house for my mother to scoop up and hide. The day I dropped an heirloom teacup and she slapped me, I began to sing "Oklahoma!" as I swept up the shards of china roses. I cleared my father's drinks before he was finished with them, and one night at dinner when he spouted about wanting silence, I surprised all of us by telling him to find a monastery. But these moments were rare and left my parents increasingly convinced that I had no sense of judgment: all common sense had perished with Randi.

After four months in Newton, I looked as if I'd been living underground. I was pale as a nightcrawler, and thin: I'd lost ten pounds and my clothes hung about me. I became disoriented in traffic and my old shyness surfaced with strangers. But I began small forays into the neighborhood, alone. Evenings at the cinema by myself. I favored independent films with offbeat characters who traveled a lot, or films where someone escaped from one country into another, took trains, or rode bicycles long distances. I would buy my ticket and hang about the lobby, reading the posted movie reviews and jumping if anyone bumped into me or asked me the time. After a few weeks, the man at the concession started giving me medium-sized popcorn when I ordered small. He said nothing about it, just took my money and smiled and went on to the next customer.

That April, I turned twenty-one. It was a mild, muddy day, and in the afternoon I took the train into the city and bought myself a spring dress, a print of blue roses, which I wore out of the store. Aunt Natalie called from New York and sent red tulips. My father left me a pair of silver earrings on the breakfast table, and before dinner he took out the Polaroid. Although we had always taken photographs on our birthdays, no one had touched the camera since Thanksgiving; there was relief and pleasure in my father's retrieval of it. He was almost jovial, loading my arms with tulips, photographing me alone, photographing me with my mother, orchestrating shots for my mother to take of me with him, and, finally, setting the self-timer and rushing over for a photo of the three of us. We laid the photos out on the table, watched ourselves emerge through the murky green and yellow stages of each print: my mother's smile a bit taut, my father's face a bit flushed, my lips together in small smiles, all of us surprised.

"Look at the two of you," my father said. "Beautiful." He kissed my mother's cheek. "Beautiful," he said. He kissed me on the forehead.

"Such a pretty dress," my mother said.

We sat down to salmon and asparagus. My father uncorked a bottle of Sauvignon Blanc and poured glasses for the three of us. He asked me about my day in Boston. He asked me whether I was getting bored in Newton.

"Maybe it's time to go to school again," he said.

I pictured Vermont, mountains, unbridled green.

"Take a look at Brandeis," he said. "Take a look at Harvard." Both schools were within ten miles of the house.

"I hadn't thought of them," I said.

"What would you want to study?" my mother said. "Anthropology? Wasn't that it?"

"Maybe," I said, "that could be interesting," even though I only wanted to watch films. My father tapped his fork against the table and then speared a piece of salmon. "Hmm," he said, waving the fork in figure eights. "Nothing wrong with anthropology, but you'd have to be serious about a field like that. You'd have to want graduate school."

"Oh."

"I didn't go to graduate school," my mother said.

"It's a different era," my father said.

"I'll give it some thought," I said.

"Abe, she can't know if she wants graduate school before she's taken any courses."

"I'm just saying," my father said. "Be practical. What's so bad about being practical? Amy, what about biology?"

I shrugged.

"Or computers," my father said.

"Maybe," I said.

"Abe," my mother said, "if she wants to study anthropology, let her study anthropology."

"Anthropology's fine. Amy, go ahead, study anthropology. Marian, don't misinterpret me."

"I think I heard you correctly," my mother said, "Anyway, Amy, we're happy to get you a car. The Green Line is a pain in the neck."

"Thank you," I said.

"We can start looking this week," my father said. "I have a patient in the business."

No one mentioned Bennington, a place I had liked, a place not so very far from Newton. I didn't say that I missed the mountains. I didn't say I'd forgotten how to be on my own but wanted to remember, if I could. Why spoil my own birthday, the shimmer of those tulips, the most peace we'd had since Randi's death? So I changed the subject. I asked my mother about her gardening plans.

Later my mother brought out the cake, angel food studded with strawberries. She sliced it and handed out the slices and sang to me. My father cheerfully mumbled along. At the end of the singing there was nothing for me to do but eat: she had brought no candles.

The lack was so striking that I found myself staring at the cake and not lifting a fork. I glanced up at each of my parents and back down at the cake. I shrugged. I blew air across the top of the slice. "For luck," I said. I stuck my fork into airy whiteness.

"Was that necessary?" my mother said.

"Was what necessary? There weren't candles," I said.

"And you know why," my mother said.

I looked down at the rose-print dress, my thin white arms. Suddenly, I felt ridiculous, a bony, flawed girl trying to pass for pretty, trying to pass for whole. I almost nodded assent. But it was my birthday. I was twenty-one. I should have been in a bar drinking champagne with college buddies. I should have been kissing a man. "Birthday cakes usually have candles," I said.

"If you don't want the cake, don't eat it," my mother said.

"What's the matter with the cake?" my father said.

"I just wanted something to wish on."

My mother bit her lip.

"Can't you appreciate that your mother baked you a cake?" my father said.

I tried to keep my tone even, but the words came out clipped. "Thanks for the cake," I said to my mother.

"What's that snottiness?" my father said.

"You think I'm going to give you lit candles?" my mother said. "After what you did?"

"What did she do?" my father said.

"Two fingers," I said. "Two fingers and there aren't even scars."

"Don't talk to me about scars," my mother said.

"Scars," I said, "show up after injuries. Some people have appendix scars. There's a movie called *Scarface* I don't think you'd like."

"Amy, be quiet," my father said.

"It's stupid, Mom," I said. "Not even one birthday candle. I would have blown it out. I would have made a wish and blown it out."

"Shut up," my father said.

"I don't want to shut up." I rose and began to clear the table. "I'll go talk somewhere else."

"You sit down," my father said. "You eat that cake."

"I'm not hungry," I said.

My father grabbed me by the arm and pushed me down into the chair. He picked up a forkful of cake and shoved it at my mouth. He held it there, gripping my forearm, until I bit into the piece. When he moved his hand away, I spit it back at him.

"That's it," he said.

I tried to make a dash for the door, but before I could sidestep him, my father grabbed me by the shoulders and shoved me back against the wall. "What's *wrong* with you?" he shouted. He was shaking me, his face fierce and red, his breath heavy with liquor and fish. "Answer me," he shouted. Twice my head banged back against the wall. I closed my eyes. "Answer me," he repeated. I began humming a two-note phrase, the first note slightly higher than the second—*see saw see saw*. I didn't move.

"*Abe*," I heard my mother say. "Abe."

His hands released, and I sensed him backing away from me. When I opened my eyes, he was beside his chair, incredulous, gazing at his palms. He sagged and looked up at me. "Amy," he said. His voice caught, and he regained it only long enough to say my mother's name. "Marian," he was begging, "Marian," and weeping. He fell back into his chair, and my mother went to him then, held him, rocked him, my father leaning his head against her belly, sobbing. Like a sleepwalker, I left the house.

Most of this took place within three or four minutes, for part of which I was sightless. Should I stick with my stream of perception, including darkness, or should I reconstruct what I did not see and film mise-en-scène from a medium shot? Should my mother be in the frame at all times?

Afterward, neither of my parents mentioned that night. The cake vanished. The photographs vanished. For a few days my father whistled comfortless, unidentifiable tunes. My mother remained watchful. I became a different Amy: sly, calculating, untouchable. I did not eat meals with my parents. Or talk. I quietly sold off the one piece of stock I owned and converted the proceeds into traveler's checks. I emptied my bank account. I scouted the house for cash.

A week after my birthday, when my mother was at the supermarket, I left a note on the counter and left Newton. I took with me no photos or mementos. My departure from the house seemed as ordinary as any other: I locked the side door, picked my way across the rain-puddled walk. I counted my change for the Green Line train, switched to the Red Line, crossed the traffic-filled blocks between South Station and the Trailways terminal. Somewhere in Ohio, I called my father's office and left a message for Barry Levitz. The buses I rode wove on across the country, through flat expanses of prairie, into mountains, stopping at Burger Kings and Pizza Huts and twenty-four-hour truckstops. I washed and brushed my teeth in the restaurant bathrooms and lived on grilled cheese and french fries. Within a few days I reached California.

For a couple of nights I stayed at the Hilton near Union Square in San Francisco, walked the city, and invented possible aliases for myself, mixing in the names of streets: Melissa Grant, Joan Vallejo, Margaret Montgomery. I renamed myself Amy Montgomery and moved to Berkeley with that name, to a shared house near Rock-ridge. For the first six months I contacted my parents only through

Barry, calling the office from pay phones.

It's me. Tell them I'm fine.

Where are you?

I'll call you in a couple of weeks.

I never said where I was and never stayed on the line more than two minutes. Was this cruel? I feared my parents would fly to San Francisco and comb the streets for me. I don't think I was wrong.

Those first months, I kept to myself. I smoked clove cigarettes and sat in cheap Chinese restaurants eating soup and reading about silent movie greats. I went to matinees alone. After a year of working in cafes, I landed a staff assistant job at KQED and enrolled in film classes. I began to live in a social world.

I have lived in Berkeley for six years: sometimes I think I stay here simply because the pomegranate trees surprise me, because of the shock of green in February, because I still find the bay beautiful. I have befriended several women. Sometimes I have boyfriends, interesting men inclined toward social justice or film, who can speak fluent Spanish or know how to backpack. I have not fallen in love.

I could say, yes, time heals. I wouldn't be wrong, but there are scars we can't always name. I cannot help but think we were disfigured to begin with, and the fire illuminated the twists to our hearts and limbs. I have visited my parents in Newton a few times. The first time, I insisted on staying at the Marriott. They came to meet me there for dinner and I wept to see them. My mother sat close beside me, stroking my hand. My father was pale and lost. "Would you come back to Boston?" he said. "My Amy, won't you come back?"

"I can't," I said. "This is all I can do."

Some nights I wake up and the air smells of eucalyptus and gardenias; my skin is warm. For an instant I could be a young girl named Amy, my sister sleeping, my father listening to Mozart, eyes closed, my mother reading in the bath. I know why theorists now write about seduction and desire. And I know why they want us to wake up, to see the seams in films, to remember that images and sounds are pasted together. How else can we keep from tumbling, blindly, into fantasy? How will we know if we have, in the larger scheme of things, been pushed against a wall?

And yet for me there is still the dream of making internal life visible. Of finding characters I can believe in. The hope that, this time, my trust will not be betrayed. There is the dream of wholeness. The dream of reconciliation. And there is my desire for a simple plot, for the unity that never quite arrives in daily life, for true closure. These days, I look for the sort of closure that is not false and is not death. Is there such a thing?

I know this: fire blooms, blooms again, marking us, dismantling what we believed inviolable. At times we can do nothing but record its stunning recklessness. Later, we sift through the ashes by hand.

What to Do in an Emergency

Elizabeth Searle is the author of A Four-Sided Bed, *a novel published in 1998, and* Celebrities in Disgrace, *a novella and story collection published in 2001. Her stories have appeared in magazines such as* Ploughshares, Redbook, Kenyon Review, Five Points, *and* Michigan Quarterly Review *and in anthologies such as* Lovers *and* American Fiction. *She received the Lawrence Foundation Fiction Prize in 2001. She has taught writing at Oberlin, Brown and, most recently, at Emerson College. She lives with her husband and son in Arlington, Massachusetts, where she is working on another novel.*

"These are stories that walk into a room and every eye turns towards them. Who is this writer, you wonder? She is Elizabeth Searle and believe me, she is for real."
JAMES SALTER, 1992

To keep Bobbie Ann awake, the housemother gave her cans to count, bread dough to punch, fresh underwear to sort by indelible black initials printed on the cloth, and Incident Reports to file but not read.

"Not that you'll find any big surprises," May Mooney added flatly, as if she meant ever, in Bobbie Ann's whole life to come. Bobbie Ann nodded, her hair dripping rain. Her eyes burned, still scalded by her latest crying jag. Obvious as a flag, she knew: what Carson used to call, at first affectionately, her red-white-and-blue eyes.

"Head-butts, seizures, big-time bites." Here May halted herself. "'Course that's all daytime drama." She lifted her fat creamy cheeks, managed a Carolina hostess smile. Scared Bobbie Ann might yet   229 bolt? Above them, rain pounded the none-so-sturdy sounding roof. The housemother, the house itself, exuded false cheer: bright orange covers stretched over the lumpy wood-framed couch, a defiantly bright green church dress billowing over the massive expanse of May Mooney's body. Her arms swelled out, round and wide as Bobbie Ann's waist.

"Rose, Belinda, Jackie J." May maneuvered into a turn, the floor seeming to rotate beneath her. On her upper arm, an extravagant purple-green bruise bloomed. Bobbie Ann blinked, realized she was composing yet another description for Carson, as if she'd be coming home to him. Sitting on his lap, telling him her day.

"Wait now." Bobbie Ann's long hair dripped onto an incident, blurring the inked word *head-butts*. "You say lots of aggression here?" Her throat felt raw; it had been days since she'd talked to anyone except her mama's—now her own—lawyer.

"Not at night, hon." May Mooney chuckled, her thick neck rippling: heavy cream, the kind that turns light when whipped. "Lucky for you, they're all—" her tongue clicked, "—dead to the world."

Lights flickered. A tall, sparsely populated bookcase swayed as they passed. A fragment of title almost stopped Bobbie Ann: *What to Do*, it began in confident yellow block letters, and her heart actually rose with dumb hopeful relief, as when Carson used to take firm hold of her bare upper arms, never quite leaving a mark.

"Usually not one peep." May chuckled again, her cheer moderately more genuine now with her own escape all but assured. What, what to do. Bobbie Ann followed May's small-sounding feet, eying the broad green rayon plain of her back, the strained seams, each thread frayed thin.

"An' Rose. Now don't let her tell you she's earned her headphones." May puffed, halted by the front door. "Oh, an' we surely can't forget Philip. Li'l Philip Purdue." Her green eyes glinted like the microscopic gold cross at her throat. "He shouldn't even *be* here." Bobbie Ann stared. Here on earth, May seemed to mean. "But his father heads the board. Joined up just so he could buy Philip a slot. When all along we'd been told, *pro*-mised, nothing but moderate to severe . . ."

Bobbie Ann looked down at her own washed-out UNC sweat-

shirt, making a vow, the sort she'd made often lately. Late nights:
after "Alfred Hitchcock Presents" and "Get Smart," after mastur-
bating and swallowing her Seconal. Another vow. No matter how
low—how much lower—she sank, she must consciously avoid joining what Mama called the Chorus of Chronic Complaint.

". . . and this boy's way past your everyday *severe*."

Bobbie Ann drew breath to question that word, but May turned
her back, opened the coat closet. "You ask me, he's down there with
those poor Mong'loid monster babies, Lord love 'em." She sighed,
wrestling with a vast mass of plastic. Bobbie Ann blinked. Since her
harried dripping arrival and May's ominously grateful greeting,
Bobbie Ann had let May quite politely bulldoze past all her attempts to confess that she hadn't done this kind of thing in years,
that she couldn't even remember what was meant by, say, severe.

"Oopsie dais-y!" May's voice rose and fell with her shiny plastic
poncho: a sweet singsong rhythm she must use with the—what
would they be called?—residents. "So." Crackling plastic settled.
Rain sizzled. "Think ya can handle it, hon?"

Bobbie Ann managed a shrug, her shoulders already hard to lift.
The same old nighttime cloak had descended inside her chest.
Hugging herself, she locked her arms against her lowest ribs. A
child-sized cage, thin curved bones Carson used to span with his
hands.

"So, so, so." May gave a mighty sigh, her flea-sized cross quiver-
ing with sparks. Her Christian spirit sending signals of struggle as
her eyes skimmed down Bobbie Ann's body? To stir up such re-
sentment, Bobbie Ann thought, it—her thirty-year-old girl-sized
body—must still look okay, even after weeks of junk food and no
jogging. She hugged herself harder, to hurt, hating her own mean
little rush of relief. Too many of her pleasures, lately, seemed mean.
"Anyhow." May Mooney tilted her delicate watch, its face as tiny as
one of her fingernails. "Any questions?" she asked, flashing Bobbie
Ann a final green glance that meant: there better not be.

After May had zoomed off to her midnight prayer meeting in a
jaunty two-door Toyota—her one chance in this life to be fast and
small—Bobbie Ann huddled on the couch and skimmed the first

forbidden incident. She blinked to clear her cloudy contacts, already too dry, worn since daylight. Would they last the night?

9pm, 4/14: R.A. commences inappropriate questions (ex: What can you do to the Who? Why is your eyeball upside down?) Bobbie Ann blinked harder, wondering.

Two weeks before—barely able to remember why, in her single year at University of North Carolina, she'd majored in special ed—Bobbie Ann had signed up at a human services temp agency called Helping Hands. Carson claimed she'd chosen it as the most pathetic place possible. Another Little Orphan Ann maneuver. Maybe so, she'd thought, lying awake in their, now her, half-baked bed. Unable, night after night, to turn off her brain, turn on her own body. So when, at 11 PM, amidst a combination thunderstorm—crying jag, the agency phoned and asked her—begged, really—to drive out to a group home and do an emergency overnight, Bobbie Ann agreed. Sniffling and fumbling to hang up, she wondered, Could this night get any worse? Daring it to, she swung onto the streaming streets and skidded round a fallen tree limb, exhilarated to see that it wasn't just her, inside her. Everything outside too was, really was, ripping apart.

After told no headphones, R.A. commences self abusive/aggr. behav. head-butts arm of couch, bites arm of Yours Truly

Bobbie Ann flipped the folder shut, chopping short May's neatly rounded determinedly cheerful words. Thunder gave a deep chuckling rumble; lights flickered. False cheer: another trap she'd vow to avoid. Bedsprings made faint rhythmic creaks. Bobbie Ann shoved the incidents off her lap, let them scatter on the floor.

"Who . . ." A hoarse female voice called from upstairs. Or was it wind? "Who-ooh?"

Shaking her head hard, Bobbie Ann reached down into the laundry basket and folded two socks together, trying to hide the ugly *PP*. Muffled movement commenced upstairs, shuffling footsteps. Even rolled tight, the sock ball showed black blurry ink on all sides. Bobbie Ann hurled it back, watched it bounce off unfolded underwear. Through a fresh staticky burst of rain, a door thumped. Steps intensified.

Looking up, Bobbie Ann held her face still, as if for inspection.

Lately, below the corners of her mouth, two matching weights had begun to form. She sucked in her cheeks, those extra pads of fat, picturing the neat white squares Mama sewed into the hems of all her curtains so they'd hang straight, even in a breeze.

The creaking wood stairs were softened by the hard rain. Bobbie Ann kept staring. Her thighs tensed; her feet pressed the floor.

"Who?"

A girl hovered in the dim living room archway. Lamplight gleamed off her glasses: dark octagonal frames, dense lenses. Bobbie Ann squinted at her thick-lipped mouth, half-open. Above, in the gentler outer circle of light, shiny black eyes, semicrossed, stared at Bobbie Ann's nose.

"Who *you*?" She shuffled closer in her nightgown, pressing colored papers to her breasts, her head bowed as if beaten down by the pouring rain. Her jaggedly cut black hair stuck out at all angles. Maybe she'd seized a pair of scissors herself. Or maybe it was a deliberate punk cut, one that would look perfectly normal on someone else.

"See Ro-ger. He's shape-ly. Isn't he shape-ly?" She was not, as Mama would say, from 'round here. Her voice held Yankee harshness. New Jersey, New York?

In the growing circle of lamplight, this girl held out a worn handful of magazine photos, their gloss long gone. Faces already outdated in Bobbie Ann's high school days. Roger Daltry and the Who. Some photos were pasted on uneven squares of construction paper. The girl stood close enough now that Bobbie Ann breathed her warm sleepy smell. Too little shampoo, too much toothpaste. Her breasts sagged under her cotton nightgown. Was she fifteen, thirty? She peered straight at Bobbie Ann's nose. "You sub?"

"That's right." Despite the pulse jumping in her throat, Bobbie Ann made her voice level. Imitation Mama. "I'm the substitute, the . . . overnight."

The girl nodded, impatient with an answer she must've heard a hundred times. "Wan' my head-phones." Her voice held no expectation.

"Well, it's . . . a little late, Rose." Bobbie Ann forced a baby-sitter smile. "I mean, everyone's asleep. Looks like you need some sleep too, hon."

Rose shrugged dismissively, maybe annoyed by the 'hon.' Or by not being asked her own name. "But we were talk-ing a-bout the Who, right?"

Her hard Yankee voice mimicked a soft Carolina rise and fall, an exaggeratedly courteous redirection of the conversation. Bobbie Ann nodded uncertainly. Nodding too, not at all uncertain, Rose settled next to her on the couch, startlingly warm and close. The lamp spotlit her top picture, an aging magazine shot of Roger Daltry as Tommy: his electrified halo of girlish curls, his angelic deaf-dumb-and-blind kid stare.

"Feel me, tou-ouch me," Rose began to sing, softly off key. Her breath was hot and minty. "Fee-eel me, heal me . . ."

Stiffly, breathing the rich unwashed smell of Rose's hair, Bobbie Ann fingered Roger. His hair blurred white around the edges from too much touching.

"Soft-as-a-kitten, in't he?"

Bobbie Ann had to nod. The crinkly once-glossy texture re-minded her of Carson's cock at rest, its limp plush skin. She tensed her fingers to keep them from trembling.

"So shape-ly. Aren't the Who shapely?" Rose reshuffled her stack to show a group shot pasted on a crudely cut construction-paper heart. An old shot, young sullen faces. Odds 'n' Sods. They stood in a row in bell bottoms and no shirts. Rose smiled, half her mouth rising. Thick chapped lips, crooked teeth, toothpaste breath. "Know how I earn head-phones?" She spoke from the live side, like an old lady who's had a stroke. "No butts," she recited. "No ques-tions, no 'gression."

"Oh." Bobbie Ann's shoulders tightened. Rose leaned closer, her glasses sliding halfway down her nose.

"I've got quite an im-ag-ination," she whispered in a house-mother tone, as if trying to reassure Bobbie Ann. "What can you, you do to the Who?" Bobbie Ann shifted. A—what was it called?—inappropriate question. Prelude to aggr. behav.?

"You can rock them!" Rose jerked the scraps back and forth, her
elbow poking Bobbie Ann's stomach, hard.

"Hey now, Rose." Bobbie Ann pulled herself to her feet. Rose
stared up at her, unnervingly expectant, her mouth half-open. Wet-
ness gathered on her lower lip. "Hey, we got to check that dough."

Bobbie Ann turned on her heel, imitated Mama's brisk housewife
strides so well she wasn't even surprised to hear Rose fall into step
behind. The kitchen doorway was solidly dark. As Bobbie Ann
halted, too suddenly, Rose bumped her.

"Sorry, hon," Bobbie Ann murmured, her voice all at once as
shaky as her hands. "Need light," she managed to add, patting the
wall hard and fast in search of the switch.

You don't really need this, Babe, Carson had told her the last
week as he'd switched on her nightlight, implying with his tone that
there was someone else, now, who did. Nineteen years old: that was
all Bobbie Ann knew, had to know.

Under bright kitchen lights, inside comforting kitchen quiet, she
punched dough. Rose leaned in the doorway, hugging the Who.
Rain crackled on the pane, low voltage, temporarily tamed. Baking
project lists and orange-red fingerpaintings hung around a magne-
tized flashlight on the refrigerator door. Bobbie Ann breathed in
cinnamon and yeast, leaned on the heels of her hands to flatten,
then reflatten, the springy pliant dough. Flour dusted her fingertips. She draped a clean dish towel over the punched lump, picturing May Mooney sunk in prayer, May's soul rather than her body
expanding. Surprised to still be capable of such a sweet special-ed-
teacher-type thought, Bobbie Ann looked over her shoulder. "Hey,
where you from, anyhow?"

Rose recited her answer, her voice flat and matter-of-fact. "I lived
in New-ark New Jer-sey till I was five and my mother started sex-u-ly
a-busing me." She paused, sucked in her spit. "Then they put me
in the Center. Then here."

"Good Lord." Mama's words. Bobbie Ann blinked, cleared her
lenses. "Are you . . . Do you like it here?" Here on earth, she
thought. "I mean, now?"

Rose nodded, impatient again. "You gonna do the count?"

In obedient relief, Bobbie Ann knelt by the lowest cabinet and began to count cans, marking ballpoint numbers on a clipboard nailed inside the cabinet door. Rose leaned on the counter behind her, breathing through her mouth. Wet intent breaths.

Five spinach, one creamed corn, six cling peaches. Bobbie Ann took care not to jangle the ring of keys hanging by the chart, not to break the peaceful rain-patter silence. Her pen scratched. Maybe Mama was right, Mama and her perfect curtains, her days divided by tasks. Two split pea and ham, one Dutch Cleanser, surely misplaced. Her pen faltered. Rain thickened.

"Who that?" Rose sucked in her wet breath.

"Oh, no-thing." Bobbie Ann hefted the powdery can, Mama's old brand. A poisonous whiff of ammonia. On the faded label, a Dutch housewife in kerchief and ruffled apron raised her broom against a spunky tumbleweed of dust. As Bobbie Ann rose on her knees, intending to shelve the can higher up, out of reach, she felt her lips quiver. Her first natural smile in weeks.

That was when—with a sky-splitting wall-quaking clap—the lights went out. A flashbulb clap: aimed straight at Bobbie Ann's foolish Mama face. God's Candid Camera. As she sank heavily onto her heels, she felt her smile give the bitter thin-lipped twist she'd made many a mental note to avoid. Rain lashed the walls and windows, holding back nothing now. Even in the dark, Bobbie Ann could feel Rose watching her, still leaning on the counter, her wet breaths coming only a little quicker. Papers shifted, the Who pressed closer. Somewhere above, a moan rose. Inside Bobbie Ann's chest, the nighttime cloak—having begun, briefly, to lift—dropped back down at twice its usual weight. She set the Dutch Cleanser on the floor with a hollow clank.

"Well, shit," she muttered, her Mama impersonation fading fast into the black.

Armed only with the bright but unsteady kitchen flashlight—she jerked it to revive it, batteries clacking like castanets—she crept back into the living room. Rose lagged behind, not letting her hand be held. As they inched toward the couch, separately, Bobbie Ann skidded. Light and paper slid wildly under her feet. The floor tilted, slammed her ass. She sat in a wide scatter of incidents, still gripping her light. Thunder gave another cosmic chuckle.

"Wha?" Rose sounded plaintive and impatient both as she stared down from above. The flashlight glared off her glasses. Night stop signs. The moan upstairs droned louder, though Rose seemed not to hear it. "Wha we *do*?"

Bobbie Ann clenched her back teeth, hot tears beginning to brew. Her tailbone ached. Years before, she'd watched a tearful Miss North Carolina tell the pageant MC she was majoring in special ed. The audience applauded. Certainly Carson, a brash business major, had been charmed at first, even impressed. After she'd quit UNC to marry him, Bobbie Ann actually had worked for a time, part-time, in a special ed class for toddlers. Mildly retarded, only mildly aggressive. Even so, she hadn't managed to duck a hurled toy truck. That evening, Carson kissed the plum-pit bump on her forehead and took hold of her shoulders and quietly insisted she quit. She had cried: tears of pure secret relief.

What to Do in an Emergency. All on its own, Bobbie Ann's flashlight sought out those bold yellow words in the bookcase, trapped them. One good thing about tears: they wet her contacts, kept the darkness clear. Shakily, she pulled herself to her feet, her breath rasping. *A Rapid Action Guide: When Seconds Count.*

When do they not? Bobbie Ann wondered, taking hold of that solid spine. Sunk on the couch beside Rose, she flipped open the oversized book and skimmed with her light down the boldfaced—no, frantic-faced—headings, each one printed on a large dictionary-style flap for easy flipping, no matter how shaky or bloody your hands.

Bleeding; Burns & Scalds; Choking; Drug Overdose; Electric Shock; Unconscious Person; Burst Pipe; Power Outage; Leaking Tank.

In her jittery spotlight, Bobbie Ann flipped pages, hearing the moan rise again like an alarm bell she couldn't keep ignoring. Rose snuggled closer. Power Outage, Bobbie Ann told herself, her fingers cold and tense. One sketch appeared over and over, each victim placed in *recovery position*: the body curled on a floor, the head low, the legs bent as if the victim might in fact be running, running on an endlessly downward slope.

. . . time to read these instructions is BEFORE an emergency strikes. Just as the middle of a darkening forest is no place to begin learning how to use a map.

Upstairs, a second moan joined the first. Bobbie Ann's grip on the flashlight tightened. But she couldn't flip the next page, her eyes swimming along italicized lines. *Bleeding* alone held infinite possibilities: *Large Foreign Body in Skin; Bleeding that Will Not Stop; Bleeding from Nose, Ear or Mouth.*

Two moans now, competing against the rain. Bobbie Ann locked stares with the bulging spotlit eyes of a child demonstrating a universal choking sign. *Immediate intervention is in order, too, if victim clutches throat or turns blue.*

A mama stretched her mouth so it covered a baby's mouth and nose, so the mama seemed to be sucking up the baby's face. Bobbie Ann turned the page hurriedly, kept turning. "Power Outage," she read out loud, flattening the words with her palm. She held the flashlight steady. "'Pow-er outages are al-ways un-expected and never pleasant.'"

"But we—" Rose elbowed Bobbie Ann, much harder than before, her Yankee voice hardening too. "We were talking about the Who, weren't we?"

She shoved her pictures into Bobbie Ann's light, hiding the page. Print showed through behind the luminously lit faces. Rose pointed. "See? That's Roger Dodger, that's Perfect Pete, an' that's Little Keithy Moon. See how lit-tle he is?"

"Hey." Bobbie Ann pushed the photos to one side, trying to take on the cool authoritative tone of *What to Do*. "Hey listen, now: 'Switch off elec-trical ap-pliances, po-tential fire hazards—'"

"You lis-ten *me*." Harder than Carson, Rose gripped Bobbie Ann's bare arm. One-handed, left-handed. With her right, she shoved her pictures back over the print. "Keithy died in 19–68." Rose's right finger froze over his tiny dazed face. Abruptly, her glasses jumping on her nose, she raised her frozen finger, pointing to the moans. "Drug over-dose!" She sang in a high-pitched fal-setto. "Keith-y? Can you hear me?"

"Shhh!" Letting the flashlight droop, Bobbie Ann took hold of
Rose's rigidly pointing fist. From her own fist, Rose's finger stuck
up, clammy cold.

"*Hear* him?" In one swift city-girl motion, Rose twisted from
Bobbie Ann's amateur grasp and swept all the photos off *What to
Do*, its pages flapping backward. Her arm jolted the flashlight beam
up the walls to the cracked ceiling and down again. The light hung
in Bobbie Ann's hand, pointed to the mass of incidents and Who
faces strewn over the floor. Bobbie Ann stared down, her contacts
all too clear.

"Who that?" Rose demanded, stabbing an ink sketch of a man in
recovery position. From Bobbie Ann's skewed angle, he looked like
he thought he was running, but really was falling. Dumbly, Bobbie
Ann stared at his bent arm: the poor guy about to pray or suck his
thumb.

"Keithy Moon!" Rose gripped Bobbie Ann's knee like a gearshift, her elbow sticking straight up. Going off, they'd always say at
the day care center. "He's in re-hab." Rose tightened her grip, her
fingers pressing bone. "He needs care," Rose whispered, this time
in a tentative reverent TV voice. The same voice she'd used to say
sex-u-ly abused. "Care, not de-spair."

Bobbie Ann could only nod, her legs stiffening against the steady
squeeze of her kneecap.

"Right!" Eagerly, Rose bent forward to nod with her. Their
heads butted, bone bumping bone. A deliberate jaw-jarring butt.
The flashlight faltered, failed.

"No!" Rose smacked her own cheek, her slap echoing in the new
dense dark. "No, bad, bad." As the flashlight flickered back on,
Rose slapped it too, knocking it out of Bobbie Ann's hand. It rolled
on the floor, lighting the Who, the ceiling, the Who. They both
watched, hugging themselves, suddenly shivering.

"Cold—" Bobbie Ann gasped as the light rocked to a halt, inches
from her feet. Her knee smarted; her bumped skull vibrated. "The
heat's off, see? We're cold!"

This was a revelation. Upstairs, both moans rose in agreement,
competing with each other.

"Cold?" Rose scrambled to her feet, her breasts swinging behind her nightgown, spotlit by the light she bent to grab. "They cold?" She backed away from the couch, barefoot, stepping between the scattered Who.

"They?" Bobbie Ann stared into the dark space where Rose had spun on her heel, the light vanishing. Bare feet pounded carpet. Bobbie Ann stayed slumped, *What to Do* weighing her down. Through the open kitchen doorway, feet slapped linoleum. Drunken applause. "Deaf-dumb-an'-blind kid—" Rose sang. Something gave a quick hard click: the cabinet hinges? A plug tugged out of the wall? "Sure playz-a mean Pin-ball!"

Above her, the moaners had quieted again, respectfully expectant, encouraged by the kitchen clatter. Tin cans clanked: yes, Rose had opened that lower cabinet.

"How you think he *do* it?" she sang, louder now, more confident. "I Don' Know!" Another can clanked, this one hollow. Powdery.

"No!" *What to Do* slid from Bobbie Ann's lap like a sled, ramming her big toe. "Don't touch that, Rose—"

Bobbie Ann stumbled up and over the shifty rustling mass of incident reports, Who hearts.

"Plays by sense o' smell—"

Keys jangled. Grit scraped under Bobbie Ann's rubber sneaker soles: bitter blue-white powder, less crunchy than sugar. "Don't—" Bobbie Ann ordered in a stage whisper, conscious of the dark listening silence that surrounded the kitchen. "Don't *touch*."

"Who?" Beyond the counter, keys jangled louder. Rose rose over the edge, her glasses askew, her jagged hair sticking up like a crown. She clutched the flashlight and key ring in one hand and raised the Dutch Cleanser in the other. More powder spilled.

"No—" Bobbie Ann lunged over the counter and seized Rose's elbow. Keys clanged; the dough bowl wobbled; the light cracked down hard on the countertop, rolled, then swooped to the floor, clattering and faltering. Everything dark.

"Where *key*?" Rose wrested herself from Bobbie Ann's grip and dropped to her knees. She slapped linoleum like a tom-tom. "Where it go? Where go, Ro-ger?"

"Shh!" Bobbie Ann dropped down beside her, groping too. Her

hands beat their own hard rhythm. No wedding ring clicks. Just

bare palms against the gritty floor.

"Who?" Crouched on her hands and knees, Rose threw back
her head. "Where go, Who? Who-*ooh*?" Her shout came out fine
and loud. Bobbie Ann's own throat tightened. Through her tear-
blurred contacts, she took in Rose's profile, its coyote tilt. "Who-
ooh!" The second shout was shriller, higher pitched. A child's
whine. Would they all join in now, a rising whining chorus of
complaint? Unmuffled, unstoppable? "*Who-ooh*!" Rose clanked the
Dutch Cleanser can on the floor, a crazed judge's gavel, poison
powder puffing up. "Who-*ooh*?"

"Hush!" Bobbie Ann clamped one hand over Rose's wet wide-
open mouth. The Dutch Cleanser thudded. Locked together like
blind wrestlers, Rose and Bobbie Ann rocked backward, hot breath
snorting out between Bobbie Ann's fingers. Rose's lips contracted:
thick chapped muscular lips. City lips. Her mouth moved under
Bobbie Ann's palm, her teeth scraping skin, closing in.

Bobbie Ann's own scream left her throat satisfyingly stripped.
Her ears echoed, full of the sound. Only the moans answered, no
louder than before. Everyone already *is* awake, Bobbie Ann told
herself, pressing her bitten hand to her stomach. Her other hand
reached for the faintest of gleams. Cold metal tube. She shook
the flashlight hard. Its weakly awakened beam illuminated Rose's
sturdy bare feet. Her toenails had outgrown their pink dabs of polish. Panting, Rose pulled herself up and stepped over the Dutch
Cleanser, bent toward the counter. Powder crunched.

Bobbie Ann tasted blue ammonia grit and sputtered, spat at the
floor. In the back of the kitchen, Rose's barefoot steps halted. Keys
jangled wearily. Squinting above the flashlight beam, Bobbie Ann
noticed that the dark had grown less dense. Metal scraped metal.
Rose sighed, tried another key. It clicked; a door squeaked open. A
supply closet? The door thumped shut; Rose stalked back into the
flashlight's range. She stepped past Bobbie Ann without a glance,
her back straight, her steps slow and steady. Her arms were filled,
now, with blankets.

Bobbie Ann lowered her hand. The meaty mound below her

thumb smarted: a surface wound, bleeding but not deep. Carpet muffled Rose's steps. Upstairs, the moans continued, slower and sleepier. An end in sight, in sound.

Bobbie Ann pulled herself up, her breasts hanging down inside her bra. Batteries clacked in their metal tube. The light seemed dimmer, the living room much less dark. Bobbie Ann's fingers tightened, cold yet sweaty on the metal. Paper rustled under her sneakers as she followed her downcast beam. Rose stood at the foot of the stairs in shadowed silhouette, bent under the weight of blankets. Her back faced Bobbie Ann, her nightgown rumpled. Hair shone on her calf.

The moans slowed almost to a stop, setting Rose in motion. They climbed slowly. Rose shouldered open the first door—a Who poster flapping, half–torn down—and stalked inside. Her roommate—Belinda?—was whimpering, curled up in her sheets. Bobbie Ann spotlit Belinda's tousled brown hair, cut short like Rose's, but more evenly. Belinda gave a suspicious slit-eyed stare. Had she tried to rip down the Who?

Rose hurled the top blanket, covering Belinda up, head and all. Underneath, Belinda mumbled, either in gratitude or complaint. Bobbie Ann stepped back. At the doorway, Rose stared over her shoulder, maybe pleased to see Belinda gone. Her octagonal glasses flashed. Leaving the door half-open, they padded over to the next.

A boy sat hunched in sheets and one lightweight quilt, arm-wrestling with himself. Jackie J.? Light shone on his dark profile, his kinky close-shaven hair. His knuckly double fist trembled. A window stood open, chill wet air drifting in. Jackie's moan was the gentlest, the lowest. Leaning back, Rose balanced on one heel. She hurled the blanket over Jackie as if over a piece of furniture, her movement bored and matter-of-fact. It hit with a cloth thud, knocked Jackie on his side. Or maybe he rolled by himself, lowering his soldierly head at last. His moan and the bedsprings' whine ceased, both at once.

Rain crackled. Bobbie Ann inched over to the window and strained to pull it shut, one-handed. The wood frame creaked as it shuddered down. Her hand hurt. Rose stood in the doorway, hugging the last two blankets, maybe waiting. One corner trailed the floor.

The last moans, the slowest and loudest, had led the others. The last dark cubicle smelled of chilled piss. Philip—this must be Philip—lay twisted in his sheets, his skinny boy's body made bulky by diapers taped on under his flannel pajamas. Oversized Dr. Dentons, specially ordered by his dad? Little Philip Purdue raised his head to stare at Rose, his hair orange in the flashlight. He blinked, his lashes orange too. Freckles covered his pale face like spots on a tropical fish. "Muhuhh?"

Here, Rose hesitated, hugging the blankets as tightly as the Who. Philip's eyes didn't shine: a pure pupilless orange. Locked in his stare, Rose let Bobbie Ann take hold of one blanket. Aiming her flashlight, she managed a sloppy left-handed throw. The blanket landed beside Philip in a heap. As Bobbie Ann stepped toward him, he wriggled under it by himself, burrowing in, curling up tight. With a last moan, he stuffed a blanket corner into his mouth and began to suck. Rose and Bobbie Ann watched, both breathing through their mouths.

Three diapers, May had told Bobbie Ann. No need to change him, she'd murmured as she left. Ought to, Bobbie Ann thought. Ought to anyhow. But she followed Rose, let Rose kick shut his door behind them, sealing in the smell. Rose shuffled over to her own half-open door and halted, unmistakably waiting. Bobbie Ann shuffled forward too, her light flooding the hall floor. For the first time, Rose stared at Bobbie Ann's bloody hand, then up. A new panicky gleam danced behind her glasses.

"Who you?" Rose asked from one side of her mouth. Suddenly playing dumb.

"Barbara," Bobbie Ann told her, trying it out. Rose hugged her blanket tighter and studied the falling-down poster on her door as if she didn't know what was wrong with it. Or only pretended not to know, so Bobbie Ann would step forward and smooth down the Who, their sheen completely worn away. Through thin paper, Bobbie Ann pressed a rolled bump of tired-out tape, making it stick.

"Where Ro-ger?" Rose asked, still using that self-consciously dumb voice. She stared again at Bobbie Ann's nose, maybe waiting for Bobbie Ann to say Roger Daltry was downstairs in rehab with Keith Moon, that Roger would sleep tight.

"He's in England," Bobbie Ann answered flatly. No trace of babysitter softness. "You know."

"Oh." Rose stared at Bobbie Ann's nose. "He 'sleep?" The quaver in her voice sounded genuine.

"I . . . don't know," Bobbie Ann answered, sticking to her course, but uncertainly. "It's different there. You know. A different time zone."

Rose gave a slow nod. Her semicrossed stare inched up so their eyes almost met. The gleam of Bobbie Ann's nose hovered between them. Rose closed her lips at last.

Downstairs, Bobbie Ann clicked off the flashlight. The kitchen was shadowy now, not dark. Her hand was bloody but dry. Bobbie Ann wiped the floor and counter, shelved the Dutch Cleanser high above the sink. She popped out the driest of her contacts, tilted back her head to squeeze drops into both eyes. In the dim living room, she slid *What to Do* onto its shelf, knelt on the floor, gathered the Who and the incident reports into a single pile. Her eyeballs burned. Her throat and hand burned too, less painfully. Her arms were only lightly marked. She had long since passed the threshold of being sleepy. She was so tired now she didn't feel tired at all. Sitting on the couch, half-blind, she folded socks. As she heard the kitchen door rattle, she let her shoulders slump.

She spent the last minutes of her shift standing in the doorway of the downstairs bathroom watching May Mooney strip Philip Purdue. Hot water exploded into the porcelain tub. With only one contact lens in, everything looked half-flattened. "Muh-muh." Philip strained his whole body toward the water. He squirmed as May peeled off the wet sweaty pajamas, expertly untaping the top diaper. Her arms jiggled, heavy but strong. No, Bobbie Ann thought. No, I couldn't do that. Philip lunged for the tub—scrambled in, splashing May's sweatpants.

"Whoa, hon." May took firm hold of his waist and tore the last diapers. Two round feces bobbed in the water, clean and natural as

miniature logs. May used his plastic underpants like a scoop, letting
him settle back, his hair afloat. Liquid fins. His orange-brown eyes
misted in the steam; his tropical-fish freckles wavered underwater.
May crammed the diapers into a trash bin, then washed her hands
at the sink, humming. Real cheer, false? The distinction seemed
silly. Philip was humming along, tunelessly. His breath made minute ripples in water, his natural element.

"So." May Mooney glanced at Bobbie Ann, her green eyes deepened by the overbright blue-green of her morning sweatshirt. Eyes
she must have wished more people would notice. "You gonna come
back sometime, hon?"

"Don't think so." Bobbie Ann swallowed, slipping her bitten
hand into her pocket. Her sleeves were rolled down. Day care, she
told herself. She'd ask Helping Hands for an ordinary day care job,
something she could stand to do while the divorce came through.
Something to keep her from moving back to Mama's. "I mean, I
know I won't. Come back."

May answered with her first genuine smile, showing China-doll
teeth. Her eyes and tiny gold cross glinted. Her initial impression
of Bobbie Ann confirmed. Bobbie Ann nodded, letting her think
whatever she wanted.

"Oh yeah." Bobbie Ann turned to the softly lit living room. Behind the couch, papers rustled. "The power's off," she told May,
realizing as she spoke that it wasn't, anymore.

"Ba-ba?" Rose stood up behind the couch and shuffled into view,
still in her nightgown. She pressed the Who photos to her chest,
the red construction paper heart on bottom. "Ba-bra?"

It might have sounded like a nonsense word, to May. Rose shuffled closer, her jagged hair sticking up on only one side, her glasses
gone, her nose marked by their purplish dents. Without lenses mag-
nifying them, her black eyes no longer blurred. Crow's feet stood
out around her squint. Definitely older than Bobbie Ann: a teenager in the 60s, at the height of the Who. She cocked her head.

"It's the temp girl, Rose." May Mooney already sounded tired of
explaining things.

"Uh-huh." Rose shifted to her slower dumber voice. She squinted
from May to Bobbie Ann's pocketed hand, leaning close, no trace

of toothpaste left. Sour grown-up morning breath. Behind them, Philip sloshed. A moan, this time, of pleasure?

"Your time sheet's in the kitchen, hon." May rotated herself toward the tub, rolling her sweatshirt sleeves further up, her bruise a pinker purple.

"You com-ing back?" Rose gave Bobbie Ann a lopsided smile. Grateful, maybe, that she'd hidden the bite. Or did Rose even remember?

"Sure I am," Bobbie Ann heard herself say, avoiding Rose's eager cross-eyed gaze. And she turned away, accidentally catching the housemother's eye. May Mooney winked. Flushing, Bobbie Ann felt Rose notice the wink.

"You come next week-end?" Rose shuffled close behind her, suspicious now.

"Gotta go." Bobbie Ann slipped into the kitchen doorway. Leftover grit scraped linoleum. "Hey." She lifted her time sheet off the counter. "You checked that dough yet? See if it rose?"

She edged toward the back door and Rose shifted the Who to one hand, then reached for the covered bowl, bending close to see without her glasses. Bobbie Ann unhooked her raincoat from the door, its plastic dry. The knob turned.

"See you." She ducked out into the dawn light before Rose could look up. Sea legs. Wobbling, she made her way down the gravel drive to her VW bug, parked askew and plastered with leaves. The air tasted like cool wet leaves. As she cleared them off her curved front window, she wondered if she could drive with only one contact lens. Inside the glove compartment were glasses she hadn't worn in years, not wanting Carson to see. She reached for the car door, but a distant tap on glass made her glance over her shoulder. Rose's face pressed the kitchen windowpane, her nose flattened, her sleepy full-lipped smile lifting both sides of her mouth. Bobbie Ann wiped wet leaf scraps off her hands. Sighing, she shuffled back up the gravel slope.

The uncovered bread dough had swollen. Bobbie Ann's stomach stirred at its sweet yeasty smell. Its flesh-colored curve nearly overflowed the bowl. Through the walls, the bathtub was draining. Bobbie Ann held on to the kitchen's wood doorframe.

"Listen," she told Rose, making her voice firm. Rose stood bare-foot by the sink, pressing the Who to one slack breast. "Good-bye."

Rose blinked. "You . . . ," her chapped lips quavered. Her voice held its hard challenging Yankee edge. "You not?" She squinted, the creases around her eyes deepening. "You *not* com-ing back?" Be-hind Bobbie Ann, Carolina morning air drifted in, temporarily clear, rainwashed. Trees dripped. Bobbie Ann hesitated. Was she about to hurt Rose just to make herself feel honest? Would Rose even remember her a day from now? Trees kept dripping. Rose kept staring at Bobbie Ann's nose. Her black eyes shone, all pupil. Nod-ding slowly and drawing breath to speak, Bobbie Ann wondered how much, without glasses, Rose could see.

Disappeared

Enid Shomer's stories and poems have appeared in the New Yorker,
Atlantic, Paris Review, Poetry, *and other journals, as well as anthologies
including* Best New Stories from the South. *She is the author of four
volumes of poetry. Among her awards are two fellowships from the NEA,
three from the State of Florida, the Eunice Tietjens Award from* Poetry, *the
Celia Wagner Prize of the Poetry Society of America, and the Randall
Jarrell Prize. Her Iowa Award–winning collection,* Imaginary Men, *also
received the LSU/*Southern Review *Prize for the best first collection of the
year by an American author. Shomer has taught as Thurber House
Writer-in-Residence at the Ohio State University and as visiting writer
at Florida State University and at the University of Arkansas.*

*"The thing one quickly senses is the will and the voice, someone saying,
in effect, 'Relax, be comfortable, I'm going to take good care of you.'
It turns out to be true. These are very fine stories."*
JAMES SALTER, 1992

"Look at my life," Fontane said. She clutched her robe together
below her neck. Fontane was a thin, lithe woman with springy black
curls that lay close to her scalp. Even in grief she was beautiful, like
a piece of sculpture in the rain. "It's as if I'm being punished for
killing people in another life."

"I know, I know." Leila Pinkerton sprinkled sweetener into a
glass of iced tea. "There's no explaining it."

"Why would the Lord give me two children if He was going to
take them away?"

"I'm sure Hiram is all right," Leila said, hoping Fontane
wouldn't get angry at the ease with which hope poured from her
mouth. Leila had never had children herself and was well past the
age for it. "I just know it in here." She pointed to her heart. "It's

only been three days. He could have amnesia, he could have gotten
lost." She stopped before saying that he could have run away. What would he be running away from?

Leila Pinkerton and Fontane Whitley were as close to friendship as they could get, given that Leila was white, Fontane was black, and they lived in a world full of people who claimed to know what that meant. They came together in crisis, like an emergency room team. At other times, a formality neither of them had created restrained them, driving them back into their separate shells. They trusted each other hesitantly, the way you trust a relative you've heard bad things about since childhood but who has always treated you with the utmost kindness.

Fontane began weeping again. Leila put an arm around her and squeezed her shoulder. "Did you search his room?"

Fontane's eyes caught fire. "Do you think I'm an idiot? We tore the house apart, hoping for a note."

"I'm sorry. I know you did. I thought you did."

"If this is some prank of his, I'm going to kill him when he gets home." She laughed at herself; then she began to cry again.

"There was nothing missing from his room?"

"Not that I noticed." Fontane stirred and sat upright.

"Like a favorite book or toy, his sneakers?"

"I don't think so." But as she said it, Fontane stood and began walking up the stairs, and Leila followed.

Leila had never seen Hiram's room, and it wasn't at all the way she would have pictured it. It was futuristic, like the inside of a spaceship. "Handsome," she said, looking around. One wall, covered with black corkboard, had posters from the video store thumbtacked all over it, and four intricate circuit boards hanging from hooks. Shelves spray-painted silver held books and magazines jammed in at all angles, including a few titles Leila had given Hiram. She believed reading kept the mind sharp, and she liked to turn a phrase herself. She'd rearrange a thought or observation in her head until she got it just right, as if she intended to write it down, though she never did. Her favorite author was Mark Twain.

"I fought the beer sign." Fontane pointed over Hiram's desk to a Miller High Life neon sign with a whale spouting a bright-blue plume of water. "That was a birthday gift from Dayton." Dayton was Hiram's father. He had refused to marry Fontane when she got pregnant at seventeen and had left town two months after Hiram was born.

Leila felt Hiram's absence more here than she had downstairs. Stuffed animals, model planes, an afghan draped across the foot of the bed: without their owner, the objects seemed forlorn. She remembered sorting through her husband's clothes after he died. She had felt sad and then had fallen into a rage. Colonel Pinkerton's ties and shirts were uncooperative messengers, not the measure of the man but a pile of anonymous hand-me-downs. It reminded her of what happened when Claude Rains removed his suit and unwound the bandages from his hands and face. There was nothing left but his cigarette and the desperation in his voice.

"Is it O.K. if I look in here?" Leila's hand hovered at the pull of the center desk drawer.

Fontane began to rummage through the bureau. "Yes, oh yes," she said. "You can look anywhere at all."

Hiram Whitley, aged twelve, had been missing officially since Monday. On the noon news that day, Hiram had been described as a slender black boy, five feet two inches tall, last seen at home on Sunday morning wearing a T-shirt and pajama bottoms. Leila, who lived next door to the Whitleys, was no alarmist. Having no children herself, she had nothing to relate Hiram's disappearance to but her own childhood, so long ago. In those days, instead of sassing, children often ran away from home or vanished into the woods for a day. She'd never known of one who hadn't come back. She imagined that Hiram was off hunting squirrels with the BB gun his father, Dayton, had given him, or exploring the bat caves formed by the interstate crossing Bellamy Creek.

But Fontane and Evan Whitley, Hiram's stepfather, were more modern, and, Leila supposed, more realistic. They were half out of their minds with worry. No doubt they were thinking of the little girl who was kidnapped last year from a department store in Palm Beach and then murdered. The killer was never found. That had happened three hundred and fifty miles to the south, in the glittery,

crime-ridden part of Florida, which seemed a crazed foreign country compared to Bellamy County. Bellamy County had hummed
along for more than a hundred years on lumber mills, tobacco,
cattle, and truck farms. The town of Waccasassa was a transparent place, like a piece of old glass with impurities in it. Its inhabi-
tants had long ago accommodated themselves to its flaws. They had
their troubles, like people everywhere. There were bar fights and
convenience-store robberies, but Leila had never heard of a child
being snatched and murdered in Bellamy County.

"Have you got any notion at all where Hiram might be?" Fontane had asked her on Sunday afternoon, when she first discovered
Hiram was missing. Hiram had made himself scarce right after
breakfast, Fontane said, probably to avoid his stepfather's weekly
attempt to persuade him to go to church.

"The last I saw him was yesterday, when he did the yard for me,"
Leila said. It had been overcast and windy on Saturday, and the
whole time Hiram was cutting her grass, she had worried about
lightning, staring through the window as the mower slowly peeled
narrow swaths of lawn from dark to pale green. "I'm sure he'll turn
up by supper."

"I tried to call Dayton, but wouldn't you know it, his phone's
been disconnected," Fontane said. According to Fontane, she and
Dayton had been on good terms only for the amount of time it
took to conceive Hiram.

After Fontane left, Leila got in her old white Valiant and drove
over to Vern's Kwik Stop, where kids often hung out to play video
games and read comic books. Then she tried the middle-school
playground. She stopped for a glass of iced decaf at Sinrod Drugs,
swiveling slowly on her counter stool as she tried to put herself—a
plump, sixty-eight-year-old white woman—in Hiram's place, tried
to divine his whereabouts.

Leila had run away once, but she was nearly an adult at the time.
It was during the war, and the Colonel was being sent to an island
in the Pacific that was so small it wasn't on the big globe at her
teachers' college. They spent his last weekend pass in a motel room
in Myrtle Beach. Her parents didn't approve of the Colonel. Too
impulsive, they said. Reckless. White trash was what they meant. He

had a thick north-Georgia drawl, and he was big and raw-boned and had crooked front teeth. She loved him, she remembered, she loved him so much that just seeing the golden hairs bristling on his arms made her feel safe. And then, after forty-three years, he had disappeared into the earth as if he had never existed.

By Monday, the Whitleys were frantic. Mr. Whitley stayed home from the lumber mill where he was a foreman to be with Fontane. It was especially trying for them, coming so soon after the death of their six-year-old, Beckah, who had succumbed the year before to leukemia. AN ANGEL CAME TO EARTH AND TOOK THE FLOWER AWAY, Beckah's headstone said. The cemetery was at the end of two miles of washboard road. Beckah's first-grade teacher and Leila were the only white people at the funeral. Leila remembered the smell of freshly turned clay, and Mr. and Mrs. Whitley standing in front of the small coffin. Hiram had patted his mother's arm and tried to act like a grownup man, but Mr. Whitley dropped to his knees and began rocking back and forth, sobbing, "Lord, O Lord, you took her away." Fontane knelt down and wrapped herself around her husband. Hiram had stood behind them, suddenly tall and alone.

Leila believed that Fontane had married Evan Whitley out of spite, to get even with Dayton for leaving her. Evan was upstanding and proper. Once, at a Fourth of July street party, Leila had asked him to call her by her first name instead of Mrs. Pinkerton. He had raised his index finger to his eye and rubbed it and blinked repeatedly, as if a gnat were trapped in his lashes.

Dayton, on the other hand, was the kind of colorful, lying, energetic man whom adults saw right through and children adored. Hiram adored him. When Dayton visited, he was extravagantly attentive. Then no one heard a word from him for six months. He drove a hot rod with airbrushed flames licking the fenders and the rear end hiked up like a scorpion's tail. He never had money, though he always had some kind of recent good time he could tell you about. For Dayton, charm was a means of locomotion, like a swift pair of legs.

When Hiram was five or six, Dayton started bringing his women around. Leila had overheard some nasty arguments. Last Easter,

Mr. Whitley had ejected Dayton from the house and stood screaming at him until he drove away, and Leila could understand why.
She didn't care for Dayton's values or his women, with their black
leather shorts and tube tops and tall boots. "They're all nurses,
according to him," Fontane had told her. Leila responded with a
questioning look. "That's how he introduces every one of those
trashy women. He says, 'Have you met Sharanda, my scrub nurse
friend?'" Fontane had burst out laughing. "He must think I have
the brains of a bowling ball." But, for all his flaws, Leila could see
that Dayton had a little fire in his soul and that the same light flickered in Hiram.

The Atlanta police had gone to Dayton's last known address on
Monday. He wasn't there. His employer said he hadn't given notice, just quit showing up. The Bellamy County police stopped by
to question Fontane that afternoon. Was it possible that Dayton
had kidnapped Hiram? Fontane was sure he hadn't. "He's never
even invited Hiram to come home with him for a weekend," she
reported to Leila later. "Hiram is just a toy he plays with when he
wants to show off for one of his girlfriends."

The neighborhood where Leila and the Whitleys lived had been
built at the turn of the century for the new middle class—for meek,
polite women like Leila's mother and grandmother, women who
held the line between public and private life and feared shame. All
the houses backed onto service alleys, as if the household functions—garbage pickup, stove-wood delivery—had to be handled
as discreetly and invisibly as bodily functions. When Leila was growing up, everything about family life was thought to be proper and
just, and you weren't allowed to talk about anything personal.
Nowadays, nothing was right anywhere in society. Just tune in
"Donahue" or "Oprah": people confessed everything, absolutely
everything, in public. The sound of the daytime talk shows was one
gigantic lamentation. Were there shameful secrets in Hiram's family? Late Monday, the police had questioned Leila privately, asking
whether she'd noted any tension between family members, any
bruises on anybody. She told them she was certain there was no

violent behavior among the Whitleys. When Hiram misbehaved, he got a "time-out," not a slap.

Fontane was not trained to be meek, but to be scrappy and vigilant. She was born to adversity, while Leila was born to the smugness typical of Southern white people of a certain class. She and Fontane had never discussed it, would never discuss it. Fontane, the solitary dancer on the music box, with long legs like exclamation points. What must it be like for Fontane to climb into her bed tonight, Leila wondered. Mr. Whitley would pat her, turn over, and fall asleep. The house would be utterly quiet. All Fontane would hear would be the sound of her own breathing, the goddam regularity of it, and a prayer repeating in her head: Please, God, let Hiram be breathing, too. Eventually her eyes would grow accustomed to the dark. Visual purple—Leila remembered that phrase from somewhere. The room would take shape, the empty hallway beyond it like a bend in a river that leads nowhere.

Leila had worked or lived next door to Fontane for seven years— two when the building was only a store and five more since Leila had moved into it. Colonel Pinkerton's Treasure Trove was a cracker cottage with Victorian touches—gingerbread trim on the eaves and porch gallery, a fancy iron fence. Inside, it was set up like a model house, the used furniture and collectibles for sale displayed in rooms organized around color themes. Leila had a knack for arrangement and for color. The attic playroom was a cartoonish blue and yellow. The kitchen bustled with green glass Depression-era mixing bowls, red-handled eggbeaters, and gingham.

At first, Fontane Whitley kept her distance. But when the Colonel died, six years ago, it was Fontane who noticed that something was wrong with Leila. Fontane liked old things; she regularly checked the new arrivals after a truck had been unloaded. She collected hand-embroidered pillowcases and anything made of copper. One day, Fontane parked Beckah, who was sleeping in her stroller, next to Leila's desk. The adding machine was plugged in and she was paying bills. Leila remembered staring at the small red "on" light. The baby dozed; the red light burned steadily. It was like a tiny traffic signal that made her want to stop doing everything.

Time passed—she did not know how much time—and the baby's eyes were open. She was grabbing at a string of plastic keys suspended above her, drool running from the corner of her mouth. Her feet kicked and her eyes watered as she reached for the toy with her whole body. Once in a while she touched one of the keys, and it clicked against its neighbor. Otherwise, the store was quiet as a folded quilt.

"Leila, honey, you're not talking today. Something's wrong with you, you're not saying a word." The voice was Fontane's. "Can't you say something?" The silence had brought Fontane hurrying down from the third floor to the front room. Usually she could hear Leila's voice, uncurling tentatively at first, then climbing, as she chattered at Beckah. "You're not even talking to the baby?"

Leila looked at Beckah and then at Fontane and burst into tears, but still she couldn't talk. The red light burned. The baby slept, then played. The Colonel had been dead for six months.

The doctor said Leila's depression was "profound"—as if, she thought, he were describing a symphony or a speech. He prescribed an antidepressant drug that gave her a great deal of energy after just a few weeks. She felt happiest in the store, each room of it like a bright nest she had woven for herself. The colors and textures suddenly brought shivers of delight, almost as if she could taste them, as if they satisfied some physical appetite. The doctor said not to worry about this odd joy; it was just her aptitude for pleasure coming back. But it was the reason she had decided to sell the house outside of town where she had lived with the Colonel and move into the store.

The police visited the Whitleys three times on Tuesday. They brought a specialist from the Missing Children's Registry, who asked detailed questions about Hiram's playmates and habits and interviewed children in the neighborhood. The church auxiliary sent covered dishes. The Whitleys' phone rang continuously with calls from well-wishers, friends, psychics, and the parents of other children who had disappeared. Two camera vans stayed parked on the street.

By Tuesday afternoon, Fontane was under a doctor's care for her nerves. She took small yellow pills every four hours and received visitors from the striped sofa in her front room. Mr. Whitley had gone back to work, but not before posting pictures of Hiram all over the county: "Missing Reward," the fluorescent-green paper said above Hiram's seventh-grade picture. Newspapers in Valdosta, Tallahassee, and Jacksonville carried the story on the front page.

Leila brought lunch for Fontane that afternoon—a platter of chicken salad with sliced cucumbers and a pitcher of Crystal Light lemonade. The Reverend Dozier Jones was there, holding Fontane's limp arm as they prayed together in front of a silent TV screen where well-dressed white people moved through spacious rooms. Fontane had taken to watching a lot of TV since Beckah got sick. She still hadn't gone back to work. Mr. Whitley said she would never have to if she didn't want to.

"Ma'am," the Reverend said, rising to his feet, as Leila leaned down to place the food on the coffee table.

"You remember my neighbor, Leila Summer Pinkerton," Fontane said.

"What a pity we keep meeting under such trying circumstances," the Reverend said. For a second, Leila imagined his voice emanating from the afternoon soap unfolding in miniature behind him.

"Lemonade?" she asked.

Leila hardly watched television anymore. Her favorite programs in thirty-five years were the Milton Berle Show and the Bicentennial Minutes. She wished they would re-run Uncle Miltie—there was nothing funnier than a man dressed as a woman, pitched forward in high heels like a gawky bird.

After Beckah died, Hiram developed an interest in movies like *Frankenstein* and *The Shining* and *Alien*. His weekends were filled with gelatinous creatures, mummies trailing gauze, and body snatchers shaped like giant snow peas. Leila was happy to let Hiram use the Colonel's VCR. He talked a mile a minute while he watched movies. Leila had difficulty keeping up with him; her attention would settle on the film or be sidetracked by a bird at the feeder in the yard. Hiram talked mostly about school. Fontane bragged to anyone who would listen that Hiram was in the gifted program, and sometimes, in front of company, she had him recite the names of all the presidents.

After lunch, the Reverend followed Leila into the kitchen and stood running his finger along the Formica counter while she washed the dishes. "I'm certain we all appreciate your thoughtfulness to Mr. and Mrs. Whitley in this time of trouble," he said. His "t"s were little firecrackers going off in the middle of words. It was probably the way he preached, drawing the words out, making them sizzle and hiss.

"Don't you remember me from the shop?" Leila turned to face him. Sometimes she couldn't bear the way her black neighbors deferred to her, exchanging nothing more than pleasantries and homilies. She wanted to grab them and shake them and scream *It's me*. She often imagined the awkwardness dissolving: a door suddenly coming unstuck in a room full of people, every face furrowed at first with alarm, then softening as though a baby with wings had fluttered through the open doorway.

"The Colonel was a fine man, a fine man." The Reverend stayed behind his mask.

Mabidda thirty, I got thirty, mabidda thirty, who'll say thirty-five, bidda thirty-five where? The Colonel used to stand at his auctioneer's podium, the walnut gavel in his hand, a cowboy hat on his head. His voice was a bullwhip, gathering the crowd in, circling, snapping in the air. Whenever Leila thought of him now, she had to remind herself of his bad traits as well as the good ones. That way she missed him less. He was too stuck on himself to adopt a child. Afraid he'd get a defective one. Being from north Georgia, he wasn't open-minded, and, if the truth be told, in the beginning he did business with his black neighbors only because there was money to be made off them.

"He was just a human being," Leila said. "You don't have to sweet-talk me."

The Reverend looked shocked. "I know he's with Jesus," he said, "the Colonel. And I hope you've taken Jesus. I've taken Him into my heart, and I am ready to go to Him whenever I'm called."

Leila picked up a knife in the sink and imagined brandishing it in his direction. *How about right now? Are you ready to go this minute?* Instead, she scrubbed the blade with a sponge until clear water danced off it. The Reverend waited as if for an "amen" from Leila, still unwilling to acknowledge her candor. "I'm in no big hurry myself," she finally said. She knew he'd find the remark too playful, but wouldn't take issue with it. A moment later, he left, promising to return the next day, urging Fontane to call him any time.

The sheriff organized a search party. At dawn on Wednesday, deputies and citizens began combing Waccasassa and its environs. It made Leila sick to her stomach when she saw volunteer fire fighters going through the dumpster behind Video World. Soon Hiram's face would appear like a reverse cameo on milk cartons, and children throughout the state would compare his birth date to their own over bowls of breakfast cereal.

Leila would have liked to join the search, but her legs and back were not what they once were. She knew the local terrain well— from the sand-hill pines near the northern county line to the swampy sweet-gum woods that fringed the Waccasassa River at the western border. Bellamy County was full of creeks, dry creek beds, quarries, and dense forests, all of which now seemed threatening. It was still possible that Hiram had run off and gotten lost; Leila believed that. When he was in elementary school, he had gone camping with Mr. Whitley and his Boy Scout troop. He knew, presumably, the basics of survival: how to light a fire, find fresh water, and sleep in safety from the snakes, bobcats, and wild hogs that Leila knew roamed Bellamy County. Still, as the days passed, the vision of him that occupied her mind changed. On Sunday, he tromped in slow motion through a field like someone in a shampoo commercial, the wild phlox and rye grass waving him on. That night, he slept in the crotch of one of the huge live oaks that lined the old Bellamy plantation road to the black cemetery. By Tuesday, his clothes were ragged and his hair was starting to mat. She saw him smeared with mud to the elbows and knees, bent over a brook, catching crawdads. By Wednesday, every imaginary glimpse of him was terrifying; he was becoming wild, a feral child. He had taken on an existence in which ferocity alone could save him. Finally, it was impossible to picture him at all—he had regressed too far from the boy she knew. Hiram had become a complete mystery. And another mystery had been revealed: Leila loved him. She felt the love deep in her body and all the way out to its edges—in her teeth and nails, skin and bones she wanted him back.

The search teams quit at sundown, having netted two garbage bags full of what looked like shreds of clothes, newsprint, and beer cans, all of it described as potential evidence.

Now, with Fontane's approval, Leila pawed through crayons and rulers and Magic Markers and gum wrappers and balled-up home-work assignments. The disorder of Hiram's desk felt vital as it touched her hands, like the boy himself. "Nothing," she said when she was done. She walked to the closet and opened the two lou-vered bifold doors. Fontane nodded her agreement. "Help me," Leila said. "You know where things belong."

The two of them bent into the dark of the closet. Fontane was a good housekeeper. At home, when Leila opened a closet or looked under a bed, dust bunnies drifted in the small updrafts. Leila rec-ognized a lavender-and-black plaid shirt and remembered a wisp of conversation, Hiram's head framed by hickory leaves. The shirt seemed ghostlike.

"Oh, my God," Fontane said. She had been squatting. Now she sat back on the floor. "My God, my God."

"What is it?"

Fontane pointed to the flamingo-colored high-tops lined up neatly at the back of the closet. "I put his sneakers there myself. They were alongside the bed on Sunday. But where are his dress shoes? Do you see his dress shoes? Black leather wing tips?"

The two of them pulled out everything on the closet floor. While Fontane pushed through the clothes on hangers Leila dumped the contents of a toy box on the bedroom rug. Legos, blocks, a small, deflated football, an old T-shirt. "I don't see them anywhere," she said.

"His good black pants," Fontane said. Her voice was shrill with excitement. "His dress clothes are gone. They're gone!" Fontane grabbed Leila around the waist and jumped up and down, holding on to her. Then she raced down the steps and into the yard, to the toolshed. Leila watched from the window as Fontane removed the padlock, ducked inside, and returned weeping and thanking God. "The BB gun's gone!" she shouted. By the time Leila made her way downstairs, Fontane was on the phone with her husband, her voice wobbly with excitement, then rushing out in a torrent. Leila hugged Fontane and sat next to her as she made one call after another.

That night Leila lay in bed thinking about the last time Dayton had visited. He had brought Hiram the BB gun against Fontane and Evan's wishes. Worse, he had taken the boy out to the Bellamy plantation road for target practice. It was a Sunday morning, and Fontane was furious and humiliated when she discovered that the gunfire that punctuated the Reverend's sermon was from Dayton's shotgun. He and Hiram were shooting mistletoe out of the live oaks. Several parishioners had seen the two of them resting in the culvert, their guns propped against a tree.

On Friday afternoon, Leila donned her tattered straw hat and pink cotton gardening gloves. She knelt on the soft rubber mat she had bought to save her kneecaps and began weeding the herbs. Fontane was arguing with her husband. Leila could hear their voices rising and falling through the open kitchen window.

The sun beat down through the torn weave of Leila's hat, dappling her hands and the ground. Then Fontane was standing beside her. "Any news?" Leila asked.

"The police keep telling me it's easier to find two fugitives than one. They don't know Dayton."

Los Angeles, Detroit, Leila thought, that's where Dayton would take Hiram, some crowded place where people disappeared into each other.

"Evan's idea of finding Dayton is to pray." Fontane reached beside the parsley and pulled out a big tuft of wood sorrel and another of spurge. "If I could kill Dayton, I would," she said.

"I bet Hiram will come back on his own. At the end of the summer, when the novelty wears off." But Leila knew that a runaway could be running *toward* something as well as away from some-

thing. She had wondered about that: which would be lonelier for
Hiram—to settle into the quiet that Evan Whitley cast around his
family like a heavy net or to listen to the laughter of Dayton and his
women behind locked doors? And what if Dayton settled down?
What if he suddenly learned about Crockpots and oral thermome-
ters and encyclopedias? Fontane would become bitter, and then,
for all her cynicism, pious. Leila could picture her in lace-collared
dresses, offering up her love for her two lost children on the un-
yielding altar of the Zion church. In any case, even if he came home,
Hiram would be changed. There would be a different light in his
eyes—a satisfied shine, or, more likely, a sullen glint.

Leila took Fontane's hand and squeezed it hard and pressed it
against her forehead, the way a magician touches and presses and
smells the article of a stranger to surmise the past or the future.

A Discussion of Property

*Lex Williford holds an M.F.A. from the University of Arkansas and has
taught in the writing programs at Southern Illinois University and the
University of Alabama. His fiction and nonfiction have appeared in the*
American Literary Review, Fiction, Kansas Quarterly, Poets & Writers,
Quarterly West, Shenandoah, Southern Review, Virginia Quarterly
Review, *and elsewhere. He has received fellowships from the National
Endowment of the Arts, the Bread Loaf Writers' Conference, the Djerassi
Foundation, and the Ragdale Foundation, among others. A coeditor of the
new* Scribner Anthology of Contemporary Short Fiction, *he teaches in
the bilingual writing program at the University of Texas at El Paso.*

*"Human relations have rarely seemed so complicated—or so tender—as they
do in these darkly funny stories. Lex Williford is a gifted storyteller."*
FRANCINE PROSE, 1993

Jenkins and Rorick had agreed to start hunting at 5 A.M., but Jenkins punched out two hours early at the textile mill so he could get back home to Dawna by three. That would give him and her a little time, he thought, maybe. When Jenkins got home, though, Rorick's old GMC was already parked in the peach orchard out front and the truck's hood was cold. Jenkins walked the clay driveway around back. At first he thought he heard the whippoorwills calling, but it was too early, too cold. Then he saw that Rorick had Dawna bent over the new deep freeze on the back porch.

"Jesus God Almighty," he tried to say, but it came out more like "Jesus got all muddy."

Which was sufficient. Rorick heard and backed away from Dawna and pulled up his Lees. Dawna slid off the freezer top, smoothed down her long Crimson Tide T-shirt, which she always wore to bed, and padded barefoot across the porch, into the house.

Rorick shoved his hands far down into his pants pockets and kept them there, but he looked at Jenkins straight on from over the porch rail.

"You and me, we spent half a month's pay apiece for that deep freeze," Jenkins said. "It's the best we could buy in Loachapoka, and now it's ruint for me." His breath hung like a torn rag in front of his face. The stars overhead were buckshot holes through a barn loft.

Rorick said nothing.

Jenkins walked up the steps, which sagged to one side and yawned under his weight. "Zip up your britches," he said, then stepped past Rorick into his house, stopping the screened door with his heel so it wouldn't slap into the frame. The mounted heads of two bucks he and Rorick had shot the year before stared down at him from over the kitchen table, glass-eyed, grinning.

In the bedroom he pulled his thirty-aught-six down from the top shelf of his closet, then laid the case at the foot of the bed, next to Dawna, and opened it. He pulled a pair of long johns from the bottom drawer and undressed, the last time, he supposed, in front of his wife. He stepped into the legs of the camouflage hunting suit he wore over his long johns, slipped his arms through the sleeves, and zipped up the front. Then he took two boxes of shells from the top drawer of his dresser, dropped them into his gun case, and snapped it shut.

Dawna was chewing the polish off her thumbnail.

"What is this?" he said. "You think I'm going to shoot you?"

She shook her head, but he didn't believe her anymore.

"Look," he said, "Rorick and me, we'll be back about noon. I want you and your shit out of here by then. You can have the Trans Am."

He picked up his gun case, walked around to the back door, and opened it. Rorick still stood outside next to the porch rail, not leaning against it, his hands far down into his pockets, to his knees, it seemed like.

"We'll have to take your GMC," Jenkins told Rorick. "We going, or not?"

"You're fucking with me, right?" Rorick said.

"That's not what it looks like to me," Jenkins said. "Your truck," he said and nudged Rorick with his gun case. "We're going hunting."

They walked the fence line for twenty minutes, Jenkins with his back to Rorick. He wasn't thinking about Rorick now, only about the way the sky grayed over the tree line behind the stubble of a soybean field. Jenkins stopped at a twisted cedar post, to cross over. Rorick tucked his thirty-thirty under his arm and held his hand out for Jenkins' rifle, and Jenkins handed it over to him. Rorick leaned the rifles against the post, stepped on the bottom wire, and held the top wire up while Jenkins ducked through, then past, the barbs. Rorick handed the rifles over the fence and ducked through himself.

Jenkins laid his rifle and Rorick's at the roots of a stunted blackjack oak and faced Rorick as he turned from the fence. He waited until Rorick was ready, then threw a quick knuckle-jab at the bridge of Rorick's nose. A loud pop echoed out over the rutted fields. Rorick wobbled on his heels a little but straightened again. Then he hit Jenkins in the throat, throwing his other fist up into Jenkins' chin in two quick sweeps.

They looked at each other a while. Rorick blinked and made a fist over his nose. Jenkins heard the sputtering whine of a chainsaw far off, and he tried to swallow. Then he and Rorick were both on the ground.

When two crows flew overhead and called out *Dawna, Dawna*, Jenkins and Rorick stood and dusted themselves off. Jenkins' shirt pocket was torn halfway down, flapping in the cold wind. He tore the rest of it off and handed it to Rorick, who used it to dab at the bubble of blood in his nostril. Jenkins waited, handed Rorick his gun, and hefted his own. They walked on together.

The two deer stands were twenty feet up in two tall pines, a hundred yards apart, across a green clearing from each other. Jenkins sat in one stand and, with his scope, sighted in Rorick, who sat in the other.

They'd built both stands together and sowed winter wheat in the

clearing one day the August before. They'd drunk a fifth of Old
Crow and woken in the middle of the clearing the next morning
without hangovers, their shirts wet with dew. Then they'd both
gone home to their own wives. Now they watched each other
through crosshairs.

Jenkins lifted his rifle barrel slowly, sighting in blurred branches
and clumps of pine needles. Then he saw a moving gray patch, a
mourning dove tucking its wings in and cooing on a limb ten feet
above Rorick's head. He squeezed off and watched the explosion
of feathers, which floated down in a fine red mist and settled onto
Rorick's shoulders and hair.

"Why don't you just shoot me?" Rorick shouted.

Jenkins shot again, dropping an overhead branch into Rorick's
lap, then aimed his rifle up at the low clouds and squeezed off three
hip shots.

"Dammit, Jenkins, it was just something that happened. It wasn't
nothing we planned on."

We, Jenkins thought. Then he couldn't think. He said nothing.
He waited for the shots' echoes and Rorick's voice to die in the
wind.

No deer had been in the clearing all morning. In a while, he
thought he could hear antlers scrape against bark in the distance.

The rifle barrel's bluing tasted like well water in a tin cup. Jenkins
tongued the smooth round barrel hole and pulled the rifle stock
in closer between his knees, pressing the barrel's mouth up hard
against the roof of his own mouth, thumbing the trigger's curve.
Then he heard leaf-shuffle at the foot of the tree, and he pulled the
rifle barrel out of his mouth. He'd had it there a while, and nothing
had happened, nothing would. He sat forward in the stand and
made ready.

"Rorick?" someone shouted. Then he heard his own name.

It was Dawna. She walked to the foot of the tree, her white Tide
T-shirt tucked into her baggy jeans.

Jenkins aimed his rifle away. "What you doing here?"

"I was afraid."

"Ought to be. You'll get yourself shot coming out here."

She looked up at him and said, "You always talk down to me, that's my main complaint. Either that, or you don't talk to me at all." She cupped her hands over her mouth and shouted, "Rorick?"

"He's in the other stand," Jenkins said. "He's asleep."

She hugged herself bare-armed in the cold, her breasts pressing against the faded red elephant on her T-shirt.

"I don't believe you," she said.

He laughed. Then he felt sick. "I'm sorry I haven't been who you've wanted me to be," he said, then laid his gun on the plywood floor of the stand and climbed down the pine's two-by-four steps, leading her by the arm across the green to the other stand.

"You better not've done nothing to him," she said, shrugging free from his grip at the foot of the other pine. "We both did what we did, but mostly it was my doing."

We, Jenkins thought again. Then he couldn't think at all.

"Rorick," he called up into the pine's canopy, "my wife wants you."

Rorick climbed down from his stand. Dawna saw the cuts on his face and said, "You all right?"

Rorick looked over at Jenkins.

She touched the base of Rorick's nose, where his eyes were purpling and swelling, and he turned his head, away from her. He kept his arms at his sides, his hands in his pockets.

He said, "You shouldn't be here."

"I want you to come back with me," she said. "Something could happen."

"It would've happened by now if it was going to. We're hunting now."

She looked at Jenkins and said, "I'll be down at my sister's."

Jenkins watched her walk back through the high grass into the clearing, her hands in her back pockets, palms out, her thumbs hooked over the back of her baggy jeans. He watched Rorick watch her, then turn away. He felt the bruised knot bulging at his windpipe. He tried to swallow.

Soon she was out of sight, and he told Rorick, "Not much luck here. What you say we try down at the river bottom?"

They waited under a wild terrace of dead kudzu vines that looped
and draped over two stooped oaks. Fresh pronged tracks in the mud
had led them there to a furrowed pile of dry grass in the shadows,
where two deer had slept the night. Jenkins and Rorick sat with
their backs to the trees, their rifles at their feet. They said nothing
for two hours.

Jenkins hadn't been able to think before, but now he couldn't
stop thinking.

Mainly, he thought about the poker games he and Dawna and
Rorick and Rorick's wife, Becca, had played Friday nights for over a
year. He tried to remember signs he might've missed, the way they
might've looked at each other over the card table's green felt, over
their fanned cards. Their grins, their little nods.

"You want another beer?" Dawna might've asked Rorick, and it
might've meant anything. And the two of them might've stood up
and pulled their chairs out from the card table to go to the kitchen
together, out to the back porch, innocent enough, just for a minute
or two.

And it might've been longer than a minute. Jenkins couldn't remember, it might've been five or ten. He and Becca might've sat
there at the card table, staring at each other, making small talk, looking down at their folded hands. And anything might've happened.

Jenkins watched Rorick lean back against the pine, fighting off
sleep, his eyes heavy-lidded, his head nodding.

"What you going to tell Becca?" Jenkins said. "You *are* going to
tell her, right?"

Rorick straightened. He opened his eyes. "What?"

"You got to tell her, she's got a right. You got to go home and
be straight with her, that's my advice to you."

Rorick was quiet. He looked out to the slope down to the Sou-
gahatchee River, where the morning mist was burning off. He was
awake now.

"Don't be telling me what to do with my wife."

"And not with *my* wife either, right?" Jenkins said. "Look, this is
it, the end of it. I mean, we're not going to shoot nothing today,
not now, not in a hundred years. It'll be noon in a while, and you'll

have to go home empty-handed and tell Becca you been fucking my wife. Then it'll all be over, and then you and my wife can keep on fucking each other."

"Let it alone," Rorick said.

"Do you love my wife?" Jenkins said. "I mean, have you loved her a long time? What I mean is, I'd like to know if you've got as much love in you as you've got gall. I've got a right."

"Stop it, man," Rorick said.

"Or've you just been fucking her because she's my wife and she's been easy because things've been hard for me and her lately, that's what I'd like to know. Was she easy?"

"Shut up."

"She looked easy enough to me. You could've been anybody, any Joe she saw walking down any road in Loachapoka, and she would've gone for you because she wanted out with me, and you just happened to be around, just happened to be a good excuse for her getting out, am I right?"

"Shut your mouth," Rorick said, gripping his rifle stock and standing in the shadows, pointing his rifle at Jenkins from the hip. "I could kill you, you know that?"

"You already killed me, friend. I been in my rut and you been in yours. My wife's been looking for a way out and you showed her a way. I loved her and you were my friend, and now you're not and now you can have her. The hell with it, it's over."

"Look," Rorick said. "There. Over there."

Jenkins looked at Rorick a long time, then back over his own shoulder.

A buck stood at the slope down to the river.

No, there were two bucks, Jenkins thought.

Rorick raised his rifle to shoot, but Jenkins gripped the rifle barrel, turned it away from the river, and said, "Wait."

"You want this one?" Rorick said. "All right, this one's yours, it's all yours. You can have this one."

"No," Jenkins said, hefting his own rifle and sighting it in. "Look again, but don't shoot."

In his sights, Jenkins saw a buck, then tangled antlers, then the

head and neck of another buck, a decaying half-carcass ending at
the shoulder, stiff black meat like jerky covered with flies, white
spine and ribs sticking through rotted meat and ratted fur, a dead
buck's head hanging from the live buck's head.

"Jesus, do you see that, look at that," Rorick said. "Jesus."

Jenkins watched the buck, its head down, dragging the carcass down to the river's edge, into the water. Skin and fur, like a balding rug, stretched over the buck's sharp-boned flanks and ribs. The buck hadn't been able to eat or drink in a long time, and it stumbled into the water and fell, its antlers locked underwater with the dead buck's antlers. The buck struggled to stand.

"It's drowning trying to drink," Jenkins said, and he ran, Rorick following him, down the slope to the river.

Rorick shot first, and Jenkins shouted, "Don't, goddammit."

Then Rorick said, "Shoot for the antlers," and Jenkins understood. He raised his rifle to his shoulder, aimed at the tangled antlers, and shot, the flying bits of shattered antler pelting the water, until his rifle's magazine was empty.

The buck stood from the water, antlerless, its head still down, until it shook its head and saw the other buck's carcass floating free in the water. It lifted its head and looked at Jenkins, then at Rorick, blinking, blowing spray out its nostrils, huffing. Then it shook its head again, slinging an arc of water out from its neck, and it bounded off, arching its back and kicking up water, up to the shore, up into the cover of scrub oak and pine along the shore.

"Jesus," Rorick said. "Jesus, did you see that?"

"Yeah," Jenkins said. "It was something."

They both stood a long time looking down at the carcass floating in the water, down at the ripples of the waves the buck had made.

"Would've made a damn fine trophy," Rorick said.

"A freak trophy," Jenkins said. "Something for people to gawk at."

"It wouldn't've been cheap to mount, but it would've been worth a million bucks."

"Not worth a damn," Jenkins said. "Not worth nothing. A man who'd pay good money for a mount like that wouldn't be worth nothing himself. No damn good, a man like that."

Jenkins and Rorick walked the logging road together, carrying their rifles back to Rorick's truck, arguing about the only buck they'd ever shot at to miss.

Rorick unlocked his door, threw his keys over to Jenkins across the roof of the cab, then opened his own door, and folded his arms at the top of the cab.

"I guess maybe you're right about that buck," he said. "But everything you said before the buck, everything about Dawna and me, you got wrong. What happened was just what happened, and it's only happened this once. You don't got to believe me, I guess. I don't blame you if you don't, but that's the way it is."

"Let's don't talk about it no more," Jenkins said, tossing the keys back to Rorick, and they both got into the truck and drove off together.

When the truck pulled into the peach orchard, the Trans Am Jenkins had driven home early that morning was still parked out front. Rorick turned his truck down the humped clay drive by the house, and Jenkins saw Dawna rocking in her glider next to the deep freeze on the back porch.

Rorick stayed in the truck, his engine still running.

Jenkins got out of the truck and walked over to the porch.

Dawna had changed her clothes. She wore the dress she'd finished on her Singer the day before, the same pattern and flowered cloth she'd bought at the Hancock's in Montgomery.

"I thought you said you'd be down at your sister's," Jenkins said, his foot on the first porch step.

"Well, I changed my mind," she said, rocking.

"I thought I told you to be out of here by now," he said.

"Well, I'm not."

Jenkins looked down at his boot, at the wood's knotted pattern under his heel on the porch step, then at the mud on the heel of his boot.

"I did you wrong," Dawna said, "I know that, but I'm not leaving till you and me talk."

"Nothing to talk about," he said.

"I don't know," she said. "Maybe there's been too much need

for talking and not enough talking. Maybe that's been the problem."

"The problem is you expect too much. You expect me to look at you and talk to you after I saw what I saw this morning. You expect more than a man can bear. You expect too goddamn much."

"I know," she said.

Jenkins looked out to Rorick's old GMC. The engine was still running. Rorick's arms were folded over the steering wheel, and his head lay on his arms. He looked to be asleep.

"Hold on a minute," Jenkins said, then scraped the mud from his boot on the corner of the porch step and walked out to Rorick's truck.

Jenkins fanned his hands back, guiding Rorick in as he backed his truck up to the back porch.

"A little to the left," Jenkins shouted. "That's good."

They lifted the deep freeze they'd bought together to keep the venison they'd kill, and they crossed out from the porch steps, stepping up and onto the tailgate. The truck's leaf springs creaked, and the deep freeze was heavy, heavier than Jenkins remembered, and he held it and lifted it and laid his end down in the bed of the truck.

Rorick slammed his truck door shut, and Jenkins told him, "You keep it a while. I don't have much use for it right now, you understand."

"Sure," Rorick said. Then Rorick was driving off, not looking around, out the day drive around to the front, to the dirt road through the peach orchard, then out to the county road down to Loachapoka.

Jenkins stood on the back porch, his arms folded, and Dawna sat on the glider, rocking. They both looked out at the naked trees and said nothing. It was quiet, too quiet, and Jenkins couldn't think of what to say.

Then he turned to her and said, "Almost got us a buck, a fourteen-pointer, at least," and she stopped rocking. "You wouldn't believe what a fix it'd gotten itself into."

It was the only way he could think to begin.

Listening to Mozart
BUFFALO, 1969

*Charles Wyatt was principal flutist of the Nashville Symphony for twenty-five
years. Since retiring in 1997 to become an amateur flutist, he has made his
living as visiting fiction writer at Binghamton University and, most
recently, at Denison University. He has completed a novel,* Falling Stones,
the Spirit Autobiography of S. M. Jones, *and another collection
of short fiction,* A Woman's Name, in the Dark. *He and his wife, Cindy,
divide their time between Ohio and Tennessee.*

"In Listening to Mozart, *Charles Wyatt displays a poignant,
compassionate sense of the small and large; he looks both ways, down into the
meticulous details of a musician's humble labor and up into the broad,
stirring, inexplicable expanse of his life."*
ETHAN CANIN, 1995

When I was discharged from the service, I called or wrote everybody I could think of who had anything to do with music. Within
a week I had been offered a position with a New Music group at the
State University of New York in Buffalo. I didn't imagine I had especially good luck. I just supposed there would be something for
me to do, and in the presence of such powerful innocence, all ob-
stacles fell away. The Vietnam War was still going strong, and I was
needed to fill in for an unlucky fluteplayer whose reserve unit had
been called up. I think I was less hostile to New Music than most
of the musicians I knew in those days, but my notion of it probably
wasn't much different. Many of my teachers hadn't even acknowledged its existence. At student recitals, the director of my music
school would grouse and grumble under his breath if he heard even
Prokofiev. To me, New Music was the refuge of intellectual odd-
272 balls, from Charles Ives to John Cage. No tunes, difficult notation,

perverse rhythms, atonality—we called it blip-blop music. I knew and genuinely liked a few pieces by Schoenberg, Berg, and Webern, even Berio and Varese. I had even spent a summer at Aspen working on a fiendishly difficult piece for flute and piano by Pierre Boulez, but I really didn't know what I'd be getting into. However, after all that marching and standing inspection, after all those orders and ridiculous short haircuts, I wasn't inclined to be too particular about civilian life.

I picked the straightest road to Buffalo from Washington, D.C., that I could find on the map. My heater wasn't working very well, so I had to stop every hour or so and drink coffee until my feet thawed out. The road didn't exactly turn out to be a major throughway and certainly wasn't straight, but there were a lot of little towns with warm cafés along the way. After a while the road got straighter and the land got flatter, but by then it had begun to snow. Just when my feet were starting to get used to the cold, I couldn't tell where the road was anymore—everything was flat and white. I tried to imagine myself somewhere else, like the early-morning fishing trips I used to go on with my father. We'd get up early, have flapjacks and coffee before sunrise in some little joint like the places where I'd been stopping to warm my feet—I'd have been sleepy, but filled with excitement and anticipation. I loved to watch the sun rise—it was almost my favorite game, to try to see that molten rind of light when it first popped up on the horizon. It *had* been fun, going fishing, at least until we got where we were going.

So there I was, peering into the snow, thinking about how seldom anything had ever come of my expectations, how big and gray those lakes and rivers had been, and how seemingly empty. It was not easy to daydream, because the car kept fishtailing. I had about given up on seeing the road again when a snowplow materialized in front of me and I followed him nearly the rest of the way to Buffalo. Behind us the wide fields, empty and white, closed over with blowing snow, and the windshield wiper on the passenger side of my old green Rambler squeaked once and died. The light inside the car became more peaceful as half the windshield snowed over.

In Buffalo the sun was shining on fresh snowdrifts, and every-thing was plowed in neat, sharp edges. I was to spend the first few days, until I could find a place to rent, at the house of one of the composers, a Frenchman with scarcely more English than I had French, Jean Claude or Jean Paul or Jean Jean (no, Jeanjean was a composer of flute études). He quickly lost interest in attempting conversation with me and returned to his study, where he com-posed with the aid of a protractor and tables of logarithms. His house was large and old. If I touched anything anywhere, a maga-zine slid to the floor. I wanted to use the telephone, but a woman in a hidden room somewhere was on the line. Someone showed me to my room. I went to the bathroom. Became lost. Found my room again, and slept. I dreamt I was fishing with many others on the banks of a large river. Everyone was pulling in fish but me. Some-how I could see the fish swimming in the river, near the bottom, their tails sweeping grandly. A woman speaking gibberish into a telephone accompanied my sleep. When I woke it was almost dark, and my heart, it was, how do you say, almost dark as a well—I was still half-dreaming, with a cartoon French accent—I sat at the foot of the stairs and telephoned my parents. I had promised my mother I would call so she wouldn't have to worry. My father answered the phone. I told him I was fine and that there was a lot of snow, that I was going to have to replace a windshield wiper. We were able to talk about windshield wipers for quite some time. When my mother got on the line I could tell she was pleased that I had had such a good talk with my father.

The next morning my first rehearsal was of a piece involving only a few other instruments and which for me consisted almost entirely of sustained pianissimo notes in the five ledger line range. This, I must explain, is difficult, even with trick fingerings and much pinch-ing and squeezing of the lips. It is not unusual for a headache to result from such straining. The composer conducted. He kept ask-ing, "Is it possible? Is it possible?" I reassured him. I understood. He *wanted* those high notes to sound painful. It was masterful. The *sound* of pain.

I met Alice in the office. I can usually tell a woman who has aspi-

rin. Perhaps this is foolish. Perhaps all women keep aspirin as a
method of introduction, a ploy passed on from mothers to daughters. Only a sensitive man would have a headache. Alice directed me
to my next rehearsal. Gray eyes, a long blond braid. She was an assistant administrator, the person responsible for distributing my rehearsal assignments, even my paycheck. She was rather pretty in an
unfocused sort of way.

"I hear you're staying with Jean Paul. You must be starved. He
doesn't keep anything but cat food in the house. Would you like to
come over to my place this evening for dinner?"

I accepted her invitation gratefully, and I had begun the ground-
work in my mind for something clever about Jean Paul's crowded
and dilapidated house, but I was too slow at it, for Alice suddenly
bustled off and left me in mid-mumble.

When I was in the seventh grade, my father found me a flute
teacher in a nearby city. He had been recommended to us by the
man who had already sold us several flutes, the proprietor of
George's Music Store. This store was rather distant from our home
town, but my father was very much at home in mercantile affairs
and willing to drive the extra mile for a good deal. He and George
had struck several arcane bargains over these flutes, and consequently my father trusted his musical judgment. The teacher's
name was Lawrence Flowers. He was supposed to be a fine teacher
but very demanding of his students. His method of teaching was
simple. He gave me a difficult Bach sonata to practice. When I came
for my next lesson, it was soon evident that I could not play the
rhythms. I had never been taught to count. Mr. Flowers told me
that if I could not play the rhythms correctly by the next lesson, he
would take the music away and give me something simpler. I went
home and learned to count. I understand now how I was moti-
vated, but I do not understand how I learned. I suppose I stared at
the music until I was struck with knowledge. It has not happened
with me or any of my students since. It was, apparently, the exclu-
sive genius of Mr. Flowers to teach in such an economical manner.

Later he played a recording of the Mozart Flute Concerto in D Major for me. It was a recording of L'Orchestre de la Suisse Romande conducted by Ernest Ansermet. The flutist, whose name I don't recall, did not play with virtuosity, but with simplicity. His playing did not call attention to itself. It was so self-effacing, there was nothing there but the music. I did not think this at the time, of course. I had never heard a flute concerto. I had never heard Mozart. I was thrilled. There was a moment in the slow movement which was so exquisitely beautiful that I thought my heart would break. Later I learned that this was a German sixth chord, resolving under the sustained flute, holding the fifth degree of the scale, the dominant; that Mozart had originally written this concerto in another key for the oboe, that he had transposed it up a step and sold it to an amateur flutist to make a quick buck. He was in turn cheated by the flutist. But that day, sitting next to Mr. Flowers, I experienced only the wonder of Mozart, and decided that I could have no higher aspiration than to perform his concerto.

Alice, I learned, was a soprano and had gone to school in Philadelphia at the same time I had. She had studied with the same woman who taught voice at my school, Madame Lavalle, a teacher with an international reputation. Alice's career plans were confused, however; her parents had been killed in an automobile crash only a year before, and this was their house, the house Alice grew up in. I had been completely intimidated when I drove into the neighborhood. I was sure I had the wrong address.

"In summer, there are pheasants wandering in the back yards," Alice said, pouring some of the cheap wine I brought. "The gardens are beautiful. But you wait too long for spring. Do you know that, downtown, there are ropes along the sidewalks for people to hold on to, to keep from being blown over by the wind?"

I told her something about winters in Missouri, a version of my snag-a-cow-fallen-through-the-ice-fishing-in-spring story.

"Do you remember playing *Lucia di Lamermoor* in Philadelphia? I heard you play the Mad Scene duet with Anna Moffo. It was wonderful. How did you rehearse with her?"

I told her that in those days every opera I played I was playing for
the first time; and that consequently my mental state often teetered
between smug arrogance and sheer terror. I hadn't known what to
expect—I was called to Miss Moffo's dressing room by a stage manager who refused to speak English; that she, however, had been gracious; and that she sang the cadenza exactly the same each time.
There was no problem in playing it perfectly, even from the distance
of the pit to center stage.

Then two of the sopranos at school had become interested in the
role and asked me to play the cadenza with them for their lessons.
They were not so steady.

"Sometimes they left out notes, sometimes they added notes. I
had to guess. When I performed it, I hadn't realized the pitfalls. It's
exciting enough without the surprises."

"But then what is the point of it?" Alice asked.

"What do you mean?"

"If you don't change it, if you don't make something different of
it, something, I don't know . . . personal, what's the point of being
a singer?"

"It's like a game with rules, I guess. If you don't like the rules,
you can always write music of your own. Or just do something else.
Besides, your voice, just the sound of your voice . . . what could be
more personal than that?"

I suppose Alice and I were both nervous. She kept getting up to
do something in the kitchen, then returning and sitting down. She
was in the next room when I began talking about Quantz calling
Italian singers fantastic dunces. I realized that she probably couldn't
hear me when she came to the door.

"Come in here, James, I'd like you to meet somebody."

I went into the kitchen, and there was a big green-and-yellow
parrot in a cage on the counter.

"This is Max. Max, I want you to meet James."

Max gave me a sharp look and ambled over to the far side of his
cage.

"I've had Max for six months. I'm teaching him to sing Cherubino's aria, 'Non so piu,' from *Figaro*."

"This I'd like to hear."

Alice coaxed and sang to Max for quite some time, but he merely shifted from one foot to the other and watched her carefully.

I began to feel a little uncomfortable and tried to distract her. "Perhaps he'd rather do Papageno. Or Papagena. Or both."

Alice was flushed with effort. "I know. This always works."

She picked up the cage and began walking from room to room, all the while singing, "Non so piu, cosa son, cosa faccio, or di foco ora sono di ghiaccio . . ."

By the time she had made her first circuit and come back through the kitchen, Max was a different bird. His pupils were dilating and contracting like a berserk camera lens. And he was making little chortling noises in his throat.

When Alice started through the house the second time I noticed the door to Max's cage was open, swinging in time to Mozart. I was just wondering to myself how I was going to tell if it was Alice or the bird singing from the next room when there was a piercing scream. I ran into the dining room, then the living room. There was another scream. In a kind of den-library I found Alice. The cage was on its side on the floor and Max was perched on her shoulder pulling beakfuls of hair from her head.

"Please get him off me. Get him OFF me," she pleaded.

When I got closer I could see that Max was using his beak and sometimes even a foot to pull at Alice's gradually unraveling hair. Perhaps he saw her braid as a puzzle, a knot to untie, some kind of challenge to his considerable intelligence. Her hair really was her finest feature, and Max was getting big hanks of it. He was proceeding rather methodically, and it seemed to me he was really enjoying himself. Alice had given up swatting at him but continued to whimper imploringly. I had to fight against a sudden impulse to bolt and let the two of them work things out.

"Please, James."

All right. I would do something. I thrust my hand in front of Max, about chest high, or breastbone high. We had had a budgie, a parakeet, when I was a kid, and that was the way you got him to sit on your finger.

"Here, Max. Climb up."

Max stopped pulling Alice's hair and gave me a bright look. He looked at my hand. Just as I realized he wasn't going to climb aboard, he bit me hard.

"Damn it. He bit me. And I'm bleeding," I announced, almost relieved to be more fully included in the reality of the proceedings.

"Get the cage! Get the cage!" Max had gone back to pulling Alice's hair.

I picked up the cage and held it as close to Max as I could, at the same time trying to keep as far on its other side as possible, after the manner of Clyde Beatty and his chair.

Max coolly hopped on the cage, pulled himself around to the open door by grabbing the bars with his beak, and climbed up to his perch, seeming quite pleased with himself.

"He seems to think of himself as more the Queen of the Night type, I think."

Alice had gone to get me a bandage and did not reply.

Alice gave me a bottle of red wine to open, and while I struggled with it, served our overcooked pasta. The wine, however, was good, better probably than I'd ever had before. We ate for a while in a kind of relieved silence.

"I'm really sorry. He's never done anything like that before. It must be the excitement. Maybe he doesn't like you."

"Maybe he doesn't like Mozart."

Alice didn't laugh.

"That was supposed to be funny."

"Oh, I'm sorry."

She looked at me a little sideways and I was reminded fleetingly of Max.

"I'm psychic, you know," she said, taking my hand and glancing briefly at my palm as if it were, I don't know, a weather report. "There's somebody else in your life. Waiting, I think. But you've got plenty of time. You're not very good with birds, either, are you?"

Nobody waits in this world, I thought.

"I don't think we should make love this time," she said quietly. "But next time would be fine."

In the fifth grade, I chose the flute to play in the school band. I had been told by my parents I could not play the instrument which had been recommended by the band director, the French horn, because it was too expensive. My parents suggested the trumpet or the clarinet. But I recall when, as a fourth-grader, I first saw, close up, a flute in the hands of a fifth-grade band student. It was that bright nickel-silver color, and the mouthpiece was so odd. It seemed to me at once more mystical and more mechanically interesting than the other instruments.

Having chosen the flute, I discovered that I could not play it. My father could produce a sound easily, but it was not in his temperament to show me how he did it. Instead, he made jokes about my ineptitude. We kept the flute hidden in the linen closet. It was rented but would have cost $140 if it were stolen by roaming gangs of flute thieves. Finally the band teacher showed me how to hold the thing and how to produce a sound. More than the sound it made, which I thought was rather ordinary, I liked the feeling of pressing down the keys against the subtle resistance of their springs. And it was a handsome sight, bright and silvery in its case, shining against a background of dark blue velvet.

The next day Alice was distant and official, providing me with a schedule of rehearsals and conferences leading up to a concert at the Art Museum in a few weeks. I rented a room several blocks from the University, and for a week I was too busy to think about anything but music. I went to sleep at night with my lips swollen and woke in the morning with my neck and fingers stiff.

Whatever plan existed for the concerts and rehearsals came from some remote bureaucratic distance. Compositions which required a conductor (most did, even those utilizing relatively small forces, because of the complexity of the music) were conducted by their composers. If a composer was not present, another composer would try his hand. These chaps were all in the same boat together, and realized probably that times might not always be as magnanimous, as propitious as these for the experimental, the difficult, and the downright repulsive. They endured each other's music with a stiff upper lip, which only occasionally revealed the sneer hiding behind.

On the other hand, some of the music in which I was involved could be managed without a conductor. There was a trio with piano and cello in which I was required to sing and play in octaves with myself. This was a difficult process which necessitated much individual practice and a nasty vibrating feeling in my head when the voice pitches and flute pitches were out of phase. Another piece, a kind of New Music golden oldie, was the "Sequenza" for solo flute by Luciano Berio. I was pleased to be asked to play something which I already knew, one which I was fairly certain would seem flashy enough to stir up a little applause. An unrelenting cascade of swirling and stuttering notes, the piece is surprisingly effective, even with unsophisticated audiences. There was not time, nor did I have the inclination, to memorize it, and page turning would have been impossible. The music opened like a roadmap and was propped up on two music stands. Some pieces required three or even four stands. The lengthy horizontal scroll of music was very much an emblem of the kind of music we were playing, functional in a sense (page-turners seldom were equal to the complexities of the notation), but also an important element of the style, like a baseball player's chewing tobacco. I decided to play the "Sequenza" on my alto flute. This, while more difficult, gave the piece a more distant color, and allowed me more freedom with contrasts of volume.

I sometimes saw Alice hurrying down the hallways, her braid bouncing behind her. I remember thinking that Max couldn't have managed to create *all* that awkwardness between us.

There was an oboe player named Fred Small who played on one of the larger pieces we were rehearsing. His specialty, I learned, was multiphonics. Multiphonics are chords, groups of notes sounded simultaneously, and it's possible to produce them on single-line instruments like the oboe or flute. The individual notes in the chords sometimes have quarter-tone or even eighth-tone relationships to each other, so the effect of the chord is often peculiar, sometimes shimmering, sometimes strident. My own impression is that they often sound like the screeching of metal on metal, a locomotive with wheels locked after someone has pulled the emergency cord. On a considerably smaller scale, of course. Freddy had written a book on the subject. He was always suggesting fingerings to me which he was sure would extract sounds from my flute capable of transforming lead into gold. After I had huffed and puffed, and spit on my music for a while, he would pretend to give up on me. But he always came back with a new one.

I asked Freddy about Alice.

"Alice. That girl in the office or the bass clarinet player?"

"I don't know a bass clarinet player named Alice."

"Oh yeah, she's on leave this semester. You'd love her. When she puts that reed in her mouth and licks it, it's unbearable. She plays well, too."

"But what about Alice in the office?"

"Oh, her. Well, she's pretty spacey, don't you think?"

At the end of the rehearsal I went by the office and asked for Alice. The woman told me she hadn't been feeling well and had gone home early. I had the evening off, the first time since my duet with Max. I thought about calling, but I couldn't think what to say. If I just drove by, maybe I'd be inspired.

Alice's car was in the drive. It was extremely cold, and the wind was making drifts, changing its mind, and making new drifts. And then I was standing on her front porch, another of the world's undecided creatures.

I finally rang and Alice, wearing a white terry robe, let me in rather quickly.

"They told me you weren't feeling well. I thought I'd see if . . ."

She started to kiss me. I hadn't even taken off my coat. The door wasn't completely pushed shut. Little wisps of snow were still shooting in around our feet. I tried to manage all the stage business while maintaining that kiss. It was obviously supposed to be a long one. Finally I had the door closed and my coat unzipped. Alice had come up for air and was holding me tightly under my coat. When I tried to lean in one direction or another she wouldn't budge. When I started to talk to her she would kiss me again. I don't know how long we were in the hall. It seemed like half an hour, but it was probably only a few minutes. Eventually I managed to get Alice a

little off balance and half dragged, half waltzed her to her bed- room. When we got on the bed, Alice moaned, "We shouldn't, we shouldn't," and I attempted to pull away, only to have her pull me back with inhuman strength. Finally, almost apologetically, we made love.

Afterward, the quiet was oppressive. I noticed there was a clock with a lopsided tick in the hallway. Then I heard somebody singing "Non so piu" from another part of the house. Of course it was Max. It wasn't half bad. It really sounded like Alice, like a real per- son, but like a person who just wanted to sing the first measure over and over. His pitch was pretty good, too. Sometimes he'd make that noise that you hear in jungle movies. A kind of gargling sound. I guess it's regular parrot singing. Then he'd go back to Cherubino.

"The reason I got this stupid parrot . . ."

I realized that Alice was crying.

". . . Is that my mother had a parrot. I grew up with cats and a parrot. It could sing like Max. Better than Max. It ate at the table with the people. 'Polly wants a cracker or an apple.' That's what it would say and stare at the damn peas or whatever. You know, with its head cocked to one side and that stupid flashlight look in its eye. Then my mother would feed it with a spoon. Its cage was always full of food and the cats would come and steal from it. They'd reach through the bars with their paws. My mother loved that bird. But it was so mean to me. If I fell down and hurt myself and cried, Polly would cry, too. Mock me. It was infuriating."

Alice slid down so the cover was halfway over her head and I had to strain to hear her.

"One time I got it to call the cats. 'Call the cats, Polly. Kitty, kitty, kitty. Call the cats.' Polly was in a good mood and called the cats. I know I didn't leave the cage door open. The cats just did it themselves. Things like that happen . . . Max . . . Max knows I can't stand him."

Max gave us a few more fragments of Mozart and then kind of dried up. It was quiet again. I think I was thinking about two things at once, about the cats and the parrot, and about me, and where I was—I could see myself on Alice's front porch like a bear come in from the forest, and here I was, in her bed, and there was something about the parrot I was supposed to appreciate . . . and I think I must have fallen asleep. Then the clock struck and startled me, and I sat up in bed and I had the clearest picture of Anna, the last time I had seen her, before she went into the hospital, and we were sitting on the floor of her apartment and she was reciting, "And James was a very small snail." I could hear her voice. It did not seem such a bad thing to be a very small snail. Then I realized where I was, and I saw that Alice had gone to sleep, too. I kissed her on the forehead, but she didn't wake or stir. So I dressed and let myself out. There was a full moon harassed by clouds that might have been those same wisps of snow in the front hall. In the places where it had melted and refrozen, the crust of snow glowed warmly. Every shape was softened, but the sound of my feet on the snow was startlingly sharp. I wondered where the pheasants were.

After almost a year of little progress with the flute, I noticed a big chart on the band room wall with a list of students' names and lines of stars after the names. A kid told me you got a star for each hour you practiced. I decided I would like to have the longest line of stars after my name. I began to practice. Most of this effort resulted in an accumulation of bad habits which required years of progressively more expensive teachers to eliminate. It seemed to me at the time, however, that I was finally learning the flute. My tone was weak and breathy, but I could play all the notes in the chromatic scale. To prove it, my father taught me to play "Stardust" in one horrifying two-hour session in my bedroom. I remember that he whistled it for me, and I suspect that, like those Lucias that were to vex me later on, he may have occasionally changed a note, and then perversely changed it back, not so much to keep me on my toes, but innocently, out of his natural fund of inventiveness.

It was my plan to learn to play the other woodwind instruments, the clarinet, the oboe, and the bassoon. But first I would master the flute. And while I did take a few clarinet lessons, I never got past working at the flute. It was like some women I have known since, always holding something back, constantly breaking my heart. The clarinet was a disappointment, and I soon gave it up. I could make

a pleasant tone from the beginning. But it was not difficult enough
to interest me. You could always get a grip on it. Playing the flute,
as a teacher of mine often told me (yet another Frenchman, a very
old man, wrinkled and stooped), looking at me sadly with his
bloodshot eyes, the smell of Pernod and stale pipe smoke on his
breath, "Playing the flute eez like trying to hold a feesh."

The next day Freddy and I were rehearsing a scene from a cham
ber opera with a string quartet. A male and a female voice intoned
loony non sequiturs about doorknobs and wallpaper while we held
more impossibly long highnotes, especially chosen, it seemed, to
create pain in the lips and cramps in the shoulders. Even Freddy was
complaining.

"'Pierrot' this ain't," he said wisely.

"Why are there such long gaps in the music with nothing happening?" I asked. "Is there another character?"

"No. I've done another piece like this. There's stuff on tape.
They probably won't even play it before the performance. You're
gonna love it."

Freddy gazed sadly at a row of reeds in a scuffed leather compact.
"Doo-doo."

"What?" Then I realized the nature of his contemplation. "Oh,
reeds."

"Doo-doo." This time with an air of finality. Freddy brightened.
"So how are you doing with the lady of the office?"

"Like your reeds."

Freddy said nothing, produced a razor-sharp knife, and began
vigorously scraping a reed, producing a sound not unlike a cat with
a hairball.

The concert was well attended and had a genuine feeling of excitement. A lot of New Music concerts I had played in had seemed
to me more like the clandestine meetings of an illegal secret society.
These people seemed happy, expansive. Even the composers were
bustling about, only a few of them surly. By intermission it was becoming apparent that the concert was a great success. Applause had
been long and enthusiastic. I loved sitting on the stage. I could look

out over the audience and see the tops of bare trees through huge glass walls. The lights of the city gave the night sky a lovely glow.

The second half began, or didn't begin, with a problem. The cellist who played in my singing piece had an attack of stomach flu or nerves and couldn't get out of the bathroom. It took another fifteen minutes before we were able to get on stage. He looked terribly pale. I had managed to croak through the simultaneous singing and playing section rather well, I thought, when the cellist dropped his bow. There were titters from the front row. If he hadn't made such a big deal of it, we could have gone on without breaking the mood. The audience never settled down after that. We were applauded mostly for effort.

Backstage, I noticed Alice. Since our night together we had avoided each other again. It had become almost a routine with us, tides or something. I was holding my alto flute when a stagehand called me. He didn't know how to set up the music stands for the Berio "Sequenza." There was Alice standing near us. I handed her my alto flute and went to adjust the music stands. After unfolding the music and balancing the stands, I went back to get my flute so the curtain could be opened and the piece begun. No Alice. No flute.

Why has she done this thing? My heart tightens in a spasm of—what, stage fright? For some reason, without my flute, I am helpless, foolish. This is all some kind of silly game with its bowing and applauding and patient listening. Alice has pulled away its mask. I feel almost like weeping.

There is a place, right under my breastbone, where I feel a kind of glowing pain. When I was a child, when I felt this, I would say my feelings were hurt. It's such an odd thing—that there is an actual, physical place in my chest I can feel hurting. Where has she gone? Why has she left me alone like this?

This is all a wave which washes over me and then retreats. I take a deep breath and the next wave is smaller, and is more like anger than anything else. I begin to pull myself together.

"Where is the blond woman holding my flute?" I ask in my most imperious, artistic voice.

I can hear that voice. Or something in it. It's a long time, years later, and Madame T., a grande dame of the keyboard, is announc- ing imperiously, "I won't go on stage until that person in the front row is removed from the hall. He has been fidgeting."

We're supposed to play the Brandenburg Concerto No. 5, and the violin soloist and I are standing together in the wings while the stage manager tries to placate the old bat. When she finally realizes he's not going to throw out a paying customer, she reluctantly agrees to go on stage. And the three of us, smiling warmly, stride into the lights. A few moments later, the violinist and I play our accompaniment figures so loudly during her harpsichord solo, she reddens and veins stand out in her forehead like caterpillars. She might have stroked out. Temperament is not without its risks.

But that evening in Buffalo, people were already scurrying about like roaches. There is always, apparently, a market for tyrants. There was a real problem, after all. Alice had disappeared, and so had my flute. A half-dozen people were wandering about backstage, calling her name. Someone was sent to scout out the women's rooms. I spread out my tails and sat down on the floor. Two hundred people were waiting to hear a solo flute piece performed, but I was no longer to be counted among them. I was thinking about how nice it would be to just get in my car and drive south until I could find some place where I could go fishing. I was trying to visualize those big fish fanning just above the bottom, when Freddy tapped me on the shoulder. He held the flute with two fingers, rather at a dis- tance from himself, as if it were distasteful. Nasty metal thing with no reed.

"She was staring out the window in the stairwell at the trees. Said she had no idea you were supposed to be playing."

The curtain was opened, and I made my entrance. The applause seemed knowing, ironic, as if it were the voice of a living thing, something at the back of a dark cave. At this point it would not have surprised me if I had knocked over both music stands.

The rest of the concert unwound normally. In the final piece, the opera scene with the long-held woodwind notes, I began to notice the strain of the evening. My back ached. Freddy's briefcase containing his spare oboe was in the way of my left foot. I couldn't get comfortable in the chair. The doorknob-sprechstimme seemed more ridiculous than ever.

Then I discovered the opera's final ingredient. The taped sounds that filled in the gaps, that floated in and out of the room like a ghost. Mozart! It was cruel. Fragments of the piano concertos, of the violin sonatas. Blowing through the room like leaves. I looked over the audience through the glass wall at arthritic trees hunched against the blue night sky. Something in e minor (a blue color to me) floated by. Freddy kicked my foot. I was supposed to be playing. I took a deep breath and joined in the musicmaking.

I saw Alice again in the post-concert melee. It wasn't easy to get through the well-wishers, but I managed. She had on her coat and had almost slipped out the stage door.

"What happened with the flute?" I asked in what I hoped was my kindest tone.

"Oh, I just didn't realize you were about to play," she said brightly. Then, after a moment. "That Fred. That oboe player. He is a very rude person."

"I'm sorry, Alice," I said.

"It's all right, James," she said, and she patted my arm.

I thought she was going out the door, but instead she took my hand and led me to the stairwell.

"See what I was looking at."

There was a nice view of trees surrendering to the night, holding their arms up wearily.

"I was looking at them, too, during that last piece."

"I was thinking about you and Max. Well, really about me and Max. I don't know if I want to be a singer. You just repeat the same thing over and over. The only difference between me and Max is that he doesn't sing if he doesn't feel like it."

"Max doesn't know what he says when he says it."

"Do you really think they don't know what they're doing?"

"Who doesn't know?"

She shook her head. Then she took my hand, and I thought she was going to say something about parrot bites, but it was the weather report again.

"It's all changed. Your waiting time is up. And where Max bit you is all better." Then she kissed the place where the bird got me, like a good mother. She left me standing on the staircase. I even called after her, but she didn't turn around. I looked at the trees and wondered what in the world it was that musicians do and why, until a guy moving sound equipment bumped into me and broke the spell.

During the long intermission someone had given me a note about a phone call. I had answered an advertisement I saw pinned to the bulletin board a week earlier—flutist needed for a touring chamber orchestra. There would be some solo work involved. I had sent my resume. The conductor of the chamber orchestra wanted me to call him. The next day I called him and we arranged an audition. The only way we could get together was for me to meet him at the Detroit airport. I played for him in a conference room. He was rather pleasant in a grandfatherly kind of way. Pudgy, white hair, glasses fallen down on his nose, a bit of the scholar. I played both Mozart concertos for him. Execrably, it seemed to me. I was humiliated. It sounded so awful. I kept saying, "Is this enough?" And he kept saying, "No, I want to hear a little more." Until I had played through all the movements. Then he said he liked my playing and offered me the job on the spot. I could start in two months. We shook hands, and I wandered around the airport for a while, slightly dazed, watching the people, watching kids who didn't seem at all interested in airplanes landing and taking off. I made up my mind to call Anna. Hobbs would know where to find her. Then it was time for my flight back to Buffalo.

When I was fourteen I played a movement of a Mozart flute concerto at the state band contest. It was the one I first heard at my lesson with Mr. Flowers. I had won a blue ribbon, and I was walking home from the high school after the competition. There had been some rain earlier, and there were puddles on the sidewalk reflecting the scattered clouds and even me, a giant stepping over them. It was springtime, the lawns were a light green, bordered with daffodils, and there were new leaves on the trees. I remember jumping up and grabbing a leaf as I walked under a tree. I was walking down the nicest street in town, holding a maple leaf in my hand, and suddenly I could hear the slow movement of that Mozart concerto in my head. I dropped the leaf and stood still to listen. I can see myself, feel myself, under the maples and elms, standing in a sidewalk puddle. I could not see what was under its surface. When I looked down at it, even though I knew there was only wet sidewalk there, all I could see was the sky.

Thomas Edison by Moonlight

WYOMING, 1878

Don Zancanella grew up in Wyoming and now lives in Albuquerque, New Mexico. He has published fiction in Shenandoah, Alaska Quarterly Review, Prairie Schooner, New Letters, *and elsewhere. His story "The Chimpanzees of Wyoming Territory" appeared in the 1998 O. Henry Awards volume. He has recently completed a novel titled* Souls Returning Soft at Night.

"Western Electric *is a diverse collection of stories about a 'new West' which in Don Zancanella's skilled hands is a compelling, witty, and highly amusing commentary about modern America. Though these stories are brought together in the context of a collection, there is a nice epic continuity to them and a wonderful naturalness of voice that is also precise and lyric. With a diversity of theme and character—from Laotian settlers in Wyoming to Thomas Edison in the West—these stories are at once accomplished, wise, and entertaining."*

OSCAR HIJUELOS, 1996

When Thomas Edison came to Rawlins, Wyoming Territory, most of the townsfolk saw only what the press releases had led them to expect: Thomas Edison, scientist; Thomas Edison, industrialist; Thomas Edison, inventor extraordinaire. A few skeptics saw through the hoopla to the snake-oil huckster peddling himself and his inventions to the diversion-starved frontier rubes. But years later, Owen Schoonover would claim to have been the only one who saw something more, who saw the original, wondrous boy in the man, the natural wizard whose ability to dream up miraculous devices outstripped even the world's ability to gobble them up.

If the crowd that met Edison at the Rawlins train station hoped for flamboyance, they were not disappointed. Riding in perched on the locomotive's cowcatcher, the great inventor emerged from a cloud of blue steam, waving his hat in greeting as the train hissed to a stop. He had shot a bear near Green River, he announced, and pulled the furry ears from his coat pocket to a rousing cheer. Yet sixteen-year-old Owen, who had expected a more dignified entrance, was surprised by nothing so much as Edison's homeliness— his tiny buckshot eyes and down-turned mouth and unkempt thatch of hair.

Thomas Edison had come west on what had been promoted as a fishing trip. The newspapers, however, speculated that it was an exploratory expedition, a search for exotic materials to be used in his proposed electrical incandescent lamp. When it became known that his itinerary included a stop in Rawlins on the transcontinental railroad, the city fathers (including Owen's own father, the railroad station master) leaped at the chance to oblige. Organizing an oversize fishing party comprised of half the town, they trundled the inventor and his own formidable entourage up twelve miles of dusty trail to Saddle Lake, on the western slope of the Great Divide. There, as everyone scurried to make camp, Owen excused himself and hiked into the woods, where he stopped, unfastened his trousers, and relieved himself on the trunk of a big spruce tree.

Two things Owen disliked were large social gatherings and camping out. If his father spotted him now, he'd accuse him of indolence, but Owen simply preferred town to the wilds and his own company to the demands of society. He grimaced as he listened to the shrieks of children, an ax splitting pine logs, and the clatter of pots and pans. Shrugging his shoulders to readjust his suspenders, he picked his way back through the undergrowth to the edge of the broad clearing by the lake. All the wagons were nearly unloaded, and the men now struggled to erect baggy canvas tents. Not far from the water, the women lit cookfires, the dark smoke rising already into the clear summer sky. And there, in the midst of it all yet coolly aloof from the hubbub, stood Tom Edison, arms akimbo, face shining in the sun.

Owen and Edison had already met. An amateur inventor himself, Owen had been proud to serve as porter when Edison's party detrained yesterday, ferrying their baggage to the hotel and showing them all to their rooms. Then, retrieving his own worn satchel from behind the front desk where he'd left it that morning, he knocked on Edison's door and forced himself on the inventor, unpacking his nitric acid battery, his electric buzzer, and his rolled sheaf of drawings before one of Edison's assistants, a tall bearded fellow, could shove him back out.

"Let him stay," Edison sighed, and the bearded man departed, but not before he had pulled Owen aside.

"He don't hear too well. Be sure you speak up," he said and left them alone.

Edison ignored him at first, stripping off his coat and vest and shoes, wiggling his toes and washing his grimy face in the basin while Owen connected his gadget to the closet door.

"It's for shopkeepers," he all but shouted. "The door to the shop opens and the buzzer sounds. You always know if someone's walked in."

"A spring-tension switch."

Owen nodded and pointed to the doorjamb.

"Where I come from, we'd call that a burglar alarm. Been done before." When Owen's face fell, he added, "You're an ingenious boy, coming up with that on your own out here." He paused for an enormous yawn. "Damn it, I'm bushed," he said. "I need a rest."

"I've got something else," said Owen. "I call it an electric singing machine. It's based on your gramophone. I haven't built it yet, but I brought some drawings."

Edison had just begun to lay back on the bed, but he sat up now, his eyes brightening, and pushed a hand through his ragged hair.

"Singing machine?"

"A carbon microphone of the kind used in Bell's telephone connected to a network of headsets. The singer's voice comes to each member of the audience through his own personal headset, thereby eliminating—"

"Let me see that," Edison said, snatching the curled drawings from Owen's hands. He spread the designs across the bed, looking at them with great interest, declaring the idea feasible, promising, marketable even, before asking once more to be left alone. But as

Owen was about to shut the door behind him, Edison called him back.

"Have you heard about my newest invention?"

"No sir," he said and watched as Edison reached his open hands toward the ceiling and drew them back tightly closed. And then slowly, before Owen's eyes, he unfolded his fists to reveal a silver dollar upon each palm.

"My newest invention. I make money out of thin air," he said and roared with laughter as he ushered Owen out the door.

Feeling at once disappointed and thrilled, Owen stood in the dark corridor and collected himself. So this, he thought, is the famous Edison, inventor of the gramophone, inventor of the automatic telegraph relay. The man who has promised to bring electrical lighting to the waiting world.

Reclining now in the shadows beneath the pines, Owen propped his head on an elbow and gazed out across the green meadow. His father, dressed as always in severe black serge and a straight-brimmed Stetson, stood on the back of a buckboard wagon shouting instructions to two town councilmen who appeared to be tangled in a length of rope. Owen felt a little guilty not helping but reminded himself that he was usually a hard worker, putting in hours at the depot every day. Since leaving school a year ago, he'd been clerk, baggage handler, and broom pusher and could soon apprentice himself to a conductor in accordance with his father's wishes. But he disliked it all intensely, preferring instead to tinker in the corner of the barn he had converted into a workshop, preferring brainwork to physical labor or the dull pencil pushing of commerce. Some nights he would stay in the barn until after midnight and then curl up on his workbench to sleep.

When at last the tent building and fire starting and horse tending had been completed, Owen got to his feet, stretched, and strode purposefully out of the trees. He had not taken two steps when he heard his mother's voice:

"Owen, you take these buckets and bring some water from the lake. And ask Mr. Edison if he wants his coffee now."

Late morning, the summer sun blazing, Owen could not imagine

anyone wanting hot coffee and felt foolish being his mother's er-
rand boy. Nevertheless, he grabbed two pails and headed for the
lake. The men had begun to fish, scattering out along the rocky
shoreline. There were so many of them it seemed only a matter of
time until lines became tangled and tempers flared. Edison, however, as guest of honor, was given a wide berth and stood perched
atop a boulder, casting out extravagantly in all directions. He
looked ungainly, as though he might tumble into the drink at any
moment, and yet his casts were graceful—long smooth arcs with
plenty of snap in the wrist. Not wishing to interrupt, Owen approached quietly and knelt at the water to fill the pails.

"My mother wants to know if you'd like coffee," he whispered.

"In this heat?"

"That's what I told her."

"Ignore her then. You're old enough to ignore your mother,
aren't you?"

"Yessir," he mumbled and then remembered Edison's hearing.
"I'm sixteen," he hollered, attracting startled glances from several
nearby fishermen.

"Tell me your name again."

"Owen Schoonover."

"Ah yes, Schoonover. Inventor of—what the hell did you call
that contraption you showed me drawings of?"

Owen lowered his eyes and poked at the mud with the toe of his
boot, unable to respond.

"Look here." Edison flipped open the lid of his wicker creel to
reveal three fish nestled in a bed of leaves. "Are these rainbow
trout?"

Owen nodded. "See the pink slash on their bellies?"

"Remarkable. First ones I've ever seen."

Owen was amazed he'd taken three fish so quickly. No one had
been at the lake for longer than half an hour. He drew his fingertips
along their length, feeling the fine-grained texture of their cool
skin.

"Tell me," Edison said, interrupting Owen's investigation, "is
that slack-jawed, lunkhead look of yours a permanent condition or
does it come and go?"

Owen looked up at him and grinned sheepishly. "You're a pretty good fisherman for an easterner," he said. Then he hefted the buckets and started to leave, only to stop short and befuddle Edison's cast.

"About your inventions. Do they just come to you out of the blue?" he asked, adopting Edison's own bald-faced tone. Edison paused and raised one eyebrow.

"Not the inventions, perhaps. But visions, yes, 'out of the blue' as you say. Man unfettered, nature remade, the disembodied voice beautiful on a cylinder of wax. Night becomes day and our bodies are released from their earthly bondage." His voice trailed off and he smiled. "I do it for money too, Schoonover. My inventions earn large sums of money."

Owen could only nod. Edison flicked his line out to crease the surface of the lake while Owen lugged the buckets back toward the fires, water sloshing into his boots as he walked. He glanced back just in time to see Edison's line go taut with a strike.

By noon fish were frying. After helping his mother he had gone searching for his own pole but discovered that his father had lent it to one of the easterners. Instead of fishing, he watched a demonstration arranged by some of Edison's men, a water trough electrified by a Ruhmkorff induction coil. Unsuspecting subjects who wandered by were encouraged to retrieve a five-dollar gold piece from the bottom of the trough, only to be shocked off their feet and find themselves surrounded by a guffawing crowd who were all the more delighted because the trick had already been played on them.

They all seem more interested in pranks than science, Owen thought as he filled his plate and found a place where he could watch another demonstration taking place at a table nearby. There, Edison had placed a small machine with a hand crank protruding from the side and a dull metal orb on top. When someone turned the crank, a turkey feather danced a few inches above the orb, suspended in midair. Owen understood the principle of static electricity and shook his head, feeling little of the wonder he knew was expected of him. An amusing contraption, but nothing more than a sideshow stunt. He bolted a few bites of fish and left.

If Edison and his party were mostly bluster, they had found their

proper audience in the citizens of Rawlins—in their small-town
eagerness to be everyone's open-mouthed fool. Owen had been
born in Chicago, but his childhood had been spent moving west-
ward, encampment to town, as his father followed the new railroad.
Though their home seemed blessedly permanent now, Rawlins remained only a ragged little settlement built along either side of the
two silver rails that came from the prairie and left again in a clean
straight line under the sun. He sometimes wondered what the cities
of the East were like. It was all he'd ever heard about, where everything came from and where anything of importance eventually
went.

Leaving the campground, he meandered up the mountainside,
looking for some way to occupy himself. The other young men his
age were all paired up with girls or fishing in boisterous groups or
off in the hills somewhere looking for game. The dense canopy of
pine and spruce closed over him, and he could hear only the sound
of fallen needles crushing beneath his feet. Then, as he passed a
granite outcropping surrounded by a tangle of brush, he heard
voices. One he recognized as his cousin George and the other as an
unidentifiable female. Therefore, he knew what to expect. Dropping to his knees, he crept along a patch of juniper and carefully
parted the branches.

George and the Pensky girl. Laura it was, rolling on the pine
needle–carpeted ground. Sweating, clothing in disarray, buttons
unhitched, and sleeves askew. Owen swallowed his laughter and
observed the earnest proceedings for a moment before creeping
back down the slope and approaching again, this time whistling
loudly and stomping his feet. George's head appeared first and then
Laura's, both of them weedy-haired and wearing foolish grins.

"It's just Owen, my cousin," George explained: "You gave us a
hell of a fright."

"Oh my, shut your eyes," Laura said, rebuttoning her dress and
regaining her composure. "I didn't know you were cousins. Don't
you work at the depot?"

"Jack-of-all-trades. Clerk, porter, freight donkey, and gandy
dancer," Owen said, only half closing his eyes and watching with

some interest as they realigned their clothing. This was not the first time he had stumbled upon George locked in passionate embrace. A year younger than he, his cousin was something of a sexual prodigy, achieving a level of skill and opportunity by age fifteen that men of twenty-five envied.

"What're you doing up here anyway?" asked George.

"Dodging my mother's chores. She'd have me washing dishes right now if I'd stayed. Besides, I'm tired of all this. I'm ready to go back to town."

"I saw you hobnobbin' with Mr. Tom Edison," George teased, winking at Laura. "Don't act like you ain't havin' a real time."

"They say he's a genius," Owen said, a little tentatively. "Later tonight he's demonstrating a model of his newest invention. Lamps that run by electricity. No oil, no kerosene, just batteries or generators and wire." He wondered for a moment if Laura was impressed by his show of scientific knowledge, but that notion was quickly squelched.

"What's wrong with a kerosene lantern," George groused. "Why do people get so worked up about gadgets?"

"George is going to ride in the cavalry when he turns sixteen," said Laura. "They don't need 'lectricity to fight Indians."

Owen had heard George discuss this ambition before and did not doubt that he would achieve it. Already as large as a full-grown man, he could handle horses and shoot straight, and he'd cut a fine figure riding over the plains in brass-buttoned splendor.

"Maybe you could be a genius inventor," said George. "You're smart and you like to fix things. You like books too."

Owen shook his head. "I've seen his gramophone. A man came through on the train with one. Human voices coming right out of a machine. That takes more than books."

"Ah, he's got you buffaloed," George said. "I've seen better tricks in a traveling circus."

When they got back to the lake, it was almost sundown, and the camp was quiet. A few fishermen remained, and a group of men played cards at a table under the trees. Everyone had retired to their tents for late afternoon naps. But as they crossed the meadow, a voice came from behind, and all three turned to see Edison seated alone on a stump at the edge of the woods, puffing on a

cigar.

"Hey, boy. You, Schoonover," he called, his voice a raised whisper to avoid disturbing those in their tents. George glanced at
Owen and grinned, elbowing him in the ribs and shoving him back
toward the trees.

"School chums?" Edison asked as Laura and George strolled
away hand in hand.

"My cousin and a friend."

"You got a sweetheart?"

"No sir. Not a regular one," he mumbled, feeling himself blush.

"Consider yourself fortunate." He fell silent then, appearing lost
in thought.

"I want to talk about tonight's demonstration," Edison said at
last.

Ever since the arrival of Edison and his party, a rumor had been
circulating that he would demonstrate a working model of his electrical lamp. Owen wondered what the demonstration could have to
do with him, but Edison's tone had become thoroughly businesslike, so he squatted on his heels in the grass and listened.

"First, they can dance to the gramophone," he began. "Women
and ministers are wild for the gramophone, but even the men like it
if they haven't heard it before. Then, when they're primed, when
they think they've seen it all, we demonstrate the lamps. The news
of Edison's latest conquest leaks out, so that by the time we reach
Chicago, rumors are rampant." He paused and jabbed his cigar at
Owen. "Business runs on rumors, you know," he said, paused
again, and continued. "When we arrive in New York, a crowd of
well-wishers meets us at the station, the newspapers print front-
page stories, and investors are fighting for a share. Or so I had
imagined."

Owen liked the momentum of the events Edison described, but
the last remark threw him. "What are you saying?" he asked.

"What I'm saying, Schoonover, is that the lamps are not ready
yet. What I'm saying is we still have not found a material to use for
a filament that has high resistance, remains stable, and doesn't dis-
integrate in a few seconds. You follow me?"

Owen nodded, even though he wasn't sure.

"Platinum, silver, titanium. Celluloid, coyote hair, or cactus spines. We've tried them all. What will work, what characteristics must it have? Two days ago I picked up the split end of a broken fishing pole and saw the frayed bamboo fibers. So tonight we try bamboo."

"People are expecting to see those lamps," Owen said, still surprised he was being told so much.

Edison nodded glumly. "So they are, so they are. But I have a plan. If you'd help me, we could make it appear that it wasn't the lamps that failed but, shall we say, the *lamplighter*. No one would hold you responsible if, while lending your assistance, you accidentally caused a malfunction."

Owen heard Edison out, occasionally fanning cigar smoke from his face as he watched the orange sun drop behind the mountains.

"You want me to be your scapegoat," he said flatly when Edison had finished.

"I'm asking you because you're a fellow inventor. Because you're the only outsider who could possibly understand. You'd be rewarded. Name your price."

"Fifty dollars cash," Owen ventured, seeing a chance for a quick killing, and then, "no, a hundred," at which point Edison laughed aloud, his voice booming out across the sleepy meadow.

The late darkness of summer finally fell, and people began to emerge from their tents in ones and twos to walk beneath the starlit sky. Kerosene lanterns were brought out to sit upon tables and hang from tree limbs, the yellow flames flickering in the rising evening breeze. Owen stood near the makeshift rope corral with George and Laura, George showing off his knowledge of horseflesh as the motley assortment of ponies and plowhorses nickered and shuffled their hooves.

"This here little bay can run, I'd wager," he said. "I'd like it if she was a notch leggier and a tad thicker through the barrel. Now this here paint—"

He stopped in midsentence, his mouth wide open. From far

down the meadow came a tinkling melody, the music of piano and violins on the night air. The horses' ears all went up, and Owen looked at Laura and George.

"It's the gramophone," he whispered, and they stood utterly still and listened. For all the scratchiness and quavering, it was remarkable. Whatever else Edison accomplished, thought Owen, these sounds will remain, the swirling strains of an orchestra on a mountaintop miles from the nearest ballroom.

Suddenly Laura bolted, dashing toward the music, the boys following, drawn toward the end of the clearing, where three or four couples had already begun to dance. Laura dragged George out among them, kicking off her shoes, while Owen looked up and down the long table where the gramophone sat and where still more of the inventor's equipment was being assembled. More condensers, more coils, batteries, loops of wire, and several transparent glass spheres, each atop a two-foot length of pipe.

"His electrical lamps." It was his father, startling Owen as he appeared beside him. "A red-letter day for Rawlins and the territory. They'll hear of us from coast to coast. Hell, they'll hear of us around the globe."

Owen wondered how much money his father and others were sending east with Edison to help bankroll his projects. In a town like Rawlins, anything from the East smacked of riches.

"Suppose it doesn't work. Suppose he's not successful."

"Nonsense," his father replied, as though the remark scarcely deserved a response. Then he explained to Owen that he'd volunteered him to power a dynamo for the demonstration. "I told Mr. Edison about your workshop and your interest in electricity. He said he'd be delighted to have you assist."

While Owen reflected on the fact that he would be participating in gulling his own father, he discovered that at his right shoulder was no longer his father but Edison, who began to speak softly, conspiratorially, as the dancing continued.

"So it's agreed, you'll help?"

"What do I do?"

"Very little. Crank one of three dynamos. You see the lamps *will* fail. We simply tell our audience that you tangled your feet in the wires and shorted the circuit or something of the sort. Who in this crowd knows one jot about electricity?"

"So I play the fool," Owen said sourly.

"It's more important than you know. My investors insist on evidence of success, but we need their money now, to carry forward the research. If they hear we've made a breakthrough . . ."

Owen didn't completely trust him, but it was too late to back out. The music stopped and Edison hopped up on a chair and began to address the gathered crowd.

"Ladies and gentlemen. Citizens of Rawlins and Wyoming Territory. Gracious hosts." His practiced, stentorian delivery made it difficult to imagine him as anything but a second-rate politician or a carnival barker—certainly not the Prometheus whose visit the newspapers had heralded for weeks in advance.

When he had thanked everyone, the mayor stood on another chair and thanked Edison and his party in return. Then it was time to commence.

"Ladies and gentlemen," Edison began again, gripping his lapels. "The story of the electrical incandescent lamp. Our problem was to find a fiber which, when charged with electricity, would glow brighter than the hottest flame but have the durability to last for hours. We tested hundreds of materials, both in our laboratories and during the course of our present journey. Our discovery, made only days ago in the wilds of the Wyoming Territory: a simple strand of bamboo fiber coated with lampblack. The serendipity of a fractured fishing pole."

Owen's father nudged him forward while Edison rambled on, something about the historic import of it all. At last he introduced two of his assistants and then Owen, embarrassing him by calling him "Rawlins's own young electrician" so that he avoided meeting anyone's eyes as he took his place behind one of the dynamos and firmly grasped the crank that projected from the conglomeration of copper wire and metal rods and gears. The kerosene lamps were extinguished, one after another, until only the pale moonlight remained.

"Start the dynamos," shouted Edison, and Owen began to turn

the crank, slowly at first but then faster and faster until it seemed to

spin by itself. He heard a high whining sound, and suddenly the
globes did begin to shine, orange at first, then yellow as the sun,
brighter and brighter, illuminating each face in the crowd in a
steady, clear hemisphere of light.

"Let there be light," Edison exclaimed. "The magic of electricity. Globes of fire."

An audible gasp of astonishment arose from the crowd followed
by a round of applause. A bedazzled smile appeared on Owen's face
as he basked in the encompassing glow.

"By God, it's working," one of the assistants wheezed, and
Owen realized they'd been turning the cranks for a long time, five
minutes at least, turning, turning, the muscles in his shoulder on
fire, but he didn't mind, so thrilled was he by the crowd and the
brilliant light. And then he saw Edison grinning triumphantly, clapping his hands in delight like a small boy.

At last Edison signaled them to stop. The lamps dimmed and went
dark, leaving round white afterimages lingering before Owen's eyes.
The crowd pressed close, and everyone began congratulating him
along with Edison and his men, pounding them on the back, touching the hot bulbs gingerly with outstretched fingers, and asking Edison how soon they might expect electrical lighting in Wyoming
and what else he had up his sleeve. The kerosene lamps were relit,
and Owen's father came and complimented his crank turning, leaving Owen to wonder if it would now be easier to convince him that
he had no desire to be just another railroad ticket clerk.

When the crowd dispersed, Owen helped dismantle the dynamos
and lamps. Buoyed by the unexpected success, Edison's assistants
joked with him and asked about hunting and fishing so that he felt
like their equal instead of only an inquisitive nuisance. After a while
Edison took him aside, and they strolled together toward the lake.

"Many thanks," he said. "A modest victory for which no one had
to shoulder the blame."

"The bamboo worked," said Owen.

"So it appears, but how well remains to be seen. For now, I think
we've silenced the skeptics. Make no mistake, the sodbusters of
Rawlins saw a wonder tonight. The word will go out, wait and see."

Owen didn't like being called a sodbuster and wasn't sure why Edison was walking with him. They stopped at the lake, and Owen tossed a few stones into the darkness, listening for the wet kerplunk. After a brief silence, Edison spoke again.

"I owe you a reward. We had an agreement."

"I didn't do anything." He figured he'd settle now for even a dollar or two, but Edison ignored him and went on.

"What I propose is that you come to work for me. We need young men like you, Schoonover. Our operations are expanding by the day. Say yes and you can be on the train with us Monday."

Owen was speechless. What did he know about Edison and his work? Was he even a trustworthy man? Inventor, famous personage, and incipient tycoon—all seemed extravagant poses. And now he appeared as some sort of rich uncle offering the glittering, incandescent world.

"This is so sudden," Owen said at last.

"You're not a goddamn bride. You can't hide your ambition. Here's your chance to escape this pestiferous backwater. I'll expect your decision in the morning."

Before Edison left, however, he showed Owen more sleight of hand. First he removed his pocket watch and disconnected the fob. Then, holding it at arm's length over the lake, he dropped it. Just as it reached the water it reversed direction and shot back up into his waiting hand. Owen shook his head and smiled, even though there was enough moonlight to see the white elastic attached to the timepiece that made the illusion work.

Owen found his bedroll in his parents' tent and spread it by the lake. For a long time he remained sleepless, staring up at the stars, wondering if he should board Edison's train or let them leave and return to his life in Rawlins as if nothing had happened. At last he slept, only to find himself awakened by one of Edison's bearded assistants.

"Mr. Edison wants to see you. Or should I say, he has something he wants you to see."

He scrambled to his feet, but before he could stretch, he was led

rapidly into the woods. They wound through closely spaced aspen
trees, down a long slope, and across a little creek, where Owen's
feet got wet, his escort marching mutely onward, until at last they
entered a small glade surrounded by enormous pines towering into
the sky. And there stood Tom Edison, flanked by three of his men,
busily assembling one more machine.

This time there were no speeches. The assistants murmured to
one another, but Edison said nothing, pausing and nodding at
Owen only to acknowledge his arrival. A single kerosene lantern
burned nearby, but it was the blue wash of moonlight that illuminated the silent scene.

"You boys work long hours," Owen said, but instead of respond-
ing with a smile, one man shook his head and frowned, another held
his finger to his lips, and Edison seemed not to hear. Then, as Owen
tried to conjure up something else to say, Edison came forward and
received into his hands the ends of two long coils of black cable,
cable which snaked back to a collection of wooden boxes, glass jars,
and shining spirals of copper wire, all instruments for which Owen
knew no name. Collarless and in shirtsleeves, Edison flexed his
knees and gave each line a vigorous shake.

"This must be our secret," was all he said.

There was a moment of surpassing stillness then, and Edison
nodded. On cue, the assistants threw a series of switches, a little
blue flash crackled at each connection, and Thomas Edison lifted
slowly, soundlessly off the ground. Inches at first and then three
feet, six feet, arms spread, a gently undulating cable trailing from
each fist, he rose. No whining bearings, no clank or roar, no shower
of sparks or hiss of steam. Only Edison calmly ascending.

Owen ran in disbelief to where the inventor had been standing
and leaped to touch the soles of his shoes, but Edison just laughed
and continued rising into the starry sky, as though his head were a
balloon pulling him upward or as though gravity had lost its grip.
Upward to the full extent of the cables, until they were stretched
tight, and he floated above the treetops, his black brogans walking
on air.

"This is what we're about, Schoonover. Not nuts and bolts and music machines. One day soon all the horses will be put out to pasture and the steam engines left to rust on the tracks. We'll travel like birds."

"I'll take the job," Owen said breathlessly.

"Come again?"

"I'll go, I'll go," he shouted with all his might. And at once he could imagine himself being pushed by a breeze, weightless, unfettered, adrift in an eastern sky.

The Iowa Short Fiction Award and
John Simmons Short Fiction Award Winners

2000
Articles of Faith,
Elizabeth Oness
Judge: Elizabeth McCracken

2000
Troublemakers,
John McNally
Judge: Elizabeth McCracken

1999
House Fires,
Nancy Reisman
Judge: Marilynne Robinson

1999
*Out of the Girls' Room
and into the Night*,
Thisbe Nissen
Judge: Marilynne Robinson

1998
Friendly Fire,
Kathryn Chetkovich
Judge: Stuart Dybek

1998
*The River of Lost Voices:
Stories from Guatemala*,
Mark Brazaitis
Judge: Stuart Dybek

1997
*Thank You for Being
Concerned and Sensitive*,
Jim Henry
Judge: Ann Beattie

1997
Within the Lighted City,
Lisa Lenzo
Judge: Ann Beattie

1996
Hints of His Mortality,
David Borofka
Judge: Oscar Hijuelos

1996
Western Electric,
Don Zancanella
Judge: Oscar Hijuelos

1995
Listening to Mozart,
Charles Wyatt
Judge: Ethan Canin

1995
*May You Live in
Interesting Times*,
Tereze Glück
Judge: Ethan Canin

1994
The Good Doctor,
Susan Onthank Mates
Judge: Joy Williams

1994
Igloo among Palms,
Rod Val Moore
Judge: Joy Williams

1993
Happiness,
Ann Harleman
Judge: Francine Prose

1993
Macauley's Thumb,
Lex Williford
Judge: Francine Prose

1993
Where Love Leaves Us,
Renée Manfredi
Judge: Francine Prose

1992
My Body to You,
Elizabeth Searle
Judge: James Salter

1992
Imaginary Men,
Enid Shomer
Judge: James Salter

1991
The Ant Generator,
Elizabeth Harris
Judge: Marilynne Robinson

1991
Traps,
Sondra Spatt Olsen
Judge: Marilynne Robinson

1990
A Hole in the Language,
Marly Swick
Judge: Jayne Anne Phillips

1989
Lent: The Slow Fast,
Starkey Flythe, Jr.
Judge: Gail Godwin

1989
Line of Fall,
Miles Wilson
Judge: Gail Godwin

1988
The Long White,
Sharon Dilworth
Judge: Robert Stone

1988
The Venus Tree,
Michael Pritchett
Judge: Robert Stone

1987
Fruit of the Month,
Abby Frucht
Judge: Alison Lurie

1987
Star Game,
Lucia Nevai
Judge: Alison Lurie

1986
Eminent Domain,
Dan O'Brien
Judge: Iowa Writers' Workshop

1986
Resurrectionists,
Russell Working
Judge: Tobias Wolff

1985
Dancing in the Movies,
Robert Boswell
Judge: Tim O'Brien

1984
Old Wives' Tales,
Susan M. Dodd
Judge: Frederick Busch

1983
Heart Failure,
Ivy Goodman
Judge: Alice Adams

1982
Shiny Objects,
Dianne Benedict
Judge: Raymond Carver

1981
The Phototropic Woman,
Annabel Thomas
Judge: Doris Grumbach

1980
Impossible Appetites,
James Fetler
Judge: Francine du Plessix Gray

1979
Fly Away Home,
Mary Hedin
Judge: John Gardner

1978
A Nest of Hooks,
Lon Otto
Judge: Stanley Elkin

1977
The Women in the Mirror,
Pat Carr
Judge: Leonard Michaels

1976
The Black Velvet Girl,
C. E. Poverman
Judge: Donald Barthelme

1975
*Harry Belten and the
Mendelssohn Violin Concerto*,
Barry Targan
Judge: George P. Garrett

1974
*After the First Death
There Is No Other*,
Natalie L. M. Petesch
Judge: William H. Gass

1973
The Itinerary of Beggars,
H. E. Francis
Judge: John Hawkes

1972
The Burning and Other Stories,
Jack Cady
Judge: Joyce Carol Oates

1971
Old Morals, Small Continents,
Darker Times,
Philip F. O'Connor
Judge: George P. Elliott

1970
The Beach Umbrella,
Cyrus Colter
Judges: Vance Bourjaily and
Kurt Vonnegut, Jr.